DAYDREAMS

NIGHTMARES AND FANTASIES

THE EMILY GAMBLE SERIES

AMIRAH J. COOK

Illustrated by
JARRELL E COOK

CHERRY BLOSSOMS PUBLISHING, LLC.

DAYDREAMS

THE EMILY GAMBLE SERIES

DEDICATION

To Jarrell.
The love of my life.
My muse, my partner.
The consistent pillar I lean on for safety and comfort.
You are, and always will be, my home.
I will love you through this lifetime and the next.
We did this together.
My only regret is not discovering a way to relive our love story,
indefinitely.
From June.

1
_____

"When the fuck will it be finished?!" His voice was beyond intimidating, bordering frightening. He sounded enraged, betrayed even.

"Whoa! Boss, we're doing the best we can, working as fast as possible. They sent the wrong marble, and now we're making the changes Mrs. Gamble requested," José said, holding his hands up while quickly glancing in my direction with a sincere apology in his eyes. He'd thrown me under the bus, and it was obvious Daniel was unpleased. He may have been the boss, but the wife always seemed to control the decisions.

I looked away, afraid to face his deathly glare. Instead, I focused on the hazardous mess we were standing in. What started two years ago as a quick real estate flip had become a complete disaster, and money pit, with no end in sight.

The building was stunning. The first time I saw it, I had to have it. I can still remember my excitement as I called Daniel over to see it. From the outside, it looked like an abandoned warehouse, but the interior was impeccable. Every level housed a complete wall of floor-to-ceiling windows overlooking the city, taking full advantage of its location. That was all the levels shared, though. Each floor was so different from the next, I chose to name them individually, in typical Emily fashion. My friends called me a hopeless romantic, always forcing things to fit my whimsical ideas.

The plan was to turn each floor into an independent loft style condo, making it the premiere building in the downtown LA real estate market. The lowest two levels contained a sixteen-car garage, giving each unit more than enough space for cars and storage, with the top four floors reserved as living spaces. Every night, I dreamed the final designs for these condos, never doubting their potential or compromising my vision.

I named the first loft Margaret, or Maggie for short. She was the smallest of all four units with a dainty feel about her. Everything was white and shiny, very plain Jane, I thought. I remember telling Daniel that Margaret was the kind of lady that didn't say a word during sex, and did whatever her man told her to. Even more vividly, I remember the smirk Daniel wore once I said it, as he looked towards the back of the loft, assuming I couldn't see his face.

Most vividly, I remember the ball of anxiety churning in my stomach, wondering if that was the kind of wife he wished he had. A blank canvas, ready to do any and everything he wanted. I was no Margaret, and our marriage was not filled with me taking orders or doing what I was told, in or out of the bedroom.

I don't know if either of us expected that in the beginning. I was the princess of every relationship in my life, and Daniel decided to follow suit while courting me. We'd wed in a fairy tale wedding 4-years prior, although he'd wanted a simpler celebration. He even suggested the courthouse once, which he pretended was a joke after seeing the look of disgust on my face. He was changing his mind and behavior to fit my vision, but I didn't stop him. I encouraged it. I was training him.

The higher you went in the lofts, the more luxurious they became. Hence, the lowest level getting such an ordinary name like Margaret. Bella was the second unit, named for her Parisian inspired finishes and French charm. Next up was Gia, which was simply the name that popped in my mind when I thought of a sexy, younger woman. Gia was filled with chrome finishes; she was the bombshell that played poker and didn't call AAA when her car broke down. Gia was fucking hot, and the loft was perfect for a bachelor, or a woman who oozed sex and watched sports.

We were standing in Giovanna, the penthouse, named for glamour that bordered gaudy. Giovanna had more marble than any other surface, and she was the main selling point when I first toured the property.

What we didn't know the day we impulsively made an offer, after I refused to slow down and think about it, was that the area had not been zoned for residential units. The previous owner had lost so much money on permits, it was on the market as a sign of defeat. It took us over a year, and 7-figures, to finally get the correct zoning for individual sale. Even after that, we still had small renovations; because of course I wasn't satisfied with the units as they were.

I watched Daniel grit his teeth during the first day of demolition, and thought how good of a job I'd done training him when he didn't say a word about ruining perfectly good bathrooms and kitchens on two levels, simply because I envisioned them on the other end of the condos. A year later, after investing every dollar we could save or borrow for the condos, we were now in the final stage of picking finishes. We were balancing this project with the greatest challenge we'd ever taken on – a divorce.

I'd like to say the stress of the real estate project ruined our marriage, but that wouldn't be the whole truth. Daniel never wanted the princess. He just wanted to marry Emily, but I wasn't willing to submit. I wouldn't let him lead. So, I manipulated my way to the head of the table with tantrums and puppy eyes. I knew he would give me anything I wanted and completely took advantage of his desire to see me happy.

Daniel would never hurt me, which was more weakness than strength when dealing with a woman like me. He was the type to ask if I was okay during missionary sex, while cradling my head and proclaiming his love in my ear. I was the type to roll my eyes and stare at the ceiling, waiting for him to come.

"Do what I tell you, and stop listening to her! She's not the fucking boss!" Daniel's outburst snapped me back to reality.

For everything he wasn't, Daniel was sexy as hell. I could see his muscles flexing through the perfectly tailored suit, his back tense while he barked orders at the crew. They all stared at him with fear in their eyes. Surely, they'd never seen him so upset.

At 6' 4", he towered over everyone in the room. The five o'clock shadow covering his flawless skin only accentuated his jawbone, as he desperately tried to contain his rage. He'd only gotten into this project to please his spoiled wife, who he now couldn't stand. And yet, his current and future financial health depended on its completion, which I continued to delay without so much as consulting him. Yeah, he was pissed.

Watching him remove his suit jacket, I couldn't focus on how mad he was, or how much I deserved it. All I could see was his perfectly chiseled frame, the outline of his six-pack engrained in my memory. We'd been at odds for so long that I hadn't seen his bare chest in over a month. Before that, it was only during peeks of him exercising in our glassed-in gym. I'd gone without his touch for 6-months, since our last pity fuck for my birthday. It was miserable, and afterwards, I think we both silently agreed that whatever we'd had was gone.

Two weeks later, I filed for divorce and he didn't so much as text me once he received the papers. Now, we were only communicating about the divorce through lawyers, living separate lives in the same home. These meetings at the construction site were the only time we were purposely in the same room. The tension was always so thick I pitied the staff, who constantly felt the wrath of both of us.

Today, I only pitied myself. I used to be able to calm him with nothing more than my body. Now, I watched as a spectator as he growled and pointed, desire pooling between my legs with no release in sight. Suddenly, his face contorted into a deep frown as he turned toward me, dropping his jacket and storming in my direction. In the ten-seconds it took him to reach me, I prayed he would pick me up and fuck me right there. I didn't care if everyone saw it. I didn't care about the divorce being called off; I just wanted him inside me.

"Why the – Why did you tell José to postpone painting the garage units?!" Daniel growled, his teeth clenched so tightly, his temples protruded just below his hairline. He was pissed, but he still refused to curse at me, even after lashing out at every worker within earshot. "Em?! Answer me!" He interrupted my gaze.

Fuck this.

2

I grabbed his wrist, because we were hand holders when we were happy. And this wasn't that. Shockingly, that was what I missed most when we first began living separate lives. Daniel was no longer the newlywed who used to look at me with googly eyes, and I wasn't the princess wife he'd never raise his voice at.

I yanked him to the elevator before I knew what I was doing. The element of surprise must have caught him off guard, because he followed willingly. He probably assumed I was leading him to an explanation, justifying my decision to further delay the completion of the project. He was wrong.

All the staff was working in Giovanna, so the elevator opened immediately after I pushed the call button. It had been idly waiting since carrying the two of us in silence just 30-minutes prior. I knew the rest of the building was empty, so I chose the third floor, hitting the button much harder than I intended.

"What are you doing?" Daniel glared down at me wearing a frown laced with disgust. He spat the words.

I felt naked; as if he knew my desires and was repulsed by the idea I would even think he wanted me. I slapped him hard across the right side of his face, just as the elevator dinged, the mirrored doors opening to Gia.

The loft was still dimly lit from our earlier check-up. I stormed towards the chrome kitchen island, no longer needing hold of his wrist. My slap would ensure he'd be on my heels. I pulled the string of my black wrap dress, effectively undressing myself with one quick motion, as Daniel turned me around by gripping my elbow.

Confusion covered his face as he slowly looked over my body. I'd always been a lingerie fanatic, but Daniel never seemed to care, claiming he'd make love to me in cotton panties because I was so beautiful. Today, there wasn't a thread of cotton touching my body. Since filing for divorce, I spent more time picking out lingerie than my clothing. It was the only thing that kept my confidence intact.

I wore a black lace La Perla body suit, with halters connecting to the top of my thigh highs. Lingerie had become my armor, a dismal substitution for the partner who protected me from everything, until our life fell apart. Daniel appeared more embarrassed than seduced. I was seconds away from breaking down in one of my notorious tantrums. Without taking his eyes off my bodysuit, or softening his frown, Daniel's full lips moved and I quickly interrupted the inevitable rejection.

"*I'm* who you're mad at! Stop taking it out on everyone else! You *need* to fuck me, and it's driving you crazy!" A smug smile curled my lips as my manicured nail poked his chest, forcing my armor to embody the confidence I lacked. I was lying, well partially.

Daniel *was* mad at me, but it was me who needed him. I yearned to feel him and the power that accompanied seduction. I turned away, dropping my wrap dress on the way to the kitchen island. I wasn't shocked when I didn't hear him follow. I couldn't look back, unable to watch the confusion morph into frustration, or even worse, annoyance. Instead, I marched to the island alone, bending over the chrome countertop.

My right cheek rested on the cold chrome as I desperately fought to slow my breathing, straining to hear any movement from Daniel. So far, he hadn't made a sound. I listened closely, sure he'd storm off to the elevators, or mumble about me being a drama queen.

Finally, I closed my eyes and surrendered to what I knew would be a humiliating experience. Daniel wasn't going to fuck me with a construction crew working on the floor above us. He didn't want that. He was probably wondering what the hell I'd been into the last 6-months. Why would I think he would do something so disrespectful to his wife, even if I were soon to be his ex?

Then I heard his tousled breath, and the pull of some type of fabric, followed by his commanding footsteps.

Oh, my God.

3

————

My heart sank further into my stomach with each step, until he reached the kitchen island. I closed my eyes and swallowed slowly, knowing he was standing behind me, looking over my lace covered body, no doubt with pity.

Everything moved in slow motion. I felt his hand yank my hair as he bent over me, pushing his erection onto the lace covering my ass to whisper in my ear through clenched teeth, "I don't want to hear you make a fucking sound."

I inhaled sharply. Daniel cursed at me. And he was hard, rock hard. His arousal pressed firmly against my lace lingerie, causing a painful surge of desire between my legs.

"Do you hear me?" He was eerily calm. I had never been nervous before sex in my life, but now I could barely speak. Feeling his warm words along my ear, I knew he was waiting for my response as his body folded over mine.

"Yes." It was more of a breath than a word, but it must have sufficed.

He released my hair and destroyed the lace between my thighs with his strong hands. I wanted to protest, as I would have in the past. It was a $700 bodysuit. But words failed me when I heard his zipper unfasten.

I reached for the inch lip on each side of the island, preparing myself, when I felt his fingers at my opening. Daniel didn't typically use fingers during sex, but this wasn't the husband I knew standing behind me. And I was slicker than I'd ever been, causing him to take a sharp breath when he felt my arousal, most likely thinking his wife didn't get that wet. But this wasn't the Emily he knew bent over the kitchen island.

I heard a kissing, or sucking sound, but didn't feel anything. The realization that he'd licked my juices from his fingers stirred me even further. Then he dug his thumbs into each side of my lower back, his fingers lifting my hips to meet his pelvis before slamming his manhood into me with one swift movement.

I gasped loudly, feeling the wind knocked out of me. Daniel didn't have a fun sized dick you could ram without warning. He had the kind of length that needed to be inched in slowly. Lifting my hips, he stretched me deliciously, forcing me to take every inch of him. Tilting his body to the left, he looked to me with a stern warning.

"Aye!?" Was all he said, and I knew it was due to my escaped gasp. I nodded my head on the now warm chrome, gripping the sides of the island for dear life.

He straightened his body and slid out of me, leaving just the tip inside to tease me. I closed my eyes and listened to my breath quicken, waiting for him to sink back into my warmth.

He surged his pelvis forward while pulling my hips to meet him, and began to move quickly in an abrasive rhythm. I scrunched my eyes closed, clenching my teeth, determined to stay silent as the painful pleasure became too much to bear. Daniel pummeled me with his manhood. I was so aroused, he slid into me with ease, lifting my hips until my feet no longer touched the ground.

Old Emily would have contested. I needed some leverage. I couldn't even push back to meet him. I was helpless, powerless, lost in sensation. Instead, I held on to the island, contorting my face to stop from screaming his name as my orgasm built inside me. The urge to pee came strong and swift, and I knew I was going to explode. Thinking of how loudly I usually climaxed worried me, so I fought to hold my orgasm at bay, intensifying the pleasure.

Daniel kept pounding, groaning in ways I'd never heard him, weakening my fight to remain silent. When I heard him mutter, "Oh my God", I lost it.

Without words or leverage, as my feet dangled in the air, my orgasm reached new levels. Pulling my breasts to the chrome island, I felt my body vibrate in a way it never had. Juices dripped down my leg as I descended from an orgasmic high. Daniel cursed behind me, his rhythm slowed before he rammed into me one last time, his body jerking as mine had just moments earlier.

I felt him spasm as he came and came again inside me, groaning loudly. I opened my eyes to see my breath fogging the counter I'd purposely had built at waist height, which was ideal for cooking. I thought to myself, *this is also the perfect height for spontaneous sex in the kitchen.*

Daniel leaned his body over mine and whispered in my ear, "Who said you could come?"

I was speechless. Before I could turn to look at him, he gently kissed my ear. Glancing back, I watched him dig into his back pocket before kneeling. Wiping my leg up to my sweet spot, he gently dabbed my swollen lips, obviously aware of how sensitive I was after his rampage.

He stood as he finished, holding my wrap dress before lifting me off the kitchen island by my waist. Keeping my back to him, he held out my dress, and I slipped each arm into the sleeves before wrapping the belt and tying a bow at my left hip. I pulled my hair to the front, trying to feel if it was completely disheveled as I looked over my shoulder to Daniel.

"After you," was all he said, nodding towards the exit. Without second guessing, I walked to the elevator, which again opened immediately after I pushed the call button, as it had obediently waited for me to get fucked in the kitchen of Gia.

Daniel pushed the button for the garage, and I looked over to my left, reminding him of the workers waiting for our direction, "They're still up in Giovanna."

He casually nodded once, and then looked up to watch the numbers decline as we descended into the garage. At some point during our time in Gia he had loosened his tie and unbuttoned his top two buttons. Now, he pulled the tie off completely, stuffing it into his back pocket without so much as glancing in my direction.

The doors opened and I felt his right hand on my shoulder before I could take a step. His fingers glided across the sweat sheen coating my skin before wrapping around my neck. Not tight enough to scare me, but enough that I knew not to step forward. He tilted his head down and coldly ordered, "Go to the house."

I began to turn towards him, when his grip tightened. Keeping my gaze forward, I attempted to tell him about my dinner date with my sister Victoria, before he interrupted me.

"Go to the house."

This time he was even more stern and cold. His grip loosened when I stepped forward, and once I exited the elevator he released me altogether.

Was he going to follow me home? Did he want me again? Was he going to confront me about what I'd just instigated and what that meant for our marriage?

I turned to him, unsure of which question to ask first, when I noticed he wasn't beside me. Spinning around, I caught the slightest smirk on his face as the elevator doors closed, with him inside it.

What the fuck?

4

I felt my eyes filling with tears as the elevator climbed to the top floor, my vision blurring as each number lit up. When the first tear dropped, I questioned why I was even crying. Was it simply the after-shock of an earth-shattering orgasm? Or did I feel cheap because he'd left me?

Daniel never behaved like that. He hadn't even checked to see if I was okay, or asked how it made me feel. Hell, he didn't even let me speak during the sex!

My big brother Elliot once told me that guys treated girls one of two ways - they either placed them on a pedestal or bent them over it. The literal interpretation was not lost on me. I felt debased. Devalued. Even worse, I wanted more of it. I knew I would go to our house, which had recently become a space for us to share as room-mates, and pray that Daniel came home to dominate me like that again.

After staring at the elevator for two minutes, watching the illu-minated light reveal its location in the penthouse, I was confident Daniel had gone back to work. I walked to my white G-Wagon and hopped in before texting Victoria.

Emily: Got fucked over at the construction site. Gotta cancel dinner. Sorry.

Giggling at my lie smeared in truth, I pulled out the garage. As I turned into traffic, I glanced up, hoping Daniel was watching me from the window of Giovanna. I was craving one of his overbearing texts, urging me to drive safely, but my phone showed no alerts.

Relief washed over me when I felt the soft vibration of my phone while driving up the driveway to our house. I unlocked the phone quickly, eager to read Daniel's text, but it was my sister.

Victoria: Cool. I'm swamped anyway. Love ya.

Walking into our home, I shivered at the coolness that was once so warm and inviting. Somberly, I made my way to the bedroom I used to share with Daniel. He'd moved into a guest room shortly after I filed for divorce, and I'd spent the last six months sleeping alone. I showered with hopeful thoughts of sleeping beside him again.

With thick white suds of shampoo falling from my hair, I replayed the past two hours in detail. Recalling my boldness and Daniel's performance brought a smile to my face. I realized it was his taking control – with the workers, and then me – that pushed me over the edge. It was a role I had never conceded, to him or anyone else, but it felt good to follow his orders.

As I washed the conditioner from my hair, I decided not to lead whatever was to happen with us from this point on. I wasn't going to question him, or seek clarity or closure. I had submitted, relinquishing my power, and I couldn't take it back. He was leading, and I was following. Simple as that.

That plan left me anxious as I stopped the waterfall shower head. Stepping into our cream and gray marbled bathroom, I looked at my thin frame in the mirror. My hair bunched around my nipples as my shrinkage curled against my copper skin. I missed my bronzed glow, in desperate need of a tan. My daydreams absentmindedly drifted to plans of a reconciliation trip on an island, and I laughed for not remaining in the backseat just two minutes after my declaration to follow Daniel's lead.

I pulled my hair into two large braids and slipped on a silk nightgown before heading to the kitchen. *Should I make dinner? Is he even coming home?*

Over the course of our secret separation, we'd digressed from knowing each other's every move, to sleeping apart, to not even telling each other about late nights or work trips. We were living detached lives and I didn't want to pretend that sex in our disaster real estate investment changed all of that, despite how mind-blowing it was for me.

Then, it occurred to me the sex might not have had the same effect on him. I did think he needed to blow off steam. And by all accounts, he'd done just that before promptly returning to work. I'd been home for an hour, and he hadn't so much as sent a text. The possibility that he was unbothered was unsettling, though unlikely.

The memory of him groaning flashed vividly in my mind. I closed my eyes, remembering his kiss on my ear and felt my nipples harden beneath the silk nightgown. There was no way he could be less than pleased with that performance.

With that semblance of reassurance, I grabbed a menu from our favorite Chinese restaurant, calling in to order my favorite. Just before hanging up, I decided to order Daniel's favorite as well. After all, he wasn't there to lead that decision.

I finished what I could of my Sesame chicken dinner, and even had a little of Daniel's shrimp Lo Mein, when I decided to turn in for the night. I did everything slowly, hoping to hear his car pull into the driveway, unsure of how he'd respond after my outburst in Gia.

Before climbing into bed, I propped the bedroom door open, encouraging Daniel to join me. After mentally running through every possible scenario, I felt myself drifting off, just as the garage door sounded. My heart fluttered as excitement shot through me like a dose of adrenaline. I knew I would be a coward and pretend to be asleep. I just wanted him to come into the room.

Listening closely as he entered the house, I heard his keys drop onto the end table in the foyer. His footsteps were the only sound in the entire house, loudly announcing his presence. In a panic, I decided to turn onto my stomach, certain my eyes would betray me with a flutter if he did decide to check on me.

Eventually, I felt his presence in the doorway. He must have watched me for two full minutes before gently walking to my side of the bed. I focused on my breathing as he hovered over me. I wanted to roll over, professing my love before begging him to come to bed. Instead, I remained still and silent, even when his hand barely touch my braided hair.

Then, I heard him glide back across the room as quietly as he entered, leaving a crack in the doorway rather than closing it completely.

The refrigerator opened and the microwave sounded, evidence that he'd found the Lo Mein I ordered for him. I wondered if he was smiling as I tried to build the courage to join him in the kitchen. I wanted to see if he would come to bed on his own, so I waited silently, listening and guessing what he'd do next until the sounds faded and I could no longer hear his movements.

I awoke without noticing I'd fallen asleep, reaching over to the empty side of our bed with disappointment. Daniel had not come to sleep with me. Taking in a heavy breath, I looked to the clock on my nightstand. It was only 6:30, plenty of time before we left for work. Maybe I'd cook omelets or pancakes.

I took the long route to the kitchen so I would pass the guest bedroom. The door was wide open, the bed perfectly made. I walked downstairs, hoping to find him in the gym, but knew from the silence at the bottom step that he wasn't there. I headed back upstairs and peeked into the garage, noticing his car was gone. He'd left for work like nothing happened.

Damn.

5

I wanted my armor more playful than usual, so I chose a colorful lace lingerie set. Bright colored thread swirled around white lace, the underwire lifting my perky breasts while the matching panties shaped my lower curves. For the first time in months, I wandered through our walk-in closet contemplating my ensemble. It was like the first day of school, or a new job. I felt strangely optimistic about the day, despite Daniel's less than warm reception to yesterday's events.

Although we'd spent the last six months living like strangers, I refused to believe he could be unaffected by sex that good. There was nothing casual about it. It might not warrant calling off the divorce, but we couldn't pretend it never happened.

A red pencil skirt paired with a colorful silk blouse accentuated my figure while elongating my legs. Buttoning the Miu Miu blouse to my neck, I left the option for cleavage. After adding a little bronzer to my cheekbones, I filled in my eyebrows and unraveled my braids, creating big waves of my dark coarse hair that had not fully dried overnight. Slipping on a pair of red Brian Atwood pumps, I smiled at my reflection in the full-length mirror, ready to take on the day.

Dashing out the door, I decided to eat breakfast at the office. The quicker I got out the house, the better. There were too many unanswered questions, and unresolved issues coursing through the silent space.

My assistant did a double take when I approached her desk just before 8 AM. I was known for not being a morning person, but her look of shock gave the impression I wasn't supposed to be there at all.

"What's wrong?" I asked, hoping I hadn't missed a memo.

"Well, you've just been so black and navy lately. It's a shock to see you in such bright colors. You look... vibrant, boss lady," Crystal lauded.

I'd hired her as a favor to a friend, but she turned out to be a Godsend. Crystal had become nothing short of indispensable, handling everything in my life – personal and professional. I was selfishly nervous when she recently got engaged, praying a resignation to start a family wouldn't follow the announcement. My face must have revealed my fears, because Crystal told me not to worry, assuring me she wouldn't be quitting anytime soon.

"I felt vibrant when I woke up," I explained, which was the truth until I realized Daniel left without a word.

"Some things came for you, I put them on your desk," she grinned like a child protecting a secret.

We went over my schedule and discussed plans for the week before I made the short walk to my office. I opened the door and stood in complete shock. There were three large glass vases filled with roses – one set was peach, another dark pink, and the last one yellow. Every rose was flawless, as if the florist purposefully selected each flower especially for me.

"Aren't they beautiful? I know Mr. Gamble has been very busy. Tracy said they're closing some major deals over there, but he still found time to take care of his favorite girl. I guess he likes the vibrant Mrs. Gamble too!" Crystal was beside herself with glee.

Like so many others, Crystal idolized my relationship with Daniel, viewing through a looking glass that altered the reality beyond recognition. She was very close with Tracy, Daniel's assistant, due to the necessary coordination to ensure our schedules aligned.

During our dating phase, Daniel and I made a pact to never share the intimate details of our relationship with anyone. Not even my nosey sisters had a clue about our impending divorce, let alone our assistants. But drastic adjustments didn't need announcements. Crystal must have noticed the change between me and Daniel, and I'm sure she made note of the decrease in calls and vacations.

If there's a reason men sleep with their secretaries in every scandalous cliché, it's because they play such a significant role in your life. The relationship is intimate by design.

"They are beautiful. He's something else," was all I could manage, looking down at my colorful blouse that matched the shades of roses perfectly.

"I left the card on your desk. Do you want coffee?" Crystal asked as I leaned over my glass desk to smell the gorgeous flowers.

"A blueberry muffin and a cappuccino with an extra shot, please?"

"No problem. I'll be right back."

I picked up the small beige envelope, sliding the card out.

I guess Gia was fitting.

I smiled remembering our argument about naming the third-floor Gia. Daniel had never understood my need to name inanimate objects, but would always humor me with participation. Once I'd decided that the third level was the sexiest loft, I set out to pick a seductive name, going as far as Googling "Sexiest Female Names", before landing on Gia. Daniel thought Gia sounded prudish, and even felt the loft was far from sexy, arguing it was more bachelor-esque.

Our time in Gia replayed in my mind as I noted how sweet it was for him to fuck me so savagely, and then send roses like a gentleman. The memory left me feeling flustered. So, he was affected.

Should I call him and thank him for the flowers? Would I have regularly called him to thank him? What if he'd only sent these because he felt obligated?

Daniel was known for being an extreme sweetheart. He might have felt like an asshole after being so aggressive. Then, I remembered the smirk painted on his face in the elevator. It was not the look of a remorseful man.

I dug my iPhone from my purse and dialed "Mr. Gamble", the only contact in my favorites. A picture of him smoking a cigar in a hammock during our last trip to Thailand popped up, a sentimental pang hitting my heart. Holding the phone against my ear, I instantly hoped he didn't answer, but after the second ring, he picked up.

6

"Hey," Daniel answered casually.

"Thank you for the flowers," I blurted, instantly cringing as I closed my eyes, trying to will some finesse.

"I didn't send you any flowers." He sounded definite and sincere.

What? If he didn't send the flowers, who could have? Did the workers hear us? Is this some sick, creepy stalker shit from someone in the building? I was speechless in my thoughts until I heard his low laughter.

"Who else would have sent them, Em?" I could hear his light smile, the one he flashed when he was playful. The one I hadn't seen in months.

"Oh gosh. I thought we'd have to fire the staff." I exhaled loudly.

"They definitely wouldn't have heard you."

I'd missed his wit. He was always so quick on his toes, so much fun on the phone.

"Yeah, you made sure of that." I could hear my smile. It was then I noticed I was pacing my office.

"You talk too much."

God, he sounded sexy, killing me with his banter. I had no wit about me, while he sounded calm and in control. Daniel was undoubtedly sitting at his desk while I walked to every corner of my office, staring out the large glass window, failing to relax.

"You left early this morning." It was an honest observation and my way of not asking any questions, a reminder I kept mentally repeating, not wanting to be the pushy version of myself.

"Technically, you could say it was late. I had a videoconference for this deal in Tokyo. I came in just before midnight to set up."

"You've been at the office since last night?!" Even I was shocked by my concern. I'd spent so much time convincing myself I didn't care what he had going on. That was easy when I didn't know, but now I had a million questions I was determined not to ask. What deal was he working on? Had he eaten? When was he going to sleep? But, I'd already asked more questions than I wanted.

"Yep. I'll just leave early today."

"Are you coming home?" Shit. Another question. And this one was way more revealing. I needed to know what was going on, but I wanted him to tell me on his own.

"Yep," was all he said. A short breath of relief escaped my lips. "When have I ever not come home, Emily?" I knew him well enough to know he was tilting his head, balancing the phone between his ear and shoulder. He was answering every question I hadn't asked, with a question.

"I don't know... Should I cook something?"

What the fuck was I doing – asking him on a date? And what was with the questions? Play it cool, Emily!

"I guess it's me who owes you dinner, don't you think?"

"Don't start being a gentleman now," I teased. Finally feeling my wit make an appearance.

"I'm always a gent – yeah, set them there. Make sure the conference room is ready." He spoke in an authoritative and commandeering tone, as he switched to business mode. Now, I was envisioning him commandeering me. The fantasy made me blush, and desperately want off the phone.

"Oh, don't worry if you're busy. I just wanted to thank you for the roses." I tried to sound casual.

"You're welcome, baby."

My heart fluttered. Throughout the divorce, I'd been 'Emily', even 'Em' occasionally. When he was preoccupied, he might revert to 'E', my nickname while we dated. But never - not one time in six months - had he called me baby. And hearing him say that, in conjunction with our rendezvous in Gia, made me want to explode. "Yeah, Tracy, that's fine."

"OkaywellI'llseeyouathome." It was one breathy word. I'd lost my wit, my cool, my mind. It was all gone.

"I'll have Tracy set up dinner with Crystal." He said, returning his attention to the call with his casual demeanor.

"Okay. Bye."

"Bye."

He resumed the conversation in his office before ending the call. *Was he just very busy, accidentally calling me baby? Did he only say it because no one in his office knew we were on the brinks of divorce?*

No, definitely not. He'd called me 'Em' hundreds of times around them, so that wouldn't have been strange. He felt different. He had to. And as awkward as that call was, I knew a dinner would be even more difficult. I'd be squirming and nervous like I was on a first date. I wanted to look flawless.

Just as I began to regain my senses, Crystal walked in holding a brown paper bag and a white cup.

"Clear my schedule for the day. I need a nail and hair appointment, asap. I'll be out, so call me and let me know where I'm going as soon as the appointment is confirmed." I grabbed my purse and took the cup and paper bag containing my blueberry muffin. Crystal stood in the middle of my office watching me strut out the door. I wasn't going to dinner with these unreliable waves.

"Yes, ma'am." She couldn't hide her shock or confusion. I didn't care, he'd called me baby.

7

———

"Tell me what you want, but no chopping! You know I love your hair!" Sonja was a great stylist, but she annoyed me with her love affair with my hair. Even her trims were stingy.

Sometimes I thought Daniel had gone behind my back, paying her extra to never cut my hair. He loved my hair long, so after I filed for divorce, I'd come to Sonja to chop it off. He was away on business, and I thought it would crush him to come home to a bald wife. In retrospect, I'm glad Sonja refused, but in the moment, I cussed her out. I mean, I literally pay her to do what I want.

Sonja lightened my hair, as I always did in the warmer months, before straightening my curls and adding layers. When she finished, my tresses bounced with every movement, shining when the light hit them.

The sun gave my hair a natural streaking effect, which looked even better when my skin was glowing with a tan. Whenever we vacationed to tropical destinations, Daniel would promise we'd move there one day. I was an island girl in another life.

Remembering my 30th birthday on Phi Phi Island in Thailand brought a smile to my face. We spent an entire day flying to get there, but the view as our speedboat arrived made it all worth it. Daniel was beaming as I jumped up and down, awestruck by the natural beauty.

He'd asked me where I wanted to celebrate my birthday months in advance, and I knew he'd spent countless hours planning a flawless trip. I can't honestly say I was grateful. The realization that I felt entitled to it left a bad taste in my mouth, as the nail technician brought me back to the present.

"Do you want me to round them or box?" She asked, holding my left hand in her hand, grazing her fingertips over my cuticles, feeling for imperfections.

"Let's do box," I replied, just as my phone rang. Looking down, I saw Daniel smoking a cigar.

Why was he calling? I thought Tracy was going to schedule our dinner. The possibility that he was cancelling created a pit of disappointment in my stomach.

"Hey," I tried to sound casual, answering as he had earlier in the morning.

"Hey. I forgot I had a lunch meeting with these guys over from Europe." My heart sank like I was being stood up for senior prom. "You're coming with me."

My eyes widened with surprise. I used to be Daniel's favorite sidekick at business meetings, but recently I didn't even know what business dealings he was involved in.

"So you're double booked and I just get shortchanged, huh?" I knew he could hear my excitement, but I didn't care. I loved going to business meetings with him.

"I never said it was a date." Ouch. I tried not to take that personal. "But I am picking you up. I'll scoop you from your office in about an hour. You'll ride over with me."

"Oh, I'm not at my office," I responded distracted, approving the first coat of polish with a nod.

"Then you have an hour to get there. Just leave your car in the garage. I'll let you know when I'm on my way."

He was still in CEO-mode, delving out orders. I wanted to

object. I'd planned to go shopping for a new dress for our dinner, but I went with his plan without debate.

"I'll be ready," I shocked myself with a lack of pushback. I must have caught Daniel off guard as well, because he took longer than normal to respond.

"Where are you? Crystal said you were out."

"Just getting my nails done."

"Oh, you were getting cute for me?"

"You wish," I smiled.

In an hour, he'd see the effort I'd made to look good for our dinner. Though neither of us allowed our pending divorce to be the reason our appearance lacked. I kept my pampering routines despite the lack of attention from Daniel, never missing my weekly appointments in addition to meeting with a trainer three times a week.

Daniel was even more rigid. Our separation seemed to make him more dedicated to his upkeep. He never missed his weekly haircut, sometimes having his barber come to the house midweek for a touch up. He worked out daily, which was when I tried to ask him anything I could think of to get a peek at his glistening body.

"Just be ready when I call."

"I will."

"What'd you get – pink or red? Those are the only colors you ever choose." He asked after a brief pause.

"Fuchsia. It's pretty. You'll like it." I started to tell him I'd picked my nail color to match my lingerie, but didn't want to sound too eager.

"Sounds risqué." I imagined him in his office, spinning in his chair. "I'll see you soon," he added.

"Bye."

"Bye." He said with a tinge of disappointment. He didn't want the call to end, and he didn't hang up, instead he sighed into the phone. I closed my eyes and ended the call.

8

I'd been back in my office for fifteen minutes, waiting for Daniel to call, when Crystal knocked on my door.

"Come in."

"I just wanted to get these packed up and ready," she mumbled as she grabbed the vase of peach roses from my desk. "Damn, these are heavy."

"No, you can leave them! I like them here," I jumped, not wanting her to move my beautiful roses to a conference room.

"Well, Mr. Gamble said to have them sent to the house," she explained as she walked out. I looked up confused, and there he was in my doorway.

Beyond handsome, wearing a light gray suit with a white shirt underneath. Top two buttons undone, no tie. My favorite. His face was freshly shaved, his mustache perfectly shaped, with just a small patch of beard on the tip of his chin.

"Don't worry. I can get you more." He smirked, the left side of his lips revealing his amusement.

An unguarded smile spread across my face. I was so genuinely pleased to see him I couldn't find my poker face. "You said you'd call when you were on your way." I placed my hand on my hip, faking an attitude.

"You said you weren't getting cute for me." He countered, raising one brow.

"Let's go." I grabbed my purse and marched towards him.

When I stepped in front of him, he touched my shoulder and then placed four fingers on my throat, similar though less restricting to his gesture in the elevator. The memory was too vivid in my mind and I felt my body freeze, desire pooling once again. Dropping his hand, he watched me pass, following closely as I made my way to Crystal's desk.

"I'm leaving for the day," I said through a shaky breath.

"Yes, ma'am. See you tomorrow, Mrs. Gamble. And I'll be sure to speak with Tracy for the details, Mr. Gamble." Crystal smiled at Daniel.

I looked to him for understanding, but he just winked at Crystal and continued to the elevator. I reminded myself to limit my questions, struggling to go with the flow.

The elevator opened, and the four women inside shuffled to make room for the two of us. There was more than enough space; but they were clamoring, nervous. After four years of marriage, I was used to women losing their cool over my husband. I just wasn't used to being one of them. It felt like a first date, filled with nerves, hoping he liked me and would want to see me again.

I led the way into the elevator, and Daniel positioned himself behind me as we traveled from the 18th floor.

"You look very nice, Mrs. Gamble." He whispered in my ear as we passed the tenth floor. The warmth of his breath against my skin made me shudder.

"Mrs. Gamble? You're pretty formal, aren't you?" I asked over my shoulder.

During the first year of our marriage, Daniel rarely referred to me as anything other than Mrs. Gamble. He was shocked when I decided to take his name after he'd assured me he was fine with me hyphenating my last name, or going by my maiden name alto-

gether. I didn't expect to be so proud to be his wife, quickly preferring Mrs. Gamble to Emily.

"The last time I was in one of these with you I was slapped in
the face. I figure it's smart to be on my best behavior," he whispered
and I laughed out loud, causing the other women to look over at us.

On the 4th floor, the elevator doors opened and a man pushing a
large cart gave the awkward look from left to right, as if we could all
shift to reveal an extra row of space behind us. If I were alone, I
would've politely shaken my head, gesturing for him to wait for the
next elevator car. But I was Mrs. Gamble now, so when Daniel
placed his hand on my midsection, moving us to the corner behind
the four women, I went without hesitation. The man pushed his
cart into the elevator and nodded to Daniel, who nodded back.

When we arrived on the ground level, Daniel kept his hand
near my waist, signaling for the man to take his cart out first. I
barely felt his kiss below my left ear. It was so gentle, so delicate. I
turned to look at him and he nodded toward the door for me to
exit.

Taking a deep breath, I walked toward the valet stand where
Daniel handed the attendee his ticket and made small talk about
the recent change in ownership.

"So, no more Jim, huh?" He asked.

"No, Mr. Gamble. He decided to move down to Florida with his
wife," the valet answered, giving his undivided attention to Daniel.

"Well, that's too bad. I'll see you later, Andy." Daniel extended
his hand and smiled at the valet as they shook hands.

"Of course. That's a beautiful car, Mr. Gamble," Andy was
mesmerized in his staring, which turned my attention to the red
Ferrari 458 Italia Convertible.

Daniel didn't drive this car regularly, and I knew he didn't drive
it to work today. He must have spent his day prepping for our
meeting just as I had. He shook his head as the valet driver raced
toward the passenger door, indicating he would open my door
for me.

"It looks like I wasn't the only one getting cute today," I smiled, sliding onto the tan Italian leather. I watched a grin spread across his face as he rounded the car, excited for our date, regardless of what he wanted to call it.

9

"Top down okay?" Daniel asked as he settled into his seat. He never rode with the top up on the Ferrari. I was suddenly grateful I'd spent the morning at the salon, confident my hair would flow fabulously in the wind.

"That's fine. How do you always know the staff at my building better than me?" I wondered aloud as he pulled into traffic.

Daniel could spark a conversation with anyone, and later use that to build a connection. There was no doubt Andy would receive a Christmas gift from us, probably a remote-control Ferrari.

He shrugged his shoulders as he looked left to right, "That kid just likes driving my cars."

Surprisingly, he drove in silence. Daniel always rode to music. Our separation was the reason I hadn't heard any new releases recently. I was eager to hear new artists, but I just relaxed, watching the city pass by.

The tension was palpable, and for the first time in a long time, it was good tension. I wondered what his meeting was all about, and if he'd want me to participate or simply serve as arm candy. He hadn't told me anything about the deal, so I didn't know if I could be of assistance. In the past, I would have researched the company so I could hold my own in their discussion, but right now I didn't care. I'd be whatever he needed, I just wanted to be close to him.

While sitting at a red light, his phone rang throughout the stereo system as his assistant's name flashed across the navigation screen.

"Trace, what's up?" Daniel answered, almost too casually. He was such a cool boss, while I was more rigid and moody. Tracy loved him, but not more than her husband, so she was good in my book.

"Mr. Gamble, your lunch appointment just cancelled. I'm sorry, they were very last minute, but I've changed your reservation to two if you still wanted to continue with Mrs. Gamble." Daniel nodded along while listening, his eyes trained on me.

"Hi Tracy," I spoke towards the speaker, smiling at Daniel.

"Oh, hi, Em! I didn't know he'd already picked you up. The Sea Club has a fantastic crab cake, and their lemon merengue is to die for!"

"Oh yeah?" I asked, staring at Daniel as he raised his eyebrows, silently asking if I still wanted to go. I nodded, and he bit his lip to prevent another grin from creeping across his face.

"Yeah, Trace. I'm going to take Em, she hasn't been. You can leave for the day, just forward the office calls to your Blackberry. Don't call me unless you really need to. And if you really need to –"

"Don't." She finished his sentence. He had been saying this to her since he hired her. Daniel worked extremely hard, but when he wasn't working, he did not like to be disturbed.

Like Crystal, Tracy was a brilliant assistant. I often joked that she could do Daniel's job for him. Interrupting his personal time was very rare, and it earned her great Christmas bonuses. He ended the call, quickly turning the corner in a maneuver I usually would have deemed too dangerous.

As Daniel rolled to another stoplight, I felt his right hand caressing my left, circling the flawless diamond on my ring finger. His fingertips moved between the creases of my fingers before lifting my hand to his face. I thought he was going to kiss my hand, or my wedding ring, but instead he touched his cheek with the backside of my fingers. Inhaling deeply, he moved my knuckles across his full lips as I watched with interest, wondering what he was thinking.

Throughout his hand massage, he never took his eye off the streetlight, occasionally looking left to right or out the rearview mirror. It was so natural, as though my fingers against his lips was second nature. From his deep breaths, I sensed he was taking in my scent, remembering the fragrance of his wife.

My fingernails ran across his lips, and I jokingly poked my index finger into his mouth. Without hesitation, he bit down with his front teeth. It didn't hurt, but it did shock. What surprised me most was the tightening in my groin, my hunger for him growing by the second. He kissed my index finger three times, continuing to watch the rearview mirror before suddenly pulling the wheel, moving to the far-right lane.

"I hate this light. I know a shortcut," he said before speeding through a parking lot. After another turn, he pulled onto a service road running parallel to the street. He swerved left and right, dodging potholes, before turning into a beautiful driveway, with an arch of lights spelling out *The Sea Club*.

Pulling up to the valet, Daniel looked over at me and smiled. "Shall we eat?"

"I'd love to," I smiled back.

10

_____

"Mr. Gamble! How are you? Shall I set up your normal room?" The young hostess asked with dreamy eyes.

"Hi, Amber. It's just my wife today," Daniel glanced in my direction. I felt like a consolation prize, instantly wondering who he'd previously brought here, and what constituted his _normal_ room.

"Of course. Good afternoon, Mrs. Gamble. It's a pleasure to finally meet you. Please follow me," she smiled at me curtly, changing to a professional tone as she gathered two leather bound menus before leading us through a dining area.

I uncomfortably maneuvered through the maze of small tables as heads turned to watch us. Women were looking to Daniel, and then at me. Men were looking at me, and then to Daniel.

Sensing my uneasiness, Daniel reached for my right hand as we followed Amber. His touch was both comforting and foreign, a level of intimacy I'd missed. When we finally reached the back of the dining area, an older man's eyes lit up as he caught Daniel's attention.

"Gamble! How are you?" He asked excitedly, rushing to his feet.

Daniel used our intertwined fingers to pull me close, positioning his arm around my body with his left palm pressed against my abdomen. His thumb touched the underwire between my breasts and from the way he applied pressure, I knew it was no accident.

"Always good to see you, John," Daniel said while extending his right hand as they exchanged pleasantries. At one point Daniel introduced me, requiring a polite smile and nod, which was all I could manage. I was too focused on Daniel's fingertips, and their strategic placement on my body.

Through my chiffon top, I could feel every move and I needed more. Lost in a daydream of him ending this torture, and ripping the silk from my body, I failed to notice the end of his conversation until his lips were gently kissing below my ear.

"Go head, baby," he whispered.

Dropping his hand from my midsection, his fingertips subtly drifted down my backside as I walked ahead of him. We reached the end of the enclosed dining area before stepping into a quieter, more dimly lit room of tables spaced for privacy. Amber was standing at the first table, and I was grateful to let go of Daniel's hand.

After a six-month drought, followed by yesterday's ravenous sex, a dam had been breached and any contact from him opened the floodgates. I asked Amber for directions to the ladies' room and excused myself.

Looking in the mirror, I forced a deep breath before undoing my top two buttons. It was time to bring out the big guns. If he wanted to play this teasing game, I was going to win. I scooped each breast into my lace bra, enhancing the cleavage. Then, I fluffed my hair while psyching myself up with a few, "you got this!" affirmations.

Strolling back to the table, I approached from behind, gently running four fingernails across Daniel's neck as I passed. He tried to hide his smile as I sat across from him.

"I ordered you a glass of Chianti," he said as I settled into my seat.

"Ooh, great. So, how do you know the hostess?" I blurted.

"I don't."

"Well, you called her by her name when we walked in," I shrugged, trying to downplay my accusatory tone.

"She's wearing a name tag, Em." Daniel responded with a slight frown, probably wondering where my line of questioning was coming from.

I honestly didn't have an angle, but I felt like a stranger in his world. All these people only knew him, when we used to be a package deal. If you knew Daniel, you knew Emily. He didn't have a favorite restaurant, *we* had a favorite restaurant. But here I was, getting recommendations on the menu from his assistant, a clear indication that he must frequent this place, and before today I'd never heard of it.

"That guy seemed happy to see you. How did he know I was your wife?" Now I was pushing it, and I knew it, but I wanted him to know I felt like an outsider.

"Emily, who else would I be parading through a restaurant?" He cocked his head to the side. I could tell it was half rhetorical, half warning. Was that what he was doing? Parading me? My stomach fluttered at the idea.

"Well, of course..." I trailed off as the waiter arrived, setting two glasses of red wine on our table before scurrying off with his tray. Resting my hands on the table, Daniel reached across to place his right hand over my left.

"Relax," was all he said, but it seemed to relieve some unwanted tension. At that moment, I decided to enjoy myself.

When the waiter returned to take our orders, Daniel said he wasn't too hungry. I seconded that, trying to rush through the meal altogether. I was dying to be alone with him, so we decided to split a crab cake.

"I think the fuchsia looks really nice," he said, lifting his hand from mine. I'd forgotten it was there.

"Thank you. The girl convinced me it was *the* color this spring." I glanced down at my hand, focusing more on my wedding ring than the polish.

It was such a beautiful and flawless solitaire stone. The simplicity was so me, and the 6-carat diamond was so Daniel. He was beyond proud of his selection, personally cleaning it every other day during our first year of marriage.

"And you lightened your hair for the summer, huh?" He asked, hiding his growing grin behind a wine glass.

"Oh, yeah. You noticed..." I blushed, running my fingers through my hair before pushing it behind my ears.

"Of course, I noticed. I always notice."

His gaze was passionate. Too passionate. I turned away hoping to break his spell.

"Thank you. You don't look too bad yourself. You know I love you in gray."

"You may have mentioned it once or twice," he smirked. He knew what I liked, and he was undoubtedly dressed for me.

The crab cake arrived to both excitement and agitation. It was the largest crab cake I'd ever seen, there was no way we could rush through it. I was hoping to split a couple of bites and be out of there, but this was the kind of dish that came with side plates. Daniel cut a piece for both of us and handed me a plate.

"This is amazing!" I closed my eyes as I chewed the first bite. It was more crab than cake, cooked and seasoned to perfection.

"Tracy said you'd love it," Daniel smiled as he watched me shift in my seat. He always found it hilarious that I danced whenever I loved food.

"Well, Tracy needs a raise. She knows me well. How is she anyway?" I asked, finishing my last bite.

"She's good. I think I'm going to lose her soon, though. She wants to do more, and she probably should, but I don't want to move her." He answered while rubbing the back of his neck, reminding me of his crazy schedule.

"Daniel, you must be exhausted. I forgot you worked all day." I put my fork down. "Did you sleep at all last night?"

"No, it would've been worse to tease myself with a few hours."

"Yeah, teasing can be torturous," I bit my bottom lip.

The passion was still in his tired eyes, and when he picked up on my underlying message, a grin spread across his face. He was prolonging what we both wanted with his charade of a date.

As the waiter approached, I asked Daniel, "Would it be okay if we just packed this up and took it home?"

"You'd like me to package it, Mrs. Gamble?" The waiter asked.

"You don't want to try the lemon merengue?" Daniel interjected, guilt creasing his forehead.

"We could take some of that home too," I suggested in a hopeful tone, praying he wouldn't force me to sit through more small talk. My thighs pressed together, struggling to alleviate my longing.

"Baby, I'm okay," he said gently, not wanting to leave early on his behalf.

"No, I'm not really hungry. It is delicious, and I do want to try that merengue," I said, more to the waiter than Daniel.

When I looked across the table, he was squinting, searching for my motive. I tried my best to relax my shoulders and remove any sign of yearning from my face. If he knew I was rushing to get home, he'd only prolong the delay. The waiter looked from me to Daniel for the final decision.

"Whatever the lady wants," Daniel said, reaching into his suit pocket.

As the waiter collected our half-eaten crab cake, Daniel handed him his black American Express card, speaking in a tone too low for me to hear.

"Thank you, Mr. Gamble," the waiter nodded before scurrying off.

"We'll have to do this over. This isn't how I saw it going. I still owe you dinner," he said. His eyes were darker now, lowered and narrowing.

"Well, you said it wasn't a date." I said matter-of-factly, quoting his earlier reminder.

"No, Mrs. Gamble, this was definitely not a date. But now I owe you one." His attention drifted, watching the waiter approach from behind me with a large white bag. He signed a receipt and placed his credit card back in his wallet before standing to take the bag, offering his hand to me.

I followed his lead as he escorted us back through the dining area and then to the valet stand. It was still early, but the sun was no longer shining. The sky had turned a light gray while we were inside. Unexpectedly, Daniel spun me around to face him, leaving no space between us, his left arm draped around my neck.

"It looks like it's going to rain," I said, looking up at the sky.

"Nah, I'll beat it."

He raised his right hand, brushing my shirt aside before asking, "Was this for me?" outlining the cleavage of my left breast with his index finger and thumb.

"Well, you always undo your top two buttons," I reasoned, flashing my best seductive smile as I ran my fingertip across his collar.

"That I do," he smirked and nodded before pulling me closer and kissing my forehead. "That I do," he repeated.

Being in public dimmed the tension between us, but the minute we were alone in the car again, it all came flooding back. We rode in silence, Daniel looking deep in thought, scanning left to right before checking his rearview mirror.

His right hand rested on the center console and I placed my left hand on top, admiring his soft skin. He looked over and smiled before lifting my hand to his face, repeating the same ritual as earlier. He was absentmindedly kissing the backside of my fingers when his phone rang through the speakers. It was Tracy, again. He gently placed my hand on his thigh, pushing a button on his steering wheel to answer the call.

"Trace! What's up?" He asked while making a sharp left turn.

"Hey, boss! Just wanted to let you know I was holding your calls for the evening and emailing over today's summary. Is there anything else I can do before heading out?"

"That's fine. I thought you left earlier. Nothing's changed, right?" He asked with concern.

"Not really. You know I think it would be better in person, Mr. Gamble. The schedule is getting even crazier. You'll have to live in a different time zone to make it happen." The anxiety was clear in Tracy's voice. I wondered how many days he'd pulled this double duty, working through the night.

"Just send me the details and draft up alternatives. We'll discuss it tomorrow." He said in a tone that meant the debate was tabled.

"Yes, sir. I'll see you tomorrow. Bye, Mrs. Gamble!" She seemed so genuinely excited to know he was with me. I bet she noticed the schedule changes as much as Crystal.

"Bye Trace!" I said, looking over at Daniel.

He was deep in thought, and when he approached a stoplight, I lost my restraint. "Is everything alright?" I asked, leaning against the headrest to face him.

"Yeah... Tracy just thinks I should go to Tokyo to close this deal. I could get done in a few days what's taking me all these video calls in the middle of the night."

He didn't look at me when he spoke and I knew why. A few weeks before my last birthday, he went away on a business trip to close a deal. It was the last straw in our faltering marriage. Time apart was the last thing we needed, but we both selfishly wanted a break from our problems. He'd went off and closed the deal, spending 10-days in Europe. I took a trip down to Miami with my sister, and it was the beginning of our separate lives.

I only talked to him once during the entire trip, and even then, it was short and unwanted. He'd come back with no plan for my birthday for the first time since I'd known him. We spent the entire day arguing as he repeatedly asked what I wanted to do. I thought he was joking, leading up to some extravagant surprise he'd laid out. In the end there was no surprise, and my 31st birthday went down as my worst ever, a fact I reminded him of more times than I could count.

I imagined Daniel had tried to retrace what went wrong as many times as I had. And although the list of fuckups was long, his trip abroad had to be at the top of the list. I wasn't sure what we were doing now, but whatever it was, I didn't want to pause it for a business trip, hoping the feelings would remain once he returned. I knew now like I knew then, time apart was the last thing we needed, but this time it was also the last thing I wanted.

My body tensed, and Daniel gently raised my hand from his lap, continuing to kiss my fingers. Leaning against the headrest, he turned to me and said, "Just relax, baby," without missing a beat in his worshipping of my fingers.

I nodded, trying my best to appear optimistic. My anxiety was evident as we pulled into the driveway. I felt the built-up desire begin to dissolve as reality hit me. I wasn't on a first date; I was in the middle of a divorce. What was I thinking?

12

Together we walked to the door leading from the garage to our home. Daniel followed so closely I could feel his presence behind me. Once I turned the key and stepped through the doorway, his hands instantly brushed my hair to the side, kissing the nape of my neck. Dropping the doggy bag, I lunged toward to the wall for support as a desperate moan escaped me. His nose was in my hair, his tender lips kissing over my ear and down my neck, while his hands reached to unzip my skirt.

I pushed the tight fabric over my hips, kicking it to the floor before turning to face him. Daniel lifted me with ease, tracing my collar bone with his tongue as I wrapped my limbs around him. Leaning back to grant him full access to my neck, my heart raced, adrenaline pumping through me. After leaving a trail of wet kisses to my ear, he grazed his teeth along my jawline until we were face to face.

The passion was back in his eyes. He stared at me for what felt like an eternity. With one hand on each cheek, he gripped my face and kissed me so deeply I couldn't breathe. His hands wandered into my hair, pushing me further into the kiss. His tongue dominated my mouth. I felt the wall against my back and tilted my head, gasping to catch my breath. Gone was the tired man from *The Sea Club*. Staring into my soul, Daniel was energized and reinvigorated.

Breaking the gaze, I slammed my lips to his, so reckless I scraped his tongue with my teeth, causing a deep moan to travel from his mouth to mine. He tugged at my hair, abruptly ending the kiss. With his eyes closed, he tilted his head back.

"Fuck," Daniel grunted, cupping my lace covered bottom. He walked through our kitchen before turning down the hallway leading to the master bedroom.

Gently touching his lips to mine, he pulled back every time I moved to deepen the kiss. He continued taunting me until I frowned, wondering why he was rejecting me. A shadow of a smile flickered across his lips, and I realized why he'd cussed earlier. This was his show; he didn't want my seduction, only my pleasure.

Once he reached the edge of our bed, he threw me onto the covers. Working quickly, I kicked off my shoes, tugging my chiffon top over my head and tossing it to the floor. Daniel shrugged out of his suit jacket before unbuttoning his shirt. By the time he was unscrewing his cuff links, I was yearning for the bulge in his pants.

As if reading my mind, he cupped his manhood in his right hand while shaking his head. I gazed up to see him smiling, watching frustration creep across my face. I couldn't take any more suspense.

Gripping my ankle, he slowly pulled me to the edge of the bed, lifting my foot to his mouth. Kneeling at the edge of the bed, he gently kissed my ankle.

His mouth was wet and warm, sending sensation throughout my body. I gasped while arching my back when his kisses trailed up my calf until his face rested between my legs. Tickling the sensitive skin of my inner thigh, he ran his nose along my panty line. Feeling him inhale deeply, I sucked in a sharp breath, realizing he was savoring the smell of my flower.

"Happy to see me?" He bit his bottom lip as his fingers caressed the wet lace between my thighs.

"Ecstatic," I breathed heavily with anticipation.

"I like these," he spoke calmly, tracing the colorful designs across my high-waist panties.

"Thank you."

He flipped me over with one hand on my hip, continuing to trace the designs along my backside. "But you might have ruined them, you know."

I could hear his smile as he slipped one finger into each side of my panties, pulling them down my hips. Lifting onto my knees, I wiggled to help him, then dropped back to my belly, feeling the lace reach my ankles.

Still on my stomach, I heard him unzip his pants and knew from the clink of his belt that they'd dropped to the floor. Running his nose along the back of my legs, his breathing alone made me shudder.

He unclasped the hook of my bra, and I lifted one arm at a time so he could remove the straps. He moved so slowly, brushing my hair aside to kiss the nape of my neck. Pushing onto my knees, I felt his bare erection, and to my surprise he gripped my hip, pulling me closer.

"I want to hear you today," he whispered.

13

Placing four fingers on my hipbone, Daniel flipped me again. Landing on my back, I was breathless from the sight of his naked body. Kneeling at the foot of the bed, he was a God. His abs were so chiseled they begged to be touched, leading to an indent at his hips that made me bite my lip. His manhood stood at attention. Just looking at him made my thighs clench together.

Overflowing with desire, I looked in his dark eyes, witnessing the passion. He was admiring my body as well, causing me to smile shyly. It had been so long since I felt the adrenaline rush of seduction. Daniel returned the gesture, though his grin was more mischievous.

He leaned down, pushing my knees open, again placing his head between my legs. Wasting no time, he flicked my clitoris with his tongue and I gasped loudly, arching my back. His hand pressed against my pelvis, pushing me down to the bed as he circled my clit with the flat of his tongue. Grasping frantically for a pillow to mask my moan, Daniel snatched it from my hand, throwing it across the room.

"Let me hear you," he commanded.

Crawling up my body, his eyes never left mine as he moved two fingers over my swollen bud, rhythmically pushing me forward.

I nodded my understanding. He wasn't giving me any crutches, forcing me to embrace the pleasure head on. Daniel slid two fingers inside me, pushing his palm against my clit. I shrieked with delight, clenching my eyes closed as his mouth moved to my breast. Swirling his tongue across my nipple until it stood tall, he grazed his teeth around the sharp tip while continuously sliding his fingers in and out of me, tapping my clit with his palm in a steady rhythm.

I reached down to push him on, but he grabbed my hand, shaking his head before returning to my breasts, this time teasing my other nipple.

I couldn't touch him? Who was this man?

I wanted to argue, but the pleasure from his mouth and fingers was making me tighten. My legs began to tense, and I knew my orgasm was coming. Slowing his fingers, he instantly halted my ascension while maintaining a high level of pleasure. Then he leaned beside me, pushing my knees towards my chest, watching his fingers slide in and out of my essence with ease.

"I want to touch you," It was a whine more than anything.

"I know," he said without looking at me.

Suddenly, Daniel pulled his fingers from my slit and leaned between my thighs. Pushing my legs into the air, he grazed his teeth along my clitoris. I erupted violently, coming so hard I felt out of my body, watching my legs shake in the air uncontrollably.

Positioning himself between my legs, Daniel smiled with my juices splayed across his lips. Wiping his mouth on his palm, he grasped my hip tightly, sliding into my needy opening before I finished riding the waves of my orgasm. Inhaling a shaky breath, my legs spread to make room for his thickness. He fit so snug. My sex clenched his length, still pulsating from my climax.

Shoving his tongue into my mouth, Daniel swallowed my moans hungrily. I tasted myself, something that would have repulsed me in the past, but now it was erotic as hell.

Gripping my hands, he interlocked our fingers above my head as he slammed in and out of me, balancing himself on his knees. It made me think of the last time I'd seen him working out in the gym. As he rolled his core wheel over and over, I watched the muscles in his back flex, admiring how sexy he was.

Now, he was exercising inside of me, every push extending my orgasm. I wondered what was making a foreign shrieking noise, and then realized it was *me*. I was moaning and gasping so loudly it was embarrassing as a new orgasm rose from my abdomen through my chest. Daniel kissed my neck, then my cheek, whispering on my lips, "Stop fighting me."

My entire body was tense with restraint, but I wanted to let go, I needed to release. Closing my eyes, I followed his movements blindly, submitting to his rhythm, rocking to meet his every thrust.

"Wrap your legs around me," Daniel whispered, finally releasing my hands.

Without question, I wrapped my arms and legs around him, running my nose along his neck. I could feel him positioning himself beneath me before he pulled my hair back, forcing me to look into his eyes. "You're about to come really hard. Are you ready?" His face was serious, worrisome even.

I nodded, thinking to myself, *I thought I did just come hard.*

With my arms and legs draped around him, Daniel sat up on his knees, wrapping his arms around me as he began to push into me, pulling my body onto his manhood in opposite motions. The feeling was incredible, our bodies collided in unison as he hit a new angle that left me speechless. I was filled to my max, afraid of the impending explosion growing like a tidal wave.

Usually, he would have asked if I was okay, but today he was left only with animalistic groans as his pace increased with every stroke. The pleasure was unbearable, I could feel myself losing control.

"Spread your legs," Daniel ordered over the crashing sound of our slippery bodies harmonizing with the melodies of my continuous moans.

Following his instructions, I released my legs, spreading them wide. His right hand remained wrapped around my back, cradling the nape of my neck, while his left moved down to my bottom, holding me in place as he maintained his pummeling rhythm.

Leaning forward, he balanced his weight on his elbows, driving me onto his length as he surged forward with force. His pace increased, falling into my warmth, and now the angle made his pelvis push into my clitoris with every plunge.

I could resist no longer. Pleasure washed over me and the strongest orgasm I had ever experienced dominated my body. I felt it in my toes, my shoulders, my breasts, my fingertips. My words became more like a chant, "I love you I love you I love you I love you I love you," repeatedly.

Daniel gripped my waist tightly, his rhythm nonexistent. He bucked like in animal as he chased his own release. The neediness and desperation in his breathing pushed my climax to new heights.

Finally, he slammed into me three last times before stiffening and pulling my hair back as he buried his face in my neck.

"Fuck!... Argh!... Baby..." his groans grew weak with his release. Kissing my neck over and over, I felt him jump inside me as he shot hot semen.

I was spent beyond comprehension. The room was more colorful than normal. My legs tingled with electricity. He brought his face to mine, looking at me with such adoration, wiping tears I didn't know I'd cried.

"I love you too, Em," he smiled between kisses, and I melted into his arms.

14

Lying on our backs, we panted in unison, lost in the moment. Daniel lifted my hand to his lips and began kissing my knuckles, the fresh stubble from his five o'clock shadow tickling my fingers. I rolled onto my side, and when his eyes landed on mine, he smirked with amusement.

"You look satisfied," he said, peppering gentle kisses along my fingers.

"I feel satisfied," I admitted through a bashful smile. How or why I was shy around my husband I could never explain. But my husband had never made me come like that.

Daniel nodded his head before frowning, turning towards me, "Are you hungry?"

"I'm starving!" I yelled, rolling my eyes.

"Me too!"

He jumped up, walking into the closet where I heard a drawer open and close. Re-emerging in a pair of boxer briefs, Daniel walked towards the bedroom door, "I couldn't even eat waiting to get you back here."

Holding myself up on my elbows, I watched him with a new

level of appreciation for what he could do with that glorious body. Once he left the bedroom, I jumped up, heading to the bathroom. Catching a glimpse of my ruined hair in the mirror, I quickly decided it was worth it. After grabbing a silk robe, I pulled my frizzy hair into a top bun as I walked into the kitchen.

"You're so sexy," Daniel said as he laid eyes on me.

"Ditto, kiddo," I replied with a smile while walking over to him. "What's up with you and hands all of a sudden?" I asked.

"I just missed your little fingers." He shrugged before taking a bite from a garlic roll. He was so sweet with such little effort.

"Where'd you get garlic rolls?" I asked, taking a bite from the one in his hand.

"I told Greg to throw as much shit as he could into our doggy bag. We have potatoes, another crab cake, garlic rolls, and asparagus." He announced, pointing to each plastic container.

"Who's Greg?"

"The waiter from *The Sea Club*. You should really start reading name tags, Em." He raised an eyebrow while watching me eye the food. "You would heat this up in the oven, wouldn't you?" He asked.

I shrugged my shoulders. We both knew I hated the microwave, but I didn't want to argue about anything. I went to open a container and Daniel lifted me like a child, sitting me on the countertop. My robe came undone, and I saw that he noticed.

Standing between my legs, he kissed my breasts before moving the silk from my shoulder to kiss there. I watched him, placing my hand on the back of his head as he made his way up my shoulder, then my neck, and before I knew it he was kissing my mouth passionately.

I wrapped my legs around him, kissing him back as he moved his hand up to my neck, tilting my head so his tongue could better dance with mine. He pulled away and my eyes refused to open, my body wanting more. When I finally looked up, he was gazing at me.

"You taste like me," I said, wrapping my arms around his neck, leaning in to run my nose along his jaw.

"You taste good," he said through a perfect smile. "I don't think you can handle anymore tonight. You change the sheets, I'll warm up the food." He lifted me from the counter, placing me gently on my feet. I stalled, not wanting to leave so soon.

I was enjoying his kisses, and although I knew my body couldn't endure another session, I didn't want to be cut off. Reading my expression, he twisted me around by my hips, kissing just below my ear as he slapped my butt, "I won't be long."

I took off towards our bedroom, glancing back as I exited the kitchen. He was watching me. Shaking his head, he began unpacking the takeout. I smiled with the hopeful passion of a newlywed.

In our bathroom, I skimmed the linen closet, selecting a gray sheet set before ripping our soiled sheets from the bed. Dings from the microwave served as the soundtrack while I moved from one corner to the next, tucking the sheets beneath our king size mattress.

When I spread the down comforter across the bed, placing all ten pillows along the headboard, it dawned on me that I'd be sharing the bed with Daniel again. Sleeping alone had been one of the worst parts of our separation. Plenty of nights, I came close to asking if we could just cuddle without any expectations or obligatory affection.

"Emily! Meet me in the TV room!" I heard Daniel yell from the kitchen.

I ran to the closet and slipped a silk nightgown over my head, spraying a little perfume between my breasts before rushing to the TV room. Daniel had warmed the food in platter dishes far too large, but he looked so proud of himself as he raised his eyebrows, awaiting my reaction.

"You did a wonderful job," I kissed his cheek before joining him on the sofa.

"I brought you a beer. Do you want wine instead?" He scrunched his eyebrows together, doubting his decision.

"Beer is perfect. Thank you," I kissed him again, allowing my lips to linger on his cheek longer than necessary. Turning to face the coffee table, I eyed the colorful platters I'd purchased in Morocco. Biting my tongue, I refused to ask if he'd put the hand painted dishes in the microwave.

Let it go, Emily, I said to myself.

15

"Bloomberg or basketball?" Daniel asked with the television remote in one hand, an asparagus spear in the other.

"Whatever you want, baby," I spoke against his cheek, throwing my legs into his lap.

He pulled my legs close while giving his full attention to Bloomberg. He'd made a plate for each of us, but I had yet to take my eyes off him.

Daniel was completely distracted, and I used that candid moment to take in his beautiful features. His dark, thick hair was cut to perfection, fading to his hairline. He must have visited his barber in preparation for our lunch date. While my skin bronzed, Daniel's was more of a golden brown. His thick eyebrows shaped his hazel eyes so perfectly, I'd asked if he tweezed them on our first date, accidentally offending him. I laughed softly recalling the memory.

"What are you giggling about?" He turned to me and I buried my face in his neck, inhaling the smell of his cologne. "You're on a sex high," he smirked before turning back to the television.

"I am not!" I shot up, trying to look as outraged as possible.

Shaking his head, he held an asparagus spear to my mouth. "Yeah, you might be mad at me all over again in the morning."

I frowned, staring at his profile as he turned back towards the television. *Is that what he thought? That this was just about sex? Was this just about sex?* My mind was so cloudy I couldn't even remember why I was mad at him in the first place. The more I thought about it, the more certain I became. I was never upset with him, we just started living separately. There was no real animosity, unless we were at the construction site.

"I was never mad at you." I said with confidence, biting the asparagus he still held to my lips, searching his face for clarity.

Is that what he thought, that I'd been mad at him this whole time?

"Oh no?" Was all he said, raising an eyebrow, unleashing a pool of guilt within me.

I was the one who filed for divorce without so much as speaking to him. Over what? A birthday party, or lack thereof? And since then, I hadn't spoken a word about the filing. In fact, neither of us had ever uttered the word to each other.

My lawyer thought my filing was a cry for attention, since I requested nothing from Daniel. Instead, I opted to give him the rights to everything in my name, while additionally maintaining control of all his assets. I even offered to remove all liability for every penny of debt we'd incurred on my impulsive real estate purchase.

When Daniel's lawyer sent back the petition, stating that he would only accept the settlement if the terms were completely reversed, my lawyer begged me to withdraw, insisting the entire process was a waste of time. But I refused. I re-sent the settlement offer with my original terms 5-months ago and had yet to hear from his lawyer. *Was* it all just a cry for attention?

I never thought about how it made him feel, or what the process looked like from his end. We didn't discuss why I wanted a divorce, or how I felt about him going to Europe without me. Instead, I threw tantrum after tantrum, pushing him further away, waiting for him to force me to address my issues.

Suddenly, I felt guilty and immature. I'd been in such agony the past six months, and it was all my own doing. I was even responsible for our separate sleeping arrangement, after asking him to sleep in the guest room. I'd hoped he would object so we could finally scream our feelings across the house.

But Daniel just clenched his jaw, closed his eyes, and said, "If that's what you want, Emily," before walking out of our bedroom. I'd only intended his stay to last one night at most, but my pride wouldn't invite him back into our bedroom. So, I cried myself to sleep for a month.

Daniel looked at me and spoke softly, "Relax, baby. I didn't mean to upset you. Just enjoy your high. I'll give you another hit tomorrow, and it'll all be fine." He laughed as he kissed my forehead. "Here, you need to eat something," he said, handing me a plate.

I sighed and forced a pitiful laugh, knowing he was right. I was on a complete high and there was no point in reliving every fuckup I'd made over the course of our disastrous year. I ate my crab cake, pushing my anxiety and guilt to the back of my conscience.

After our meal, Daniel watched the end of his favorite show, *Brilliant Ideas,* as I kissed him repeatedly. I started on his shoulder, working my way up to his neck with soft gentle kisses. His perfect smile swept over his face when I cuddled his neck with my nose before kissing the small dimple on his cheek.

"I'm not giving you another hit today. I'm sorry, but you're cut off. I don't want to encourage this type of addiction." He somehow managed to keep a straight face during his fake speech.

"Well, can you just sleep with me then?" I asked as innocently as possible.

He looked over me and blinked slowly. Without a word, he lifted me from the sofa and headed towards the bedroom. Pausing, he looked at the dishes. I reminded him that Marla would clean in the morning, which was all the encouragement he needed to continue walking.

We brushed our teeth side by side in our bathroom as I peeked over at him and smiled. I felt like my best friend could finally stay the night for the first time, overly excited about every normal routine we got to share.

Pulling the covers back, I climbed into bed, waiting for Daniel to finish in the bathroom. He came into the bedroom and immediately walked into the closet, opening drawers before shutting off the light and crawling into bed wearing only pajama pants.

He pulled me close, wrapping his arms around me as he inhaled deeply. I never felt safer or more at ease than I did in Daniel's arms. I exhaled thinking of how perfect the day had been, and looked up to Daniel, whose eyes were already closed. My husband was exhausted.

"I love you, Daniel," I whispered in case he was already asleep.

"You love the dick, Em. But he loves you too, so go to sleep," he smiled without opening his eyes.

"Don't say that! That's not funny!" I feigned offense.

He smirked and kissed my forehead before drifting off to sleep.

16

I couldn't sleep, but didn't want to leave Daniel's grasp, so I lie awake staring at him, my perfect man. Daniel had always been the ideal husband, according to my sisters and girl-friends. I'd listen to tales of their horrific relationships, thinking how Daniel would never do those things to me. The truth was he treated me too good, or maybe I just didn't know how to accept his love.

My parents gave me everything I ever wanted as a child. Rather than being grateful and obedient, I chose to act out, confident I would never be punished. The youngest of four daughters and one son, I was spoiled rotten. My sisters constantly claimed rules didn't apply to me growing up, but I never saw it that way. I knew my parents loved all their children beyond words, I was just best at exploiting their love to get what I wanted.

By the time I left Los Angeles for college, I could no longer recognize when I was being manipulative. It had woven into my character so seamlessly, I couldn't tell where it stopped and I began. I remember building up tears before calling my father from the front steps of Meridian Hill Hall during my second year at Howard

University, concocting a story on the fly about seeing a rat in my dorm room.

Once I was confident he'd bought the story, I revealed my need – a private apartment. The truth was, I'd been caught smoking weed with my roommate Monica, and we'd both been kicked out of student housing.

My parents wouldn't have given me any grief about the trouble. My mother thought the dorm rooms were beneath me anyway, but I didn't want it the honest way. I needed to be the victim, and by the time I ended the call with my dad, he was apologizing for what I'd seen, guaranteeing he and my mother would be on their way in two days to find an apartment for both Monica and me.

Until then, he instructed us to stay at one of the four boutique hotels he owned in Washington, D.C. I was halfway through bragging to Monica when I realized the timer for the call with my dad was still counting. I frantically tapped my phone screen to end the call and sat stunned, certain he'd heard my crying conveniently end along with our conversation. He knew I was lying.

A few days later, he and my mother arrived from Los Angeles, as promised, and me and Monica were the only sophomores living in a penthouse apartment. My father never mentioned my lie, or even led on that he knew about it at all.

Lying in bed with Daniel, I wondered if my life would've been different if someone, anyone, had ever called me on my shit.

In the deepest level of my subconscious, I wanted Daniel to be the person to put me in my place. It wasn't fair to expect him to fix me, especially when he was so well put together himself. There was nothing I would change about Daniel, especially now that he wasn't fucking me like a fragile doll that may break at any moment.

We'd had rough sex before, especially after a night of drinking, but never anything like this. *Did he always want to fuck me like this, or was this just built up aggression?* The six-month sexual hiatus seemed to transform him into a new person altogether.

Had he been fucking someone else? Before my thoughts could make it through the proper channels to form an actual conclusion,

I decided I didn't care. Honestly, if another woman had turned him into this sexual beast, I'd send the bitch a Christmas gift. She deserved it. Deep down, I knew Daniel could never betray himself in that way. His integrity was too strong. Wasn't it?

I tried to shake the thought from my mind. Here I was again, getting caught up in my imagination rather than just enjoying the moment. I looked at Daniel sleeping so peacefully beside me, his arms intertwined with mine, my left leg draped across his sculpted body. I wanted to lie in bed with him all day so this feeling would never fade. Syncing my breathing with his, I forced myself to relax. Finally, my eyelids grew heavy and I drifted off to sleep.

I awoke to gentle kisses on my lips. Blinking slowly, I struggled to focus my vision. Daniel was leaning over me, his right knee on the bed.

"I'm leaving, baby. Keep sleeping. I told Crystal you'd be working from home today," he said before kissing me one last time and standing. He was fully dressed in a dark tailored suit with a crisp white shirt. Top two buttons undone, no tie. It was too early for this type of temptation.

"Nooo! I wanted to play hooky and stay in bed today," I whined. I thought we'd at least have breakfast together.

"I tried. I have two meetings and a bunch of calls I can't cancel. I won't be too late, and I'll take you to dinner to make up for yesterday's lunch," he said, leaning down to brush my hair from my face.

"I don't want to go out to eat," I argued. My arms stretched above my head as a deep yawn escaped me. My silk nightgown rose above my thighs, exposing my swollen lips. I watched his gaze shift downwards, a smile spreading across his face.

"Yeah, I know what you want, fiend. I'll try not to be long. I've heard the withdrawals can be pretty bad. Drink a lot of water," he smirked and walked towards the door.

"I love you," my voice was still raspy, making me sound sexier than I intended.

"You love the dick, Em," he smiled with only the left side of his mouth, his hand on the doorframe as he caught his last glimpse before leaving.

"Stop saying that!" I squirmed, feeling his stare all over me.

"I love you too." The words were muffled through the wall as he walked down the hall, leaving a trail of cologne in his absence. I was left feeling giddy like a teenager. God, I loved him.

After trying and failing to go back to sleep, I reached over to my nightstand for my iPhone. He'd already texted me.

Daniel: I love you too.

I sat up and smiled, crossing my legs as I unlocked my phone to respond.

Emily: Has it ever occurred to you that maybe you're on a sex high?

After sending the text, I climbed out of bed, sauntering to the bathroom. My phone buzzed.

*Daniel: This escalated from denial to accusatory very quickly.
As your dealer, I'm concerned.*

I smiled. Why did we ever stop texting? He was so much fun. Oh yeah, I filed for divorce.

Emily: I want to taste you.

I bit my bottom lip, awaiting the swoosh sound following a successful delivery.

Daniel: You just made my dick hard in a meeting, so I'm terminating this conversation.
Emily: I accept your defeat, Mr. Gamble.
Daniel: I look forward to taking you to church later. I had no idea you spoke in tongues.

17

Daniel never responded to my text. I wondered if he'd really gotten hard in his meeting. The thought made me smile as I dialed my office.

"Mrs. Gamble's office. Crystal speaking, how may I help you?" Crystal sounded cheery and professional.

"Hey Crys! What's going on?" I immediately cringed. I had never called her Crys. I was not a fun boss, that was for sure.

"Mrs. G! All's good on the home front! How are you?" She answered after a pause, surely trying to work out why I'd called her Crys. Bless her heart for trying to play along with her 'Mrs. G' nonsense.

"I don't really have anything going on, do I?" I asked, although I knew the answer.

My work had suffered considerably during my separation from Daniel. I bought Cherry Blossoms Publishing, on my 25th birthday, with my first trust fund disbursement. I wanted to write, but was too scared, so publishing other writers seemed like a great alternative.

My first year was pretty shitty. No one wanted a 25-year old boss, which made gaining my staff's trust more difficult than I'd anticipated. In my second year, I made a point to always remain sternly professional. It garnered a lot of respect, but made my job too formal. I often felt like I was going to work rather than running a company.

I spent my third year hiring and firing talent, as the publishing industry drastically changed. I needed a new team that didn't think the eBook was going away, and anyone over fifty was hard to convince.

In my fourth year, my company began to run without me. I went in for appearances and purpose, but my team was undoubtedly the star of the show. It had remained that way since, but during the past year, I was absent even when I did occasionally make it to the office.

"Oh, you're all good. You did have a hair appointment, but I figured you'd want to cancel since you saw Sonja yesterday. Did you still want to go?"

I touched my hair and thought I *should* go, but the idea of spending three hours in a salon didn't sound appealing.

"No, cancel it. Call me if you need me. I'll be home." I said, wishing we shared a saying like Daniel and his assistant Tracy.

"No Problem. See you tomorrow, Mrs. G!" Crystal was excited to use my new nickname.

"Bye Crys!"

Daniel was nothing like me in business, or life in general. His parents didn't own a hospitality empire. He was completely self-made, launching his first business from a dorm room at Stanford, where he received a full scholarship to play basketball.

He always joked about how disappointed his family was when he chose to attend Stanford, doubting he'd ever win a national championship. But Daniel never planned on becoming a basketball star, he only wanted the education and prestige that accompanied a Stanford degree. Everything was always a calculated business move with him. By the time he graduated, he'd sold his image sharing app in Silicon Valley, pocketing more than he would have earned as a first-round draft pick. His family wasn't impressed.

Now, he ran Tower Enterprise Group, the most successful consultancy firm in southern California. When I met him at my 25th birthday party, and asked what he did, I thought he was full of shit when he told me he was a consultant.

"And what's that mean?" I asked, my voice laced with condescension.

"It means that if you can afford me, I can solve your problems," he answered bluntly. I melted, instantly captivated by his bold confidence.

"I can definitely afford you," I quipped.

"It doesn't look like you have too many problems, though," he flashed his perfect smile, taking my breath away.

Scanning the over decorated birthday party Monica had planned, I imagine he wondered what a brat like me could ever need help with. I was so lost in Daniel's eyes, I forgot all about Eric, until he was wrapping his arm around my hip, introducing himself as my boyfriend.

I dated Eric my entire four years at Howard, and he'd taught me a lot – how to crack any iPhone code, when to know your boyfriend's fake sister actually loves sucking his dick, and the art of faking an orgasm.

We had all but broken up when Monica sent him a pity invite, and he had the audacity to drape himself over me all night like we were madly in love. Ruining my first conversation with Daniel was the last straw.

"You're a lucky man," Daniel noted to Eric before excusing himself to take a call.

Daniel later told me he'd never seen someone so pretty give such a dirty look. He assumed I was going through a break-up, and figured he'd see me again. But patience was never my forte. In true pushy Emily fashion, I Googled him and showed up at his consultancy firm with the first disbursement from my trust, determined not to blow through my money like my older siblings.

Tower Enterprise Group researched publishing houses before presenting the best options. I acquired a smaller company, based on a rare recommendation from Daniel, and renamed it Cherry Blossoms Publishing, an ode to my years in Washington, D.C.

My plan was to work with Daniel to get to know him better, but that quickly proved impossible. Daniel was serious about his business, never even engaging in small talk. In every meeting, he sat quietly, studying me from across a long mahogany table.

Occasionally, he would make a note, or whisper to one of his colleagues, but mostly he seemed to observe in silence. He didn't need to vocalize his opinions, because every presentation or recommendation was preceded by a head nod from him. His influence and status was discreet, a rarity in LA, where everyone was defined by their title.

After the closing, Daniel dismissed his team, leaving just the two us in the conference room as I signed the final paperwork.

"The commission line is blank," I pointed out.

"Let me see," Daniel leaned over, the scent of his cologne swirling between us as he reached for the contract, scribbling quickly and then passing it back to me.

"Mélisse? The restaurant?" I asked, reading his neat handwriting.

"That's the fee."

I stared at him in disbelief. I'd been certain he wasn't interested in me. After a brief pause I responded sharply, "No."

"No?" Now, he was the one shocked.

"I can go to Mélisse on my own. If you want to have dinner with me, you need to cook the meal."

We spent our first date in his penthouse bachelor condo, eating the most amazing lasagna I'd ever had. Two years later, on our wedding night, he confessed it was Stouffers.

The doorbell snapped me from my trance, and I grabbed my robe before heading to the door. I opened to a young Latino man holding a huge white box, extending an iPad turned towards me with a stylus, passively requesting my signature.

"You use iPads for deliveries now? That's posh," I remarked while signing before accepting the package. Closing the door behind me, I sat the box on the kitchen island, revealing fifty long-stem white roses. Reaching for the card attached to the top of the box, I shifted my weight from one foot to the next with excitement.

COCAINE WHITE

FOR MY FAVORITE ADDICT.

I threw my head back, exploding with laughter. He was too much. I reached for my cell and shot him a text.

Emily: While they don't compare to the real thing, my roses are beautiful.
Daniel: What can I say? I'm an enabler.
Emily: What happened to a vase?
Daniel: I thought that's what Greece was for.

I smiled, reaching into the cabinet above the oven, searching for the red stained-glass vase we'd gotten during our vacation in Greece. We'd met a stain glass artist while exploring Crete, the largest of the islands, and commissioned her to create five vases for me in various colors. It had been two years since they arrived, but I loved them just as much as I had in Greece. They were stunning.

Emily: Just when are you coming home? Dealers don't get to take breaks, you know.
Daniel: Believe me, the minute I can leave, I'm out of here.
Emily: Are you missing me?
Daniel: Always, baby.

I smiled, deciding to set something up for him to prove he wasn't the only one with tricks up his sleeve.

"Mr. Gamble's office. Tracy speaking," she answered.

"Hey Trace, don't say my name. I don't want Daniel to know I'm calling," I answered, slightly whispering as if anyone could over-hear me.

"Oh... Oh, okay. That's fine. How can I help you?" She stuttered.

"I want you to set up an appointment for Daniel, either a chiro-practor or a masseuse, depending on what his schedule allows," I said.

"Oh, okay. Probably the first one, not much time." Tracy sucked at talking in code, but I could tell she was excited. I wondered what she liked more – the sneaky aspect or the fact that I was doing something sweet for him.

"That's fine. And Trace, do me a favor and call me when he leaves the office, so I can know he's on his way."

"No problem, Mrs. – Rogers." Tracy said before chuckling. She was really enjoying herself.

18

Marla had cleaned the house spotless by the time I gave her a grocery list. I hadn't enjoyed grocery shopping like I used to, so I let her do it for me. It wasn't fun without Daniel's suggestions and random requests for healthy shit a client recommended. Since we began our separate lives, I didn't do much cooking, often eating out or making simple meals for one. Daniel and I used to cook together, despite his lack of skills. He was excellent at chopping, but more than anything, he made the best company in the kitchen.

After showering, I decided to blow dry my hair while waiting for Marla to return. I'd sweat out Sonja's hard work during yesterday's activities, and then slept without a scarf, leaving my hair in a tangled mess beyond repair. Once it was straightened again, I braided two pigtails that hung down to my breasts.

In our massive walk-in closet, I picked up Daniel's shirt from the previous day. Bringing the soft fabric to my face, I inhaled his aroma slowly before deciding to wear it around the house. I could hear his voice in my head as I fastened the buttons. *Fiend.*

Before long, Marla was back and stocking our cabinets and refrigerator as I helped, organizing and mentally planning meals.

We were just about done when I heard my phone ringing from the bedroom. I turned to take off as Marla asked if there was anything else I needed.

"No, that's it for today. Thanks, Marla. Can you please lock up on your way out? I'll see you next week!" I called over my shoulder while jogging towards the bedroom.

"Hello," I answered.

"Hey, Mrs. Gamble. Mr. Gamble is leaving now. I'm not sure if he's gone for the day, because he still has several calls, but he's definitely on his way home." Tracy sounded excited and confused, probably wondering what the hell was going on with us.

"Thanks, Trace! I owe you one!" I ended the call, running to the closet.

My top drawer was reserved for lingerie, and I already knew which one I wanted. It was a red, La Perla Maison bodysuit made of satin silk with white and silver embroidery. The neckline was low, super low, and it made my boobs appear a full cup larger. The back was completely sheer, riding up my ass in a way that exaggerated my curves.

I'd bought it months ago, when it first debuted at the Rodeo Drive location, but even on my most confident days, I deemed it unfair to hide it beneath clothes. This was the type of lingerie someone had to witness. I slipped it on and looked into the mirror as I buttoned the closure between my legs.

Easy access was a bonus. I smiled at my reflection, certain Daniel would go crazy when he saw me. Concealing the lingerie beneath his oversized shirt, I fastened the buttons on my way to the TV room. Sitting on the sofa, I tried to slow my breathing, flicking through channels.

Black Mass was playing. I loved Johnny Depp, and Daniel had taken me to the premiere in San Francisco on opening night. I looked over at my phone, but no messages. Daniel was planning a surprise attack, but he was walking into an ambush.

His car pulled into the driveway and I started speaking aloud to myself.

Calm down, Em. Look natural. The key turned and I willed myself to focus on the movie. When he walked into the TV room, holding his phone to his ear, a smile spread across my face.

"Yeah, Rob mentioned that in the meeting," he said into the phone before smiling, walking towards the sofa.

Reaching down, he looped his forearm behind my back and I instantly wrapped my legs and arms around him as he lifted me from the sofa. Daniel wasn't holding me at all, his hands were hanging at his sides, as I clawed into him.

"I couldn't wait to see you," he kissed my ear. "I'm still on a call, so be quiet," he whispered before tapping his phone screen, placing the caller on speakerphone.

I motioned as if I was zipping my lips shut and he kissed me deeply, controlling me with his tongue. Walking through the house, he kissed along my neck as the man continued rambling on speakerphone. Once he reached the kitchen, he stopped, placing me on the center island.

"Well what would be the point of the addition?" He asked before setting the phone at the edge of the counter. Gripping the nape of my neck, he kissed me passionately while unbuttoning my shirt with his free hand. I couldn't make out what the guy was saying on the call, his words blurring together in my mind. Daniel stopped kissing me abruptly, his face still buried in my neck.

"But that's not what the proposal stated," he argued with a hint of annoyance in his voice. Straightening, he glared down at the phone.

"Exactly, Mr. Gamble. I'm not sure if it's a contingency or if they're trying to pull a fast one," I heard the guy on speakerphone say before launching into another ramble.

With my shirt fully unbuttoned, I leaned back on my palms, waiting for Daniel to look over and see my lingerie. When he finally glanced in my direction, his eyebrows moved together as the left side of his mouth curled upwards. Taking a step back, he tilted his head left, and then right, never taking his eyes off me. He moved close, running his fingers along the embroidery along my breasts before bending down to gently kiss my cleavage.

"I don't know, Ralph. It seems kind of pointless to me," Daniel said, leading a trail of kisses from my breasts to my neck, stopping at my ear, "This is my favorite one yet. You're beautiful," he whispered.

I beamed, trying to hide my teeth through my smile. He straightened again as Ralph recited statistics through the speaker. Daniel traced the silver design of the bodice, running his right hand over his head, then down to the back of his neck. I wondered if he'd met with the chiropractor before his eyes locked with mine, and every other thought evaporated.

Smiling mischievously, he bent down, gently lifting my left leg. He kissed upwards from my calf before taking soft but shocking bites along my inner thigh. Each nibble made me jump from the sharp pain, but he immediately kissed each bite with his tongue, setting off a stream of sensation.

He did the same to my right leg before pushing me back on the kitchen island, raising my knees, while moving my ass forward. It reminded me of a gynecologist visit, my legs wide open as though I was in stirrups. Moving his face between my legs, he kissed and licked my opening through the bodice. I felt his finger beneath the fabric, and then he nibbled my clitoris through the bodysuit.

"Hahhh!" I yelped loudly.

19

D aniel shot up, his head cocked to the side while his lips curled upwards with satisfaction. He pressed his index finger to his lips.

"Is everything okay?" I heard the man ask through the phone.

"Yeah, that's just my wife." My eyes widened with shock at his honesty. Daniel smiled and shrugged. "Could you give me the full details of the model? I have the paperwork in front of me, but I really want to know how *you* see it. Don't hold back, Ralph. This is what I pay you for, and I want to know as much as you can tell me. I'll try not to interrupt you at all," he said, raising his eyebrows. I smiled knowing full well what his plan was.

"Oh, well, sheesh. Mr. Gamble, I guess for me it all starts with the prototype and its inefficiencies..." Ralph's voice grew insignificant as I relaxed onto the coolness of the countertop, focused on Daniels touch.

Fearing his eagerness, I sat up to show him the buttons between my legs. He nodded, motioning for me to lie back. There was no way he was ripping this one. Forget the $900 price tag, you couldn't find this body suit anywhere. All the La Perla stores had been sold out since it launched. Pushy or not, he wasn't destroying another negligee.

Slowly, he unbuttoned the bodice, purposefully dipping his finger into my essence with every motion. Once it was unlatched, he touched my abdomen until I looked up at him, placing his finger to his lips as a warning. I nodded and he gently folded the fabric of the bodice, exposing me completely.

"I see what you mean," Daniel said to the phone before diving face first into the wetness between my thighs. I closed my eyes and arched my back, reaching for anything I could grasp.

I felt the shirt I was wearing and balled it up, biting into it as Daniel fucked me with his mouth. He alternated between licking and teasing my clitoris before inserting his tongue deep into my warmth.

He kept randomly repeating, "Mm Hmm", as though he was following along with the call. It felt like a vibrator pressing against my clit, each tremor sending a strong sensation up my spine. When he grazed his teeth along my most sensitive spot, I held my breath. The inevitable surge came hard and fast as my orgasm poured out of me, tensing every muscle in my body.

"I *gotta* have you. Come on," Daniel announced bluntly.

I popped my head up confused, looking over at the phone, which he was sliding into his pocket. "I'll tell him it died. This won't take long," he explained, pulling my legs toward him as I sat up. I wrapped limbs around him as he carried me to our bedroom. Kissing his neck repeatedly, my sex clenched, yearning for pressure.

"I wanna play with these," he said while tugging at my braided hair.

Daniel threw me onto the bed roughly, seeing the sheer back of the bodysuit for the first time. His eyes lit up as he undid his belt. "Leave that on and come here," he demanded. I crawled backwards to the foot of the bed on all fours.

Without warning, Daniel slammed into me, grabbing one of my pigtails in each hand. He pulled my braids so tight my eyes rolled. My ass bounced from his force, rushing to match his rhythm. He released my hair and grabbed my waist as I threw myself into each thrust, arching downwards, gripping the sheets for traction. I knew it wouldn't be long. This position always made Daniel come. It was my go-to when I was aiming for a quickie.

Glancing over my shoulder, I saw his head tilted back in ecstasy. His shirt was open, revealing his abs as they flexed with every plunge. He was groaning loudly, his pelvis surging to a relentless rhythm, thrusting in and out of me. I knew I didn't have long, so I moved quickly, turning my body around as he looked down with confusion. Before his brows could form a frown, his dick was in my throat.

"Whoa!... Em!... Baby..." His words turned inaudible as his hips involuntarily kept surging forward, shoving his length past my lips.

"No, baby... What are you – Oh shit..." He groaned before biting his bottom lip. His hips kept moving, almost gently, pushing himself into my mouth.

Sheathing my teeth, I swiveled my head slightly from left to right in a swirl, moving back and forth, taking him in and out of my pool of saliva. I looked up at him, still on all fours, and the pleasure was obvious. His head was cocked back, his hand resting gently on the back of my head as he rocked forward, never losing the rhythm.

"Fuck!... Em... Baby..." He muttered between biting his bottom lip. Slurping noises were the only other sound as I continued to swirl my head, taking him as deep as I could manage, trying to taste the root without gagging.

Of course, I'd sucked Daniel's dick before, but nothing like this. It was usually half hand job half sucking, just waiting for him to come, grossed out by my own spit. But watching him lose himself, cussing and groaning, felt almost as good as climaxing myself.

I felt so powerful. I didn't want it to end, enjoying this vulnerable state too much. He looked down and noticed me watching, biting his lip as his hips kept rocking forward. I could've come on the spot. Exaggerating my swirling motion, I opened my mouth wider, taking him deeper.

"Emily. I'm about to come," he said seriously, looking in my tear-filled eyes as I fought off my gag reflex.

He was warning me, and subtly asking, *do you know what the fuck you're getting yourself into?*

My nod was imperceptible, but I know my eyes spoke loudly as I silently begged him to do it. For a split second, disbelief flashed in his hazel eyes. Ending our stare down, I focused on his pleasure, increasing my speed as he dug his fingers into my hair, his thrusts growing with aggression as he groaned loudly.

"Emily... Uogh..." he groaned. I knew he was close, so I moved even faster, begging my jaws not to quit as they tightened, stretched beyond capacity. He grabbed my head, one hand on each ear and shoved his manhood down my throat, holding it there as his hips slowed to a standstill. I felt him spasm against my tongue as hot, thick semen hit the back of my throat.

With my eyes closed, and his hands over my ears, the sounds were intensified. I could hear myself swallow. His moans sounded distant. His hips rocked leisurely, just a little, and I slowed my motions until I'd milked every drop. Opening my eyes as he released his grasp, pulling his softened length from my lips, he stared at me like I'd grown a third eye.

Feeling a warm liquid slide down my chin, I wiped it with my index finger and licked it clean. He raised his eyebrows in utter shock as I climbed off the bed. My red bodysuit had rolled just above my belly button, so I smoothed it down, strutting across the bedroom knowing he was watching.

"Really?" He asked as I reached the bathroom door. Turning around, I bit my bottom lip to hide the smile begging to spread.

"What?" I asked as innocently as possible.

"I gotta go take this call after *that*?"

"Hey, stop slanging dope," I shrugged before walking into the bathroom.

I saw his head fall back as I walked through the door, and heard his laughter from the next room. I couldn't believe I had done that.

Sober. What the fuck? Maybe I *was* an addict. I already wanted more of him.

I let my braids loose and poured a cupful of mouthwash. As I began gargling, Daniel appeared in the bathroom fully dressed.

"This addiction is getting out of hand, Mrs. Gamble," he grinned from the doorway.

I laughed, causing me to spit the blue liquid into the sink. "You're trying to kill me," I joked.

"I think it's the other way around, actually," he raised his eyebrow before walking over to me. "What's gotten into you?" He asked.

I thought about how shocked he must have been. Daniel had only come in my mouth once before – on accident, while drunk, and I spent the whole night dry heaving, certain his semen was stuck in my throat.

"Blame the dealer, not the addict," I said, looking directly into his eyes.

He flashed his million-dollar smile and kissed me gently on the lips.

"I have two more calls, then we'll get dinner."

"Whatever you want," I said. And I meant it.

20

————————

My phone buzzed loudly from the nightstand, jolting me awake. After dinner, Daniel and I had relaxed with a glass of whiskey before falling asleep. Opening my eyes with the confusion that follows a night of hard liquor, I glanced around the bedroom. Daniel slept silently beside me, his right arm heavily draped across my chest. Hoping not to wake him, I reached for the nightstand awkwardly, grabbing my iPhone without disrupting his hold.

"Hello," I whispered, not bothering to see who was calling.

"You're up! I figured your entrepreneur ass would be. I'm getting everyone together for lunch today. Can you leave your little publishing empire?" Olivia asked with a giggle. My oldest sister spoke four languages fluently – English, Spanish, Italian, and Sarcasm.

"What time is it, Liv?" I grumbled, covering my eyes with my right hand.

"A little after 6. I'm feeding Ava," she paused, speaking baby talk to her infant daughter before continuing. "So, are you in, hot shot?" She asked, knowing the answer. I never told Olivia no, even when she deserved a taste of rejection. She was more like a second mom than a sister.

While our father built his hospitality empire, our mother tagged along, hoping to deter his search for new mistresses. Olivia was left in charge, because although Elliot was the oldest, he was a boy, so responsibility seemed to skip over him altogether. As the oldest daughter, Olivia was happy to assume the role.

She was the type of girl who scribbled her future children's names across notebooks in grade school. My mother would beam with pride whenever she retold the story of 8-year old Olivia being asked what she wanted to be when she grew up. With a bright smile, she had replied, "A mommy." That was Olivia.

"Olivia. I love you beyond words, but please don't call me before nine. Text me the details. I'll be there. Love you. Bye." I responded mechanically, removing the phone from my ear.

"Bye," I faintly heard her response.

When I looked over, Daniel was staring back at me. As our eyes met, he grabbed me into his arms, burying his face in my neck.

"Liv still bossing you around?" He asked, rolling on top of me, balancing his weight on his elbows.

"I've been summoned to lunch with the Delley girls," I announced through giggles as Daniel nibbled my neck.

"I wanted to stay in bed with you all day," he whispered, his soft bites turning to kisses.

"Can you?!" I practically yelled with excitement, ready to cancel everything.

He lifted his face so we were eye to eye before smiling and shaking his head. "I wish. But I'm clearing one day this weekend to fuck you all day."

I failed to hide my teeth as a bashful grin covered my face. Daniel rolled over quickly, lifting me as he turned. I ended up straddling him.

"What are you doing?" I giggled as he sat up, lifting my silk nightgown over my head.

"I'm about to watch you come," he explained matter-of-factly, lying back with his hands on my hips.

~

After Daniel left for work I began the preparation for lunch with my sisters, trying to find the perfect outfit that wouldn't warrant too many questions. They picked up on everything. We were so close they could sense when something was bothering me.

Keeping my marital issues a secret had been difficult over the past 6-months. I'd become a master of deflection, learning to keep them talking to avoid answering questions about myself.

No one would ever suspect anything was wrong with my marriage. They all thought we were madly in love. I think all women looked at Daniel, and the way he treated me, and assumed that if there were problems, I was a fool. Maybe they were right.

Now that I no longer had anything to hide, I was even more nervous. Looking too happy would warrant questions about what had changed and why I wasn't happy before. My sisters overwhelmed me with little effort. Whenever we were together, I shrank into my 7-year old self.

I looked forward to each meeting with them like children look forward to going back to school. The excitement would undoubtedly wear off quickly, yet I still spent an entire afternoon selecting my outfit.

I decided to wear a high waist pair of chinos I'd recently found at a vintage thrift store on La Brea. Marla had retrieved them from the cleaners with the stiffest crease I'd ever seen. I joked with her that they could stand on their own. With a pair of 6-inch wedges, the hems barely grazed the floor.

Pairing the khakis with a red, ruffled off the shoulder midriff slimmed my waist while creating an illusion of height. My barely there abs peeked through, and I made a mental note to eat light or the whole outfit would be ruined with a food baby. My hair was in a slick top bun to accentuate my shoulders. The 4-carat princess cut diamond studs Daniel gifted me for my birthday completed the look.

Walking out the door, I realized my G-Wagon was still at work. I called Daniel, because that's what I did whenever my life wasn't perfect.

"Hey, baby," he answered on the second ring.

"Hey. I was heading out to lunch and just realized my car is still at work." I said, thinking no further explanation was necessary.

"Oh," he paused. "Just take another car, Em. We have four cars. It's not that big of a deal." I could tell he was amused by my dilemma.

"You think I'm being dramatic," I rolled my eyes.

"*You? Dramatic?* That's absurd," he said.

"I don't need your sarcasm right now, Mr. Gamble," I countered, looking through the key cabinet. "I don't want to drive the Audi," I whined.

"Take the 458, baby," Daniel was trying for patient but he was beginning to sound annoyed.

"That car is too much pressure," I admitted. He loved his Ferrari too much. Every time I drove it, I was anxious I'd damage it.

"How about this – I'll send a car for you, then you can hang with Victoria at lunch," he was smiling now. Victoria was only one year older than me, and known for being a complete lush. We never went through less than two bottles of wine when we linked up.

"That's actually not a bad idea. Will it take long? I'm supposed to be there in 30-minutes."

"Being as I have nothing else to do, I'll bump this to the top of my priority list, Mrs. Gamble." I could tell he was pleased. Daniel loved solving my problems. No matter how big or small, he enjoyed handling any and everything for me.

"Thank you, baby," I sang.

"My pleasure. Tell your crazy sisters I said hello."

"I will," I laughed.

"Bye, Em," he sighed.

"Bye, Daniel."

I sat at the breakfast bar, debating if I should have a glass of wine when my phone buzzed. It was Daniel.

Daniel: Car will be there in 10-minutes.
Emily: Damn. That was fast. What car service is it?
Daniel: It's not 1992, Em. It's an Uber.
Emily: I could've called an Uber.
Daniel: Are you telling me or reminding yourself?
Emily: Screw You, Mr. Gamble.
Daniel: Is that a promise?
Emily: Bye, Daniel. Thanks for the car.
Daniel: Let me know when you get there.
Emily: Will do.

21

W hen I arrived at the restaurant Victoria was already on her second glass of Chardonnay. My oldest sister Olivia was passing around her phone, displaying a slideshow of Ava, her 6-month old daughter.

"Bring your little skinny ass here!" Yelled Denise.

She was three years older than Victoria, one year younger than Olivia. Growing up, we always broke into two sets of sisters due to the age difference. Me and Victoria were thick as thieves, but too young to hang with Olivia and Denise.

Denise was actually her middle name. She preferred to shorten it to "Niecey", for a more urban vibe. We'd all gone through a rebellious 'hip hop phase', as my mother called it. But Denise never grew out of hers. Our father was born and raised in Inglewood, so we knew enough to play the part, but none of us were hood. Hell, we had trust funds and inheritances.

"Skinny? I'm thicker than a snicker," I joked as I scooted into the half circle booth, bumping hips with Denise. "What we drinking, Vic?" I smiled to my partner in crime.

"Eh. It's actually kinda shitty, but it'll get us there," she shrugged, raising the bottle before pouring me a glass.

"Did you drive?" Olivia asked, always the responsible one.

"No, I got an Uber," I answered casually, not wanting to admit Daniel had scheduled it for me.

"Twinsies!" Yelled Victoria. "We can share one home!"

I winked in agreement. We always made sure to get a little one on one time to reveal everything we didn't want the older two to know.

"I want to throw Daddy a birthday party this weekend," Olivia announced, revealing the reason we'd all been summoned to lunch.

"Aww, that's sweet," Denise said.

"Emily, can you handle the food?" She started down her list of chores.

"You want me to hire a caterer?" I asked over my wine glass, sharing a side eye with Victoria, who was sitting between Olivia and Denise. I wished she were sitting next to me so I could nudge her.

"Or you could come over early and cook with mom. I guess we could all help," Olivia suggested as though she'd been thinking about it.

"You want to live out *Soul Food* so bad," Victoria butted in. "Don't nobody want to miss the whole party, cooking all day. We wanna be cute and smell good. Keep that barefoot and pregnant shit over there," she laughed.

"I know a good caterer. I'll set it up," I quickly added, trying to save Victoria from a verbal lashing.

Remembering Daniel's request to let him know I got there safely, I shot him a quick text.

Emily: Liv is throwing dad a bday party this weekend.
Daniel: Cool. I'm picking up the last part of his gift today.
Emily: What'd you get him?
Daniel: Just some man shit.
Emily: Do I need to get something sentimental?

Daniel: Nah, we're all set. I'm walking into a meeting. Enjoy your lunch.

"You're smiling like a 16-year old texting him! Don't you think it's about time ya'll drop the newlywed act? You've been married for like a million years." Denise quipped before sipping her wine.

"Four, actually. Well, almost five. Shit, we're about to have an anniversary." With all the divorce drama, I'd forgotten our fifth wedding anniversary was a month away.

"Well, I'm sure Mr. Moneybags will buy you an NBA team or something," Olivia rolled her eyes.

"What's wrong with him buying her nice things?" Victoria asked with an attitude. She'd always been my bodyguard, especially with my sisters.

"I just think he spoils her. It's outrageous." Olivia explained with a shrug.

"Speaking of him buying up all of Los Angeles, why would he want a restaurant? I heard he was buying that Sea Bar, or whatever it's called, over on Melrose." Denise asked, turning to face me.

I was stunned.

He was going to buy *The Sea Club? That's* why everyone knew him there? How could he not tell me that? I'd have to ask him about it later. For now, I put on my poker face, knowing Denise was watching my every move.

22

"I t's the Sea *Club*," I corrected Denise confidently before adding, "It looked like a good investment. But I think he's decided against it. Their crab cakes are amazing, though! Have you been yet?" I detracted. Olivia and Denise were explaining why they hadn't been while Victoria looked at me with the all-knowing sister eyes.

For the next hour, we laughed and updated each other on our lives over three bottles of Chardonnay. Denise was dating another rapper. We all kept our comments to ourselves, knowing it wasn't worth the argument. She said she may bring him to Dad's party and Olivia choked on her wine, causing Victoria to bust out laughing.

Olivia's husband Andrew was stressed at work, and as always, she was trying to convince him to quit being an accountant and just live off her savings. I was the only one of the girls to invest any portion of my trust fund.

Olivia spent hers moderately, while Victoria lived a bit more lavishly. At least Victoria worked as an interior designer, and her husband Mike was an engineer, so I always suspected she had a lot left over.

We all assumed Denise had spent her entire trust on the dirtbags she dated. Victoria and I had a running joke that Denise secretly owned a record label with all the rap careers she'd funded over the years. She always had boyfriend drama better than reality TV.

Olivia assigned chores to each of us and we agreed to arrive at our parents' house early, to help with the set up. Victoria fought to hire a cleaning crew, refusing to do dishes. I thought it was fine, and Denise argued that if Victoria covered the bill, she didn't care. Victoria shot me a look when she said that, another note in our mental indictment that her trust was wiped clean.

When it was time to go, I casually asked Victoria to schedule our Uber, not wanting to let on that I didn't know how. She didn't object, and before long we were kissing and hugging the older two as Olivia gave out last minute reminders. As usual, I ended up paying the bill, and Denise suddenly needed an extra meal to go. I bit back my laugh, signing the receipt before leaving with Victoria.

"Mike wants to have a baby!" Victoria exclaimed as I climbed into the backseat.

"What? But you don't want kids. I thought you both agreed," I said, smiling at the driver, embarrassed by my sister's outburst.

We'd had "help" our entire lives, but I'd never been the person to continue talking while the waiter refilled our glasses. Unlike my sister, I would never climb into a car without addressing the driver.

"I guess I don't, conceptually. I'm not some Olivia robot wife. I've never felt like I *needed* kids, but now I'm really considering it," she paused, watching my reaction. "Don't look at me crazy. *You're* the one who said you'd never get married and now you're like the poster child for bliss."

"I didn't want to get married, in a general sense. I wanted to marry *Daniel*. There's a difference," I said, raising my eyebrows to emphasize my point.

"That's how I feel about kids. I want *Mike's* kids. I'd love a little Michael running around. And maybe a little Victoria too, but no more than two."

"That's dope, Vic. I'm happy for you. You'll make a cool ass mom, and Mike will be a great dad. I better be the God mom!"

"You'll be their aunt, silly. You can't be their God mom, too," she laughed.

"I at least need an extra title that distinguishes me from Olivia and Denise. Maybe I'll be *Supreme* Aunty, or something like that," I joked.

"You're a dork, you know that?"

We both laughed as Los Angeles passed by. Despite how many times I'd entertained the idea of moving, there was no better place in the world than California. Eventually, I wanted homes in other cities, but I couldn't permanently live anywhere else.

"Danny-boy didn't tell you about buying the restaurant, did he?" She hesitantly asked.

"Stop calling him that," I feigned disgust. Victoria coined the nickname when I first started dating Daniel, but it never grew on me.

"Don't avoid the question." If anyone called me on my shit, it was Victoria.

"No," I sighed, looking out the window.

"Don't sweat it. Let him have his business and take care of his own shit. He doesn't use your money, so be grateful for that, and keep it moving. Besides, if he was serious about buying it, I'm sure he'd tell you first. Daniel is good about shit like that. He always thinks of you. That's why I love him."

I struggled to focus on her advice after the subtle hint that Mike uses her money. "I try, but I don't like being left in the dark, Vic."

"You never know how true stories are anyway. This girl I work with swore she knew Danny-boy, claiming her home girl went out on a date with him. I almost cussed her out," Victoria huffed, but my heart sunk into my stomach.

"What home girl?" I asked before I could stop myself. I wasn't ready to tell my sister about my problems at home, but insecurity rose heavily in my chest, wondering what Daniel had been doing during our separation.

Victoria turned to me with shock. "Who cares, Em! Daniel would never do that to you. You can't bother yourself with bullshit rumors."

I nodded, trying to calm my heart rate. The driver merged to the right, readying for his exit, and I knew I only had a few more minutes with my best friend. "Get her name, Vic."

I felt her gaze, but chose to focus on the city passing by the window rather than expounding. There was nothing more to say.

"Okay." She answered so quietly I thought she was talking to herself.

We barely spoke for the rest of the ride. When I got out the car, I felt empty inside. It was the first time I'd ever lacked trust in my marriage. I wasn't sure how to face it returning to the home I thought we'd restored.

23

Boisterous laughter greeted me when I opened the front door. Daniel must have had friends over, something he hadn't done in months. We used to entertain and host parties all the time. That was a little difficult when we weren't speaking to each other, so we'd done away with it altogether during our informal separation.

I sat my purse on the kitchen island before making my way to the empty living room. Following the laughter, I continued to the room Daniel refused to call a man cave. Located at the back of the house, it overlooked the pool with an incredible view of the city.

Like the rest of our home, I'd designed the room alongside Victoria. It featured a pool table and full bar facing a huge television with all the gaming systems, although Daniel never played them. The walls were decorated with framed sports paraphernalia, but my favorite part of the room wasn't visible. Knowing how much Daniel loves cigars, the design included unique ventilation, so the smoke never escaped. It was the definition of a man cave.

"There she is! What up, baby sis?" Jason rose from his seat to lift and spin me around. He was Daniel's younger brother by two years, but since Daniel was three years older than me, I was his little sister. As Daniel's only sibling, it meant the world to me that Jason had always treated me like family.

"Jay!" I squealed in his bear hug. "I haven't seen you in forever," I smiled as he put me down.

"I know! I've been in Chicago for a bit. Plus, your man works too much. He's never trying to let me clean out the bar," he joked, nodding to the fully stocked bar in the far corner.

Daniel made his way across the room, kissing me on the lips while scanning my face. Silently, he inquired about my lunch with my sisters. He could never predict my mood after seeing them. Sometimes, I'd come home in tears feeling bullied. Other times, I'd be head over heels about how much I loved them, claiming some spiritual connection to each of them. Sisters are complicated like that.

"I shared a car home with Victoria. We had fun," I smiled at Daniel before returning my attention to his brother. "My dad's having a birthday party this weekend, Jay. Wanna come?"

"Aw shit! Mr. Delley is having a party? What'd you get him, D? An island?" He asked with a laugh. Daniel just shook his head, standing behind me while massaging my shoulders. I shrugged awkwardly, stepping closer to Jason to avoid Daniel's touch.

"Denise will be there," I teased.

When we first met, Jason jokingly asked if I had any sisters. I told him I only had one that wasn't taken. After introducing him to Denise at a family function, he whispered in my ear that he wasn't interested, and I fell out laughing. Since then, Daniel and I had a running joke that he liked her. I never told him that Denise was genuinely interested in him, fearing it would ruin the joke.

"Baby sis, ain't nobody checking for your crazy ass sister. I've never met anybody that wanna be hood so bad," he said while shaking his head. I laughed while Daniel came to her defense.

"Don't call her crazy, Jason."

We both knew he was serious, because he used his full name.

"He was just playing." I tried to save him, to no avail.

"*You* call her crazy!" Jason quipped.

"*I'm* married in," Daniel said with a grin. We all laughed before I excused myself.

I told Daniel I wanted him to spend some time with his brother, but the truth was, I needed some time to myself. Victoria had dropped a bomb on me, and the longer it sat with me, the more it made sense.

The restaurant, the sex, his new routines and rituals. My husband was a new person, but I couldn't bring myself to believe it was at the hands of another woman. Daniel wasn't that guy. He'd never made me believe he could betray me. The anxiety rolled in my stomach like a tumbleweed, growing larger by the minute.

I was standing in front of the refrigerator, absentmindedly picking at my cuticles, when I noticed Daniel standing at the corner of the kitchen. He walked toward me with concern in his eyes.

"What's the matter, baby?" He asked, cradling my neck with both hands.

"Nothing. I'm just tired," I said, feeling uncomfortable in his grasp. After days of submitting to extreme vulnerability, it suddenly felt bulky and ill-fitting.

"Let me run you a bath," he suggested, scrunching his eyebrows together as he strained to read me.

"No, no. I'm fine, but that is a good idea. I think I'll take a bath. Enjoy Jay. He hasn't been over in a minute." I shrugged away from his touch without making eye contact. Something was off, but I wasn't ready to face it. I needed time and space. Before he could respond, I dismissed myself.

"I won't be long," he called after me. I heard the need in his voice; the fear that I was running away. I wanted to take off without explanation. Instead, I stopped, slowly spinning on my heels before responding.

"I'm just tired. I'll be fine. I promise."

I started running the bath before undressing. While I loved our oval shaped lagoon bathtub, filling it was no easy feat. Daniel and I had shopped for it when we first bought the house, literally sitting in bathtubs to find the perfect fit. Remembering that time brought back the joy I'd recently rekindled with Daniel.

We were young and open to heartbreak, happy to risk it all for passion. I was both naïve and ambitious, a dangerous combination. Daniel was everything I'd ever wanted, but I hadn't yet learned the value of timing. I was far from ready to accept the lessons he'd teach me.

As I reached into the cabinet that stored my bath toiletries, I questioned if I was finally open to learn. Opting for a little of everything, I added oils, salts and bubble bath, leaving the waterfall faucet running as I strolled through our bedroom naked. After picking a nightgown from my lingerie drawer, I noticed a pile of clothes wrapped in plastic on the plush sofa in the center of the closet.

By the time I finished hanging the freshly pressed clothes in color coordination my bath was ready. Wrapping a scarf to cover my hair, I sunk into the bathtub, taking a deep sigh as the hot water rose around me.

I knew I had to ask Daniel about buying *The Sea Club*. I just wasn't sure how I'd bring it up. I couldn't decide if I truly cared, or if I'd just been embarrassed to be called out by Denise.

Then, I relived the most devastating blow – the possibility that Daniel had gone on a date with a mystery woman. The memory hadn't slipped far from my thoughts since I heard it. There was no way I could mention it without enough facts to begin the conversation, but I planned to get to the bottom of it.

The idea of Daniel betraying me just didn't sit right. Regardless of how I tried to shape the story, nothing felt plausible. I'd done enough to push him away, but for some reason Daniel remained the man I married. I couldn't honestly say I would have done the same. The realization brought on a new wave of guilt as I sank deeper into the water that was a bit too hot for comfort.

I tended to polarize everything in life. It was black or white, and rarely did I accept in-between arguments. Now that Daniel and I were back on, I wanted in on everything, despite the unreasonableness of my argument. I was still rationalizing my feelings when I heard the knock at the door.

24

"Come in!" I yelled over my shoulder, straining to see the door from the bathtub.

"I come bearing gifts," Daniel announced, holding an eighteen-year-old bottle of Macallan whiskey in one hand, and two glasses in the other.

"You always know what I need," I sighed, thinking *liquid courage*.

He poured three fingers of the amber liquid into each glass, offering one to me before pulling a thin orange rectangular box from his back pocket.

"It's dark chocolate, almonds, and orange peel. I put your dad on to eating chocolate with whiskey, now he thinks I'm Willy Wonka." He smiled while squatting to sit directly across from the bathtub.

"Tracy found a little boutique in Santa Monica that makes different chocolate. They had this one as a sample and I knew you'd like it. I got some for us and some for your dad," he continued, scooting on the floor until his back rested against our over-sized glassed in shower.

"That was thoughtful." I opened the chocolate before continuing, "You could've pulled up the chair." I said, nodding towards the loveseat that matched the light gray swirling throughout the marble.

"I think I should be eye level for this." Daniel swigged his whiskey. I followed suit, sipping slowly before placing the glass on the small roundtable beside the bathtub. "So, what's up, Em?"

I sighed, reluctant to bring it up. I took another sip and decided to just go for it in a roundabout way.

"You're buying *The Sea Club*?" I turned to see his reaction. He didn't look shocked, as I'd expected. Instead, his eyebrows rose with curiosity.

"I thought about it, but it didn't make sense. You know I've never wanted a restaurant. They're money pits. But the owner is Tracy's Godfather, so I entertained the idea. A loan was a better fit. Why do you ask?" He sipped his whiskey.

"So, that's why everyone knew you? The hostess, the guy in the dining area who seemed shocked to learn you were married, the private room, all of that?" I asked with more sass than I intended.

"Well, I think the guy was gawking at you for the same reason every other guy was staring – because you're beautiful, and you were wearing the hell out of that skirt."

I rolled my eyes at his explanation, urging him to continue.

"As for the private room and the hostess, Tracy did some marketing for the restaurant, and her Godfather paid back the loan in 2-months. He wanted to give her something in return, because she wouldn't charge him. So, we let him cater some meetings at the office, and we hosted some there, in a private room." He glared at me, asking *'anything else?'* with his eyes. I paused, hoping for discernment that never materialized.

"I'm an outsider in your life, Daniel. When we went to that restaurant, everyone knew you, but they'd never heard of me. We used to share everything. My whole life has been on standstill for 6-months, personal and business, but you kept going without me. It's awkward. Today, my sister asked me about you buying a restaurant and I felt like a fool for not knowing," I confessed.

"Denise?" He asked.

"Yeah."

He nodded slowly as if he already knew it would be her. I broke off a square of the chocolate and passed the bar to him.

"It didn't really matter that it was Denise. It mattered that I didn't know," I said softly, running my index finger over the intricate designs molded into the chocolate.

He raised his eyebrows again, smirking sarcastically before refilling his glass. Lifting the bottle towards me, he silently asked if I wanted another. I shook my head and he screwed the cap back on.

"What?" I asked in response to his smirk.

He sipped the whiskey then sighed, leaning his head against the glass wall of the shower. Without lowering his chin to face me, he began speaking, talking towards the ceiling.

"Em, you do this thing where you make impulsive decisions and just walk away. You feel moved to take drastic steps without considering how they'll affect anyone else – and I actually think that's fine. You're not making the decision for anyone else; you're making it for yourself. But you don't even think about how the decision will affect *you*. That's what I can't wrap my head around," he said, finally lowering his chin to face me.

"What does that mean?" I asked, genuinely confused by his statement.

"You stopped talking to *me*, babe. How could I share anything with you after you shut me out?" He asked, his eyebrows furrowed.

"Why didn't you try to come and talk to me, or move back into the bedroom?" I turned away from him, not wanting to see his reaction.

"I didn't file for divorce, Emily." He said sternly.

"If I wasn't saving my hair for my dad's party, I would sink under this water right now." I spoke softly as guilt rushed over me. He'd said the d-word. The elephant standing in the middle of our love fest smiled after finally being acknowledged.

"I don't get it. You set fires and just walk away without looking back. You expect me to realize the house that I love is on fire, get myself to safety, bandage my own wounds, put out the fire, then come searching for you to make sure you're okay, beg you to tell me why you started the fire, and then bandage you up. It's ridiculous, baby."

The emotion was clear in his voice. Feeling his glare against the right side of my face, I refused to face him. Choosing to stare straight ahead, I struggled to focus on the vase of peach roses as tears began to blur my vision.

"I don't think anyone has ever described me so accurately in my life," I paused. "I know I'm wrong, but out of curiosity, why didn't you say anything to me about it?" I glanced over to him. He didn't look mad, instead concern was on his face.

"Do you have any idea how embarrassing it was to have my lawyer call me to his office and see that bullshit you sent? He thought you just wanted to upset me. You know how private I am, Emily. And you go and file something that's public record? For what? Attention?" Frustration began to seep through his voice.

"Why would you think I wanted attention?" I asked, knowing my choice to focus on such a small detail would frustrate him further.

"Because you asked me to take everything you own!"

He clenched his jaw, taking a deep breath before continuing, "You asked me to leave you with absolutely nothing. Did you think I would accept that?" He leaned forward, resting his arms on his bent knees as he spoke.

"No," I admitted quietly.

I always knew Daniel would never accept the divorce terms I proposed. As much as I didn't like to admit it, it was becoming apparent that everyone was right. I did want to upset him, and it was an undeniable cry for attention. Only, it didn't garner any response from him. Daniel completely ignored my tantrum, a first for me.

"I can't do this," he sighed, moving to stand up.

"Where are you going?" I asked, shocked. We were finally talking, and he's leaving?

"I'm getting upset. I need to calm down." He spoke with a determined clarity as he walked to the door, leaving me alone in the bathroom.

Yanking a white towel from the towel warmer, I climbed out the bathtub, wrapping myself while following him into the bedroom.

25

"**N**o, let me hear it! Tell me!" I yelled at Daniel's back as he stood in the middle of our bedroom. I may have sounded confident, but I was begging. I needed to know what he wasn't saying.

"Emily, do you want a divorce?" He turned and looked at me, his mouth tight, far past upset.

"No! I've never wanted a divorce, Daniel. That's what I'm saying," I pleaded.

"So why haven't you withdrawn the petition?!" He exploded before inhaling deeply and lowering his voice. "You're in here fucking me all day, pretending to be as in love as when we first met. But every day, I call my lawyer and he says nothing has changed. What are you doing?"

"I *am* in love – even more than before. These past few days have been the best in a very long time – I've loved every minute with you. I wasn't thinking about the divorce, Daniel. I haven't even been to the office in two days," I rushed the words, hoping he believed them.

"Because you've set the fire, and now you don't want to look back." He shrugged, holding his palms up, as though he'd proved his point.

"Well, tell me how you really feel," I rolled my eyes.

"You're constantly antagonizing me. You listen to your miserable ass friends, watch all that bullshit reality TV, and you miss drama in your life. So, you make the shit up. You *want* me to disrespect you and cuss you out. It's crazy!" He yelled, raising his hands above his head in exasperation.

"Well, I understand that sometimes I deserve it." My voice was just above a whisper, as I stared at my feet. Daniel was silent, and I glanced up to see an unidentifiable emotion sweep over his face. Was it disgust?

"Is *that* what you think? That you *deserve* to be disrespected? *By me?* Emily, I'm never going to disrespect you. Ever! And as much as I'd like to attribute it to honor, it has nothing to do with you. I'd never disrespect you because you're a part of me. *You're my wife,* Emily.

"I think about you in everything I do. I'm always thinking about you and how my decisions affect you. If you wanted to be treated like a girlfriend, you should've said no when I asked to marry you. But you said yes. You're my wife, and I don't take that shit lightly. I'm always going to treat you like a queen, because that's how I want you to represent me. That's not changing," he barked, shaking his head.

"I know. I mean, I don't want you to slap me or anything. I just know what I did was stupid and I don't want to manipulate you. I know that I deserve to be treated well, I just... I don't know... I sometimes feel like you have me on a pedestal and I can never live up to how you see me. It all comes so easy to you," I looked into his dark eyes as the frustration faded away.

"I'm glad it looks easy," he chuckled. "Emily, I would do anything for you. Everything I do is for you, for *us.* You wanting anything makes me crazy. I'll move mountains to make your dreams come true. I poured every penny I had into what I knew was a bad investment, just because you wanted a bullshit condo building.

"Then, I worked my ass off to make sure we'd be straight regardless of what happened to that fucking building, and you didn't even care. We could not make a dollar from those condos and we'll still be in a better position than we were when we bought them. And yet you make decisions on the property, without even consulting me. Like it's a dollhouse!" He wore a light smile as he finished, as though it was truly unbelievable.

"I've never cared about the money," I whispered, still looking at him.

"That's a privilege. And I work very hard so that you can continue to not care about money – so that if anything ever happened to me, you'd be set for life without your father so much as lifting a finger. Emily, I do so much to place the world at your feet and you look down your nose like it's supposed to be there.

"Yes! I should've taken you to Europe with me! But I had so many meetings, trying to build our reserves back up, I barely slept the whole ten days I was there. I missed you so much, but when I called just to hear your voice, and remember why I was working so hard, you didn't even want to talk to me!

"You told me you'd call me back and never did. So, yes! I was spiteful and didn't plan anything for your birthday. But, so help me God! If I had known it would push you to file for divorce, I would've rented out the fucking Staples Center! You act like I didn't do *anything*," he argued, motioning towards the earrings I was wearing, one of several birthday presents he'd gifted me.

"It doesn't matter... Even if you didn't do anything, or get me any gifts, I shouldn't have reacted that way. I was wrong, and I'm sorry." I said with a small smile as I walked towards him. He took a step forward and wrapped me in his arms.

"You're my world, Em. You can't do shit like that without even talking to me. I deserve that much."

"Thank you for not divorcing me and leaving me penniless," I said, my words muffled in the tightness of his arms.

"I should've took all your little money," he said with a light laugh before kissing my forehead. His last sentence made me think of what Victoria said in the car, and I popped my head up.

26

"I think Mike has used some of Victoria's trust fund," I said conspiratorially.

"Man, she's bought him at least four businesses. They've all went bankrupt within two years," he said casually.

"What? How do you know that?"

"Your dad told me. He checks the balance on all your trusts. I don't know if he can see a line by line list of transactions, but he knows enough to know what you do with it. That's why he likes me. You're the only one that has more money in your trust than he put in it. Plus, you have the publishing house, and you don't pay for shit. Your sisters don't really have anything left. Elliot flipped his pretty good though," he nodded with pride speaking about my brother.

"Really? I always figured Denise didn't have anything, but I thought Victoria and Olivia were okay," I passively asked, looking up to him.

"They're not broke. Your dad wouldn't let any of you fail. But they can't maintain their lifestyles from their trusts. And Denise... *Fucking* Denise, bringing up *The Sea Club*. I'll fucking buy *Denise* if I want, and it *still* won't be none of her business," he laughed.

I wanted to defend my sister, but I knew he was only joking. I also knew she somewhat deserved it for stirring me up intentionally.

"I always thought my dad couldn't afford to go broke because of my mom. I guess it's more because of us," I huffed.

"What do you mean?" Daniel picqued with interest.

"My mom has always been open about the fact that if my dad goes broke, or picks another mistress, she's leaving him." It was a known fact in my house from the time I was a teenager. Christine Delley would never be with a broke man. Honestly, I couldn't imagine my mother living on a budget. I always respected that she knew her limits. And after my dad's years of infidelity, she added that to her list of deal breakers.

"Baby, I'm tired. You've worn me out. I have an early morning, so let's get some sleep," Daniel changed tones before kissing my neck.

Daniel fell asleep fast that night, but I tossed and turned, contemplating if he had more to reveal. Victoria's disclosure still bothered me, but after considering the possibilities, I decided it was best to wipe the slate clean.

Daniel loved me, and after all he'd told me, there was no doubt in my mind that he was committed to our marriage. I slept wrapped in his arms, feeling safe in our bond.

The next morning, Daniel dropped me off at Cherry Blossoms Publishing so I could finally retrieve my G-Wagon from the parking garage. I walked into the office and greeted Crystal, chatting with her for an hour about office gossip and her sister moving to Philadelphia, which to her was as far as the Philippines. She always gawked at my fashion and today was no different. I wore a black blouse donning a huge bow at the neck, with black high waist slacks. My bun had made it through the night, and I left my diamond studs in from the previous day.

When I finally made it to my office, I asked Crystal to get my lawyer on the phone. It took half an hour for Ms. Angela to walk me through the steps of withdrawing the divorce petition, followed by another 30-minutes of her lecturing me about my impulsiveness and immaturity.

More than my personal counsel, Ms. Angela was my Godmother and mentor. She'd known me my whole life and felt cornered by my decision – obligated to file the paperwork, knowing it was some sort of game to me. By law, she couldn't tell my parents, though my mother was her best friend.

Because we were still in the mediation phase, I was assured the proceedings would end immediately. Unfortunately, the filing would remain public record. That stung, but I accepted there was nothing I could do. Regardless, I felt relieved when I ended the call.

Thirty minutes later my phone vibrated. It was Daniel.

Daniel: Meet me at the house.

His lawyer had called him. I knew it. I started to text him a long message explaining how I hadn't been in the office for two days and needed to catch up, but I deleted the whole paragraph, asking the only thing that mattered.

Emily: When?
Daniel: Now.

I grabbed my purse and proudly informed Crystal I'd be out for a while. I pulled into our driveway to see Daniel leaning against his Ferrari, his feet crossed as he loosened his tie with a smirk. I jumped out the G-Wagon and walked over to him as he unfastened his top two buttons. When I stood in front of him, he glared at me for a long moment before hoisting me into the air. I wrapped my legs around him as he cupped my ass, staring into my eyes.

"So, you're not leaving me?" He asked, his eyes shining while the left side of his mouth curled upwards.

"Not in a million years," I beamed before leaning in to kiss him. He put one hand on each side of my face and kissed me with more passion than I'd ever felt. "Don't pull no shit like that again, Emily."

I shook my head and he kissed me again while carrying me into the house. Gentle kisses on my lips marked every step.

"I'm going to let you call Crystal in a couple of hours, but you're not leaving for the rest of the day," he whispered in my ear as we reached the bedroom.

"You're staying in bed with me?" I asked, ecstatic.

"I'm going to fuck you until my name is all you remember," he whispered before kissing me so deeply I was panting when he pulled away.

"I'm so sorry, baby," I whispered.

"You're going to be," he laughed.

We stayed in bed for the rest of the day, finally releasing the love and hurt we'd bottled up over the past six months. I screamed his name while he dug into me, chanting my undying love with every orgasm. We made love and I cried, releasing my guilt wrapped in his arms, draped in his kisses.

27

It was the day of my father's birthday party, and I was experiencing the most severe sex high of my life. Daniel had bent me in ways I didn't know possible after biting and licking every inch of my body. I was obsessed with him. As he stood at the edge of our bed, telling me his plan for the day, I looked up at him squirming with lust.

"You're making me feel guilty for doing this to you. You actually look high, Emily," he smiled at me.

"I feel high," I laughed while stretching, "Are you thinking of cutting me off or something?" I asked.

"Not for a second," he shot back as his perfect smile crept across his face.

"So, tell me the plan. I'm listening," I yawned, crossing my legs. Daniel walked around the bed to sit next to me before pulling me into his lap.

"You're going to go to the party and set up with your sisters. Then, I'll come as soon as I leave my meeting." He kissed my lips between each step.

"Okay. Do I need to take the gift?"

"Hell no! You're not getting my credit."

"Can I see it?" I asked, realizing I didn't even know what *we'd* gotten my dad for his birthday.

"Sure," Daniel lifted me in one swoop and walked towards the kitchen. After sitting me on the center island, he reached into a cabinet, retrieving two packages. One was a rectangular shaped wooden box, the other a teal colored oval cylinder shape.

"This," he said while holding the teal cylinder, "is what we usually drink. It's a good whiskey, but we go through them all the time. I take one of these whenever I go over there. But this," he paused looking at the wooden box with admiration, a wide grin transforming his handsome face. "This is a 50-year old Macallan. He's gonna shit himself when he sees this."

Daniel looked genuinely proud of himself. I loved how close he was to my father. Although, I was a little jealous of his gift, knowing I'd never be able to think of something so perfect for my dad. They'd bonded in a way a man never bonded with his daughter. It was bittersweet.

"Do you want me to get a bag or anything?" I asked.

"No, it's cool. I got a bag from the chocolate store. I'll just put it all in there," he said, still staring at the wooden box. "I've never even gotten this for myself. I can't wait to see him open it." He shook his head slowly.

"Don't forget to leave us some chocolate," I poked my bottom lip out.

"As much as it pains you to not have an integral role in this gift, trust that it's all taken care of. You just show up and be beautiful. Your husband will handle everything else," he said before glancing at his watch and continuing, "I have to go. You're riding with Victoria, right?"

I nodded while swinging my legs from the island.

"Let me know when you get there, okay?" He kissed my forehead.

"Yes, sir," I said, nodding with each syllable.

We kissed once, and then again. Desire brightened his eyes as he struggled to leave. Usually, I would have helped him pull it together, but I was so smitten I kept wrapping my legs around him, deepening every kiss. Eventually, he willed himself out the door. Once I heard the lock turn, I laid back on the kitchen island, hot and bothered. When I made my way to the refrigerator, the cordless phone rang.

"Hello?" I answered as if it was a mistake.

"Emily! Where are you? I've called your phone like ten times!" Olivia sounded frantic on the other end of the line.

"I'm sorry. What's wrong?" I asked, wondering how long I'd been away from my cell.

"I couldn't find the number to the caterer you set up – what time are they coming?" She asked out of breath, like she was handling a crisis.

"Jesus, Liv! I forgot I had a house phone. You're impossible!" I didn't even try to hide my displeasure.

"Well, I'm the one handling all the stress of the party! For me, it's not just a fun event," she snapped.

"*You're* the one that threw the party, Olivia! That's usually how it works. Hire a party planner next time." I exhaled into the receiver, relieved and annoyed. "Shit! I'll be there before the caterers. I pray you've had a glass of wine before I arrive. Bye!" I said sternly.

"Okay, but don't eat. I've got a little brunch set up for us. Love you. Bye, baby sis!" She rushed the words in her cheery voice as if she hadn't just pissed me off.

I slammed the phone back onto the receiver, rolling my eyes before a chuckle escaped my lips. Damn, she needed a life. I checked my phone before heading to the bathroom. I only had two missed calls from Olivia. She was so dramatic. Hopping into the shower, I washed my hair. Following the previous day in bed, my hair was unsalvageable, so I decided to wear my natural curls.

I'd just finished the hour-long process of leave-in conditioners, diffusers and mousse, when my phone dinged with a new text message. It was Victoria.

Victoria: I'm leaving in an hour, baby girl.

Emily: Sweet! Are you wearing a dress?
Victoria: Duh.
Emily: See you in an hour.

I chose a navy maxi dress with a chiffon overlay, covered in pink and white flowers. The length effectively hid the fact that I wouldn't be wearing stilettos, a habit my mother found unladylike, but at least I'd be comfortable. The dress flowed beautifully, making me appear 3-inches taller.

My curls fell down my back, grazing the top of my dress. I pulled the front section of my hair into a top bun, not wanting to take anything away from the semi-sweetheart neckline. My cleavage was very understated, but hard to miss. I wore my diamond stud earrings for the third day, and added a light layer of foundation and bronzer before filling in my eyebrows. As I finished applying mascara and eyeliner, my phone vibrated. I knew it was Victoria before I looked at the screen.

Victoria: Pulling up now.

28

"Flip flop twins!" Victoria yelled, kicking her foot in the air as I settled beside her in the backseat. I laughed, lifting my dress to show my flip-flops, before acknowledging the driver with a kind smile and nod.

"Are those Chanel?" She asked before touching my curls, showering me with compliments. I tried my best to reciprocate; praising her straightened hair, which was longer than mine, flowing down her back. If you asked me, Victoria was the prettiest of the Delley girls. Her skin, just a smidge darker than mine, was stunningly clear. When we were growing up, people always told my mom to put her in modeling. And she dressed the part – by far the most fashionable.

Today, she wore a short coral colored dress with a belt to accentuate her tiny waist. We were halfway to my parents when we stopped gawking over every detail of our outfits.

"Did Olivia call you?" I asked tilting my head. She rolled her eyes while shaking hers.

"If that girl don't get a damn life! I can't wait for this party to be over so she can leave me the hell alone. She's been stressing me about the cleaning crew all day. Like, Olivia, the party hasn't even started. Why are you worried about the cleanup? Does she think I can't book a damn cleaning crew?"

We laughed, poking fun at our oldest sister until we were pulling into the driveway. My parents sold our childhood home in the city while I was in college, opting to move into a gated community deep in the valley. My mom was ecstatic when she moved into her dream home, although I think she was most excited to keep my father away from the temptations in the city of angels.

Regardless of her reason, she loved everything about the house. The exterior was very valley-esque – yellow clay structure draped in ivy vines, with a dark red Spanish roof. It was always landscaped to perfection, featuring an 8-car garage, huge pool, and a full-sized basketball court.

The long driveway led to a landing the size of a small parking lot, which would be perfect for the party today. Olivia was standing out front with two young men dressed in all black, who she appeared to be berating.

"This bitch done hired a valet?" Victoria huffed, rolling her eyes.

"First task is finding the wine," I turned to her and we both laughed.

Olivia motioned towards the backyard, so the driver pulled around before letting us out. The house was transformed with party décor. String lights were positioned across the lawn, already prepared for the evening. There were bouquets of white roses on every surface in site, with centerpieces on the larger tables. It looked amazing. Despite our critiques, and lack of help, Olivia had done a great job beautifying the place.

The décor was even more extravagant inside. Olivia hired a full staff, which added to the opulence. She'd turned a sitting room into a buffet style area to serve food. There was a bar in the corner with another young man dressed in black standing behind it.

The walls of the sitting room were lined with tables draped in white linen. The first table held stacks of white ceramic plates, bowls, and cutlery held in chrome containers. Most of the tables were empty, reserved for the catered food that would arrive later. But the final table was already set with every dessert you could imagine. There were cakes, brownies, cookies, chocolates in glass vases, and cupcakes with festive icing.

I was taking it all in, impressed by Olivia, when she snuck up behind us.

"This, is why I've been bugging you two," she said with a sigh.

"Liv, you did all of this in two days?" I asked in disbelief.

"More like five," she said, waving her hand, motioning for someone behind me to move something.

"I am beyond impressed, Olivia. This looks amazing! You need to start event planning."

"Yeah, right," she quipped before noticing my admiration. "Oh, gosh, you're serious! Emily, I didn't do all this myself. I hired people to help move things and do the brunt work. I just did a lot of pointing, really." She smiled, glancing around the room. She was being modest, but I could tell from her smile that she was proud.

"That's all it takes, Liv! You just need to get the right people around you and manage a team. It's your vision, and that's what's invaluable." It was shocking how much I sounded like Daniel.

"Spoken like an entrepreneur," she sighed looking away. "Emily, I don't know how to do any of that stuff. I just like throwing parties."

"Daniel can help you. Don't let this go. You love doing it and you're great at it. You *need* to be getting paid for it." I volunteered Daniel without hesitation.

"Thanks, baby girl," she hugged me. "You look like a baby doll, as always. Where's Daniel? You know dad has been asking about him since he woke up. You? Not so much," she laughed as Victoria emerged holding a bottle of wine and three glasses.

"There's a bar right there!" Olivia snapped her a sharp look, pointing at the stocked bar.

"Yeah, but this is the top shelf shit," she said, holding the wine bottle in the air. "I had to go down to the cellar for this," she smiled before asking the bartender to open the bottle.

My parents had an impressive wine cellar beneath their house, and we all went shopping whenever we visited. Daniel was the only one who added to the collection, which reminded me to let him know we'd made it safely.

Emily: Your precious cargo arrived, safe and sound.
Daniel: Glad to hear it. I'm leaving the office now. I'll be there in
an hour.
Emily: Can't wait.

Denise walked in the back door and we all jumped to greet her as Olivia instructed the bartender to bring another wine glass. Two young ladies served trays of miniature waffles topped with fried chicken, drizzled with maple syrup. My mother joined us, wine glass in tow, and we laughed together, preparing for another Delley party. Before we knew it, the caterers were arriving, setting up their trays as guests began to trickle in.

29

My brother Elliot arrived with a date, shocking everyone. He was fawning over his new girlfriend Tiffany. She was stunning and sweet – about my height, with light brown skin and short, curly hair streaked blonde. Wearing Chanel from head to toe instantly put her in Victoria's good graces.

Olivia was more reserved with her acceptance, always a mother hen. I liked Tiffany. She seemed sweet, if clingy. She held on to my every word and quickly became my shadow. I wondered if Elliot had told her I was his favorite or something. It was obvious she wanted to be friends.

Despite being slightly annoyed, I agreed when Victoria whispered that we had to take her under our wing, because Denise was being downright nasty to the girl. I had to shoot her a look more than once as she interviewed Tiffany, asking everything short of a detailed account of her sexual history.

As if on cue, my dad and brother joined us from the living room. Elliot looked to me for a silent judgment on his girlfriend. I gave a slight nod of approval and he beamed with pride. My dad started asking about the food when he abruptly stopped, prompting everyone to follow his eyes to the back door.

"There he is!" He yelled as Daniel walked towards the kitchen. He was dressed down in a pair of jeans and a black Polo shirt. My dad started walking over to meet him, excited like a child on Christmas morning.

"My main man! What are you, like 92 now?" Daniel smiled before hugging my dad as though they hadn't seen each other in years. His right hand held a structured bag overflowing with tissue paper. I couldn't help but think to myself, *he did good.* "This is for you," he said, handing the bag to my dad.

"Awww shit!" He exclaimed, accepting the present. Moving his weight from one foot to the next, my dad failed to contain his excitement. Daniel scanned the room quickly, winking when we locked eyes. I smiled and puckered my lips.

"Anybody else want to give me a gift before I open this? Because you know my Dan is hard to follow!" My dad hollered. Guests sauntered towards the commotion with curiosity.

"No, open his. I'll wait for you to get drunk before giving you mine," Elliot laughed before shaking Daniel's hand, pulling him into a hug.

My dad walked to the massive kitchen island, setting the gift on the marble countertop as everyone waited to see what he would reveal. Daniel stood next to him, barely smirking, but I knew how excited he was. My dad removed the tissue paper and threw his head back.

"That better not be what I think it is!" He yelled. Daniel's grin was instant and contagious.

"What is it?" Elliot asked as everyone watched in anticipation, unable to see into the bag.

"Open it!" Daniel prodded.

First, my dad lifted the teal cylinder from the gift bag, holding his hand up to gesture it wasn't the spectacular part. Then, looking to Daniel, he smiled while raising the wooden box.

"It's a 50-year?" He half read, half asked Daniel in disbelief.

"Are you fucking kidding me?" Elliot yelped, moving towards my dad to see the box.

"The anniversary edition!" Daniel added, his hands on my dad's shoulders as he playfully shook him.

"How'd you find it?"

"I know some people."

"You'll have to introduce me," my dad said to Daniel, pulling him into a bear hug, "Thanks, son! Let's go get drunk!"

"Let me kiss my lady first," Daniel said, his eyes on me.

"She ain't going nowhere," my dad joked when Daniel moved around the breakfast bar, placing his hands on each side of my face.

"You look amazing," he whispered on my lips before kissing me softly.

"All of that over some damn liquor?" Denise quipped.

"It's just hard to find," Daniel brushed her off.

He made his way around the kitchen, complimenting my mom and sisters as he hugged each of them and kissed them on the cheek. Victoria introduced him to Tiffany, who looked at him with googly eyes, annoying me yet again.

"And it's expensive as fuck!" Elliot added, examining the bottle now that my dad had removed it from its wooden box.

"Of course, it is," Denise muttered while Daniel made his way back to me.

"You can't buy this. The only people that would sell it don't know what it is," my dad explained, marveling at the gift.

"Well, yeah, you could always sell it, Pop. I bet they go for a fortune on eBay," Daniel suggested before kissing my shoulder.

He was the only one of our husbands who dared to call my father anything other than Malcolm, or Mr. Delley. After our wedding, Daniel revealed my father encouraged him to call him 'dad' while we were dating, but he told him he wouldn't feel comfortable doing that until he made me his wife. Their bond was independent of our union.

"I ain't selling this! I'm trying to drink it, if you'd leave my baby girl alone for two seconds," he argued, grabbing the other bottle of whiskey he'd neglected since pulling it from the bag. He handed the oval cylinder to Olivia's husband. "Here, ya'll can have this."

I heard Daniel chuckle behind me before catching my dad's glare. He kissed my other shoulder, bending to whisper in my ear, "I'm off to get drunk."

"May the force be with you," I whispered before lifting onto my tippy toes to kiss his soft lips. He threw his hands up, motioning that he was ready to go, and all the men made their way outside.

"You're watching him walk away like he's going to war! Ya'll need a room," Denise teased.

"I think it's so cute," Tiffany gushed.

"I might not have a thousand-year-old whiskey, but I don't see why that should stop us from getting drunk," Victoria said, raising her wine glass.

We all reached for our glasses, lifting them in agreement. Eventually, the women moved to sit at the dining table near the patio, while the men sat outside, smoking cigars and drinking whiskey. My dad sat with his new Macallan within arm's reach, laughing loudly while retelling stories about his childhood in Inglewood. He went into his cellar, bringing out a 25-year Macallan to share, reserving the 50-year bottle for him, Daniel, and Elliot.

Friends and family drifted in and out to wish my father a happy birthday, eat, and drink. We met all the new additions to the family as babies ran around the backyard. My mother constantly asked when her younger daughters would be giving her grandchildren, and we collectively rolled our eyes. It was a typical Delley party, full of laughs and libations.

As the sun began to set, my mom dragged us outside to admire the new roses blooming in the backyard. All the women followed her around the garden, directly in front of the men sitting in lounge chairs. I glanced up and caught Daniel staring at me with a look so lustful I gasped. He noticed and smirked as my dad got up to walk into the house.

When my mother decided to move the tour further into the backyard, eager to show off new trees she'd had planted, I decided it was time for a break. On my walk past Daniel, I ran the tip of my nails along his forearm.

"Where you going?" he asked.

"I gotta pee," I whispered.

"Where's your phone?"

"Inside, I think," I hadn't seen it since we arrived.

"Go get it," he said, looking up from his seat with desire in his eyes.

As I made my way to the kitchen, my dad had just finished refilling his ice bucket.

"Somebody's phone is going off, baby girl. Can you shut that thing up?" He asked, pointing toward my phone. I nodded as I picked it up, shocked by the message from Daniel.

Daniel: I want to fuck you right now.

I inhaled sharply, smiling as I climbed the stairs to a restroom away from the party. The dark powder room, decorated with mahogany wood and black accents, smelled of lavender. When I closed the door, I felt it push back as Daniel barged through the threshold, quickly closing and locking the door behind him.

"Daniel, what are you doing? My dad almost read that message!"

"I don't care," he shrugged, stepping towards me. Ignoring my outrage, he kissed my neck while cradling my head with both hands. "I want you. Now."

30

"Baby, there's a whole party downstairs. Anyone could come up here," I whispered, but he was completely undeterred.

"I don't care. I *need* you," he kissed me, pushing his tongue into my mouth before biting my lower lip. "You know how to be quiet. I'll be quick. I swear. *Please*, baby?" The desperation in his voice made my knees weak.

"You'll be quick?" I asked, reaching for his belt buckle. He nodded quickly, smirking as he sprung into action, dropping to his knees.

"What are you doing?" I asked in a shocked whisper.

"I *gotta* taste you," he said, lifting my dress before dipping his head underneath.

Before I could process what was happening, my panties were sliding down my legs and Daniel was circling my clitoris with the tip of his tongue. I gasped, gripping the vanity for support. He'd hoisted me onto my toes as I literally sat on his face.

Forcing my body to rock back and forth, he pushed my ass in rhythm, rapidly moving his mouth around my sweet spot. Sliding two fingers into my slickness, he hummed against my clit, and I moaned loudly. Frantically, I turned on the faucet to muffle the sounds in case anyone walked past the bathroom.

My breathing was heavy and intense as tidal waves built deep in my pelvis. I pressed against his tongue greedily, aggressively riding his mouth as my orgasm climbed through me.

"Baby, I can't take it," I whimpered, gripping his head through my dress.

"Mm Hmm," he hummed, pushing his fingers deeper into my warmth. My head dropped back as he massaged my g-spot. I feared someone would hear the inevitable explosion I was nearing.

Suddenly, he removed his fingers and roughly licked along my labia before gently sucking my clitoris. I exploded, leaning against the vanity as I lost control. Covering my mouth, I fought to quiet the moans as my climax seeped out of me, my body tensing with a strong urge to cry.

"Oh, my God," Daniel said, rising from his knees while unfastening his belt. "I've never seen you come that hard. I need you."

Those three words again. Stronger than desire, bordering distress. Possessing the weakness of such a powerful man was intoxicating. Moving quickly, I gathered the soft fabric of my maxi dress, equally as eager to feel him.

"It's not gonna take me long," he shook his head, biting his bottom lip.

Gripping my waist, Daniel lifted me into the air. I wrapped my legs around him as he walked to the wall, propping me against it. The surface was cool against my back, and then I felt his warm hands behind me, unzipping my dress just enough to free my breasts as he kissed me all over while unbuttoning his pants.

Leaning his forehead against mine, Daniel closed his eyes as he lowered my body onto his erection. I watched the pleasure alter his handsome face. We were nose to nose as he bit down on his lip, a quiet groan escaping him. He pushed me further until his length was fully sheathed by my essence. His lips lazily drifted across my neck.

"Baby, we have to be qui – " I tried to rush him, but he cut me off.

"Shhh... Just let me feel you, baby," he breathed heavily in my ear before continuing. "It's not even fair that you don't get to feel this. I swear there's no better feeling than being inside you, Emily."

His words were like a prayer as his mouth hovered between my ear and neck, his hands guiding my hips. Slowly, he began to lift me up and down, thrusting his pelvis in the opposite rhythm so we collided with pleasure. "I love fucking you," he whispered in my ear.

"It's yours, baby. I'm yours, Daniel." My words were breathy, spoken directly into his ear. He groaned loudly, moving forward once more, coming instantly. Taking a half step backwards, he wrapped his arms around me, squeezing tightly as he erupted.

Through clenched teeth, he grunted my name, his hips still rocking forward as I contracted my sex to extend his climax. After loosening his grip, he kissed my breasts, then my shoulders and neck, before landing on my lips.

"That was the sexiest thing you've ever said."

"You following me in here was the sexiest thing I've ever seen," I smiled, rubbing my nose against his.

"If watching a man go crazy is your thing," he joked, raising one eyebrow, gently kissing my lips.

"Watching *my* man go crazy over *me*. There's a difference," I corrected him. He smiled bashfully, a smile I'd never seen from him. After one last kiss, he lowered me to my feet.

It was so erotic that we were both fully dressed, our passion for each other too strong to waste time undressing.

"Let's get you cleaned up," he said, brushing his hair down with his hands.

Combing the cabinets, I found a hand towel and wiped my juices from his manhood before cleaning myself. "You need some mouthwash," I opened the medicine cabinet, sure my mother would have it fully stocked.

"No," he shook his head. "I wanna taste you for the rest of the day."

I crinkled my nose, "That's disgusting!"

He smiled, straightening his shirt before buttoning his pants and buckling his belt. Rushing him to the door, he fought for a few more kisses before I could shove him out.

"Take your panties," he laughed, shoving a piece of wet lace into my hand. I gasped, quickly shutting the door behind him before returning to the vanity. Looking at my smeared mascara in the mirror, I shook my head just before the bathroom door swung open.

31

"Ya'll nasty!" Victoria said in a singing manner before laughing.

"You scared the shit out of me!"

"Come here," she walked into the bathroom, leading me to sit on the toilet. Reaching into the medicine cabinet, she opened a pack of makeup remover wipes. With precision, she wiped beneath my eyes, removing the excess mascara and eyeliner that bled with my orgasmic tears. I stared up at my big sister feeling like we were teenagers again.

"Em?" She looked down her nose with a weird emotion in her eyes. I couldn't read it, but I knew something was wrong.

"I don't need a lecture right now, Vic."

Despite being so close in age, Victoria could easily switch from best friend to disciplinarian without warning.

"I don't care if you fuck in every room in this house." Her tone shocked me even more than the words.

"What's wrong?" I leaned back, trying to read her.

"I feel like this might be the best time to ask you this," she said, taking a deep breath.

"What?"

"Are you divorcing Daniel?"

A lump appeared in my throat as my sister glared at me with hurt in her eyes. We had always been inseparable, but I'd cut her out of such a huge decision in my life. Now, it was coming back to haunt me.

"You are?" Her hands dropped to her side in frustration as she backed away from me.

"No, Vic. No. It was stupid. I didn't want everyone in my business, but we're fine now." I spit the words out, hoping they could heal the betrayal.

"Daniel went to dinner with the girl." She dropped the bomb abruptly, without care or warning.

My heart stopped.

Crashing from such an intense sex high, I opened my mouth to shoot a quick response, but nothing came out. I was free-falling. My stomach tensed with anxiety beyond description.

Did I hear her right? The words left her mouth so fast, I refused to believe me ears.

During my handful of perfect days with Daniel, I forgot everything Victoria had mentioned about the dating rumors. My body rocked back and forth and my stomach stirred with the need to purge.

"Relax, Emily!"

My sister kneeled to rub my back, her face sad and guilt-ridden, as though she'd done something wrong.

"When?" I ignored her advice.

"I just found out. Trish just called me."

"When did he go to dinner? Tell me what she said." I couldn't look at her.

"Why didn't you tell me you filed for divorce?" She was hurt. I could hear it in her voice, but couldn't focus on that.

"Tell me what she said, Vic." I looked in her eyes as one tear slid down my cheek.

"It's probably nothing, Em. Don't overreact."

"Victoria!" I yelled so loud she jumped.

"Her name is Lana Boyden. She's some type of accountant, lawyer, something professional like that. She told Trish you and Daniel were separated. I denied it, but you know Trish works at the courthouse, so she looked it up." She paused, glaring at me.

"What else?"

"I guess they went to dinner. Trish said the girl was really hush after she told her we grew up together. I don't think it's anything, Em. Daniel is in love with you."

My mind was blank, so I focused on my breathing, fearful I would faint. When I didn't respond, Victoria slowly began removing bobby pins from my hair, releasing my top bun. Without a word, she put me back together. Running a hairbrush under the faucet, she brushed my hair into a ponytail, wrapping the ends around before pinning it into a bun using two bobby pins.

"So, everyone is downstairs?" I wiped my cheek as I stood.

"I think it's just family left. You know Daddy's friends don't stay long after the food is gone," she failed to make me laugh.

If my mother had taught me anything, it was how to pretend everything was perfect in public, regardless of what was happening behind closed doors. My father cheated on her for years, but she still accompanied him around the world, sometimes attending events aware his mistress was also in attendance.

I'd never imagined that type of life for myself, but in that bathroom, I knew I had to make it through the night with a strong front.

"It's fine, Vic. I'll talk to him about it."

It was a lie. I didn't want to talk about it at all. What could I ask – if everything he'd ever told me was a lie? This was the reason I ran, because some things weren't worth learning more about.

"Let's get back to the party," I nodded, convincing myself everything would be okay. Victoria forced a smile before following along.

We walked down the steps, my stomach in knots as I tried to maneuver through my rambling thoughts. Victoria was right, the crowd had thinned out significantly while I was upstairs with Daniel. We stayed in the kitchen, behind everyone, watching the party.

My mom was sitting at the dining table with Denise and Olivia, a fresh bottle of wine between them. Closer to the kitchen, in one of the living rooms, my dad sat with Daniel, Elliot, and another man I'd never seen before. He looked so out of place I felt uncomfortable for him. With tattoos covering his neck, he wore a black hooded sweatshirt, and what looked like skinny jeans.

"Is that Denise's boyfriend?" I whispered to Victoria.

"Yes! Emily, he has on bedazzled Louboutin's," she huffed, nudging my elbow with hers.

"Shut up!" I played along, peering to see his feet as if I cared what kind of shoes he wore. My thoughts were stuck on Daniel and the mystery woman he'd been seeing.

Taking a bottle of wine from the chiller, my big sister quietly poured us each a glass. I'm not sure what Victoria was watching, but my eyes were trained on the back of Daniel's head. He was joking with my dad and brother while Denise's boyfriend watched television.

"You should've let me push the 458," my father said with a slick smile.

Daniel twisted, reaching into his back pocket before pulling out a set of keys and tossing them at my dad.

"I thought you might say that." Without seeing Daniel's face, I could envision his smile. "I have to call a car anyway. Keep it for the week."

Grinning like a child, my dad caught the keys as Elliot put his hands over his eyes in disbelief. "I'm staying here for the week!" My brother laughed.

"What I don't know won't hurt me," Daniel said to Elliot, insinuating that he too could drive his Ferrari.

I tried to convince myself that it was all okay. I wanted to forget what Victoria had told me so everything could get back to normal. Daniel was here with my family, the life of the party again. I should've been grateful. I almost lost it all, and now I had a chance to repair our marriage.

"Emily, it's not that deep." Victoria startled me.

"I know, I know," I repeated the mumbled words before taking a sip of wine.

"He loves you." She repeated the observation, and I nodded without turning my attention away from him.

Across the room, Olivia rose from the dining table, walking over to the arm of Daniel's chair. "Ya'll should stay the night," she said, first to Daniel and then to the entire room.

"We can all stay here and have breakfast in the morning. Everyone has been drinking too much anyway," she motioned towards the men.

"You know that's up to your sister, Liv. Whatever she wants is my move," Daniel answered, looking up to Olivia.

Seemingly defeated, Olivia turned to go back to the dining room, her eyes lighting up when she spotted us.

"There you go!" She announced loudly. Both rooms turned to face us as I took a deep breath, knowing it was time to pretend. We picked up our wine glasses and headed back towards the party, my shoulders heavy with uncertainty.

32

"Your sister wants us to stay the night," Daniel said when I entered the room.

"I heard," I scanned his face for a truth I suddenly felt missing between us.

"Whatever you want to do is fine with me," he tugged at my hand, pulling me into his lap.

I shook my head, "If everyone else stays, I'll consider it, but I wanna go home."

I *needed* to go home, to be with my thoughts and think through this new information. Had Daniel been pretending, the same way I was now? Could he hide an entire relationship from me?

He's a new man.

It was a revelation I'd had a few days prior. Jokingly, I thought I wouldn't care if Daniel had been with another woman, but now it was all I could think of. I wanted to know everything about Lana Boyden, a name engrained in my memory.

Who was she? And what did she have with my husband?

There was no doubt in my mind – Daniel couldn't love another woman. That was off the table, but six months was a long time for a man to be deprived of sex. Maybe it was just that, a sexual release. Could I forgive that?

"Is that okay?" Daniel's hands gripped my hips, jolting me back to reality.

"Huh? Ye-yeah," I answered reflexively, stumbling over my words.

"Yes! Slumber party!" Olivia raised her hands in celebration.

"Wait. What?" I asked, turning in Daniel's lap.

"Everyone else said they would stay, so Olivia asked if we would." He squinted, and I knew I wasn't doing a good job of wearing a strong face.

"Oh, uh... Okay," I climbed from his lap needing distance.

Back in the kitchen, I stood alone in a corner as everything appeared to move in slow motion. Elliot was joking with his girl-friend while my mom and dad shared a slice of cake. My sisters sat together laughing, while their significant others sat at the opposite end of the dining table. None of it felt real.

The night passed slowly, one glass of wine at a time. I found it best to stay with my sisters, because looking at Daniel made me want to curl up and cry. Unaware of my new information, he seemed to thoroughly enjoy himself, joking with my dad and brother.

I was the first to call it a night, grateful to be alone in the guest bedroom Daniel and I shared whenever we stayed at my parents.

I'd just finished my shower when I heard Daniel enter the bedroom. My heart raced with anticipation. I'd decided to play it cool, not wanting to start any type of confrontation until we returned home. But when our eyes locked, all rules went out the window.

"Who is Lana Boyden?"

"Huh?"

I swallowed slowly. He stalled, and that was never a good sign.

"Who is Lana Bolden?" I repeated the question, a little less eager to hear his response.

"Um, she's a financial advisor," his brows scrunched together as he answered.

"You went to dinner with her?"

"I went to a dinner *meeting* with her." His confusion morphed into amusement as he watched me fidget with anxiety.

"Daniel, just tell me the truth." I was tired of pretending. For half a year, I had put on a show for everyone in my life. I didn't want to do it anymore. It didn't matter what he'd done, but I needed to know.

"The truth about what?" He said, a mix of a huff and a chuckle escaping his lips.

"About her!" My voice cracked as the emotion shot through me.

"Baby, you're tripping." He shook his head, turning away.

His dismissal hurt more than anything else as he climbed into bed, claiming he was too drunk to deal with me.

"Daniel, I'm serious," I pleaded. I needed to know what happened between them. It had to be more than a dinner meeting for the woman to go around bragging to Victoria's friend.

"I'm serious, too. I'm going to bed. We can talk in the morning."

I stood at the end of the bed in shock. Still draped in a bath towel, I dressed in a nightgown hanging from the bathroom door.

Daniel was snoring loudly when I returned to the bedroom. I watched him sleep, debating if anything good could come from waking him. I was alone, needing answers that only he could give.

Just then, a loud noise startled me as Daniel's phone vibrated against the wooden nightstand. Unfazed, he continued sleeping, but my heart skipped wondering who would be calling him so late. Could it be her? Lana Boyden, calling in the middle of the night?

It had never occurred to me how much privacy Daniel had living in a different bedroom. Although we lived together during our separation, I never knew much about his plans or how he spent his time. Was he entertaining women? In our home?

My blood pressure spiked at the thought of another woman in our house. Before I could stop myself, I reached for the phone with unsteady hands.

33

An alert for a new email popped up on his screen, but there was no preview. My thumb sluggishly tapped the notification, opening his email account.

"Uhh," Daniel groaned in his sleep and I panicked, racing to the bathroom.

I'd never gone through Daniel's phone before. We didn't have that kind of relationship, because trust was never an issue for us. Now, with my back to the door, I sunk to the tile floor, my chest rising and falling in waves.

The email was an advertisement from Emirates, our favorite airline. What should have been a relief left me feeling cheated. I'd fought through too much anxiety to settle for a message about discounted flights.

Old relationship advice from my mother replayed in my mind, something about not asking questions you don't want the answers to. I couldn't focus on reasoning or foresight, as my fingers typed the letters into the search bar without permission.

I stared at her name with disdain for a stranger. Lana Boyden. My thumb hovered above the blue search button, something deep inside trying to stop me from delving into the unknown. I was one click away from finding whatever Daniel hadn't scrubbed from his email history, but my intuition told me to stop.

Daniel deserved privacy. I knew that much. It was an invasion to read his private messages. After a night with my father, and a new bottle of whiskey, he probably was too drunk to have a serious conversation. If I could just wait for the morning, he'd open up and give me the answers I was prepared to steal.

It was wrong, but before I could back out of the application, my thumb tapped the search button. Five emails populated instantly.

Meeting at Sea Club
FOUND IN TRASH

From: Lana Boyden
Lana@BoydenFinancial.com
Date: April 17, 2018
To: Daniel Gamble
Gamble@TowerEnterpriseGroup.com

You can walk out of dinner all you want, Daniel, but it won't be as easy to get me to walk out of your life. The ball is in your court, you have my offer.

Just a reminder – I have photos, videos, bank statements, receipts, and more. You may not care how this unfolds, but I'd hate for your pretty wife to learn her fairy tale life is all a sham.

Pay the money, or I will contact her. Trust me, Daniel, I'm not the type of woman who bluffs. You should know that by now.

Lana Boyden
Executive Analyst at Boyden Financial

"Pray like it all depends on God, but work like it all depends on you."

Re: Meeting at Sea Club
FOUND IN TRASH

From: Daniel Gamble
Gamble@TowerEnterpriseGroup.com
Date: April 17, 2018
To: Lana Boyden
Lana@BoydenFinancial.com

Lana,
I'm not the best target for extortion. Like I told you at dinner, I have nothing more to say to you. Forget we ever met.

Gamble
CEO Tower Enterprise Group

FWD: Meeting Confirmation for Lana Boyden
Found in Trash

From: Lana Boyden
Lana@BoydenFinancial.com
Date: April 21, 2018
To: Daniel Gamble
Gamble@TowerEnterpriseGroup.com

Any suggestions on what I should wear to my meeting with your wife, Daniel? You know how important a first impression can be. Tootles!

Begin Forwarded Message:
From: Cherry Blossoms Publishing Booking@CherryBlossomsPublishing.com
Date: April 19, 2018
To: Lana Boyden
Lana@BoydenFinancial.com

Hi Lana!
Thank you for contacting Cherry Blossoms Publishing.
This email is to confirm your meeting for April 22, 2018 at 10:30 AM.
We look forward to meeting with you and discussing how Cherry Blossoms Publishing can help you reach your publishing needs.
If you have any questions, do not hesitate to call the office directly.
See you soon!

Cherry Blossoms Publishing Team
This is an automated email. Please do not respond.

Re: FWD: Meeting Confirmation for Lana Boyden
FOUND IN TRASH

From: Daniel Gamble
Gamble@TowerEnterpriseGroup.com
Date: April 21, 2018
To: Lana Boyden
Lana@BoydenFinancial.com

Cancel the meeting. What do you want?

Gamble
CEO Tower Enterprise Group

Re: FWD: Meeting Confirmation for Lana Boyden

FOUND IN TRASH

From: Lana Boyden
Lana@BoydenFinancial.com
Date: April 21, 2018
To: Daniel Gamble
Gamble@TowerEnterpriseGroup.com

Well, that was easy, so I'll return the favor.

$100,000 in cash, and $5,000/month for two years makes me go away.

Otherwise, I take everything to your wife. No warnings, no questions.

I'd send proof that I cancelled the meeting, but I figure you trust me. If your wife met me, I'm sure you'd hear all about it.

Pleasure doing business with ya.

Lana Boyden

Executive Analyst at Boyden Financial

"Pray like it all depends on God, but work like it all depends on you."

My vision was blurry by the time I finished reading her final smug email. I was exhausted from the words as I inched toward the toilet, vomiting every drop of alcohol I'd consumed. After dry heaving for several minutes, I gathered my strength to see a shell of myself staring back from my reflection.

I'd aged a decade from five emails, but I wasn't going to put myself through any further turmoil. I tried talking and giving Daniel an opportunity to explain. With a quick tap on his phone, I forwarded the emails to myself, gently placing his iPhone on the bathroom vanity.

My fingers trembled as I grasped the door knob, returning to the sounds of Daniel's hard sleep. With one last glance, I said goodbye to the life I knew, unwilling to pretend for another moment.

The house was silent as I crept down the stairs, careful not to make too much noise. I didn't want to alert anyone about my departure, and I doubted my ability to handle a conversation without breaking into tears.

From my calculations, I had about five hours before Daniel would wake up, wondering where I went. That gave me plenty of time to get the hell out of dodge, and that's exactly what I planned to do.

NIGHTMARES

THE EMILY GAMBLE SERIES

DEDICATION

To the readers who made this series bigger than my daydreams, taking me on a journey that led to a full throttle career. I appreciate your faith, enthusiasm, and unrelenting pressure to get this book out. Hehe. You're my folk. I needed you more than you'll ever know.

PROLOGUE

Groggy and dehydrated, I rolled over, reaching for Emily. After a night of drinking, I was craving her. She was gone, most likely downstairs cooking breakfast with her sisters. The aromas were already creeping up the stairs, but I wasn't quite ready for the family affair.

Looking to the nightstand, I began searching the bed for my phone. The night was a blur. Staggering into the bathroom, I had to admit how subtly quality liquor crept up on you. I caught my reflection in the mirror, shaking my head as I noticed I'd fallen asleep fully dressed.

My phone vibrated, drawing my attention to the vanity as I struggled to remember leaving it there. My assistant was alerting me of a new request in the contract negotiations for a deal in Japan. With the potential to break into the Asian market, it would take Tower Enterprise Group to the next level. But respecting Japanese business etiquette was proving to be a timely concession.

I'd been working around the clock for weeks, and Tracy knew time was of the essence. Typically, my time away from work was off limits for business, but for this deal I was willing to make an exception.

Quickly, I responded to her message, instructing her to contact the legal team with my approval to make the adjustments. Before the email had sent, I was texting Emily.

Daniel: Come back to bed.

Anticipating Emily's arrival, I hopped in the shower, stalling with the hopes she would soon join me. The urge to relieve myself was strong, but as always, I wanted to reserve everything for her.

After lathering my body with every soap and bath oil lining the built-in shelves, I finally accepted my wife wasn't going to join me, stepping out the shower smelling like a bouquet of roses. There was still no sign of her in the bedroom, but the voices from downstairs were growing louder. It was only a matter of time before she would come upstairs, upset by my delay.

Emily lived for these moments, but I quickly learned she wasn't satisfied with private quality time with her family. She needed us both there, a public display of how happy and successful she was. Coming from a broken family, it wasn't something I was used to.

No one in my family cared about my happiness, or how well Emily and I got along. I lived in a mansion and drove a Ferrari, there wasn't much left to prove to them.

Like many things, I adjusted this part of my life to accommodate the woman I loved. In the grand scheme, it was miniscule. A few hours mingling with the Delley family was far from a chore. It was the first time in months I'd spent time with my in-laws, reuniting in their family home was a breath of fresh air. Although, I was certain Emily's parents' relationship was not one I aspired to model my marriage after.

Descending the long stairwell, I paused, surveying the room before making my entrance. Mr. Delley was an early riser. From the accordion glass doors that led to the massive backyard, I could see he was already on a call. Pacing the same patch of cement, he was speaking in what looked to be an aggressive tone.

I had some business to discuss with him, but it looked best to save that for later. By the time I made it to the living room, my stomach was speaking in complete sentences, the liquor from last night demanding food.

"Good morning!" Tiffany greeted me first as I sat in a loveseat at the edge of the room.

"Good morning," I smiled, nodding to both her and Elliot. He sat beside her, his arm wrapped tightly around her shoulder as if she might run away any second.

"It'll be a good morning once they finish that food!" Elliot yelled towards the kitchen.

"Tell your little girlfriend to come help and we might finish sooner!"

I didn't need to look up to know that was Denise. She was always looking for an argument. To my knowledge, Tiffany was the first woman Elliot had ever introduced to his little sisters. Denise had been bullying her since she arrived.

"Hey, Daniel. You want some coffee?" Olivia asked. Emily's oldest sister was the most nurturing of them, constantly concerned with every-one's well-being.

"Good morning," I called out before adding, "No, I'm fine. Thank you."

The Delley women were in the kitchen, and I knew well enough to stay as far away as possible. Besides, I liked to have my morning coffee with Emily.

Reaching for my phone, I checked to see if she'd responded to my message, but there was only a new email from Tracy. For the first time, I didn't want updates about the deal. I was yearning to touch my wife.

"Where's Em?" I asked Elliot after scanning the room.

"She's in there," he nodded towards the kitchen without turning away from the television.

"Ya'll wanna watch something else?" Denise's new boyfriend asked from the opposite end of the sofa, slouched like a teenager. I'd barely had a conversation with him during the party, at least not one I could remember.

"Nah, you good, bro," Elliot answered. We continued to watch Sports-center in silence, a mindless activity I gave up in college.

Just then, Victoria walked into the living room carrying a tray of mimosas. "I've been assigned waitress for the morning."

I chuckled, but to my surprise she never looked in my direction. As Emily's best friend, Victoria had always been my favorite of her sisters. I liked to think we had the closest bond. I could tell she was in a foul mood, probably over a quarrel with her sisters. I knew I'd hear all the details from Emily on the ride home.

"Daniel! Can I talk to you?" Mr. Delley barked from the backyard.

"Of course," I jumped up, quickly making my way across the room. The look on his face said whatever he needed was urgent. I had a feeling I knew exactly what it was.

"I need to contract you for a new deal," he wasted no time cutting to the chase.

"I actually wanted to discuss some business with you," I massaged my hands together, certain this would be a difficult conversation.

"I need this to stay between us," he began before Olivia poked her head out the glass doors. "What is it, honey?" Mr. Delley asked, shifting to a kinder tone.

"Sorry, daddy. Daniel, is Emily hungover? I knew she was drinking too much last night. I should have stopped her," she winced regretfully.

"What do you mean? I thought she was cooking with ya'll," I questioned, walking towards the back door.

Upon re-entering the house, I knew something was off. Everyone turned to me. It felt each of them were aware of something I wasn't privileged to.

"Victoria," I called across the island when I entered to the kitchen. If anyone knew what was going on with my wife, it was her. "Where's Emily?"

She finally looked to me, hurt swirling through her almond shaped eyes. Gone was the little sister I'd regularly send clients, hoping to keep her flailing interior design business afloat. She was harboring something, but I couldn't be sure what it was.

"She's sleep," she frowned, answering me with an attitude for the first time since we'd met. While she was clearly upset, I didn't think she was lying.

"Sleep where? Daniel, she's not upstairs?" Mrs. Delley began to panic.

My stomach sank when the four women began moving in circles, concern transforming their faces. Glancing toward the living room, the rest of the party was moving in, crowding around the kitchen island as the news made its way throughout the house.

"Emily's gone?" Mr. Delley asked, the frustration clear on his face before he was distracted by another phone call.

"Oh God!" Mrs. Delley yelped as though Emily was a six-year-old child.

The women began running up the stairs, searching every room as they called her name. Elliot and his girlfriend stood to the side speaking in whispers. He was probably explaining the impulsiveness of his youngest sister.

"Shawty left last night, dog," Denise's boyfriend said. I hadn't even noticed him standing beside me. Glaring at him from the corner of my eye, I tried to bite back my annoyance. I didn't take anyone dating Denise too seriously. "She dipped out in the 'Rari at like three this morning."

"She what?"

"Look, this ain't my business. But I saw her leave. If you need it, I got ways of finding anybody. Just say the word."

1

_____

"Miss. Delley?"

My head snapped, recognizing my name after a long delay. The young blond man curled his lips, but the smile didn't reach his eyes. I could sense his concern, and knew I deserved it.

"Yes, is everything okay?" I forced a fake smile of my own, eager to be alone with my thoughts.

"I'll just need the American Express you used online," he explained the obvious.

I was a mess. Still flustered from the nightmare that had officially carried into the morning. After a quick scramble at the house, stuffing a bag with unnecessary odds and ins, here I was. A fashionable vagabond.

"Oh, yes... Of course," I nodded, lifting my leather denim Neverfull bag onto the granite counter. As I dug for the matching wallet, a pair of pink lace panties fell from the bag. The embarrassment seeped through my pores as I stuffed the underwear into my pocket.

"Sorry, I'm just," I struggled to explain, grateful for my last second decision to wear the oversized shades I'd found in Daniel's car. The thought of my husband turned my stomach, causing my teeth to clench as I envisioned his face.

"Don't worry about it, ma'am. We can handle it after your appointment. You will still be partaking in the spa day, right?" The blond guy asked while typing on his keyboard.

Too tired to insist he not call me ma'am, I simply nodded before accepting the thin white envelope he handed me. Peeking inside, I noticed one room key, along with my valet ticket.

"Will you be needing a second key?" He asked, misreading the disappointment on my face.

My stomach fluttered at his question. Of course, he had no idea I'd just left my husband, making this the first time one key was sufficient.

"It's fine. Where is it?" I asked, a soft grunt escaping me as I lifted the Louis Vuitton bag from the counter.

"The elevator is just up the hall, ma'am. You're on the top floor, as requested."

"My name is Emily... Matthew," I squinted to read his name tag, again thinking of Daniel. He made a point to address everyone by name, treating janitors and board members alike.

"Of course, ma'am... I'm sorry. Of course, Miss. Emily," He stumbled through the correction, unable to drop all formalities.

After refusing the bell hop's assistance, I walked to the elevator alone. The last thing I wanted was forced small talk during a long elevator ride. Dropping my bag, my shoulders slumped with the weight I'd been carrying, literally and figuratively. Leaning my head against the mirrored wall as the elevator car ascended floors, the heaviness of my decisions began to sink in.

It was all surreal. Operating on autopilot, my body was working solely on adrenaline after a sleepless night. From the time I learned the truth about Daniel, and what he had been up to during our rocky time, my feet had been moving as swiftly as my mind.

The drive back to the city from my parents' estate in the valley was quicker than normal, as I struggled to disguise the unavoidable truth. Over and over, I tried to recount the words of the emails, hoping to be wrong, but I knew I wasn't.

Standing in our bedroom, the one Daniel and I had only recently begun sharing again, I admitted I could no longer recount even a word from the series of emails. All that was left was the emptiness in my gut, the shame in my chest, and the tension in my shoulders. I may have forgotten the words, but the way they made me feel was burned into my soul.

The soft bell of the elevator brought me back to reality. I reached for my overflowing bag before making my way to the room. It had been a long time since I'd stayed in a hotel not owned by my family. But if I knew Daniel, he was already searching for me, and a Delley Retreat would never conceal a drop of information from my father.

The Britton Hotel was in Downtown LA, the last place my family would expect me to hide. Glancing around the room, I couldn't stop pointing out missteps made in the design. The King-size bed was far too large for the room. The designer was either greedy or forced, squeezing a plush lounge chair and ottoman in front of the only window, impeding on the view of the city.

Tossing my bag onto the lounge chair, I plopped down on the ottoman, taking in the details of my new home. The bright red theme dated the room, which I imagined was trendy a few years back. A geometric design on the bedspread was duplicated on an accent wall opposite the window. Tacky.

Instantly, I began to ponder other options. The room was too cluttered to stay for long. As I walked into the bathroom, I noticed where all the square footage had gone. It didn't pair well with such a tiny hotel room. With both a standalone soaker tub, and large glassed-in shower, the bathroom felt more spacious than the living area. To make matters worse, fire engine red tiles lined the bathroom floor and wall. The space was as relaxing as a disco.

A soft knock at the door sent me into a panic. Was it possible Daniel could find me so quickly? I'd been extra careful, booking with my corporate credit card, using my maiden name. He had no idea I kept a credit line completely detached from him, a lesson and wedding gift from my mother.

Tip toeing across the thin carpet, I peered through the peep-hole to see a small Asian woman dressed in a light pink uniform that reminded me of scrubs.

"Hi, I'm Megan. Are you ready for your spa day, Miss. Delley?" Her voice was calming even through the door.

"Hi, Megan. I thought I was supposed to come downstairs?" I asked while opening the heavy door.

"Oh, no. You ordered the VIP package. We come to you," she smiled before reaching for a cart I hadn't noticed.

Moving aside, I made room for her as she navigated the tight space like a pro. As much as I was looking forward to a bit of pampering, the idea of unwinding felt impossible.

"Let's start with a bath," she suggested, making her way to the bathroom before running the water. It was the first time I'd fully entered the bathroom, after being disturbed by her arrival. I'd completely missed the vanity at the far end of the large room.

I plopped down, feeling the fatigue as I watched her add one oil after another into the white ceramic bathtub. Megan quietly prepped her tools and clean towels like a doctor preparing for surgery. I only hoped she could revive me from the hell I was in.

"Ready?" She turned to me when the water had reached a level that met her satisfaction.

Without a word, I stepped out the maxi dress I'd been wearing for nearly 24-hours. I could still smell Daniel on it. The memories of our passionate erotic episode a few hours earlier lodged in my throat.

"Should I have this laundered?" Megan asked.

"Burn it." I ordered as I sunk into the steaming water.

2

Megan had done just what I needed, nursing me back to health with a spa day that was worth every penny. I tipped her a crisp one-hundred-dollar bill, one of many I'd taken from the safe before leaving the home I shared with Daniel.

"Thank you," she gratefully nodded as she gathered her things.

Not only had Megan bathed me, but she washed and conditioned my hair, wrapping it in a silk scarf before adding a large white towel for what I thought was more aesthetic than anything. Afterward, she'd given me a massage for what felt like hours, allowing me to sleep as she magically managed to paint my fingernails.

"Do you really want me to burn this?" She asked, lifting my maxi dress from the floor. "It's a very expensive dress," she added, a look of shock on her face.

"You keep it," I smirked, noticing she was about my size. Her eyes lit up, and I felt even better.

"Thank you, Miss. Delley," she smiled as she backed her cart of goodies out the room. "Reception will come up to verify your card. I was told they thought you would be coming down," she added.

"Oh, right. No problem," I assured her, forgetting all about my mishap at check-in.

Although it had only been a few hours, I felt like a new person. Far less frantic than the woman who had checked in with lace panties falling from her purse.

When the door closed behind Megan, it seemed to take the oxygen with it. Suddenly, I felt forced to deal with the mess I knew was happening whether I acknowledged it or not. Digging through my purse, I decided it was finally time to face the music. For the first time since I left my parents, I looked at my phone.

Eighteen missed calls and seventy-three text messages, mixed between all my family members. The last call from Daniel was only a few minutes prior. *Fuck.*

I threw the phone on the bed. Maybe I wasn't as ready as I thought. A little time could do my body well, or at least that's the excuse I gave myself. Before lying down, I shoved my phone under a pillow and reached for the remote to the television.

An episode of *Girlfriends* was playing, and I took it as a sign the Universe wanted me to relax for a day. It had always been my favorite television show, but I hadn't rewatched an episode since the series finale.

I'd just settled into bed, feeling even more relaxed, when a soft knock at the door interfered. Remembering Megan's reminder, I disregarded the panic and quickly searched through my wallet. Pausing at the mirror, I wondered if it were inappropriate to answer the door wearing only a towel wrapped around my body to match the one on my head.

Another soft knock. I decided they'd seen plenty women in less than towels working in hospitality, and made my way to the door.

"Here you go," I extended my hand holding the credit card before glancing up to the tired eyes staring back at me.

We stood in silence. Shock halting my words, while another emotion appeared to have captured Daniel's. Instinctually, I took a step backwards, unsure of my next move.

Gripping the towel, I felt naked, but it had nothing to do with my clothing, or lack thereof. He was staring through me in a way that made me question everything I'd felt since discovering his truth.

I felt... guilty. A strong need to cower and explain myself took over me. I was no longer the fierce woman who had brazenly taken his car in the middle of the night. Now, I was the kept wife, staring at the man who had directly affected every major decision of my adult life.

Daniel's jaw tensed as his eyes moved past me, taking in the room.

"You're having a fucking spa day?" He finally asked, catching me off guard.

How was *he* angry? The memories flooded back, and my own anger re-emerged. There was no reason for me to cower. I was right. He was wrong. I repeated those two short sentences until I found my voice.

"I saw the emails."

I had a much better response. One I'd practiced the 45-minute drive from my parents' house, but now the four words rolled off my tongue as all the accusation I needed.

"What emails?" Daniel's handsome face contorted, half frown half disgust.

"The emails from Lana Boyden."

His eyes widened imperceptibly. It was only a split second of recognition, but I caught it. The realization pushed my shoulders back as I stood taller, even more confident in my reaction.

I might have forgotten every word in those emails, but that woman's name was fixed in my memory. I watched as Daniel swallowed slowly, inhaling through his nose, his lips pressed tightly together.

"Hi, uh, Miss. Delley?" The blond man from the front desk appeared out of nowhere. Next to Daniel he looked even more frail. Daniel looked from Matthew to me, then back to Matthew. I knew exactly what had caught his attention.

"Here you go," I handed him the card. He awkwardly reached past Daniel to inspect the credit card before nervously returning it.

"Perfect. Sorry, it's just protocol," he explained to Daniel, which annoyed me.

"Oh, I'm not staying with *Miss. Delley*," he glared at me when he spoke my maiden name, confirming my assumption.

"Thank you, ma'am," Matthew returned his attention to me, his cheeks the color of beets as he realized his misstep. "Oh, I'm sorry. Uh, thank you... Miss. Emily," he added before scurrying off.

We were back where we'd left off. Daniel seemed more the offended than the offender, shaking his head slowly as he scowled at me.

I clenched my lips, trapping the words I'd been practicing, as they searched for gaps between my teeth, eager to cry foul. I didn't need to explain anything. I refused to give Daniel a way out.

"Enjoy your spa day," he finally said, releasing his grip on the door as he turned to leave.

"What?" I stepped forward, just as he turned back to me. There was a look on his face, one I couldn't read. The gust of air between us smelled of a distant life, one that now only brought pain.

"Give me my keys."

I couldn't believe my ears. *He was putting me out?* Asking for the keys to a house we'd built together? My mother's insistent advice to have my name added to the deed rang loudly in my head as I turned away, feeling the tears burn at the corners of my eyes.

Don't you fucking cry.

The keys were still on the side of my bag, easy to find. I forced my head up as I glided back to the doorway, handing Daniel the keys he'd so arrogantly requested.

To my surprise, he removed the key to his Ferrari before handing me the keychain with our house key still attached. "I'll have someone drop off your car."

He turned to leave again.

"Are you serious?" I asked in disbelief. I didn't chase after him this time, certain he would turn around. He did.

"I woke up and you were gone, Emily. I was worried about you. Now, I see you're fine." He spoke the words like each one hurt, over pronouncing every syllable as he fought for restraint.

"And what about Lana Boyden?" I spat, hating the taste of her name in my mouth.

"Emily, if you left in the middle of the night without an explanation, I'd hope you have all the answers you need. I don't have any for you." He turned to leave, and I felt frozen by his coldness. "And call your family. They're worried sick, but I'm done explaining your bullshit."

The door slammed loudly, punctuating his declaration. My hands went to my chest as my legs gave out. My bravado could only last so long. I fell to the floor realizing my biggest fears were true.

He didn't even care to explain himself, discarding me like an old thought he couldn't remember believing in.

Even in my state of shock, I fought for dignity, covering my mouth to mask the cries I refused to let Daniel hear. He was gone to who knows where. My imagination ran wild with the possibilities of him returning to Lana Boyden.

3

Meeting at Sea Club
FOUND IN TRASH

From: Lana Boyden
Lana@BoydenFinancial.com
Date: April 17, 2018
To: Daniel Gamble
Gamble@TowerEnterpriseGroup.com

You can walk out of dinner all you want, Daniel, but it won't be as easy to get me to walk out of your life. The ball is in your court, you have my offer.
Just a reminder – I have photos, videos, bank statements, receipts, and more. You may not care how this unfolds, but I'd hate for your pretty wife to learn her fairy tale life is all a sham.
Pay the money, or I will contact her. Trust me, Daniel, I'm not the type of woman who bluffs. You should know that by now.

Lana Boyden

Executive Analyst at Boyden Financial

"Pray like it all depends on God, but work like it all depends on you."

Re: Meeting at Sea Club

FOUND IN TRASH

From: Daniel Gamble
Gamble@TowerEnterpriseGroup.com
Date: April 17, 2018
To: Lana Boyden
Lana@BoydenFinancial.com

Lana,

I'm not the best target for extortion. Like I told you at dinner, I have nothing more to say to you. Forget we ever met.

Gamble
CEO Tower Enterprise Group

FWD: Meeting Confirmation for Lana Boyden
FOUND IN TRASH

From: Lana Boyden
Lana@BoydenFinancial.com
Date: April 21, 2018
To: Daniel Gamble
Gamble@TowerEnterpriseGroup.com

Any suggestions on what I should wear to my meeting with your wife, Daniel? You know how important a first impression can be. Tootles!

Begin Forwarded Message:
From: Cherry Blossoms Publishing Booking@CherryBlossomsPublishing.com
Date: April 19, 2018
To: Lana Boyden
Lana@BoydenFinancial.com

Hi Lana!
Thank you for contacting Cherry Blossoms Publishing.
This email is to confirm your meeting for April 22, 2018 at 10:30 AM.
We look forward to meeting with you and discussing how Cherry Blossoms Publishing can help you reach your publishing needs.
If you have any questions, do not hesitate to call the office directly.
See you soon!

Cherry Blossoms Publishing Team
This is an automated email. Please do not respond.

Re: FWD: Meeting Confirmation for Lana Boyden
FOUND IN TRASH

From: Daniel Gamble
Gamble@TowerEnterpriseGroup.com
Date: April 21, 2018
To: Lana Boyden
Lana@BoydenFinancial.com

Cancel the meeting. What do you want?

Gamble
CEO Tower Enterprise Group

Re: FWD: Meeting Confirmation for Lana Boyden

Found in Trash

From: Lana Boyden
Lana@BoydenFinancial.com
Date: April 21, 2018
To: Daniel Gamble
Gamble@TowerEnterpriseGroup.com

Well, that was easy, so I'll return the favor.

$100,000 in cash, and $5,000/month for two years makes me go away.

Otherwise, I take everything to your wife. No warnings, no questions.

I'd send proof that I cancelled the meeting, but I figure you trust me. If your wife met me, I'm sure you'd hear all about it.

Pleasure doing business with ya.

Lana Boyden

Executive Analyst at Boyden Financial

"Pray like it all depends on God, but work like it all depends on you."

"**D**amn, Emily! Why didn't you tell me?" Victoria asked after reading the email exchange between Daniel and Lana Boyden.

Only one year my senior, she was more like a best friend than a big sister, and the only person I trusted with the newly discovered information. Forcing her to secrecy, I invited her to the hotel before sharing all I'd learned.

"I knew you'd tell me to think it over," I explained, shrugging my shoulders. My eyes were red and puffy from hours of crying, my body exhausted and dehydrated.

"I don't know, sis. There's not much to think about here. I might have told you to take it easy on the dramatics, but that's it."

"The dramatics?" I snapped, offended.

"Emily, you left in the middle of the night. Daniel was distraught. Mom thought you'd been kidnapped!" She stared at me in disbelief.

"Right," I rolled my eyes. "Someone broke into a huge estate and only took me and a Ferrari." My words laced with sarcasm.

"You're right. We all should have put it together that you'd secretly read Daniel's emails, learning about his private extortion, and decided to leave in the middle of the night. I honestly don't know how we failed to connect those dots," she shot back, twisting her lips with annoyance.

I turned away. I hadn't called my sister over for a lecture, or as a reminder to be more calculated when learning of my husband's infidelity. I had my mother for that.

"Sorry," she scooted towards me as we sat on the edge of the bed, so close our thighs touched. Needing the comfort, I leaned my head against Victoria's shoulder as she wrapped her arm around me. "I guess I knew," she finally added.

"I thought you would," I whispered, my voice tired and weak.

"I feel responsible for all of this," she admitted.

I popped my head up, witnessing the guilt crease the space

between her lips and nose, which looked so much like mine, I understood why people mistook us for twins.

"How could this be your fault?" I turned to face my sister, my eyes wide with curiosity.

"Are you serious?" She turned to me before continuing, "If it weren't for me, you wouldn't have had a name to search."

She was right. Victoria did spread the rumor she'd heard about Daniel going to dinner with another woman. And when I'd asked her to find the mystery woman's name, she didn't fail in her research. But still, blaming herself for my husband's infidelity was absurd.

"Vic, you're my sister. If you hear my husband is cheating on me, you're supposed to tell me."

The words had replayed in my mind, but hearing them for the first time was more than I could bear. "He's cheating on me, isn't he, Vic?"

"Well, it doesn't look good," she answered after a long pause, glancing at the phone still displaying the email thread between Daniel and Lana. I'd been refusing to acknowledge her so informally, but it seemed we were sharing a man, so I might as well get familiar with the bitch.

"He didn't even try to explain," I blinked slowly, recalling his brazenness.

"That's Daniel. You left him looking stupid. His ego was bruised," she shrugged as if that explained it all.

"I left *him* looking stupid?" I shot back.

"I'm not defending him, Emily!" She held her hands up innocently. "I don't know if he's cheating, but he's definitely hiding something. That much is certain. You gave him an opportunity to explain himself and he passed. Sometimes no response *is* a response."

Falling back on the bed in dramatic fashion, I threw my hands in the air, looking up to the crown molding outlining the ceiling. The hotel room wasn't half bad, now that I'd gotten used to it. It was no Delley Retreat, but it was nice.

"What do I do now?" I asked, knowing Victoria didn't have the answer.

"This is why mom says to always have your ducks in order before the confrontation. You went to him with big guns and no ammo, baby girl." Her voice rang with disappointment.

"I hate that we have so much advice about how to deal with an unfaithful husband," I sighed.

"Word." Victoria nodded before falling back on the bed, mocking me. I laughed, watching her eyes light up at the sight of my smile. "Let's order some room service, *Miss. Delley*," she teased before reaching for the menu on the nightstand.

"I think he was more upset that I'd checked in under my maiden name than anything else," I smirked recalling the disgust on Daniel's face.

"I remember when I was decorating your house, the artwork for the living room arrived, and the man said it was for 'Miss. Delley'. I was in the backyard, but I could hear Daniel from the front door. 'That's my wife! Her name is Mrs. Gamble!'" Victoria laughed as she impersonated Daniel's barking voice.

I forced a soft laugh, but inside I was broken. I remembered the artwork she was referencing. One she had chosen for aesthetics, although it was far from my preferred style. One evening after dinner, I admitted my distaste to Daniel and he excitedly leaped from the table, removing it that instant.

It turned out we both hated the painting. Too afraid to disappoint the other, we'd lived with it for months before my admission. Standing in our living room, the now empty wall the clean slate we needed, we vowed to never hide our true feelings from one another again.

The memory replayed like a vintage black and white film, as I questioned when we broke that vow, and how many others had since been severed.

"Should we get two or three meals? You look like you need a burger," Victoria glanced over the menu.

"I don't even think I can eat," I answered pitifully.

"Three. Definitely three," she nodded confidently before reaching for the phone.

4

————————

"He didn't say *anything*?" Victoria asked before dipping the last French fry in a mountain of ketchup.

"Not a word, but I saw something in his eye. It wasn't guilt, but he knew what I was talking about," my words faded as I tried to make sense of it all in my head.

Standing before me, Daniel was nothing but angry. He tried to pass it off as concern, but I knew it was a shock that I'd left him in the way I did. My impulsive decision was beginning to set in. It was impossible to ignore the absurdity of my behavior with it reflected in my sister's eyes.

"Why didn't you just wait to talk to him? Emily, mom was scared to death when we realized you were gone." She paused, shaking her head as if she wanted to stop herself, but the words continued. "I was mad at Daniel when I woke up. I couldn't even look at him. But when we were all calling and texting you, I actually felt bad for him."

"Don't take his side," I rolled my eyes, appalled by her swift change of course. "You read the emails," I reminded her.

"He's wrong, Emily. I'm not denying that, but now so are you."

"In what way?" I boldly challenged her, tilting my head defiantly.

"Do you want a divorce?"

The adrenaline drained from me quickly. The word I didn't even want to think of stopping me in my vengeful tracks. I'd just escaped the gloomy trail leading to the demise of my marriage, unsure if I wanted to welcome back the dark cloud that had hovered over my life for half a year.

"If you don't, then what are you leaving?" Victoria asked, taking my silence for an answer.

"I asked him who Lana was last night and he took me for a joke. Literally laughing in my face," I recalled before continuing, "he needed to know I was serious."

"Mike could barely make it to the room last night. They were drunk as hell. What did you expect? Now you're holed up in some over decorated hotel, for what? What's your plan, Em?" She tilted her head pitifully.

Glancing around the room, my confidence diminished with every question. I wasn't sure what I wanted, since my plans rarely included an ending. I did know I wanted Daniel to feel what I'd felt after reading those emails, and despite everything that followed, I'd succeeded in hurting him.

"Then explain him not answering today, Victoria. Is he still drunk?"

"He's humiliated, Emily! And now you still don't get answers. You had the winning hand and threw it in. This makes no sense!" She flailed her arms in the air, confusion evident in her gorgeous features.

"You sound like him," I sneered, turning away from her on the bed, wishing I hadn't invited her over.

Reading my cues, Victoria scooted to the edge of the bed, wrapping her arm around me. "Look, I know you were mad. I get it. The emails are hard to read and I'm not married to the man. But, you want answers, and this is the wrong way to go about getting them. You've got to put your big girl pants on and face him, Emily."

Despite her soft tone, Victoria's words felt like daggers. There was no way I could possibly go to him after how he'd treated me; dismissed me.

"So, I'm supposed to cower to him to figure out why he is secretly paying a woman six-figures?"

"No, you were supposed to wake up this morning with your questions ready, because he would have no choice but to answer. Instead, you made a scene, to which he naturally reacted, and now there are two problems to face." Victoria answered matter-of-factly as her phone vibrated on the nightstand.

"I'm not cowering," I said more to myself, as my sister frowned, looking at her screen.

After typing quickly, she returned her attention to me, disregarding my declaration. "Whatever you're going to do, you can't stay here. At least come and stay with me and Mike while you figure this out," she offered, surely knowing I'd never move into her small townhouse.

"I just need some time to myself. I have to work through this on my own," I reasoned.

"Don't get too caught up in what you think you know. I'm good at reading people, and Daniel is in love with you, Emily. I didn't see a cheating man yesterday," she argued as she gathered her things.

"You're taking his side," I rolled my eyes, happy to see her go.

"If you wanted someone to rile you up, you should have called Denise," Victoria smugly added before making her way to the door. Our older sister Denise had never been a fan of Daniel's, or stability. If I'd called her, we would probably be ransacking Daniel's office by now.

Annoyed and alone, I called the front desk with an attitude, requesting room service return to retrieve the evidence of our binge eating.

5

The morning came with a sliver of clarity. After a good night's rest, I could see Victoria's side a bit more clearly. While I still wasn't ready to check out of the hotel, I did want answers from Daniel, and I was willing to admit how wrong I was in my approach to obtain them.

Rising earlier than usual, I drove to our house with a knot of anxiety looming deep in my abdomen. After our last encounter, I wasn't sure how Daniel would feel about an unannounced visit. Hoping not to alert him of my arrival, I used my house key rather than entering through the garage as I normally would.

From the moment I entered the foyer, I knew something was off. The strong smell of cigar smoke filled the air as soft mumblings from the kitchen greeted me.

"Oh, Mrs. Gamble! You don't want to see this," Marla warned me. Holding her hands in the air, our housekeeper tried to block my view of the broken stained glass shattered on the floor. She'd swept everything into a neat pile, but the destruction was still visible.

"Where's Mr. Gamble?" I forced a brave voice, turning away from the evidence of my favorite vase.

"He wasn't here when I arrived. He asked me to come early, said you were away on business," she said.

"I see," was all I added before excusing myself to the bedroom.

Unsure whether Marla had already cleaned the master suite, or if Daniel had failed to sleep, I noticed the immaculately designed bedroom with fresh eyes. All ten pillows lined the headboard just as I liked, an image ripped from the pages of a home design magazine.

Sitting on the edge of the bed, I found the courage to do what I couldn't at the hotel – finally check the messages Daniel left after learning of my absence. Starting with the texts, I braved myself with a deep breath.

Daniel: Come back to bed.
Daniel: Did you take the Rari out?
Daniel: Where are you?
Daniel: You can't even answer my calls?

My stomach tensed knowing there was more. It was one thing to read the words, but I still had to hear his voice. Daniel had left three voicemails, something he rarely did. The first was standard.

"Em, it's me. Call me."

The second, a bit more panicked:

"Emily, your mom is worried. Call me back."

The last was more in line with the man who greeted me at the hotel:

"I cannot believe you're pulling this shit again... Emily, please just call me back."

My eyes clenched hearing the pain in his voice, but nothing he said could erase the anger I still felt for him and his audacity. Suddenly, I was grateful for his absence, realizing I wasn't quite ready for the inevitable confrontation.

Scrolling my phone, I shocked myself with the selection before placing the phone to my ear.

"Mrs. G! Good morning," Crystal's voice was cheerier than I'd expected. She had stuck to using my new nickname, which made me feel a little less intrusive about my early morning call.

It was over an hour before she was due in the office, but Crystal was eager as always. I didn't deserve an assistant as proficient as her. Cherry Blossoms Publishing wouldn't survive without her.

"Hey, I need you to come ready to work today. I know I've been really lax, but I want an update on everything that's going on at Cherry Blossoms," I heard myself say, unsure of my intentions.

"No problem!" She excitedly responded. "I've been taking notes on everything. I can clue you in before the morning status."

"Sounds good. I'll meet you at the office," I smiled before ending the call.

For everything my publishing house wasn't, I knew it could be a great distraction. During my marital dispute with Daniel, I hadn't been involved with much of the business, but I was ready to jump back in full throttle if it meant getting my mind off our new battle.

A war mentality inspired my outfit selection for the day. With my hair slicked into a top bun, I dressed in an all-black Chanel pant suit with a simple white blouse underneath.

On the way out the door, I texted Daniel.

Emily: Thanks for having my car dropped off. I stopped by the house, wanted to talk before work.

Driving through the city, I glanced over to my phone at every opportunity, anxious to see how he'd respond, if at all.

6

"Good morning, Mrs. G!" Crystal had managed to beat me to the office, still ahead of her scheduled start time. Making a mental note to give her a much deserved bonus, I led her to my office, ready to get caught up on the business I'd been slowly falling out of love with since the day I bought it.

In some ways, I always felt Cherry Blossoms Publishing was more Daniel's idea. He was the entrepreneur. I often found myself hiding behind his expertise rather than discovering my own.

Over the course of our private separation, I considered selling it altogether, ready to start anew. But there was still too much love there for the business I had transformed in just a few short years.

Daniel might have been responsible for my endless flow of sound business advice, but it was my hard work that resulted in our consistent growth. Cherry Blossoms Publishing was now the most successful black owned publishing house in California, a feat I was extremely proud of.

"I know I've been out the loop lately, but I want to get back in the swing of things," I said, tossing my Neverfull bag onto my desk chair.

"Don't worry, boss lady. I knew you'd want me keeping an eye on things. I've been ready for this day," Crystal began.

I turned to see her flipping through a stack of papers attached to a clipboard. When she finally looked up, she was beaming with pride as she ran down the projects and clients on the docket.

Together, we went over the business in detail. Crystal updated me on the new authors we were slated to sign, and the releases scheduled for the quarter. A possible acquisition on the horizon was what really sent her into a frenzy as she gushed over the possibilities.

"The publishing house is based out of New York, but the owner wants to jump ship and move out west. Rumor has it, he's interested in Hollywood. Madison has had a few video calls with him, and every time, all the ladies in the office crowd around the conference room for a peek," Crystal blushed.

"He wants to sell the company or partner together?" I questioned, more concerned with the business.

"Initially he wanted to merge, but I think it's strictly acquisition talk now," she nodded quickly, catching her slip in professionalism.

"Okay, I'll introduce myself on the next call," I said, jotting down a reminder to speak with Madison, the head of our acquisitions division.

"He's coming in for a meeting today!" Crystal failed to hide her excitement.

Watching her nervously straighten the hem of her dress, I noticed her outfit for the first time. Unlike her usual business casual attire, Crystal wore a short and flirty black shift dress that stopped just above her knee. Her hair fell in big curls framing her face. Even her bronzer couldn't disguise her blushing.

"Tell me about this mystery man, since it seems the whole office is already up to date," I huffed, glancing through the double-sided mirrors lining my office.

It was my favorite detail of the office design, much of which was Daniel's doing. Positioned in the center of the eighteenth floor, I had an unobstructed view of the main entrance, watching everyone without living in a fishbowl.

"His name is Quentin Bolden. He founded Laney Publishing less than a decade ago, and it's already grown to be a powerhouse on the east coast. Mostly into non-fiction, with an emphasis on celebrity deals. They do a lot of tell-all type exposés. I thought he would be sleazy, considering their reputation, but he's very charismatic," she emphasized the last word. "From what I gather, he's looking to completely change industries, moving into something with movies, but Madison has been very tight lipped about it. I think she likes being the point person on this one," Crystal smirked.

"Mm Hmm," I nodded. I'd never heard of Quentin Bolden, but I was intrigued from her short description. "They're the ones publishing all the reality star memoirs, right?" I paused, searching my memory for details. "Didn't they get sued for defamation by a network?"

"Yes! That's them! It was Roxanne the Diva. She'd signed an NDA and lied about it in her book deal. They settled out of court."

"I see. Is he trying to dump his garbage on us?" I wondered aloud, not understanding the benefit of the acquisition.

"No, they actually have a really good roster of new writers. The celebrity attachment just gave them notoriety. Plus, Madison says he's willing to sell for less than the company's worth. But, you have to meet him. He's just..." Crystal waved her hand, biting her bottom lip with desire.

"Do I need to call Jamal to come supervise?" I teased, mentioning her new fiancé.

"Don't you dare!" She shrieked, covering her eyes with her free hand. "I can look, I just can't touch."

"You're a mess!" I giggled before glancing at my watch. "What time is the status?"

"In fifteen minutes," Crystal answered, regaining her composure.

"Let's get ready, then."

Every day at Cherry Blossoms Publishing began with a morning status. As the company grew, the divisions functioned more and more independently. We needed regular meetings to keep everyone on the same page. It was the perfect time to re-introduce myself as the glue that had brought them all together.

While I was nervous, I was more excited. It had been so long since I was heavily involved in the day to day operations, and for the first time, I was noticing how much I'd missed it.

Wanting to make an impression, I arrived at the meeting early. Greeting the head of every division, I could read the shock and confusion on their faces. Nervously, they settled into the leather seats surrounding the long chrome table, another detail Daniel had chosen.

"Don't worry. I don't come bearing bad news," I announced, hoping to relieve the palpable tension. I could see the relief on their faces as I continued. "No one is in trouble. You've all been doing an incredible job. As you know, I like to be hands off in my leadership. But as we continue to grow, I want to play a more integral role in the business I love so much."

I felt empowered standing before my incredibly talented team. Each of them was a respected leader in their field, but they were all looking to me for instruction. I was the boss.

"First, I want to change the way we communicate. In the past, I've always been quite formal, something I thought best after acquiring this company at such a young age. But that's not really who I am, and it's not something I want to continue. From now on, I'd like you all to call me Emily, not Mrs. Gamble, and no boss talk.

"Everyone in this room knows your title, as well as mine. So, let's skip the formalities and fluff talk. As we go around the table, only share what we need to know. Save what can be an email for emails. This meeting should only include need to know information. Everything else can be discussed privately."

Madison smiled, nodding her head in appreciation. Nodding back, I silently granted her permission to start the meeting, as I knew she always did.

Leaning back in my chair, I listened closely, taking notes as necessary. Christian, the head of our fictional division, pitched his untraditional new approach to the low season.

Summer was well regarded throughout the industry as a down time in sales. The weather was too nice for cuddling up with a book. Kids were out of school, or going back, and people didn't tend to buy as many books as they did in the cooler months.

"But all I see is opportunity," he smirked.

Christian was a white man in his mid-thirties. He had a flair for the dramatics, starting as our marketing director before transitioning into fiction. Let him tell it, his life is a fairy tale, so it was a natural fit. Nodding along, I encouraged him to continue, intrigued by his enthusiasm.

"We're going to flood the market with our new writers. These are the best of the best, our class of undiscovered talent." Christian stood as he continued, circling the conference room while using hand gestures to emphasize his plan.

"Sure, the numbers will be lower than typical fall releases, but they'll snowball and gain traction. It's a new territory no one's exploring, sticking with standards set by New York in the seventies. Let's shake it up!" He challenged with two fists held above his head.

The room fell silent as he made his way back to his seat. The confidence in his plan was evident by his rosy cheeks, flush with excitement.

"I love it," I broke the silence, sending heads rolling my way.

"Really?" Christian asked.

"Of course! What do these writers have to lose? The competition is less stringent, and you'll make sure they have the best roll out." I raised an eyebrow with my last statement, delicately making it more of a directive than a suggestion.

"Yes! Of course!" Christian beamed with pride.

"I have some really great book festivals we can participate in this summer," the head of public relations piped up.

"There we go! You two sound like you need to have lunch. Let's get a meeting on the docket for the end of the week so I can see everything in writing," I smiled, feeling like I hadn't lost a step.

7
_____

"Mrs. Gam – I'm sorry, Emily," Madison stopped me at the end of the meeting.

Everyone was excitedly filing out the conference room, as she lingered behind waiting to catch me alone. Madison had been with the publishing house before I bought it, one of the few employees to stay through the transition. Leading the way, she'd helped me change the culture of the company, proving herself to be an asset.

"I know the name change will take some getting used to, don't fret," I laughed, hoping to ease her embarrassment about using my formal name.

The truth was, I no longer wanted to hide behind Daniel's last name, a shield I'd picked up the second I dropped my father's. Besides not needing a constant reminder of my husband and his betrayal, I wanted to stand on my own for the first time.

Mrs. Gamble would be at home crying, awaiting Daniel's response. I didn't want to be her. Not after 6-months of living in limbo, terrified I'd be outed for not living the picturesque life I portrayed.

Books had always been my escape from the dysfunction that was my childhood. Between my parents' long absences, and my father's habitual infidelity, I'd witnessed unhappiness even money couldn't fix. Now, I wanted to discover new talent and provide the necessary respite for a new generation of readers.

"I wanted to talk to you about a potential acquisition out of New York," Madison began, quickly grabbing her stack of paperwork as she noticed my movement towards the door.

At just over five feet, Madison made up for what she lacked in height with personality. Her excitement kept her cheeks rosy, a benefit for her pale skin.

"Crystal was catching me up on things this morning. So, you have a meeting today?" I asked, speaking over my shoulder as Madison followed me towards my office.

"Oh, great. I didn't know if you had heard. I was going to share all the details once it was a concrete offer. It wasn't a secret or anything," she explained nervously.

Turning on my heels, I startled her as I reached for her wrists. "Madison, you don't have to worry about doing your job independently. It's the reason I wanted you to head acquisitions. I respect your opinion and judgement. If you think it's a good opportunity, I'm eager to hear all about it," I smiled, releasing her wrists as she dropped her shoulders. I could see the tension roll off her slim frame as she exhaled deeply.

"That's such a relief. I've been communicating with Quentin for weeks," she said, a subtle smile revealing a dimple in her right cheek.

"Yes, I've heard you rather enjoy your video calls with Quentin," I raised my eyebrow with suspicion before turning to continue my walk. "Glad you're on a first name basis," I added with a smirk she couldn't see.

A quintessential book worm, Madison rarely had her hair styled, preferring a sloppy bun, usually with a pen stuck through it. But today her dark brown hair was straightened to perfection, pinned behind her ears as the blonde highlights added a needed pop to her look.

"Oh, he's very personable," she reasoned, following closely.

"I bet." I turned to face her once again as I arrived at my office. "I'll be accompanying you on the meeting today. Let's see how personable this Quentin Bolden is," I smiled, letting her know I was only teasing her.

Madison blushed like a school girl. We made plans for her to debrief me on all the details an hour before the meeting, and I made an executive decision to change the location to off site.

"We want to wine and dine him. Have Crystal set up a lunch. I know a place on Melrose with great crab cakes."

Alone in my office, I felt like I'd just completed an intense work-out. My adrenaline was pumping as I reached for my phone. I'd purposely left it in my office during the meeting, hoping to leave Daniel awaiting my reply.

My heart lit up at the icon indicating a new message, but I was quickly disappointed to see it was from Victoria, checking in on me. Unsure of how to respond, I sat my phone on my desk, contemplating my next move.

It was unlike Daniel to ignore me, but there was still no response from my earlier message. Scrolling through our text thread, I skipped over his last desperate messages, choosing instead to read the playful banter that preceded the chaos.

We'd just rediscovered the lighthearted nature that made us fall in love, and now I was left on read for over four-hours. Before I could stop myself, I was dialing his office, biting my bottom lip as I nervously twisted the huge diamond on my ring finger.

"Mr. Gamble's office. How can I help you?" Tracy answered. She'd been Daniel's assistant for so long she often felt like family. Now she was on the inside while I was on the outs. A strange resentment fell over me as I realized she must have known about Lana Boyden. Nothing happened on Daniel's schedule without Tracy knowing.

"Hi Tracy. Is my husband in?" I heard myself ask. Never had I spoken to her with such formality.

"Hi, Mrs. Gamble. I'm so sorry I didn't greet you properly. There's so much going on today. I can transfer you to Mr. Gamble right away," she said in an apologetic tone. Instantly, I regretted my coldness.

"No, it's fine. Don't worry," I rushed, ending the call before she could respond.

Running my manicured nails along my neck, I stood behind my desk feeling deflated. I was losing it, trying to find answers without asking questions. A dark cloud hovered above LA, threatening to interrupt the regularly scheduled sunshine. I couldn't ignore the irony.

Before I could begin to question if my marriage was the gray cloud of my life, my cell vibrated against my mahogany desk. It was a gift from Daniel, one that never truly fit my style, but I'd always kept it hoping not to hurt his feelings.

My heart stopped as the photo of Daniel lounging in a hammock flashed on the screen. Nervously, I tapped the green button to answer the call before lifting the phone to my ear.

"Just make sure they have all the paperwork ready," Daniel's voice was authoritative and borderline angry. He paused for a second before continuing, "Hello? Emily?"

"Hey," was all I could manage.

"Do you need something? Tracy said you called – No, get Rodrick on the phone. Tell him I need him in person. Today."

My heart sank hearing the name of his lawyer. Tracy had mentioned things were busy, but it sounded like a madhouse.

"I texted you," I blurted.

"What?"

"I texted you. You didn't respond," I repeated, shrugging my shoulders as if he could see me nervously pacing my office.

"Emily, I don't have time for this today," he growled, speaking closer to the phone.

"You don't have ten seconds to reply to my text? You're *that* busy?" I shot back, finding my voice.

How dare he put me off. In his deflection, Daniel had done a good job of making me feel like the guilty party. I wasn't going to let him hide behind work. I wanted answers about the emails that still haunted my thoughts. I hated how many times I'd read them, and kicked myself for refusing to delete them.

"Yes, Emily. I am *that* busy. What do you want?"

"Are you seriously yelling at me in front of your staff?" I asked, appalled.

"My God," he mumbled under his breath before exhaling. "I had to step into my office since you want to play this game. No one knows your life isn't perfect, Emily. Your secret is safe. Now, what do you want?" Daniel didn't even attempt to hide his annoyance.

"I stopped by the house this morning. You weren't there," I rushed the words before my courage dissolved.

"Yeah, I guess I was out philandering around the city at five this morning," he snapped.

My stomach dropped before filling with rage. If there was one thing I hated, it was when people made light of things that bothered me. "Do you think this is fucking funny?"

"Watch your mouth," he sneered.

"I'm serious, Daniel," I nearly screamed into the phone, glancing up to make sure I wasn't causing a scene outside my office.

"So am I."

We remained silent on the phone, trapped in a verbal standoff, neither of us willing to go further. I can't be sure of Daniel's reasoning, but I was worried I would go too far, saying something I couldn't take back.

"Mr. Gamble, everyone is ready," I faintly heard a woman's voice in the background.

"I'll be right there," he answered, followed by the loud sound of his office door closing. "Enjoy your hotel, Emily."

I stared at the phone in shock as the call ended before the screensaver appeared, a recent picture of Daniel and I lying in bed together. Our eyes were hazy from love making. Looking at it brought tears of uncertainty to my eyes.

"Mrs. G! Madison is ready for the debriefing," Crystal announced through my intercom system, jolting me back to the present.

"I'm on a call, give me five minutes," I lied, rushing to my private bathroom to regain my composure.

8

———

"This place is really nice," Madison remarked as we made our way through the dining room at the Sea Club. Just like the last time I'd visited, the large dining area was filled to capacity.

The ambiance seemed more fitting for evening. Subtle blue lights darkened the restaurant despite the bright afternoon. People spoke in hushed tones overshadowed by the soft jazz playing in the background. The vibe exuded secrecy and exclusivity.

I could feel the eyes on us as we navigated between the circular tables covered in white cloth. Status was everything in LA. Bypassing the normal dining area indicated our importance.

Crystal had requested a private room so we could focus on business without distractions. But as we settled into our seats, I could think of nothing but Daniel. He was the one who had introduced me to the restaurant when things were much better between us.

Even in the worst of our disagreements, he'd never been so nasty to me. I'd replayed the conversation in my mind repeatedly. Every time, I struggled with understanding his need for a lawyer. The thought of Daniel filing for divorce, impulsively reacting the same way I had, left me anxious.

What started as an optimistic morning had taken a turn for the worst, leaving me insecure and fearful. I'd bitten off more responsibility than I could chew by imposing myself into the meeting, but it was too late to back out. I forced a brave face, absentmindedly nodding along as Madison pointed to figures on a financial report.

"Oh, here he is," Madison abruptly snatched the paper from the table, shoving it into her leather work bag as she rushed to her feet.

A bit slower to react, I took a deep breath, readying myself for what was sure to be a long lunch. I pushed my shoulders back, mustering all the confidence I could manage, when my eyes landed on him.

"Good to see you in person, Madison," the man I'd heard so much about spoke to my head of acquisitions, but his eyes were trained on me. "I don't think we've had the pleasure of meeting," he extended his hand as I stood from the table.

"Yes, this is my boss," Madison began before I interrupted her.

"Emily. Nice to meet you, Mr. Bolden," I forced a smile as I accepted his hand.

"Please, call me Q," he flashed a charming smile. I could see why the women in the office had been gossiping.

Quentin Bolden was a sight for sore eyes. In my stilettos, he was at least a foot taller than me, his muscular frame indicative of an athletic past. His eyes were trained on me as he sat down, apologizing for his delayed arrival, although all three of us knew he was early.

"We were just getting caught up on business. You're fine," Madison gushed, waving her hand as her face reddened in his presence. Quentin was dangerously attractive. No one would deny that.

With only inches of white tablecloth separating our hands, I noticed he was the same caramel complexion as me, making his green eyes even more striking. A thin beard framed his baby face with precise lines indicative of a recent shape up. Dark bushy curls balanced out his look, giving the illusion that he'd just rolled out of bed. Quentin was handsome and he knew it. He was the type of man accustomed to getting what he wanted.

"I guess I've passed some sort of test to be sitting at the table with you," he smirked, looking directly into my eyes.

"I'll be handing out final grades after the meeting," I winked playfully. "I was expecting more of a team," I explained, motioning towards the four empty seats. Suddenly, the private dining room felt a bit overzealous.

"I don't like to involve too many people in my business. I'm more of a private man," Quentin reasoned in a way that felt like a double entendre. "I just can't believe I haven't met you in all these months of negotiations," he said, placing his elbows on the table as his unruly eyebrows scrunched together.

"No, we wanted you speaking with the best. Madison is the head of acquisitions, so she handles all of this. I'm actually learning from her," I turned to Madison, who seemed happy to be acknowledged.

"I've been catching Emily up on how well we can work together. Your New York office will be a great addition for us. We've been thinking of expanding to two offices, so your employees won't even have to relocate." Madison excitedly handed him a sleek proposal complete with potential updates we would make to his existing office, projected numbers, and a list of authors we'd like to keep on board.

"I don't like to talk business without a drink," Quentin objected. I quickly signaled the waiter standing just outside the glassed in private room. Dressed in all black, the young man with long locks pulled into a stylish bun entered the room with a smile.

"Ready to order?" He asked.

"Do you ladies mind if I order for the table?" Quentin asked.

"Whatever you want," I held my hands out, regretting the words before they'd made their way to his ears.

I could see from the smirk on Quentin's face, he knew why I wished I'd said something else. Thankfully, Madison was too flustered to pick up on my blunder as she happily nodded along to the suggestion of wine.

"2007 Sassicaia." Quentin announced flatly.

"And Bobby, can you please bring a basket of garlic rolls?" I added with a smile, noticing the waiter's appreciation I'd used his name. Leaving us with the menus, he quietly exited the room.

"Sassicaia is fine with you two, right?" Quentin asked, looking to me and then Madison.

Madison laughed awkwardly before chiming in, "Is that a white wine? Reds can be too heavy for lunch."

The shock on Quentin's face made me laugh softly. He was a wine snob. I could see it in the disgustful glare he sent across the table.

"I've never been a huge fan of blends, but I'm happy to accommodate you," I smiled, deflecting the attention from Madison.

"If I could get that in writing for the negotiation portion of this meeting, that would be great," Quentin quipped, his eyes revealing just how impressed he was with my wine knowledge.

Sassicaia was a Cabernet Sauvignon and Cabernet Franc blend, one of many wines Daniel had introduced me to during an intense wine tour in Tuscany. I was beginning to resent how much of my business advantages were a direct result of his subtle teachings.

We shared a light laugh as Bobby returned with the bottle of wine and three glasses. After a slight nod from Quentin, confirming he had selected the correct bottle, Bobby quickly uncorked the wine. Offering the cork to Quentin for approval, the waiter then inserted an aerator into the bottle and poured a small glass for tasting.

I had to fight the urge to roll my eyes as Quentin swirled the wine around his glass, sniffing dramatically before taking a sip. It was only a two-hundred-dollar bottle of wine, for Christ's sake.

Bobby poured three glasses before leaving us again. I could sense Madison was as eager as me to get to the point of the meeting, so I wasted no time getting back on track.

"So, we're ready to talk business now?" I asked with my wine glass in hand.

"Whatever you'd like," Quentin smiled. His charm was irresistible. I felt myself falling into a trap.

9

We'd just finished lunch after discussing more about Quentin's impending move across the country than the business at hand. I'd learned he was an Army brat, spending his childhood moving at least twice a year. He spoke Portuguese and German, both from the years his family was stationed abroad.

When Madison brought up the acquisition, he seemed to skirt around the details, inserting a barely relevant anecdote about his travels around the world. I couldn't be sure if he was purposefully deflecting, or just that into himself.

"I'm going to go freshen up," Madison said, looking directly at me with a silent signal to follow.

"That's fine. We'll meet you out front," Quentin smiled curtly, letting us both know he'd picked up on her cue.

Madison slowly maneuvered from her seat, glancing over her shoulder before leaving the two of us alone. There was undeniable tension between me and Quentin. Not quite sexual, but mysterious, as if there was deeper meaning lurking beneath our words.

"You know, at some point you are going to have to discuss the deal," I started the second the door closed.

"I thought it would be better discussed between you and me. Why have you been avoiding me?" He asked in a tone that would lead an outsider to believe we had a history.

"Excuse me?" I countered, taken aback.

"You sent me through weeks of inquiries before you would even come to the table. Why is that? Are you always this selective with who you get into business with?" He didn't miss a beat.

"Actually, I'm typically much less selective. This is the first acquisition meeting I've attended this year."

"So, I should feel special?" He squinted before flashing a perfect smile. I turned away, annoyed by his charm.

"Quentin, you're trouble," I sighed, reaching for my bag.

"I thought I told you to call me Q." He rushed to catch me as I quickly exited the private room.

"A dozen calls with Madison, and she wasn't granted nickname privileges?" I asked without glancing over my shoulder. I could feel him following me.

"Nah, that's just for you."

Without turning, I knew he was smiling as we walked through the busy dining area. Scanning the room, I searched for familiar faces, suddenly feeling subconscious about walking through a restaurant with a man who wasn't my husband.

I bet Daniel didn't flinch parading Lana Boyden through here, I thought to myself just as Quentin demanded my attention.

"You know my asking price is too low, right?" He asked rhetorically as I waved to the hostess.

"Have a good day," she said, her eyes devouring Quentin.

"I do know that. I also know you will never sell at that price," I turned to face him, watching that grin spread across his face yet again. He had dimples.

"That would mean I've been wasting your time," Quentin held the door open for me, his tone a bit mischievous.

"You're too smart for that," I brushed past him, smelling his cologne for the first time.

"You're right."

"Then what *are* you doing, Mr. Bolden?" I faced him again, stopping before we reunited with Madison, who stood watching us from the valet stand.

"Q," he corrected me, raising his eyebrows seductively.

"What are you doing?" I asked with attitude, tired of his overly flirtatious strategy.

Quentin paused, studying my face before running his tongue across his lips. "I want to merge. I need an LA base."

I nodded, appreciating his honesty. I'd suspected he didn't want to sell his company from the moment Crystal filled me in on the negotiations. Acquisitions were typically short and sweet, but he'd dragged things on for weeks because he never had any intention of selling his company.

Glancing over to Madison with disappointment, I knew I'd have to do more research on the man standing before me. Less than a week before, I'd stood in the same spot with my husband, gazing into his eyes as hope brewed in my chest for the first time in months. I felt like a new woman living a different life sizing Quentin up, the tension between us growing by the second.

"So, you've been wasting Madison's time?" I asked, noticing the different shades of green in his eyes.

"No, Madison has been wasting mine," he shot back, glaring over to the valet stand, where Madison fidgeted nervously. I was losing my patience, and Quentin seemed to notice, choosing to elaborate further. "I've been asking for a meeting with you since my first phone call with her. This is what I want," he moved his hand, pointing to me and then himself.

"What is *this*?" I questioned, crossing my arms.

Quentin smiled, inhaling deeply before running his tongue along his lips again. "I can see you feel misled. That wasn't my intention. Can we start over?"

I wasn't sure how to read him just yet, but something told me he wasn't the type of man who walked away without a fight.

"I'll be in touch, Mr. Bolden," I extended my left hand, watching his eyes catch the sparkle of my wedding ring before a grin spread across his face.

"I know you're married, Emily," he tilted his head as he spoke. Taking my hand in both of his, our eyes locked in a weird stare down.

"Do you?"

"I do." He said without any further explanation or apology.

Snatching my hand from his, I stormed towards Madison, grateful when I didn't feel Quentin following. He didn't call after me as I'd expected he would, but nothing that man did was predictable.

"What happened?" Madison asked as we climbed into the back-seat of our waiting town car.

"We got played."

10

—————

Two nights had passed since I'd spoken to Daniel when the hotel phone rang, jolting me from my sleep. Rolling over with an attitude, I answered the phone in the cheeriest voice I could muster without opening my eyes.

"Thank you," I blindly moved to hang up the phone, as I had every other morning, when Matthew's squeaky voice caught my attention.

"I'm sorry. I just noticed you're scheduled to check out today," he paused, insinuating what we both knew.

The young blond man had called the bell hop to assist with the two large suitcases I'd packed while Daniel was at the office. He knew as well as me, I had unceremoniously moved into the hotel.

"Extend it a week," I grumbled, hearing his apologies as I slammed the receiver onto the base.

Tossing the down comforter to the side, I slipped my feet into the awaiting slippers, murmuring a complaint under my breath. I still couldn't believe I'd resorted to living in a hotel. With Daniel acting so out of character, and me back to working 12-hour days, I barely had time to make plans for lunch, let alone the mess I'd made of my life.

Work had quickly become my haven, an escape from the questions I was too afraid to ask. The writing was very clear on the wall – Daniel had no intention of being honest, or even open, about what happened between him and Lana Boyden.

I hated how much I knew about her. Late nights alone in a hotel room had turned me into a detective. One thing was undeniable: Lana Boyden was gorgeous.

Staring deep into my computer screen, I scrolled the website of her family business wondering if Daniel saw me in her. The similarities were too obvious to ignore. The daughter of a hedge fund manager, I had no doubt she too was a trust fund child. That had to make her extortion more humiliating for Daniel. She didn't need his money. It was solely for revenge.

From her business profile I learned she was a financial analyst with a golden complexion and long wavy hair. My stomach turned staring at her perfect smile, wondering if she had any idea how much trouble she'd caused in the life of a stranger.

Each night, I closed my laptop with tears in my eyes, uncertain of how Daniel and I could ever recover from such a betrayal. Especially when he refused to talk about it.

These were the thoughts clouding my mind as I pulled into the office before the sun made an appearance. I'd become the workaholic who showed up to the office first, but it was nice to get a start on the day before the eighteenth floor came alive.

"Hold it, please!" I heard as I stepped into the empty elevator car.

Madison rushed in holding a stack of binders, her long hair pulled into a sloppy bun with a mechanical pencil tucked behind her ear.

"You're hitting the ground running, aren't you?" I teased as I released the button, allowing the elevator doors to close.

I could sense the embarrassment when we left the meeting with Quentin. Madison was great at what she did, but we both knew she should have seen through his stalling strategy.

"I wanted to catch you before the morning status," she explained out of breath.

"I've got a few minutes. What's up?" I glanced down as subtly as possible, noting her gray sweats and New Balance tennis shoes. She was back in her comfort zone, which made me more confident in what she had to share.

"Quentin doesn't want to sell his company, but that's actually better for us," she began, watching me closely for a reaction.

"I'm listening," I nodded just as the elevator sounded, opening to the eighteenth floor.

I greeted the cleaning staff by name as they finished vacuuming the carpets and cleaning the windows. Madison followed closely, keen to share her new findings.

"His reputation is too salacious to inherit. But if we can keep clients separate and share distribution, the deal could increase our annual profits by twenty percent while doubling our market share."

"Twenty percent?" I repeated the unbelievable projection.

On the drive from our lunch meeting, I'd made it very clear that Quentin was not someone I wanted to go into business with. He was right, I did feel misled. What I hadn't told Madison was, the man was too attractive and tempting to be around if it wasn't necessary. The way he looked at me set me on edge. If I could avoid any interaction with him, I would.

"Twenty percent!" Madison smiled, thumbing through one of her binders.

Handsome or not, there was no way I could ignore an opportunity that advantageous. For the next hour, I diligently listened as Madison highlighted all we stood to gain from a merger with Laney Publishing. She was proud of her research, which in my eyes redeemed her previous fumble.

Just as we were wrapping up, my cell phone rang. A call from my mother. I sent her to voicemail before heading to the morning status. She immediately called again, something out of character for her. Again I dismissed it, incorrectly assuming I could put it off for later.

11

"After yesterday's meeting, I took it upon myself to develop a new rollout schedule for the summer season," Christian enthusiastically opened the meeting.

Emboldened by my encouragement, he had moved forward with restructuring the schedule. I was both proud and aware of the tension in the room. Many eyes rolled throughout his presentation, evidence of the pushback he was receiving from peers.

Most departments would be affected by the drastic change unlike anything we had ever done at Cherry Blossoms, but I still supported the initiative. I was watching with excitement when Crystal popped her head in signaling for me to step out of the meeting.

So intrigued by Christian's PowerPoint presentation, I waved her into the meeting instead, watching as she nervously crossed the projector before making it to my seat.

"Your mom is calling and she says it's an emergency," she whispered.

Annoyed, I glanced at my cell phone – twenty missed calls in the five minutes I'd been in the meeting. That was completely out of the ordinary for my mother. Turning to Crystal, I could see she too understood the rarity.

"I think it's important, Mrs. G," she urged me with her eyes. I reluctantly relented, following her out the meeting to answer my mother's insistence.

Crystal followed me to her desk, where I lifted the phone receiver, giving her a nod to dial my mother back. The look of concern on Crystal's face troubled me. I was just about to warn her of my mother's tendency to blow things out of proportion, when the panic shooting through the phone hijacked my attention.

"Get over here! They're taking everything!" My mother's voice wasn't one of anger, but a fearful cry, an emotion I'd never heard from her. My stomach dropped as my eyes looked to Crystal for assistance I knew she couldn't give.

"Mom, calm down," I breathed, my voice lacking the conviction I'd hoped for.

"Put that down!" My mother screamed, her voice cracking. "They're taking everything, Emily! Get over here!"

"Mom, *who's* taking everything? What's happening?!" I screamed, embodying her panic as though I was there.

"No! No!" She cried before returning to the call. "They're arresting your father! Get to the house!" Her words left me frozen, unable to move or offer any support.

A man's voice took over. "This phone is now property of the federal bureau of investigations."

The call ended.

Standing in shock, I heard Crystal's voice, nodding without fully processing the words. Everything was moving in slow motion as the phone began to ring in my ear. I'd forgotten I was holding the receiver until I heard Tracy's voice.

"Hi, Mrs. Gamble, would you li–," she began before my sobs interrupted her cheery tone.

I didn't realize I was crying until I was fighting through the tears to speak. "Daniel! I need Daniel," I managed after a short delay.

"Mr. Gamble didn't come in today. He isn't answering his cell, but I can try again if you'd like," she offered. I dropped the phone, leaving without another word.

Forcing a deep breath, I rushed to my office to pull myself together. I tried Daniel on his cell, but it immediately went to voicemail. I felt lost, in desperate need of his instruction, forced to handle things on my own for once.

Wiping my eyes, I grabbed my purse. Hoping to avoid watchful eyes, I took the back route to the elevator. Surely, the entire office had heard my outburst. I didn't want to face anyone.

The drive to my parents' house was a blur. It was a miracle I made it unscathed. My mind was anywhere but on the road. When I finally made it to the valley, the nightmare worsened.

You could sense something was off from the driveway. Three garage doors were open with no cars in sight. I approached the front door just as a young black man exited with an overflowing cardboard box.

"Get it out! Take everything to the lawn!" I heard as I rushed to the living room, following the harrowing sounds of my mother's cry.

"Mom! What are you doing?" I asked when I finally found her in the sitting room.

She was frantically directing an army of people as she struggled to open a small safe sitting on the glass tabletop.

"Emily!" Her voice cracked as she ran to me. She shoved a stack of papers into my hand before draping her arms around my neck. Hugging her thin frame tightly, I felt her shudder with hollow cries.

Carefully, I moved to the sofa, gently setting her down although her fingers remained clasped at the nape of my neck. Struggling to see around her small body, I searched for a familiar face in the sea of people urgently moving throughout the house.

"Mrs. Delley," a soft voice called. Both me and my mother turned to answer.

"Do you want this outside as well?" The woman I'd never seen raised a sculpture my parents had brought back from a trip to Nigeria years ago.

"Everything! Put it on the lawn. If they want it, they can have it!" She yelled, her face contorting with disgust.

"Mom, who are these people?" I wondered.

"Your father's ruined everything! Now he can have his shit! I'm done with it," She threw her hands in the air, her lips pursing as she fought back another cry.

"You're putting dad's stuff out?" I asked in disbelief, watching everyone with newfound understanding.

"They already took everything. Now, if they come back for more, it'll be on the lawn waiting for them," she shrugged, satisfied with her reasoning.

Glancing over her, I noticed the red stain on her lips for the first time. She had been drinking. My jaw clenched realizing she was in no state to make decisions. Quickly, I moved from one room to the next, giving new instructions.

Everything was in disarray. It seemed every drawer had been emptied, every trash can overturn. The entire house was a mess, just like my mother, who yelled from the sofa.

"It's all a fraud! All of it! They'll come for the rest of this," she waved her hand, her chest heaving as the cries racked her shivering body.

"Mom, just relax," I tried to calm her.

The kitchen was the most intact room I'd come across, so I took the small break of normalcy to catch my breath. The stack of papers she'd shoved in my hand felt like a dumbbell. It grew heavier as I finally read the bold print. It was a warrant to search the house in part of an investigation against Malcolm Delley. Tears blurred my vision before I could read more, searching for Daniel's name.

I knew he had business with my father, but I didn't see his name mentioned anywhere in the warrant. It was only a slight relief as I wondered if my own home had been destroyed in search of evidence that couldn't exist.

There was no way my father had committed any crimes. This all had to be a misunderstanding. One that would result in an expensive and public apology after my father's lawyers were finished.

"Turn it off! I don't want to hear it!" My mother screamed.

I turned to see CNN on the main television, my father's smiling face just above the breaking news headline. Before I could argue with my mother to quench my thirst for information, my pocket vibrated. It was Victoria.

"Vic! Where are you? You need to get to the house," I answered, panting as I rushed the words.

"Turn to CNN," she said. Her voice eerily calm.

"I saw. Mom doesn't want to watch it. You've heard what's happening?" I asked, confused by her tone.

"Turn on the fucking news, Emily!"

My legs trembled as I entered the living room, slowly pressing the button on the remote control. An older white man with graying hair spoke with shameful eyes.

"... It appears to be the largest scandal to rock the hospitality industry. One of fraud and embezzlement on the grandest scale. We have exclusively confirmed that Delley Retreats falsified documents, illegally securing governmental contracts worth tens of millions of dollars. The scope seems to grow by the hour, as more information comes to light. What's most interesting, is this web of fraud would have gone undiscovered if not for the brave and heroic act of a whistleblower. Willing to lose everything, this individual has risked both anonymity and reputation for the greater good, outing a fraud that has gone undetected for decades. Ladies and gentlemen, welcome Lana Boyden to the program."

12

———

"Em! Em! Are you there?" Victoria screamed into the phone, but I was lost in a trance, staring at the television.

The screen was split in two, with the newscaster on the left and Lana Boyden on the right. The woman I'd researched so much about was detailing the crimes my father allegedly committed, her face as smug as I'd envisioned it reading her emails to Daniel.

She claimed to have proof of a massive fraud committed by my father, one spanning decades, that would leave hundreds of investors penniless. My thoughts drifted back to her emails and the threats she made to Daniel – to expose my fairy tale life.

I'd assumed her threat was directed towards Daniel, revealing an affair that would destroy our marriage. But it appeared she had information to devastate my entire family. My stomach turned with a mix of anxiety and guilt. I'd pushed Daniel away, upset at his refusal to explain himself, and now it was obvious I was wrong.

"Emily! Answer me!" My sister's screams cut through my thoughts.

"I'm here, I'm here," I whispered, my voice weak with regret and confusion.

"I don't know how much Daniel knew, but I think he was trying to prevent this," she stated the obvious.

Just then, a loud sound from the front of the house demanded my attention. The front door swung open as my father emerged, flanked by two men I knew to be his lawyers, and a handful of other faces I didn't recognize. They were speaking in voices too low for me to hear, but the despair on my father's face needed no translator.

In all there were nine men, including my father. I was watching him so closely I didn't see Daniel until he turned to close the door. My heart raced when he slowly followed the entourage, his eyes red with exhaustion, his neck tie loosened.

"I gotta go," I murmured before ending the call, my hand absentmindedly releasing the phone onto the ground.

My pride dissolved. I dashed across the room, bypassing my father and his flock of lawyers until my arms were wrapped around Daniel's waist. Caught off guard, he stumbled back half a step before regaining his balance. He didn't speak, but I heard him clearly when his arms did not welcome me, but instead remained at his side.

"I need to talk to your father," he finally said, patting my back gently.

"Daniel, I didn't know," I looked into his eyes. His indifference was crystal clear even through my blurred vision.

"We'll talk later," was all he said before leaving me.

Alone in the foyer, I watched him follow the flock of men in dark suits to the back of my parents' home, where my father had a large office and adjoining conference room.

My heart sank, certain I'd gone too far this time. I'd pushed Daniel further than he was willing to return from. Never had he looked to me with such blank eyes, the love completely missing from his gaze. My world was crumbling around me, and I wanted nothing more than to sink to the ground, curling into a fetal position until everything returned to normal.

My mother's loud screams sent me running to the back of the

house. Daniel was holding her back as she swung uncontrollably, trying to get to my father who watched her with pity in his eyes.

"I hate you!" She bellowed, her voice screeching with emotion. "Look what you've done!" She swung again, this time slapping Daniel's shoulder.

"Ma, calm down," he managed, tilting his head to miss another of her weak blows before wrapping her in his arms. She fell meekly into sobs, murmuring about how much of her life she'd wasted.

"Mom, come here," I took her into my arms, searching for Daniel's eyes.

"Keep her here," he grumbled without facing me. Turning before I could respond, Daniel followed the team of lawyers towards my father's office.

My mother collapsed dramatically, taking me down with her. We settled on the marbled tile floor, gripping each other for the support we so desperately needed. Acting as each other's anchors, we allowed our tears to flow freely. Although we were crying for two separate reasons, we shared the same truth knowing that neither of our lives would ever be the same.

It was there that Victoria and Olivia found us. My older sisters rushed to bring us to our feet. Our tears had long ago stopped, but the sorrow and shock kept us frozen in the state of mourning. Mourning what, I wasn't sure. The life we'd lost; or possibly the realization that that life never truly existed.

"Where's daddy?" Olivia asked, searching my face for answers.

"In the back. With the lawyers." I spoke in choppy sentences, matching my thoughts.

"Have you talked to Daniel?" Victoria asked.

"In the back. With the lawyers." I repeated, my body limp as I sunk into a sitting chair, exhausted.

"I'm going to talk to him," Olivia announced as she made her way to the back of the house. My eyes followed her, wanting to tell her it was of no use, but my lips didn't part.

Victoria's arms felt like a blanket, the warmth I'd expected from my husband. I hugged her too tightly, yearning for security. It was impossible to process all that had happened since I spoke with my mother at Cherry Blossoms.

My life had been an emotional whirlwind. Three hours felt like a lifetime. I was fatigued from processing so much so quickly. Victoria rubbed my back gently, but my eyes were dry. Focus had finally begun to set in.

"What do you mean?! That's my father! I need to speak with him!" Olivia's shouting startled me and Victoria. We both jumped to our feet, following her cries.

She was standing outside the office, speaking to someone only willing to crack the door. As Victoria and I joined her, I was disappointed to see an unfamiliar face, hoping for another opportunity to search Daniel's eyes for any sentiment of emotion.

"Ladies, we will only be a few hours. There are some things we need to discuss with your father and they are extremely important. Please, just give us this time and then he can answer all your questions as he sees fit. I promise you," he pleaded with his eyes, looking from Victoria to Olivia, and finally to me.

"Let's give them some time," I suggested, turning with my arm wrapped around Olivia's waist.

"No, we need to know something now! Look at mom," Olivia stopped my movement, turning to face the door. "Do you see what you've done to her?!" She yelled into the office. From the slit in the doorway, I could see the top of my father's head, but he refused to acknowledge us. "Look at our mother!" Olivia's voice cracked in a tearful cry.

I took her weakness as an opportunity, steering her back to the sitting room where my mother remained on a leather loveseat, stiff as a statue. On an adjacent sofa, Victoria and I guided our oldest sister as we fell to the patterned fabric.

My shoulders dropped. I was defeated. Shut out by another man I loved. It was all too much to endure in a day. I needed a reset, a relief of sorts. But there was none.

"This is what happens when you put blind trust into a man," my mother's voice was calm and emotionless.

Turning with my sisters, I watched her shake her head from side to side, gripping her knees with frail fingers. Her lips pierced tightly as she exhaled through her nose, her cheekbones rising as though she'd recalled a funny memory.

"I should've known," she sucked her teeth. "He'd been taking more 'work calls'," she raised her eyebrows as she used air quotes. "And here, I thought it was another affair." She huffed, flashing a half smile that didn't reach her tired eyes. "I wish it was another affair."

With that, she rose, pressing her manicured nails into the skin of her knees as she fought for strength. We watched her walk to the back of the house, where we had just been rejected.

While our mother had regularly talked to us about the trials of infidelity, the lack of sass and spunk that usually accompanied the unorthodox advice was sobering.

The soft knock could be heard from the sitting room, but her words were too soft to carry. Unlike Olivia, her plea seemed to be less emotional, and from the reaction I discerned it was more convincing.

Within seconds, the men streamed from the office, each looking to have aged significantly from their short meeting. Daniel was last in the parade, passing the sitting room as he rubbed his forehead with the palm of his hand.

My instinct to chase after him was halted by Victoria's grip on my wrist. "Give him some time," she whispered.

I watched him follow behind the team of lawyers as they made their way to the backyard. It felt like a funeral, and in some ways, I guess you could say it was. The solemn energy kept me and my sisters trapped on the sofa in silence.

"Where's dad?" My brother's voice was panicked. I hadn't heard him enter the house.

"In the back," I sluggishly pointed over my shoulder.

"Emily, can I talk to you?" Daniel's voice released a spurt of energy. My neck snapped in his direction, my feet moving to the edge of the room before I could nod.

13

Daniel's fingers wrapped tightly around my wrist as he pulled me into a guest bedroom off the main hall, closing and locking the door behind us.

His eyes scanned the room before landing on me. "Did your father ever ask you to make any withdrawals or deposits from any of his accounts?"

"No." I answered flatly. My father had never involved me in any of his business dealings.

"Not even a simple, 'drop this off at the bank' errand, or anything like that?" He asked, moving closer, his eyebrows scrunching together with suspicion.

"No. I don't know anything about my dad's business. Why? Am I in trouble?" I wondered aloud.

"No, we shouldn't be. As long as the only money you've accepted is through your trust, you'll be fine. It seems your dad made sure that money was always legitimate," he spoke at the floor, rubbing the small patch of hair on his chin between his thumb and index finger.

"Daniel, what's going on?" I asked, reaching for his arm.

I pretended not to notice when he brushed my touch away,

rubbing his hands together before turning to face me. "Your dad was arrested today."

Blinking slowly, I waited for more of an explanation. When Daniel just stared at me blankly, I pried. "I know that. I saw the news," I paused, wondering if he knew that included learning about Lana.

"That's bullshit. They're sensationalizing it," he scowled.

"So, it's not that bad?" I could hear the hope in my voice.

"It's bad," he nodded quickly, changing his approach as he saw my shoulders drop. "But not as bad as it's being reported."

"I saw Lana Boyden on the news." I added, watching his jaw tense as he looked at me for the first time. He'd glanced at me before, even searched my face for truth. But in that moment, he was staring into my soul.

"I didn't know, Daniel," I stepped forward, closing the gap between us as he raised his hand, stopping me in my tracks.

"Not now, Emily." He turned away from me, glancing over his shoulder to add, "If you think of any time you may have done anything involving your father's business, I need you to tell me immediately. Do you understand?"

I nodded, unable to speak. Although I couldn't see his eyes, he appeared to accept my voiceless response. Unlocking the bedroom door, he let himself out, closing me inside alone.

14

My stomach dropped watching the door, hoping Daniel would return. His cold departure didn't shock me as much as my reaction, or lack thereof. My lip quivered in anticipation of the tears that never came.

Maybe I was used to his rejection, or too numb from an afternoon of crying. Either way, I left the bedroom with my head held high. My eyes landed on Victoria's as she perked up, racing towards me.

"What happened?" She asked.

Looking towards the back of the house, I saw Daniel speaking with one of the lawyers, an older man with a thinning head of white hair.

"Nothing," I answered, watching Daniel's conversation, his questions still lingering in my head.

It was what he hadn't asked that left me curious. All his questions were about me, and my collusion with my father. What about his? Did Lana Boyden only have information on my father, or was my husband also tangled up in the web of lies? Her extortion was a steep price for an innocent man to pay.

My feet sought answers before I had questions, carrying me

across the house with an unexplainable sense of urgency. Daniel noticed the curiosity on my face, dismissing the lawyer just as I approached.

"I need to talk to you," I said more calmly than I expected the words to roll off my tongue. Avoiding the watchful eyes of lawyers and my sisters, I led him to the guest room we normally used – the last bedroom we had shared.

Daniel followed in silence, but his annoyance was obvious from the moment I locked the door. Sitting on the bed, I could tell he was exhausted from the way his body fell onto his elbows at the first feel of the soft mattress.

"Why did Lana reach out to *you*?" I asked, my arms folded across my chest defensively.

Daniel perched, his eyebrows rushing to meet each other as he tilted his head with disbelief. "What are you asking me, Emily?"

"Do you have business with my father?" I swallowed the lump in my throat, treading in what I knew to be muddy waters.

Daniel stood, his lips curling slightly at the corners before his jaw tightened. Slowly, but intentionally, he walked towards me, his glare making me uncomfortable.

"If you're asking me if I was looking out for me or you, the answer is neither." He barely released his jaw to speak, the words forced through his teeth.

"So, you did pay her?" I spoke over the drumming sound of my heart beating heavily in my ears. My intuition told me to back off, but my curiosity was steering.

"Are you fucking serious?" Daniel barked, his harshness splitting the tightness in his jaw. His aggression was so intense I flinched before recommitting to my defiance.

"You heard me," I tried and failed to match his intensity before he moved to brush me aside, reaching for the doorknob.

"I answered your fucking questions!" I yelled, shoving at his arms until I was again blocking the doorway.

"Watch your mouth," he growled.

"You just cussed at me!" I reminded him.

"Emily, move." He closed his eyes as he spoke my name.

"No! Answer me!" The emotion was creeping into my voice, a neediness tethered to each syllable.

Clenching his fists, Daniel turned his back to me before placing both hands on his forehead, rubbing across his scalp furiously.

"Emily, I need you to move." His voice was eerily calm, a threat disguised as a request. One I intended to ignore until he glared over his shoulder, an anger I'd never seen brewing in his eyes. Without thinking, I slid one step to the left, clearing his path. Turning away from me, he diverted his eyes, leaving the room without glancing in my direction.

My head dropped back against the wall. The urge to sink to the ground was overwhelming. Still, I found it impossible to cry as I normally would. Unsure of whether the emotion was trapped or nonexistent, I exhaled deeply, feeling my chest rise and fall as I looked to the ceiling.

Ten minutes later, I emerged from the bedroom as if nothing had happened. Because everyone was still running around in organized chaos, no one seemed to notice my absence. My mother sat on a sofa in the living room with my sisters huddled around her. Denise had arrived, and she seemed to be taking everything the hardest. With her head on my mother's shoulder, she wept as though our father had died.

"Dad told mom everything. She can't tell us. She has the marital privilege thing, but if we know, we can be ordered to testify," Victoria whispered as I settled next to her.

"There's nothing to worry about, darling. It's just business. Your father will fight it as he would any other obstacle." My mom's face was stone, her mask of 'everything is okay' securely back in place.

"Glad to hear it," I couldn't hide my disdain as I rose to my feet.

"Where are you going?" Olivia asked with shock.

"If all is well here," I said sarcastically, looking to my mother. Only she knew how we had both cried earlier, and I couldn't stand to watch her pretend for my sisters. "I need to get back to the office."

There was no business at the office and no way I was returning. I just needed an excuse to leave, creating distance from the family that had proven to be more fraudulent than I'd suspected. I turned to leave just as the disbelief spread on their faces, all except for my mother. She was committed to her character.

"Emily, we need to talk about this!" Olivia called after me.

"It's fine, sweetheart. I've already talked to her." My mother's reassuring voice made my stomach turn.

I'd just made it to the front door when I felt the soft touch on my elbow. I turned to see Daniel, his eyes softer, but still void of the emotion I was used to.

"I need you to take me to the house."

Hearing nothing but the first three words, I nodded too eagerly, agreeing without a thought of his recent behavior. Forgetting his dismissal and rejection, I made myself available to him, cancelling every hypothetical plan I'd made for myself. I followed him to my G-Wagon, parked haphazardly in the driveway, reminiscent of the disheveled state I'd arrived in.

15

I knew I'd made a mistake before I reached the 101 South Highway. Daniel hadn't spoken a word, instead spending his time scrolling through his phone, typing away feverishly as I drove in silence.

My hope of a resolution was being swallowed whole by the deafening stillness. Daniel appeared oblivious despite my frequent glances in his direction.

"Trace!" He excitedly answered a call. "I know, I know... It's been a crazy day," he rubbed his forehead as he listened.

"Yeah, I saw her," from the annoyance in his tone, I suspected he was speaking of me. Any doubt I had melted away when he glared in my direction. "She's fine," he added.

I'd never felt smaller or less significant, sitting across from him as he treated me like a paid driver. What was worse, Daniel didn't even treat his employees as harsh.

"We have to reschedule everything for tomorrow, or tonight if we can. I need to get a little sleep, but I'll be ready to start in a few hours," I saw him glance at his watch through my peripherals.

Stuck in standstill traffic, a motorcycle zoomed between the lanes. I hated myself for leaning closer to Daniel, unwilling to miss a second of his one-sided conversation. It was the only insight I had into his life, a desperate glimmer.

"I don't know if we can make that. Hold on," he paused, putting the phone to his chest before turning to me. "Get off here and take Sepulveda," he ordered before returning to the call.

I glanced over in disbelief, appalled by his audacity. He either didn't notice or chose to ignore me altogether. Watching the rearview mirror, I waited for my opportunity before zipping across two lanes just in time to make the exit.

For the rest of the ride, I drove like a bat out of hell, disregarding speed limits and racing through yellow lights. Daniel continued his conversation with Tracy, though I'd stopped listening.

I'm not going to be like my mom, taking a back seat, clueless to what the fuck you have going on, I thought to myself as I pulled into our driveway.

Despite Daniel hopping out the car without speaking a word to me, I was certain he expected me to follow. Shock coated his face as he turned just in time to watch me back out the driveway.

Fuck this.

16

Again, I drove on autopilot, passing through the sunny city I loved. Stopped at a red light, I peered out the window, closely watching two women share a laugh. Frowning, I wondered how anyone could find happiness or humor on such an awful day.

A loud car horn alerted me of the changing light and I absent-mindedly made a left turn, veering into the parking garage. I'd made it back to the office with no intention of returning to work. I parked in my designated spot and walked into the elevator car, grateful it was empty.

A small smile played on my lips as the elevator doors opened to the eighteenth floor. Cherry Blossoms Publishing was as busy as I'd left it. People moved rapidly in every direction along the grey carpet that perfectly matched the matte walls.

The monochromatic design was calming despite the buzzing energy. Two employees stood chatting beneath the large chrome letters of the brand name I'd spent days brainstorming. An ode to my years attending Howard University in Washington, D.C., Cherry Blossoms Publishing was more than a business to me.

The center of the office served as a lobby, with a small waiting area for clients, and a large reception desk to prevent stragglers. I'd designed the space to look professional, stylish, and important, all the things I wanted to be.

"Did you see the first draft of the cover? I told Lenny he better have an improved visual by day's end," a woman with a stunning caramel complexion spoke to a colleague as they approached me.

"It was so amateur hour," the other woman responded before they both spotted me, a swift but subtle shift in their tone.

"Hi, Mrs. Gamble. I love your hair like that," the caramel toned woman smiled before returning to her private conversation without slowing her stride.

"Mrs. G! I wasn't expecting you back," Crystal chimed, rushing to meet me.

"I didn't know I was coming back," I admitted.

With each step towards my office, I waited for it, preparing myself for the inevitable stares from employees. Surely, they'd heard the news of my father's indictment, a humiliating truth I couldn't deny or avoid.

"I was going to email you an updated schedule. I cancelled your status with Madison, but she's still in the office. So, I can set that back up if you want," Crystal read from a clipboard, looking up briefly for my reaction as I rounded my desk.

"Crystal, do they know?" I asked, unable to ignore my insecurity.

"Do who know?" She frowned, abandoning her notes to give me her undivided attention.

Lifting my hand, I motioned towards the hallway just outside my office. From the double-sided mirror, we could see them walking about as if nothing had changed. But I remembered my outburst. Anxiety pooled in my belly imagining their reactions.

"About your father?" She asked quietly, moving closer to my desk as though our conversation could be overheard.

"Yeah," I answered in a tone so low I questioned if she'd be able to hear me.

"Yes. It was all over the news," she reasoned, her lips piercing with disappointment. I could tell she wanted to shield me from the embarrassment.

"Then why are they..." my words faded as I watched the office move in every direction, carrying on with the day's events.

"Acting like professionals who have a job to do?" She answered with sass, turning to face the glass wall. "I made it clear that anyone who couldn't be professional would need to find another profession." She flashed a dangerous smile.

"You what?" I shocked myself with the laugh that flowed with my words. The day had been filled with many things, but laughter wasn't one of them.

"Mrs. G, you've given me a lot of liberty since I started working for you. I've always acted as your eyes and ears when you're not here, and you've never limited me to the traditional roles of an assistant. I've led meetings and sat in on deals my peers couldn't dream of. So in your time of need, don't feel alone. I'm holding you down like I always do," she smiled, sliding a sheet of paper from her clipboard.

"I emailed this memo addressing the news story they'd obviously heard about. Just a quick reminder that it had nothing to do with them. If anyone can't find a way to capitalize off the new attention we'll be receiving as a publishing house, they're in the wrong industry."

I stared at her blankly, amused by her bold approach. I knew she was right, but I wasn't sure I would have been able to confront the issue as fiercely as Crystal had. She was invaluable on my team.

"What would I do without you?" I smiled with gratitude.

"Let's hope we never have to find out," she smiled and we shared a laugh that was quickly interrupted.

"You really came back to work?" My sister's voice was an alarm, jolting my thoughts. Victoria's eyes were red and puffy.

"Give us a minute," I motioned to Crystal, who nodded before taking Victoria's order for a ginger ale and leaving us alone.

17

Sitting across from each other in my office, Victoria slumped into the soft brown leather as she described learning the news about our father. Like me, she was at work when my mother called frantically. Her husband Mike was unable to get away from the office, so she drove to my parents' home alone, as distracted as me.

"He doesn't even seem phased by all this," she dropped her shoulders. Confusion spread through her perfectly arched eyebrows as she sought to understand my father's calm demeanor.

"That's why I left. If he's not making a big deal of this, I'm surely not. And mom is just..." I shook my head thinking of her performance.

"She's so strong," Victoria's voice cracked recalling my mother's behavior. "She was the one who gave me strength; the only reason I can still hold my head high."

I swallowed the revelation I'd planned to share with my closest sister, finally understanding my mother's behavior. She knew I could handle seeing her at her weakest, but my sisters needed her to be their rock.

Realizing my mother's vulnerability sent a wave of immense

pride through my chest. She trusted me with a side of her my older siblings could not bear. In that moment, I vowed to keep her secret forever.

A soft knock at the door excused us from the difficult memory. Crystal made her way through the office carrying a glass vase holding about two dozen red roses. Frowning with curiosity, I watched my assistant carefully place the vase on the table between me and Victoria.

"Danny boy sent you flowers," my sister whined romantically.

Crystal shot me a glare that confirmed my suspicion – the roses weren't from Daniel. Red roses weren't really his style, and two dozen was less than half his normal order.

"No, these aren't from him," I reached for the card just before Crystal closed my office door behind her.

"Well who the hell is sending you roses?" She perked up, leaning forward in her seat.

"There's a guy from New York who wants to merge his publishing house with mine." I spoke carefully, deciding how much I wanted to tell my sister.

> *PLEASE FORGIVE ME.*
> *I MADE A MISTAKE.*
> *LET'S START OVER.*
> *Q*

Reading the card in Quentin's deep voice, I fought the warmth rising in my cheeks. It had been so long since I'd received flowers from anyone other than Daniel. The differences were evident. Daniel didn't sign his cards, and he would never write something so generic. His messages were always filled with wit, written in a coded language only the two of us could appreciate.

For the second time, I was displeased with how easily Quentin Bolden's words could be misconstrued. Nearly impossible to excuse as a coincidence, I decided he liked the dramatics. Given the recent books his publishing house had released, it made sense.

"I might not be a big shot CEO, but aren't roses a weird business proposal?" Victoria snatched the card from my hand before I could stop her. I watched her brows rise as she read the card before looking over to me. "And this card – if Daniel read this he would have some questions."

"Trust me, Daniel wouldn't care what I was doing with him." I hated what felt like Daniel's abandonment, but pretending things were okay between us felt even worse.

"You don't mean that," Victoria giggled.

"But I do." I turned to face her, glaring into my sister's eyes until she diverted her attention back to the note.

"Why do New York men have to be so damn extra?" She joked, lightening the mood. Unable to remain upset, I felt my lips curl into a smile.

Draping her arm over my shoulder, Victoria relaxed beside me on the leather love seat. It was the first time we'd embraced since she burst into my office. I hadn't admitted how much I needed my big sister until my body melted into hers.

"His name is Quentin. He wants to work together, but I think he's a bit obnoxious. His business looks good on paper, but it's almost too good to be true." I vented, resting my head on her shoulder.

"You don't want to ask Daniel about it?" She asked after a brief pause, tip toeing back to the taboo topic.

"He won't talk to me," I murmured, waiting for the judgment that never came. Instead, Victoria gently touched her cheek to the top of my head, and we rested that way for a long moment.

"Just give him time. He seems to be helping Dad. It's probably been weighing on him," she argued as she lifted her head, defending Daniel yet again.

"I don't know," I sat up. Leaning from one side to the other, I gently massaged the tension in my neck. "He acts like my reaction was baseless. Fine, he wasn't having an affair. But he knew dad was being investigated for fraud, and he secretly paid a woman off to hide it."

The words had been floating in my mind and motivating my actions, but it was the first time I'd heard them so clearly. I knew I was wrong, but I didn't deserve the silent treatment from Daniel. I'd suspected the wrong type of betrayal, but he wasn't completely innocent.

"Daniel thinks he inherited the duty of protecting you from reality. It's what mom and dad always did – making us think life was perfect. He tries to carry that torch. Maybe you're all grown up now, ready to see the truth," she mockingly pinched my cheeks as she spoke the last sentence.

Daniel did try to make everything right for me. In a way, I'd encouraged it. I loved letting him fix problems I could manage on my own, confusing stroking his ego with being a good wife. It led to me becoming more of a liability than an asset, a position I never wanted to be in.

"I never thought of it that way," I finally said, noticing my sister's attention had been stolen by the movement outside my office.

Ignoring my comment, she walked towards the glass wall waving her hands dramatically before launching into jumping jacks. "They really can't see me?" She asked when no one reacted to her show.

"It's a double-sided mirror, Vic. You can see them, but they see a reflection of themselves," I explained the obvious. While no one in my family visited my place of work often, Victoria had been enough times to know how private my office was.

"It feels so..." she paused, waving to my undeterred staff passing the window. "... outdated."

"What?" I huffed, reaching for my glass of ginger ale, silently noting how nice the roses smelled.

"I don't know. It's got an interrogation room vibe. Even these chairs," she pointed towards me. "This office just doesn't fit you."

Another knock at the door turned our heads before Crystal revealed herself. This time, with two more glass bottles of ginger ale, which she left on the coffee table before turning to leave.

"Crys," Victoria began, casually using a nickname that never felt right rolling off my tongue. "Don't you think my baby sister should let me re-design her office?"

Crystal grinned, the kind of smile that revealed her true thoughts before they fell from her lips. "It could use a facelift, Mrs. G," she scrunched her nose apologetically as she turned to me.

"Then it's settled. We're getting rid of this stuff," Victoria announced proudly as I rolled my eyes.

18

_____

Four days had passed since I dropped Daniel off at our family home. Things were less predictable than after I'd filed for divorce. Refusing to respond to my calls or texts, Daniel had left me in the dark about where we stood. The uncertainty was driving me crazy. As the weekend came to an end, I found myself driving to the construction site where our troubles really began.

Since Daniel had taken control of the real estate investment I'd turned into a money pit, there had been significant progress. A member of the construction team proudly informed me that three of the four condominiums were finished with renovations. Giovanna, the penthouse, was the only level still under construction.

Slowly, I walked through each apartment admiring details in the finishes. The lowest level, which I'd named Margaret, was even more dainty than I'd remembered. The crown molding added character, making the condo feel anything but brand new.

Margaret was the only unit with a walkout porch, but I wasn't sure how to utilize the extra space. Daniel had added a small garden, complete with a white wrought iron table and matching chairs. A petite rosebush stood at the edge of the perfectly green grass. It was ripped from the pages of a fairy tale.

Hoping not to disrupt the staff who were busy at work, I took the stairs. Even they had been thoughtfully designed. Paintings hung at every landing, accompanied by large fern plants, making the stairway an extension of the apartments.

Bella, the second level, had been upgraded with furniture that resembled a Parisian café. Two soft pink Victorian chairs sat in the center of the loft. A white coffee table between them held a stack of design books. Settling into the lux fabric, I thumbed through one of the books, impressed by Daniel's attention to detail.

Upon entering Gia, my favorite of the four lofts, I was filled with memories of my last time in the condo. Running my finger-nails along the chrome kitchen island, my abdomen tensed remembering the way Daniel dominated me in that very space. Gia would always be where I got the courage to fight for my marriage.

As I re-entered the stairway, heading to the top floor, I made up my mind to do that again. The final apartment was shaping up to be everything you would expect from a Los Angeles penthouse. The unobstructed view of the city was vastly impressive.

Looking around the large loft, I watched the staff actively working together. Two men were painting an accent wall at the back of the apartment, while another man carried a large loveseat covered in plastic over his shoulder. Stepping back, I made a path for him as he apologetically smiled without breaking stride. Marveling at Daniel's productivity, I didn't notice him approaching until his unkind eyes locked with mine.

"I wasn't expecting you, but we need to talk," he spoke calmly as he opened a manila folder before gently placing what looked to be a contract on the table. "I need you to sign this."

My heart dropped as my eyes glazed over the black font, certain he was turning the tables on me, requesting a divorce. Just when I thought things between us were salvageable, and I was willing to be the catalyst to the change, he was showing me he'd had enough.

"It's a change of control contract. I need your consent," Daniel said casually as my vision blurred.

"A change of control?" I turned to face him.

Unbothered by the concern in my voice, Daniel tore a small bag of Skittles open, popping a few into his mouth as he looked down at the paperwork. "Technically, it's a request for consent to change of control."

"What does that mean?" I felt my temper building. He knew he was speaking over my head, and his refusal to return my eye contact felt suspicious.

"You need to give me complete control to finish and sell the condos." His jaw tensed as he chewed the candy, looking towards the back of the loft.

"I've already done that," I argued, my voice rising with frustration, begging for his undivided attention.

"You've already *said* that. This will make it official. Legally," he nodded towards the paper as he poured more candy into his hand.

"And what does that mean for me?" I wondered, hearing the worry in my words.

Daniel finally turned to me, staring as he moved his hand to his lips, tilting his head back as the Skittles fell against his tongue. "Have a lawyer read over it if you want, Emily. It's written in plain English," he lifted his hands in exasperation.

"Fine, Daniel." I spit the words out. Snatching the pen from his suit jacket, I signed my name so forcefully I feared the paper would tear.

"Great," he smirked. Carefully retrieving the pen from my hand, he looked over the document, his jaw slowly compressing with each bite of candy.

"Let me walk you out," he strolled through the condo after carefully placing the contract back into the folder. "It's best if you leave me to finish on my own," he called over his shoulder, confident I'd followed.

I felt duped. Almost instantly, I regretted following his instructions blindly. I was frozen in shock – persuaded by what initially felt like a warmer reception than he'd given in recent times.

I'd gone to the condos hoping for a reconciliation. Watching the elevator doors close, with only me inside, I felt less optimistic than ever. My chin fell, but no tears followed. Again, I was past crying as my stomach tensed with what felt like anger.

How could he?

19

That night, sleep was impossible. Lying awake until my eyes burned with fatigue, I replayed the day's events in my mind. While the hotel had never felt like home, it was even more uncomfortable after my interaction with Daniel.

Emily: We need to talk.

I texted him after arriving back to my room. I wasn't sure what I needed, but I knew only he could give it to me. I waited for two hours, staring at the phone every few seconds before accepting he was ignoring me.

Emily: Really? The least you can do is respond, Daniel.

Still, nothing.

Left with my curiosity and imagination, I scoured the internet to understand a change of control contract. The results were harrowing. One after another, I read horror stories of spouses and business partners being deceived into signing over their rights to property and investments.

A popular divorce blog listed it as the first step to a legal separation; a preliminary division of assets. The contract gave Daniel free reign on the condos. Legally, I had no say in any decisions, including how much he sold them for. The worst news was after signing that paperwork, I no longer had any legal right to any of the profits.

I felt sick to my stomach remembering the smirk on Daniel's face as he examined my signature. My father's stern advice to never sign a contract without first having it looked over by a lawyer looped repeatedly in my mind.

I wanted to believe Daniel would never defraud me, but the events of the past week made it difficult to trust anyone.

The loud ringing of the hotel phone was a relief, the signal I'd made it through what felt like an endless night.

"Yes. Thank you. Please send my breakfast up," I answered the phone groggily, kicking my legs to the side of the bed.

For all that hotel life wasn't, I had to admit room service was one of my favorite perks. Seeing my breakfast rolled in – French toast, fresh fruit cut into cute shapes, and a flat white coffee topped with a flawless design – made me feel a little better about my sleep deprivation.

The longer I sat with it, the more I accepted my exhaustion had nothing to do with a lack of sleep. I was tired of waiting, tired of pretending, tired of hoping things would right themselves.

Daniel had always been the one to take control. I'd allowed it to my own detriment. Remembering the last instance I'd taken control, and the lustful satisfaction it brought me, was all the motivation I needed to change course.

With every bite of breakfast, a plan developed. There was no reason to sit in a shitty hotel wallowing about Daniel. There were still cards to be played and ways I could rectify my mistakes. I had the power, I was merely forgetting how to wield it.

After a hot shower, I was ready to confront Daniel in a way he couldn't ignore. He might dismiss me at the construction site, and he would probably do the same if I showed up to our house unannounced. There was only one place Daniel wouldn't risk getting out of character, his office.

Rose gold buttons along the off white asymmetrical shirt dress felt more like armor than the white lace bodysuit I wore beneath it. With straightened hair falling over my shoulder, I knelt to buckle the clasps of my rose leather Jimmy Choo Lancer pumps, feeling invincible.

A seductive smile played on my lips the entire drive to Daniel's office. Desire coursed each time I accelerated, racing through the city as though I was late for an appointment.

"Mrs. Gamble! I wasn't expecting you," Tracy's eyes doubled in size as I walked towards her tall desk.

"Just wanted to pop in on my husband," I smiled, seeing the shock fade from her narrow face.

"He's in a meeting," she informed me with disappointment.

"I'll wait for him," I assured her, turning the corner towards his office.

Treating the hallway as my personal runway, I strutted through Tower Enterprise Group like I owned the place. Just as I passed the glass walls lining the conference room, I spotted Daniel. Sitting at the head of the long mahogany table, he squinted with concentration as another man spoke.

My passing averted his attention, and he glanced up, double taking when he realized it was me. Rushing to his feet, I smirked watching him point with direction before rushing towards the glass door, waiting for it to close before addressing me.

"What are you doing here?" He stepped towards me, his eyes narrowing with disapproval.

"We should go to your office," I forcefully suggested, watching his eyes drift to my hips.

Shaking his head subtly, he gripped my elbow, leading me the rest of the distance to his office with an urgency I'd lacked.

"Hi, Mrs. Gamble!" A young woman called as we passed an open conference room.

"Hi," I waved with my free hand as Daniel continued to steer me.

"Daniel," I whispered as we approached his office, snatching my arm free as soon as we were out of view.

"Are you serious?" He growled, storming across the large office before pressing a button on his desk, alerting Tracy to hold his calls.

"Well, you won't answer my calls. I figured I'd catch you the only place you seem interested in maintaining relationships," I flipped my hair over my shoulder, taking a deep breath.

This wasn't going how I'd intended, but I wasn't ready to retreat. In the back of my mind, I hoped he would see the dress hugging my body and forget everything going wrong between us. I wanted him to show me how he felt, make me remember the fire that burned between us.

"You haven't called me." His voice deepened as glared from behind his desk.

"Fine. You're not answering my texts," I corrected myself, rolling my eyes.

"You said you wanted to talk. So, talk." He walked around his desk, crossing his arms as he leaned against the glass top.

20

Daniel was dressed like he was expecting me. The suit did little to disguise his broad shoulders, the masculinity exemplified by pristine tailoring. He was even more handsome scowling, his thick eyebrows furrowed so deeply they almost touched.

"Daniel, I made a mistake." I swallowed, watching him exhale deeply as he stood in silence, refusing to engage. "I read an email that made me believe you were hiding something from me and I reacted. I wanted to talk to you, but I didn't have patience. I panicked, and while I was wrong about what you were hiding, I was right that you were hiding something."

Willing more confidence, I shifted my weight from one foot to the other before taking two steps towards him. Shrinking under his coldness, I froze when he unfolded his arms, turning away from me.

"That's it?" He asked, smirking as he sat in one of the leather chairs centered in the massive room. It was the first time I noticed how similar they were to the chairs in my office. Taking his place, I leaned against the desk, crossing my arms as he had.

"What do you mean, 'That's it?' I want to talk about it. That requires participation from you," I explained, the attitude clear in my tone.

"If you wanted to have a conversation with me, you shouldn't have ambushed me at my office, disrupting a meeting."

He didn't even look at me. His eyes fixated on the coffee table before slightly adjusting the magazines on the glass top.

"Then you shouldn't have ambushed me with some shady contract to push me out of the condo deal."

"What?" He turned to face me, standing before I could find the words to answer him. Closing the distance between us in three short strides, he stood just inches from me, glaring down his nose as his jaw tightened with fury.

"What did I sign, Daniel?" I asked softly, trying to back pedal from the accusatory tone I knew was below the belt.

"I already told you what you signed. So, ask me what you really want to know," he growled. Our faces were so close, I could feel his words on my face.

"I want to know what's happening between us. You've been so cold to me," I answered honestly, my voice barely above a whisper.

"Now you're the victim, huh?" He shook his head, biting his bottom lip as he flashed a dangerous smile. Walking away, Daniel took a deep breath. "You want to know what's happening with us, Emily? You're dealing with the repercussions of your actions."

"And what about *your* actions? And your secret meetings? If I hadn't read those emails," I said before being interrupted.

"What? If you hadn't gone through my phone to read some deleted emails, what, Emily?" He barked. If his office weren't soundproof his entire consultancy firm would have heard his question.

"How could you keep something like that from me? I tell you everything!" My emotional need to be understood battled with my brewing anger.

"I was protecting you!" He argued, which infuriated me. I was so sick of everyone treating me like a helpless housewife in need of protection.

"Yeah? And how did that work out for you, Daniel?" I challenged, tilting my head defiantly.

I watched his temples protrude, his eyes closing in frustration. Loosening the Pratt knot in his tie, Daniel's chest rose and fell as he sighed. He walked away, focusing on the skyline displayed from the large window lining his office.

He brushed his hair forward with the palms of his hands, as he always did when he was frustrated. I wanted to go to him, to find an end to the unbearable tension.

"Why are you so intent on fighting with me?" I asked as I neared him, feeling the emotion cloud my vision.

"I'm intent on fighting with you?" He stepped back, a humorless laugh transforming his face with what would look like amusement to a stranger. "You storm in here, dressed like a model, demanding forgiveness without so much as an apology." His face turned to stone as he faced me.

"How are you mad? I'm the one staying in a hotel, unable to get so much as a response from my husband," I pleaded.

"You're staying in a hotel because you're stubborn. That's of your own doing," he waved me off. "What did you think, Emily? You'd parade through here, we'd fuck in my office, and things would be better?"

Inhaling sharply, I looked away, shocked by his bluntness and accuracy. Tugging at the hem of my dress, I felt exposed and humiliated, rejected yet again. He was right. I did have visions for his office, thinking we could patch things up with sex. The possibility that he could be uninterested had never crossed my mind.

Pouncing on my shortcoming, Daniel slowly walked towards me, his brows framing his eyes as he frowned. "You think very highly of that slit between your legs," he smiled menacingly, continuing when I didn't respond.

"You got amnesia in your pussy, baby?" He asked, tilting my chin upwards with his index finger.

Instinctively, I swung to slap him, but he leaned back, barely dodging my lashing as a playful grin spread across his face.

"You're being an asshole!"

"That's what you want, right?" He shrugged, still smiling, pleased with his performance. "According to you, I'm the type of man who would have an affair, and then pay a woman off to hide it from you."

He glared across the room, enraged. "You bombarded my office to question me about tricking you out of some money? Really, Em? Why would you even want to be with someone you think that low of?"

"Is that where we are?" I swallowed the emotion clogging my throat. Feeling threatened and attacked, I fought back. "You're not the only one with a lawyer, Daniel. You should know I can have papers drawn up just as fast as your little contract." I was flailing, desperate to hurt him as he'd hurt me.

The smile fell quickly from his face as he stormed towards me so quickly my stomach dropped with fear. "I fucking dare you to send me divorce papers, Emily."

Just then, his office door swung open. A short Latino man flushed with embarrassment when our eyes met. "Oh, Mr. Gamble. I'm sorry, I was just delivering the notes from the meeting."

"It's fine. My wife was just leaving," he spoke at me, his eyes hiding none of the fury he felt.

Piercing my lips together, I forced myself to contain the emotions dying to pour from my eyes. Lifting my purse from his desk, I was careful not to so much as brush against him. The thought of his hands touching me was repulsing.

Storming through the office, I managed to smile at Tracy before squeezing into a packed elevator, gritting my teeth for strength until we reached the garage beneath the building. Walking as quickly as possible, I rushed to the car with tears falling before I could unlock the doors. Alone in the parking lot, I sobbed until the cries threatened to choke me, my body fighting the need to purge all I'd digested in Daniel's office – the rejection, disrespect, and humiliation.

Whatever I thought could happen between us was wrong. My plan had failed miserably, and I couldn't imagine ever trying again. My phone vibrated in my purse, and I scrambled to find it, desperate for a distraction. It was a text from my mother.

Mom: I'm on my way to The Ivy. Meet me there for brunch.

21

"I'm not going to divorce your father." My mother sat poised across the round table of The Ivy, one of her favorite restaurants in the city. The colorful floral arrangement added a bright pop of color against the sharp white tablecloth.

The décor was vibrant, matching the audience of the outdoor dining area. Two men sat perched on a blue Prius across the street. Large cameras hanging from their necks identified them as paparazzi. I was still in a trance after my blow up with Daniel, trying to make sense of how things had escalated so quickly.

"Did you hear me, Emily? I said I'm not divorcing your father," she repeated.

"I know, mom. I didn't think you were," I smiled pitifully, unable to focus.

"Those things I said," she began, licking her teeth as she nervously twisted the large diamond on her ring finger.

"We don't have to talk about it, mom. I know you were upset," I reached across the table, covering her hand with mine, hoping to relieve some of her stress.

"It's just," she inhaled before taking a large gulp of white wine. "I never talk to my girls like that. I don't want to taint your image of your father. He's a good man. You know that, right?" She searched my eyes.

"Yes, I know," I managed. Her words sent me back to thoughts of Daniel. He too was a good man; one I had pushed to the edge. In a way, I felt responsible for his reaction earlier.

"What's the matter, baby?" She leaned across the table to touch my arm.

"Me and Daniel just got into a huge fight," I admitted, feeling the tears rebuild in my eyes.

"Drink some wine, honey," she urged. I giggled softly at her answer for everything. Leaning my head back, I inhaled as much oxygen as I could manage, blocking out the tears before taking a sip of wine.

"More. Drink more, Emily," My mother instructed, following her own advice as she waved her finger, signaling a refill to the waitress.

"He was so mean to me," I recoiled.

"What happened?" She asked as the waitress arrived with the bottle of wine.

"Leave the bottle, sweetheart," my mother rudely waived the waitress on. Her eyes trained on me, imploring me to answer.

"I went to his office," I sighed, exhausted just thinking of the backstory she would need for context. "I was going to confront him."

"About Lana?"

"You knew?"

"I've learned," she corrected me.

"And what do you think?"

"I think Daniel thought he was protecting you," she said before pausing as she refilled our glasses. My stomach sank with disappointment, assuming she would mirror Victoria's feelings. "But of all my children, you're the only one who has never needed protection."

A tear slid down my cheek, feeling understood for the first time in a long time. My mother quickly pushed a napkin across the table, her lips piercing into a flat line at my public display of emotion, something she would never do.

"I don't know what to do," I cried quietly as the diners around me laughed and joked, oblivious to my sorrow.

"What do you mean? You have an entire company. You have friends. You have family. You have a shit ton of money." My mother waved her hand with every reminder. "You have more than enough to keep yourself busy while Daniel remembers who the hell he's dealing with."

"I don't need to prove myself," I twisted my face, disliking the notion.

"If you showed up to Daniel's office in *that* dress, you definitely think you have to prove yourself," my mother snickered as she sipped her wine, nudging my glass towards me.

"He didn't even flinch," I embarrassingly recalled before sipping the wine, enjoying the bitter taste.

"Of course, he didn't. You wreak of desperation, honey," she huffed with arrogance. "You've looked like a lost puppy ever since you ran away from home." She sipped her wine through her laughter, completely amused.

"You find this funny?" I raised an eyebrow.

"Oh, sweetheart. You have the winning hand and you don't even know it," she flashed a mischievous smile before again refilling our glasses. "You are who you are without Daniel, and he has nothing to hold over you. If you'd decided to go through with the divorce, you'd be fine and he knows it. There are no children. You'd be happily remarried within a year, and he'd be gutted."

My mouth dropped at her frank analysis of my life, casually mentioning the divorce I'd thought she knew nothing about. With another wave of her finger, she ordered a second bottle of wine. This time I didn't flinch. We were undoubtedly going to need more alcohol.

"You knew about me filing?" I whispered, suddenly concerned with someone overhearing our conversation.

"You think one of my daughters could make a public filing

without my knowing?" She huffed, smiling behind her wine glass. "My best friend filed the petition, for Christ's sake."

"She can't tell you what we talk about!" I argued.

"No, but she can ask me how you're doing, and how Daniel is doing, and I can hear the concern in her voice," my mother stared at me with the mother all-knowing eyes.

"Why didn't you say anything?" I asked.

"For the same reason I didn't say anything when you two decided to buy that shithole warehouse downtown, or when you suddenly stopped coming by the house. I knew you'd come to me like this one day," she paused as the waitress arrived.

"Can I get you two anything else?" The thin blonde woman asked.

"Yes, we need to have a little food with the wine. Do you want your regular, honey?" She asked and I nodded. "Okay, she'll have the lobster pizza. And bring a nice big salad with it," my mother smiled with squinted eyes that silently dismissed the waitress.

"Being a mother is the most difficult task for an independent woman. I anchored myself to a man when we chose to start a family. As much as I've wanted to move alone at times, you children are half your father's. And because he's a good father, I couldn't make a single impactful decision without first discussing it with him. There was never a clean break, we'd tethered our lives together.

"And when you all grew from babies, things only became more complicated. Between you and your siblings, I have five pieces of me running around the world, making decisions with youthful arrogance. And I'm forced to wait for you to realize you need me, when you used to run to me for help with everything."

She smiled as she spoke the last sentence, like it was a fond yet distant memory. Again, she nudged my glass towards me and we both took a large gulp.

"Emily, you're no damsel in distress, but you like to pretend you are. You have since you were a child. You'd nudge yourself in the smallest nook you could find, and then scream until someone came to pull you out. I was worried you felt neglected and were seeking attention, but the gleam in your eyes would always make me think otherwise. It was a game to you, or at least that's what I thought. But you've never stopped playing that game, always pretending to be stuck, when of all the people I know, you have the most opportunity."

Silenced by her scrutiny, I did the only thing I could, refill our glasses. I knew in my heart she was right, even remembering the game I would play as a child. Whether she used the word or not, it was manipulation. I'd spent so much time worried I was manipulating Daniel, I never considered I could manipulate myself. Pretending I needed saving, when I could crawl from my hidden nook whenever I chose.

The waitress arrived with my pizza, and my stomach growled with approval as the aroma wafted through my senses. Forcing my mother to eat more than salad, I placed two slices on a plate and sat them on her side of the table before devouring my lunch.

Knowing she'd already said enough, my mom let me eat in peace, digesting both my lunch and her revelation. I'd gone from the lowest of lows to a strange place of empowerment. By the time my mother paid the bill, I was feeling more like myself than I had in months.

"Let me use your phone. Mine is dead." She tossed her phone into her purse, waving her fingers in anticipation of mine.

"I'm riding with you," I said, feeling stuffed and tipsy.

"You think I was going to let you drive?" She asked over the reading glasses she'd put on to use my phone. I watched as she tapped with a deep frown creasing her forehead.

"Do you need help?" I asked, standing from my seat.

"No! No, I've got it," she quickly tapped a few times on my phone before I could make my way around the table. Retrieving my phone, I giggled at her stubborn attitude, confident she hadn't successfully contacted her driver.

"You're the reason I'm so independent, you know?" I wrapped my arm through hers as we made our way through the dining area.

"Yeah, but you're much smarter than I was at your age." She said plainly, as though it were a fact not a compliment. "Take the rest of the day off," my mother instructed as we walked to her waiting car, proving she was more tech savvy than I'd expected. "Check out of that God-awful hotel, and get a suite."

"That hotel is two hundred dollars a night," I argued, despite my own disapproval.

"So, how much is a nice hotel?" My mother asked before climbing into the back seat, sending me into a fit of giggles. Nothing was more subtly direct than my mother's insults.

"I barely spend any time there. I've been at my office more than anything," I explained, noting the pride in my voice.

"You've always loved your job, baby," my mom turned to me as I settled beside her in the back seat. "Get back to that, but first take a day for yourself. Enjoy this time alone, because believe me child, Daniel is going to come back around. And when he does, you need to know what you want."

Her purse began to vibrate loudly. A tipsy laugh tickled my lips. "I thought your phone died," I recalled. My mother was the worst with phones.

"So did I," she yelped, leaning her shoulder into mine as we laughed together, letting the wine work its magic.

22

Following my mother's advice, I booked the premiere suite at the Four Seasons Beverly Hills, requesting they retrieve my belongings from The Britton Hotel. At the rate they were charging, picking up my luggage was the least they could do.

My first stop was to visit Sonja, my trusted hair stylist. Though I wasn't interested in going full *Waiting to Exhale*, I wanted a change. Always happy to assist in a makeover, Sonja gleefully presented options. I chose the most drastic change, a golden copper color to transform my long tresses.

Sonja was nervous I'd regret the bold selection, so it wasn't until she'd finished styling my hair with voluminous wand curls that I saw the transformation. Much brighter than I'd anticipated, my already highlighted hair was bolder than anything I'd ever done.

"Over time, the color will fade," Sonja assured me when my mouth dropped open, staring at my reflection.

"Then you're going to have to touch it up. I love it!" A smile spread across my face staring at the woman in the mirror. My hair change was only the start. A woman bold enough to have vibrant hair tumbling down her back deserved a new wardrobe to go along with it.

"Em! Why didn't you call me?!" Monica gasped when I walked into the ready to wear department at Neiman Marcus. Positioned on historical Wilshire Boulevard, it was just a short walk from my new hotel.

"I need a new look," I smiled as Monica wrapped me in one of her bear hugs. We were thick as thieves in college, but life had drifted us apart as I focused on my career and marriage, and Monica jet set around the world, dressing Hollywood's biggest stars.

"It's been too long since we hung out! You picked the perfect day to stop by. My schedule is blank!" She laughed, looking me up and down before hugging me again.

"I didn't know if you'd even be here." I told a half-truth. The reality was, I didn't know if Monica would be excited to see me after I'd missed so many holidays, birthdays, girls' trips, and failed to keep up in general.

My mother was right, I had a lot of friends, but I hadn't been a great friend to any of them. Seeing the genuine smile on Monica's face was all the confirmation I needed. If there was ever anything I'd done to upset her, she'd forgiven me. And as always, she was going to be there to help me through this next phase.

"We just got a new shipment! I was going to pull a few things for you anyway," Monica flashed her infectious smile as she wrapped her arm around my shoulder, leading me through racks of clothing.

Although I hadn't seen her in months, Monica had continued to work as my stylist, sending me the latest fashion from her travels. She'd made quite the name for herself since college, but she was never too busy to answer my calls.

"I want to try some bold color," I nervously suggested, knowing how quick she was to reject my bad suggestions.

"Well, you have no choice now. Is this recent?" She ran her fingers through my hair, as only close friends can do.

"Just got it," I smiled bashfully as she showered me with compliments.

"It suits you." She nodded, smiling with her eyes before

hugging me again. "I'm just so happy to see you. I needed some good news today."

For the next three hours, we caught up on each other's lives, though I left out the details of my troubles with Daniel. I told her about my dad's legal troubles, which she had already read about online, and she told me about her latest falling out with a celebrity client.

After explaining my determination to take my career more seriously, Monica picked what she described as a "Modern Boss" wardrobe. Between sips of champagne, I tried on dresses, pant suits, separates, and shoes. Once I'd given her feedback on my favorite cuts and colors, she took notes to create the full concept package. She promised to send over enough for a full makeover, complete with coordinating accessories, and even a few new lingerie pieces.

"I'm staying at the Four Seasons," I declared after we'd finished playing dress up.

Monica's smile faded, her eyes narrowing with concern. "So, that's what brought you here?"

"That's not the only reason," I rushed to explain, hoping she didn't feel used by my impromptu visit.

"Em, you don't have to apologize for having a life. We're not teenagers anymore. We can't share every detail of our lives. You might ignore my pointless texts, but whenever I really need you, you're there. And I'm here for you," she smiled. I exhaled deeply, grateful for her understanding.

"Things were so much simpler then," I rolled my eyes, thinking back to our days at Howard.

"Yeah, until it was time to drag your ass to class!" She reminded me and we both laughed, recalling how bad of a student I was. "Seriously, you always knew what you wanted to do. School was only delaying that."

"I don't know about all that," I raised my eyebrows doubtfully.

"Trust me. I knew you would be running your own company

249

even back then. You're an all-in type of person. You throw yourself into everything full throttle."

I stood in silence, hoping the disbelief wasn't evident on my face. Monica had always been an objective observer in my life, able to see me more clearly than I ever could.

"It's funny you say that. I've been getting back into my business and it's a breath of fresh air. After I bought it, I kind of faded into the background," a nervous laugh escaped me as I searched for the words. "I was so focused on being Daniel's wife."

"It's not a bad thing. I do it too. It's something I've been learning about myself in therapy. You don't have to choose between your roles, Em. You can be a business woman and a wife."

Her words were as comforting as the arms she wrapped around me. For so long, I'd allowed titles to define me. Every decision was based on how others would perceive it. Impressing people was exhausting. In the middle of Neiman Marcus, I hugged my friend with a rediscovered confidence, determined to focus on myself.

"Thanks for this, Monica. Really," I hugged her one last time.

"Oh, you'll be getting my bill," she said, and we both laughed. "But seriously, I get it. Take your time, there's no judgement here. Whatever you decide is best for you is best. I'll always be here, no matter what."

Maybe it was the whirlwind of emotions, or my nonstop drinking throughout the day, but I was overwhelmed by the time I made it to my suite. With barely enough energy to wrap my hair, I buried myself in the lush bedding, drifting off to sleep after what felt like the longest of days.

23

woken by a knock at the door, I rubbed my eyes, unsure of how long I'd slept. Crawling from the bed, I stumbled through the living area of the suite before squinting through the peephole. Daniel stood with a bouquet of roses, chewing the inside of his cheek nervously as I gasped with shock. I hadn't expected for him to come around so quickly.

"Baby, I can hear you. Can we just talk for a minute?" He called through the door.

Before I could put up a fight, my instincts took over, opening the door. Unlike the angry man he'd been in his office, Daniel was relaxed. Still dressed in a suit, he was seductively formal, although he'd ditched the tie. Stepping through the doorway, he looked around the suite before turning to face me, his eyes weary as though his day had been as rough as mine.

"I see you've upgraded," he broke the ice, flashing a half smile that made my stomach tense with need.

While I hadn't forgotten how nasty he was to me, I still missed him. Knowing nothing would feel better than being wrapped in his arms, I invited him into the sitting room, offering him a drink.

"I don't know if I should have anymore. I started drinking the moment you left my office," he admitted, leaning back on the sofa as he stretched his arms.

"Me too, but they have Macallan, and I didn't want to drink it alone."

Returning from the small bar in the corner of the room, I placed two glasses on the coffee table as I sat beside him. So nervous my hand shook, I managed to pour us each a drink before turning to face him.

"Emily, please forgive me. I still can't believe the things I said," he spoke sternly, his jaw tense as remorse covered his face.

"You've never talked to me like that," I whispered, the memory still fresh.

"I never want to," he added, reaching for the drink before finishing it all in one gulp.

Following suit, I lifted the heavy tumbler from the table. Sipping slowly, I watched Daniel over the top of my glass. His eyes were trained on the table. I imagined he was struggling to find words to express his feelings.

"I don't even know how we got here. I thought we were finally over this rough patch. Then things got even worse. It's been moving too fast for me to slow down," he turned to me, his eyes reddening with regret.

"My world crumbled when I read those emails," I recalled, emotion cracking my voice. Taking another sip of the liquor, I forced a deep breath.

"So did mine. I know how much you love your father. The last thing I wanted was someone ruining that. I didn't know what else to do. We were already on rocky terms. I didn't want you to have to deal with that too," he explained, twisting his lips as he tried to make sense of his actions.

"The news of my father was nothing compared to how I felt when I read the emails," I explained before finishing my drink. "But I should have never gone through your phone," I added quickly, hoping to take some accountability, but Daniel didn't allow it.

"It was never about that. We've never had secrets. You can always look through my shit. I deleted it because I didn't want you to find it. In some way, I knew what I was doing was fucked up. It just felt like the lesser of two evils," he shrugged, subtly shaking his head as he reached for the bottle, refilling our glasses.

"Did my dad know she'd contacted you?" I heard myself ask, trying my best to tread as carefully as possible.

"I don't know what he knew," Daniel exhaled loudly. "Every time I tried to talk to him about it, he had a reason to brush me off. I didn't really want to have the conversation, so I let him. I never thought it would cost me everything."

I watched as the turmoil appeared to eat him alive. I hadn't thought of how much he must have been going through, learning his mentor wasn't who he said he was, while also dealing with an impending divorce.

Daniel had always looked like a superhero to me, unshaken by everything life threw at him. But now, I saw him breaking, the weight on his shoulders too heavy to bear any longer. My heart broke realizing how lonely it must have been for him. Away from his hometown, Daniel had always been clear that I was his family, and I had deserted him.

My need to remind him of our bond rushed over me as a tear slid down his cheek. Quick to hide the emotion, he aggressively wiped his face with both palms. It wasn't planned, or what I'd anticipated when I opened the door, but I climbed on top of him, straddling his large frame.

"You didn't lose me, baby," I whispered, kissing his cheek as I cradled his head in my hands.

"I fucking love you, Emily. I would never betray you," he looked directly into my eyes, gripping the nape of my neck.

"I love you too," I managed before our lips collided, his tongue seeking refuge against mine.

Our bodies moved in choreographed motions, his hands lifting my silk nightgown to reveal a lace negligée. His eyes narrowed with hunger gazing over my body before gripping a handful of my hair, savagely kissing my neck while tearing at the lace.

"Ahh," I moaned loudly, tilting my head back as his kisses drifted to my collar bone.

Desperate to feel him deep inside me, I tugged at his belt before fighting with his zipper as he chuckled in my ear. "Slow down, baby," his words were warm and familiar, an endearing tone he hadn't used with me in far too long.

"I want to feel you," I begged, just as I'd managed to unfasten his pants. Lifting himself briefly, Daniel pulled his boxer briefs just low enough to free his erection, which heavily fell onto my stomach.

Rising on my knees, I positioned myself above his length before lowering my body to take every inch into my warmth. I gasped at the fullness as Daniel plunged deep inside me, hugging me so tightly I strained for air. With his mouth pressed against my ear, I heard the barely audible moan as he stretched me, holding my hips in place so I felt him in his entirety.

"I love you," he growled as he lifted me by my waist, manipulating my body to fall onto him at an angle he knew too well.

"Daniel," I moaned, my body instantly remembering his dominance. He was so controlled, his breathing calm and steady, as I panted with every thrust. My hips winded dangerously, my fingers gripping his neck tightly.

"I missed you," he groaned, kissing my neck sloppily.

"Daniel... Baby," I cried, the sensation rising from the depths of my stomach. Lifting on my knees, I moaned loudly as I fell onto his manhood.

"I know, baby... I know," he whispered before tugging at my earlobe with his front teeth.

My body melted into his as he took over, increasing his pace. One hand gripped my hair, the other guided my hip, forcing our bodies to collide. Lifting his hips from the sofa, I could feel the control seeping from him as he too raced for a release.

"Fuck!" He growled as his body began to tense, bracing for an explosion.

"Daniel!" I cried, just as my orgasm began to take over. My arms wrapped tightly around his neck, rising and falling on his length as our bodies greedily fought for more.

I was teetering on the edge, ready to let go and pour into a pool of unleashed desire, when a soft ringing grew louder and louder, until it was all I could hear. Reflex took over as I reached with muscle memory.

"Good morning, Mrs. Gamble. This is your wake-up call. Will you be needing a car this morning?"

"Thank you."

Slamming the phone onto the receiver, I noticed the pillow clamped between my legs before angrily climbing from the bed, rushing to the shower.

24

"**M**rs. G, you're looking fabulous! Love the new look," Crystal admired my hair as she followed me into the makeshift office I'd began using while Victoria finished redecorating.

"Felt like it was time for a change," I announced with a twirl, feeling confident.

Monica had sent over the first delivery of clothes. I'd chosen a belted vintage button down dress. The copper details in the flannel print went well with my hair, and the tulle teasing at the hem of the full circle skirt added a subtle sex appeal.

"Well, it looks good on you," Crystal nodded her approval.

"Thanks. What's up for the day? I know I missed so much yesterday," I rolled my eyes, a bit regretful of my day off.

"No, you're fine," Crystal looked to her clipboard. Moving closer she whispered, "I told everyone you were vetting a managing supervisor, a new position you wanted to fill. Now the whole floor is on their A-game."

I laughed, instantly relieved as I accepted the printout. Crystal knew how much I hated staring at my phone, so she printed a schedule every morning, color coded by the level of importance.

"Looks good," I remarked as I looked over the day, mostly filled with statuses and follow up meetings.

"Madison and Christian both want to add a short meeting to your schedule. I told them I'd speak with you about it," she added. I knew Madison wanted to continue discussing the merger, but I wasn't sure what Christian, the head of the fiction department, needed.

"Okay, set them up," I nodded, happy to be back in the swing of things. In recent months, no one cared to run ideas by me, but thankfully my team had taken to my return with enthusiasm.

"One more thing," I nervously called to Crystal before she left me with the briefings for the morning status.

"What's that?" She turned on her heels.

"I need you to find me a psychiatrist," I looked up just in time to see her remove the worrisome frown.

"Any special requirements?" She asked, returning to her normal professionalism.

"A woman..." I puckered my lips, considering the question for the first time. "...Black... And in the city." I nodded, satisfied with my prerequisites.

"Done." Crystal nodded before turning to leave.

The morning status meeting was scheduled to be like any other – with every department head giving a brief update on what they had been working on. Reading through Crystal's notes from the previous day, I jotted down a few follow up questions to ask, excited for what used to be a chore.

My mother was right, I had always loved my job, but my conflicts with Daniel had made it impossible to focus. Determined not to let that happen again, I decided to jump in head first, making a list of projects for Crystal to add to my schedule.

I wanted to meet with every new writer we'd signed during my six-month hiatus, introducing them to the woman who signed their checks. Writing had always been my dream, but after realizing I wasn't as good as I thought, publishing the talent I admired so much felt like the perfect middle ground.

I'd just finished thumbing through the binder of new talent when my cell buzzed, a call from Victoria.

"Are you done with my office?" I feigned an attitude as she giggled on the other end of the call.

"Well, how are you this morning, baby sis?"

"I'm sitting in what used to be a storage room, pretending it's an office." I answered, glancing around the dark and windowless room, a gloomy change in environment.

"Well, I should be done in less than a week. I just need to talk about the final selections," she continued.

"A *week*?" I screeched.

While I'd tried to keep things light and fun, my sister's insistence to go overboard with her design was frustrating. I only agreed to the renovations to give her something to focus on, knowing our father's legal issues were weighing so heavily on her. Now, she was delaying my full return to work.

"Trust me! It will be worth it!" She argued. I could hear the humor in her voice.

"What new selections do you need approval on?" I rolled my eyes, returning to the mention of changes she wanted to make.

"Umm, I never said approval," she corrected me. "I just need to talk about the budget."

"That sounds like some approval to me," I snapped back.

"If I ensure you it'll be worth it, can you just sign the check?" She asked, her voice teetering on whining.

"How much?" I asked flatly.

"Who can put a price on comfort, really?" She countered, avoiding answering.

"They're ready for you, Boss Lady," Crystal said with a soft knock on the door.

Nodding, I held one finger in the air, signaling I'd be there shortly. Gathering my notes and work bag, I cradled the phone between my ear and shoulder as Victoria rambled on about how she needed a little more room in the budget.

"Fine! Just make it fabulous, and hurry the hell up!" I moved to end the call.

"You won't regret this!" Victoria yelled back just before I hung up, sending me into the meeting with a smile on my face.

25

"**M**rs. Gamble – Emily," Christian quickly corrected himself. We were filing out the conference room after a successful morning status. "I've been trying to get on your schedule for a few days now. Do you think we could talk, just for a few minutes? I'd love some feedback on my ideas for the summer roll out. I think you'll love what I'm working on."

Christian beamed with pride, teetering from one foot to the other, fighting to contain his excitement. Dressed in a flannel button down shirt with a matching bowtie, he'd deemed us twins after seeing my dress. Nothing impressed me more than initiative and persistence, so I wanted to reward his dedication.

"Okay, I think I have a few minutes," I began before Crystal interjected.

"Sorry, no you don't, Mrs. G."

Christian's face dropped instantly, shooting Crystal a look that made me pity her. "But, I had..." I looked to my printed schedule, searching for what I thought was a free hour and a half following the status meeting.

"Something else has come up, but Christian, I can get you in afterwards. How's three today work?" Crystal lifted his mood instantly.

"Perfect! Prepare to be blown away, Emily!" He grinned before leaving me alone in the conference room with my assistant.

"Was that a cover or did something really come up?" I quizzed once the door closed.

"You have your first session with Dr. Lorraine Cathway, 'the premiere therapist for today's modern professional woman', or at least that's what her website says," Crystal smiled as I stared with incredulity.

"Don't worry! I vetted her thoroughly. She's the real deal," she added.

"Today?" I yelped, not expecting to open up to someone within hours of admitting I needed help.

"There's no time like the present, and I have a driver downstairs so you don't have to worry about anything. Just go, have an open mind, and be honest," Crystal advised.

"Was that on her website too?" I smirked.

"Oh no, that's from personal experience," she smiled, silently showing her support without knowing what was troubling me.

I took longer than necessary to get to the lobby. My nerves sent me into a fit of anxiety anticipating my first therapy session since high school. During one of my parents' particularly rough patches, my mother insisted we all speak with a professional to work through our feelings.

I didn't see the point of it then, but later missed the weekly release of thoughts. Therapy was something I'd been putting off for months. There was no doubt I'd been bottling up more than I could manage.

Crystal had found a therapist within walking distance to the office, making the car ride completely unnecessary. Still, I used the few minutes to gather my thoughts, jotting down things I wanted to discuss and problems I felt she could help me resolve.

"I'll be waiting here," the driver's deep voice intruded on my quiet planning.

"Oh, okay," I glanced out the window to see an old building that looked more like a ranch style home than a doctor's office. The beige limestone looked both ancient and well maintained. A narrow path of granite stones led to the red front door, a blatant contrast in color.

Stepping inside, I instantly noticed the aesthetic carried through to the interior of the office. Low ceilings dated the space that was sparsely decorated. A large painting hung on the opposite wall, with one chair placed on either side. A closed doorway, which I imagined led to the doctor's office, was positioned to the right of the reception desk.

"Hello," I announced myself as the older black woman glanced up with a bright smile.

"Oh, Mrs. Gamble, have a seat," she extended her hand towards the two waiting chairs.

"How'd you know my name?" I wondered aloud.

"Dr. Cathway doesn't just take on anyone. She researched you even more than you probably investigated her," she smiled just as the elusive door opened.

"Hi, Emily. Come on in."

Dr. Lorraine Cathway had a regal poise that made me comfortable from the moment I sat on the sofa. Her long gray hair was neatly pulled into one thick braid that fell to the middle of her back. As I'd suspected, there were only two rooms in the entire building. The front waiting area, and what appeared to be the largest office I'd ever seen, though it was nothing like I'd expected.

There wasn't a desk in sight, or a chaise lounge I'd imagined from my familiarity with psychiatrists in television shows. Instead, the room was set up like a loft apartment, complete with a small kitchenette.

"Do you live here?" I asked, settling onto the black velvet Victorian sofa.

"No, but I could," Dr. Cathway tilted her head slightly as she sat on a loveseat across from me.

"I find it's easier for people to get comfortable in a comfortable setting. So, here we are," she held her hands up, presenting the most unique office I'd ever seen.

"It is comfortable," I forced a smile.

"But you're not. Do you want a cup of tea?"

"No, no... I just wasn't really expecting to meet with you so soon. It was only this morning when I admitted I needed to talk with someone," I rushed to explain, not wanting to offend her.

"And what set that thought in motion?"

Inhaling with wide eyes, realizing I'd walked right into the one topic I neglected to jot down, I decided to forgo the list altogether. "An erotic dream about my husband," I refused to look up and see the reaction on her face.

"Surely an erotic dream about your husband is perfectly healthy. Ideal for many, in fact. Tell me why it bothered you to the point of seeking me out."

"My husband and I are... estranged," the word tickled my tongue. "Well, that might be a strong word. We're not seeing eye to eye."

"Did something happen yesterday, leaving him in the forefront of your mind when you fell asleep?"

"We had a blow-up argument in his office." I finally looked up, but her light brown eyes were without judgement.

"Do you want to talk about this blow up?"

"I didn't," I puckered my lips. "But, I guess it's the things I don't want to talk about that are probably bothering me, huh?"

"This isn't a linear type of solution. I imagine you deal with a lot of problems in your life that can easily be broken down into measurable steps, but this isn't one of them. I can't tell you what issue will unlock inner peace within you, or how to clear your mind. I can only help you work through what you're willing to share."

I watched her for a long pause, admiring her poise and the calm patience she exuded. My staring didn't appear to make her uncomfortable in the least bit. In fact, her eyes seemed to soften with every passing second. Strangely, I trusted her, from that very moment. She was right. I wouldn't be able to think my way through this. I'd have to surrender, finally.

"My parents are rich. Well, really my dad's rich. But they don't have a prenup, so if my mom ever left him, she'd make out alright. So, I guess they're both rich," I reasoned with a shrug of my shoulders.

"He owns hotels across the country; boutique hotels, very high-end. I inherited a bunch of money and entitlement from his success and the life it afforded me, went on to buy a publishing house because I'm too afraid to be a writer myself.

"Got married young. Well, not teenage young, but relatively young. My husband's name is Daniel. He's..." I paused for the first time, looking to the ceiling for the right words to describe him.

"Daniel's very well put together. He's always been that way, or at least as long as I've known him. There's a certain conviction about him. Like he knows exactly what he's doing, what he wants. I don't have that. I'm more of a whimsical person, which I guess goes back to the writer at my core. I like to make up stories, and I'm my favorite protagonist.

"Daniel was cast as the hero of my life novel, but I don't think he knew he was auditioning. I loved him from the day I met him. He wasn't impressed or intimidated by me, and that was... rare."

Again, I paused, glancing at Dr. Cathway. She maintained her poise, watching me carefully without judgment, silently encouraging me to continue. I felt safe.

"He helped me buy my publishing house, and for that I'll always be grateful. I only bought it to prove to him I was a big shot. He was a CEO of his own consultancy firm, and I was – Malcolm Delley's youngest daughter. I wanted him to think I was important; that I was serious about something like him, but I wasn't. I was just a young kid with too much money.

"When he asked me to dinner, I was half shocked. He'd paid me no attention during the entire process of negotiations," I recalled, the memory bringing a small smile.

"Everything about our courtship was storybook. We didn't date,

Daniel courted me. He was so mature, and he treated me so well. I think I've always feared that was an act, probably because of my dad. He puts on this front like the sun rises and sets on my mother, but he's a womanizer. A workaholic addicted to success. I saw so many similarities between him and Daniel, I assumed the uglier traits my father possesses would eventually appear.

"Anyways, my husband and I had a weird 6-months – I filed for divorce, but I didn't want a divorce. He didn't sign it, and we lived as roommates in our house for a while. Finally, I ambushed him for sex out the blue, and we started to rekindle our flame. Things were good, well kind of. We hadn't really worked through what happened between us, but we were remembering how we felt about each other.

"Then, I went through his phone, because my sister heard he'd gone on a date with a woman. I found what I thought were emails extorting him about an affair. I left. Like always, he chased me. But when he finally found me, he didn't play the role of hero, and I had somehow turned into the villain. He was angry, dismissive, all these things I didn't know him to be.

"Turns out the woman was extorting Daniel because she'd discovered my father was a fraud. *Is* a fraud, who knows. Honestly, that part isn't shocking. My dad has always been a fraud, I just thought it was limited to his personal life. Now, my husband is irate with me for even accusing him of cheating. But he did betray me, hiding such a big secret and paying a woman six-figures, which must not have been worth it, because she still told. Maybe he didn't pay her?" I questioned myself.

"I don't know, but he's been ignoring me. I went to his office to seduce him, thinking we could try again. He was..."

Again, I was at a loss trying to describe Daniel. I was apprehensive to say his behavior wasn't who he was, and I wondered if that hesitation was a silent admission that I didn't really know him.

"He was rude. And mean. He spoke to me like he wanted me to hate him, or at least divorce him. No one talks to me the way he did," I looked across to Dr. Cathway to hammer this point home.

"I cried my eyes out after I left his office, then had lunch with my mom. She lifted my spirits, but I was still confused and hurt by Daniel's choice of words. Then, I went to sleep and dreamed of fucking him, but it wasn't even fucking. It wasn't an angry, aggressive erotic dream. It was needy. He cried. I've never seen him cry."

Dr. Cathway stared at me for what felt like an eternity. Unsure if she expected me to continue, I waited for further instruction. Eventually, she nodded, piercing her lips before they parted just enough for her tongue to slide from the left to right corners of her mouth.

"I think you need that tea, Emily. Let's move to the kitchen."

26

I emerged from the limestone ranch a different person. Dr. Cathway hadn't given me any answers, but she did grant me the permission to be free. Opting to walk back to the office, I inhaled without obstruction for what felt like the first time in my life.

Never had I heard my story so bluntly told, and for it to come from my own lips was even more impactful. I was seeing myself with fresh lenses, not the rose-colored ones I preferred to use. Dr. Cathway didn't know me, and I felt no obligation to be anything for her.

I didn't notice the soreness in my jaw until I walked past an ice cream shop, craving the coolness. I'd talked so long I needed a few minutes of silence before returning to work. After ordering two scoops, one vanilla, one coffee, I sat alone in the parlor.

I was blown away by my vulnerability – confused about whether to applaud or scold myself for revealing family secrets. I'd been raised to keep our problems at home, and despite what her reputation might be, Dr. Cathway now had all the dirt I'd worked so hard to conceal.

She could expose me if she wanted, my whole family even. Yet, I didn't care. The freedom I felt was worth any repercussion that could follow. And when my mind did begin to contemplate her possible betrayal, I quieted the fear with a declaration that I would sue her for every penny she had if she chose to sell my secrets.

I returned to the office refreshed, and from the look on Crystal's face, it was evident.

"Do you want to resume today's schedule, Mrs. G?" She asked.

"Call me Emily, Crys," I smiled, feeling indebted to her for not only finding Dr. Cathway, but also for pushing me to go before I was ready. "And, yes, let's keep with the schedule. My sister said my office will be ready in a week, but until then, I need something better. Set me up in the conference room."

"Will do, Emily!" She nodded, turning to get started on her new task.

Slowly, I strolled through the eighteenth floor, avoiding my temporary closet of an office. The open area in the back of Cherry Blossoms Publishing was an extreme contrast to the professional grey lobby.

Designed to spark creativity, a bright mural of a playground covered the furthest wall of the large room, with colorful beanbags scattered throughout. Perched in the doorway, I listened in on a brainstorming session discussing new ways to approach the ever-changing publishing market.

The heated debate captured my attention, as the digital media team argued whether to go with or against online trends. A few randomly placed tables were covered with notebooks, abandoned by their owners when the discussion drew them away.

"I don't care if the top ten sellers are following a reverse harem trope, that's stupid. We're not shifting focus to accommodate every change in charts we know can easily be manipulated." A thin woman argued, pulling her fire red hair into a ponytail as though she was preparing for a fight.

"Fine. If you want to be left behind, you're making the right move. Everyone else will dominate the online charts, but we'll have our integrity. And now that I think of it, my landlord did say I can pay in cashier's check, money order, or integrity. So that works well, Katie," an overweight dark skin man shrugged as a few of his peers laughed at his rebuttal. Wearing a baseball cap turned to the back, and a graphic t-shirt that had seen better days, I remembered hiring him. Racking my mind, I tried to recall his name until Katie helped.

"Cool, Tyler. Be sarcastic; make light of the truth. The trends are bullshit. We can both name three ways to get to the top of the charts without selling one fucking book. So, how are we even arguing about their validity?" Katie shot back, her face flush with passion.

"Because we also know how to capitalize from the top of that list. We know how to get there without selling a book, and we know how to sell ten thousand books once we're there." He held his hand up, motioning as though he were dropping a mic.

"And then what happens, Tyler? You hook someone in to a story you've forced a writer to create, based on a trend. It's not their style, their voice, or their passion. And then, when the trend changes next quarter, you're back to square one. If you want to make a few bucks online, you've got the winning formula. But if you want to develop writers, you're going to fail. And everyone in this room knows it!" She screamed the last sentence as she turned to look around the room, challenging anyone to disprove her theory.

When her light eyes landed on me, she blanched instantly, apology clear in her eyes.

"Don't mind me," I smiled before waving and dismissing myself.

"Really? You guys weren't going to tell me she was there?" I heard Katie gripe as I proceeded to the next open discussion.

The office was buzzing with new ideas and talent. And because of the thoughtful design, conversations were open, encouraging collaboration. Nothing about it was new, but it felt like a foreign experience. I was overwhelmed with pride by the time I circled back to my office.

Victoria had gone so far to conceal her design changes, there was cardboard plastered against the windows into my office.

Curiosity was just about to get the best of me, my need to see what she was doing growing by the second.

"Ready for our status?" Christian's cheery voice turned me around.

"Is that now?" I glanced at my watch.

"Yep! And Crystal says we can use the conference room."

27

It had been two weeks since my father's arrest when Quentin Bolden successfully landed a meeting with me. Partly due to my apprehension about dealing with him, but mostly because I was that busy.

Crystal had done a great job seamlessly integrating me into every faction of the business. I'd met all the new writers, hosted a team building event with the executives, and began scheduling an afternoon getaway for the entire staff. Things were going great.

But regardless how much time passed, Madison was adamant about the possibilities of a deal with Quentin Bolden. After much back and forth, I decided to put my personal feelings aside, willing to talk business if he agreed to keep things more professional.

"I hope I didn't keep you waiting," Quentin's deep voice stole my attention.

"Oh, sorry, lost in my thoughts," I rose to greet him, extending my hand as I forced a smile. "We have a lot to discuss."

"That we do," he smiled, more innocently than he had during our initial meeting. He was less flashy than I'd remembered him, but more handsome.

"I feel like an ugly step child. Why are we meeting here?"

Quentin asked, frowning as he took in the details of the conference room. Mostly charcoal gray, with chrome accents, the room was sparsely decorated by design. I didn't like the idea of meeting with distracted people, so I'd stripped the room of everything but the narrow chrome table and seventeen chairs placed around it.

Sitting at the head of the table, I smiled looking to Quentin, who sat to my left. "My sister's redecorating my office. Supposedly, it should be finished today," I clarified.

The formality of our meeting location didn't cross my mind. Victoria had extended the timeline for redesigning my office twice, refusing to so much as allow me to retrieve files from my desk for fear of ruining her grand reveal.

"So maybe I'll get to see the new and improved digs on our next meeting," Quentin hoped.

"Maybe," I replied, the left corner of my lips curling upwards.

He was less obnoxious without an audience, that much was clear almost immediately. I could tell Quentin was more serious about this meeting from the tailored suit he wore. Navy so dark it could easily be mistaken for black, making his crisp white shirt more striking. His skinny necktie had a simple pattern, stripes of blue and white with subtle hints of powder pink. Listening to him apologize for our miscommunication, I silently wondered how much thought he'd given to his wardrobe selection this morning.

"I'm glad to start over," I assured him once he finished his monologue.

Crossing my legs, I leaned back in my chair. Oversized buttons lined the center of my suede sleeveless shift dress. Slipping one hand into each of the two large pockets positioned against my thighs, I sat silently, forcing Quentin to continue.

"I know you've done your research about my company, but that's not really what I'm about," Quentin carried on, adjusting the simple knot that made his tie even more chic.

"So, what are you about, Mr. Bolden?" I tilted my head in preparation for his next sales pitch.

"I really wish you'd call me 'Q'," he began, licking his lips.

When I failed to respond, he continued. "I named the company Laney Publishing after my grandmother. She raised me alone, and the only thing she loved more than me was books," a genuine smile spread across his face at the thought of his grandmother.

"She was a high school English teacher in Harlem, where I grew up. She would force me to read as a form of punishment," he smirked. "I read a lot of books growing up."

Piercing my lips, I fought the effect of Quentin's infectious smile. I was intrigued. He was right, I had read more intel about him than I'd wanted, but nothing mentioned his grandmother.

"She was ecstatic when I started the business. I knew she was proud, but I wasn't making any money."

"Most businesses aren't profitable in the beginning," I chimed in.

"Sure. But, my grandmother didn't care anything about that. I was taking peoples stories and sharing them around the world. Well, at that time I was barely sharing them around the city, but I was sharing them," Quentin raised his hands and shoulders simultaneously.

"She would come to every hole in the wall bookstore I could convince to open their doors, allowing my writers to share their work. I felt like I was failing, but she always made me believe I was doing the right thing, even if I wasn't getting the right results."

"What results were you looking for?"

"Money!" His eyes lit up as he answered, followed by a soft laugh. His candid smile made him even more attractive. "I was young. I thought that was all that mattered."

"And I'm guessing your values have since changed?" I led him to the conclusion.

"My grandmother left me a hood fortune when she passed," his eyes lifted to meet mine, his smile fading.

"A *hood fortune*?" I repeated, unsure of what he meant.

"It was more money than I'd ever known anyone to have, but it was far from what people like you inherit," he lifted his hand to point to me.

Leaning forward, I felt the disdain rising to my chest. "You don't know what I've inherited," I started my tirade, but Quentin didn't allow me to finish.

"I don't mean that in a bad way. That's my goal in life – to leave my children with more than I knew existed. That's why I want to partner with you," his voice was tender now, his eyes softened with openness.

"I used my small inheritance to build a successful business, but all it makes is money. What I love about Cherry Blossoms Publishing is the confidence you give your writers. It's like money is only a byproduct of what you create, not the driving force behind the business. That's what I want; to get back to the reason I got into publishing in the first place. I have the cash flow. You have the talent. We need each other more than you think," Quentin's eyes were pleading without desperation.

He was a man who knew what he wanted, and despite everything else, I liked that. I would've never thought he had any respect for the art I valued so much. Learning otherwise left me a bit conflicted.

"I appreciate you stopping by," I said, uncrossing my legs as I moved to stand.

"Don't kick me out yet," he rushed to his feet, holding his hands up defensively.

"I'm not kicking you out. I just need to think about what we've discussed. That is your full pitch, right?" I reasoned, a soft chuckle falling from my lips as I straightened the non-existent creases in my burnt orange dress.

"Well, yeah," he paused. "In the mirror, it felt like a longer speech," he flashed his smile again. I imagined that smile had won him many negotiations.

"So, you were practicing this in the mirror, huh?" I chuckled at his honesty.

"Longer than I'll admit to."

We stood in silence for a pregnant moment. I wasn't sure if Quentin was sizing me up, but that's exactly what I was doing. His pitch was good, a much better approach to make the emotional sale, but I wasn't entirely convinced. It didn't take much research to discover how passionate I was about writing, and I did not put it past him to exploit that connection.

"Can I at least have a tour of the office?" Quentin asked, towering over me.

"A tour?"

"Yes. A tour, led by you."

Playfully rolling my eyes, I left the conference room, feeling his presence follow closely behind. Had he requested a tour two weeks ago, I might have shied away, unsure how my staff would react to my presence. But after spending early mornings and late nights getting to know everyone and every project, I was a bit excited at the prospect.

While the Cherry Blossoms office wasn't the grandest in the city, I was proud to show Quentin around. It was obvious he was a people person. He had a question for every person we encountered, asking what they did and how they liked working for me.

After an hour together, I found myself laughing with ease, much more relaxed than I had been preparing for our meeting. We were finishing up our tour of the office when Quentin stopped to admire the view from the eighteenth floor.

"Damn," he mumbled under his breath before turning to me. "Everybody told me the view was enough to make you switch coasts. Now I see why."

"Wait. This is your first time visiting my city?"

"Second. Our first meeting was my first trip, but I was only here for a day," he explained.

"You're kidding me," I said unbelievably as we resumed the walk around the office. I'd read his financials, disinterest was the only reason he'd neglect the trip.

"New York has everything. And when I decide to get away, I want to go where they're speaking a different language," he reasoned.

"Half of LA speaks a different language. You just haven't been to the right neighborhood," I argued with a smile.

"Yeah, neighborhoods are tricky out here. My driver has been clowning me all day. I went to visit a friend who has a studio out in Inglewood. I couldn't believe the famous Rodeo Drive was in the hood," he began when I burst into laughter.

It was a mistake I'd heard out of towners make, blindly trusting the GPS systems without understanding the difference between Rodeo Road and the world renown Rodeo Drive. The former, located in west LA, had nothing more than a name in common with the tourist attraction.

"Okay, so you gonna clown me too?" Quentin nodded sarcastically as I covered my mouth, trying to cap the laughter that refused to stop. Just imagining him peering out the window in search of high end retailers, when he was closer to Crenshaw Mall, sent me into a fit of uncontrollable laughter.

And that's how Daniel saw us.

28

"You alright?" Daniel's tone didn't match the warmth in his eyes.

A weird tinge of guilt traveled down my spine as I struggled to regain my composure. "What are you doing here?" Pronounced cheek bones revealed my amusement.

Daniel's brows rose with shock at my response, and then Quentin spoke, cutting through the thick tension. "Quentin Bolden," he announced, extending his right hand.

"Daniel Gamble," he emphasized our last name as they shook hands.

"Well, I was just leaving. Thanks for the tour, Emily. The city of angels has lived up to its name." Quentin smiled, shaking my hand before nodding to Daniel and excusing himself.

I didn't notice the stares from the office until Daniel leaned in, speaking in a hushed tone, "Can I talk to you in private?"

Glancing around, my attention sent everyone scrambling, rushing to return to work.

"Um... Sure," I managed, finally recovering from Quentin's hilarious story.

Daniel led the way purposefully, his Testoni leather lace ups announcing our path. Paired with a beige tailored suit, I admired Daniel's physique as I followed him through the office. Distracted by my mental attempt to count the days since I'd last seen him, during our blow-up argument in his office, I almost allowed him to ruin my sister's surprise.

"Oh wait! We can't go in there!" I touched his arm just before we reached my office.

"Why not?" His distaste for rejection was clear.

"Victoria is redesigning it, and you know how she gets about her reveals," I shrugged, sure he could remember the week we lived in a hotel while she decorated our home.

Pushing the lust filled memory to the back of my mind, I led us to my temporary office. I was relieved when Daniel instinctively held the heavy door to the conference room.

"Why is she redecorating your office?" He asked as the door closed behind us. I leaned against the wall, unsure if I wanted to sit for whatever had brought him to my office.

"It was never really me," I scrunched my nose. "She came by and decided it needed a facelift."

"I picked most of the furniture," he recalled, the first hint of a smile dancing on his lips.

It had been so long since I was alone with him without an expectation or agenda. Now, at my office, I felt more confident than ever. Watching Daniel fidget with the cuff link at his right wrist, I realized he was the one on his heels.

"So, what brings you here?" I pounced.

"I've been trying to apologize to you. I should have never spoken to you the way I did when you came to my office, Em. I regretted it instantly," he searched my eyes.

"I forgave you a while ago," I assured him, seeing the disbelief on his face.

So much time, alone and with Dr. Cathway, had passed since our explosive argument. The first few days were difficult. I desperately wanted to reach out to him, but pride stopped me. Trusting my mother's advice, that Daniel would eventually come around, I decided to focus on myself. Between work and my mended social life, I hadn't spent much time harping over the details of our dispute.

His eyes scanned from my feet to my eyes before looking towards the door. "Who was that?"

As his eyes locked with mine, I understood the strangeness in his demeanor. "Are you jealous, Daniel?" I let the words fall off my tongue.

"Why would I be jealous?" He flipped it.

"Q is a business prospect," I answered, using Quentin's nickname for the first time as I pushed my hair behind my ear.

"Q?" Daniel repeated.

"Quentin."

"Hmm... He's in publishing?"

"That's what business I'm in, if you remember." I paused, watching him struggle to read me. I could feel the tables turning, fighting my inclination to gloat in the small defeat. "So, what brings you here, Daniel?" I asked again, using his name to emphasize formality.

"Why haven't you seen your parents'?" He asked, pulling out a chair.

"I have. Me and my mom have lunch every week. I'm actually going to meet her after my session," I crossed my arms defensively, unsure of the motive for his questioning.

"Session?" He froze. His hand still on the seatback.

"Oh, yeah. I started going to therapy the day after our blow up. A really nice woman I found in the city," I explained without the shame I expected to accompany the admission.

"I sent you to therapy?" He raised his eyebrows, a mix of shock and guilt creasing his forehead.

"I wouldn't say that. There was a lot I had been bottling up. It was overdue."

"Baby, I'm sorry." His words didn't adequately express the hurt in his eyes. He wanted to reach for me, I could feel it. When I turned away, he sighed, choosing to take a seat instead.

"Why did you ask about my parents?" I ignored his overdue, under-delivered apology.

"You haven't seen your father. He thinks you're avoiding him," Daniel looked up to me with soft eyes.

For so long, I'd wanted him to care without much concern for the source of his emotion. I just wanted to know he still loved me. But now, seeing his brows furrow with the nurturing concern of a caretaker, I was annoyed. He wasn't genuine, disguising how he truly felt as interest for my relationship with my father. Four sessions in with Dr. Cathway, and I could spot deflection from a mile away.

"I'll talk to him," I uncrossed my arms, bringing my hand to my waist as I took one step closer to Daniel's chair.

He perched taller, his lips parting slightly as if he had a thought, but decided against sharing it. He wanted me. It was a signal I would always be able to read. The same signal Quentin had given me just minutes before Daniel's arrival.

"I can set up a lunch with the three of us," Daniel offered, as though it would be a concession on his part.

"No, don't worry yourself. Thanks for stopping by to check on it, but I'll handle it," I smiled without showing my teeth. "Come on, I'll walk you to the elevator."

Daniel's chuckle afforded me the first genuine smile I'd seen from him in weeks. His straight teeth, full lips, and that glorious tongue, all working together to subtly seduce me.

"What's so funny?" I rhetorically asked, fighting the growing urge to straddle him in the conference room.

"Nothing. I see you're busy," Daniel rose from the chair, buttoning his suit jacket.

"Why did you really stop by?"

Daniel paused, licking his lips before swallowing slowly. Watching his Adam's apple adjust, I felt my Kegel muscles tighten. Narrowing his eyes, he looked to me like I was a different woman than he remembered. In many ways, I was.

"Desperation, I guess." He finally admitted, and I softened up, even if only slightly.

"And what are you desperate for?" I tasted the seduction on my tongue as I closed the gap between us.

"Not what you think," he smiled, his hand dropping to my hip. With his thumb on my hip bone, I felt myself losing the edge. "I like your hair," he used the other hand to touch my copper curls.

"Thank you," I turned, releasing my hair from his grasp. Needing space, I backed away, his aura too commanding.

"I just want to talk, Em. That's all I've wanted. I swear," he held his hands up innocently.

"That's not what I just felt." My heart raced from his touch, my body yearning for him.

"Of course, I miss you. All of you," his eyes scanned my body. "But more than anything, I want you to know I'm sorry. And I'm ready to talk whenever you are."

"Okay, maybe we can talk later. I have to get to my session and then meet my mom," I looked to the door, not trusting myself to stare into his eyes again.

"I'll let you get back to your schedule, but I would really like if you could call me later." He calmly pleaded before exiting the conference room, holding the door open for me to follow.

"You'll have to invite me back when Victoria finishes the office." Daniel made casual conversation during the short walk to the elevator.

"You don't need an invitation. I'm not as harsh about unannounced visits," I answered facetiously.

"I deserved that," he nodded, half smiling as he looked over to me.

"See you later, Daniel," I smiled as the elevator arrived, purposely excusing myself without embracing him. I could feel his eyes on me every step of the way, but I refused to turn around. It was his turn to chase me.

29

"Where'd Danny boy go?" Victoria asked as I turned the corner leading to my office.

"Oh, he was just stopping by," I lied, but my sister wasn't buying it.

"He told me he was trying to get you back. You've been avoiding him?" She moved in closer, whispering.

"Is the office ready?" I noticed the cardboard missing for the first time as I moved towards the door before she could jump in my path.

"Wait! I have to announce it," she grinned, excited to reveal her work.

"You're so dramatic," I shook my head, crossing my arms as she carried on.

"You're my baby sister, and by far the most successful woman I know. I wanted you to have an office that spoke both to your personality, and your boss status. So, without further ado, here is your new and improved office!" Victoria eagerly opened the front door, which was no longer made of glass, but instead a thick oak stained with blush undertones. A gold nameplate hung at the new entrance, 'Emily Gamble', with 'CEO' in cursive beneath it.

I'd expected nothing more than a change in furniture, but as I walked inside, I realized how seriously my sister had taken the project. It felt like a completely new room.

Gone were the masculine finishes, replaced by an inspiring colorful pallet. A neon yellow tufted sofa was the centerpiece of the room. In front sat a contemporary coffee table, featuring a mini bar beneath the glass top, with two fire red womb chairs and matching ottomans positioned on the opposite side. A vibrant, multi colored rug stole my attention. Looking so much like a painting, I had to kneel to touch it.

"It's dope, right?" Victoria asked, following me around the office wearing the biggest grin.

Two thick white metal rope chains hung from the ceiling, holding my desk, which was essentially a thick sheet of glass. Carefully, I tried to move it, but it didn't budge.

"It's just an illusion," Victoria explained, watching me closely. "It's not really hanging like this – it's actually reinforced steel. You couldn't move this desk if you wanted to."

My computer was the same iMac pro, but she'd added graffiti to the back, tagged like an alleyway. My name was painted in block letters, my maiden name added in smaller font at the bottom corner. The largest of the tags was 'Cherry Blossoms Publishing', which brought a tear to my eye as pride bloomed in my chest.

"It's not actually on the computer. It's an overlay. All your files and everything are intact. I didn't mess anything up," Victoria added, still following closely.

Towards the front of the office was a small area for group work. A wooden base the same neon color as the sofa made a three dimensional 'X' shape that held a circular glass table top. Four clear silicone chairs surrounded the table, with a white hanging hammock finishing up the corner décor.

"Okay, I have two more things to show you, and then I'm done," Victoria nervously announced, taking my wrist as she led me to the back of the office.

She'd managed to convert what used to be a dated sink and

toilet to a modern bathroom equipped with a small shower and sleek, square shaped toilet. I was blown away as she dragged me back to my desk.

"Now, I know how much you loved your two-way mirror windows, but they were just so outdated. I've been watching you in your environment, and I don't think it's the vibe you need as a boss. You like to engage with everyone, and you want them to be able to see you," she explained.

It was the first time I noticed the wall of windows lining my office were now clear. Every passerby was gawking at the new design, smiling with admiration. While I used to enjoy the mysteriousness behind my two-way mirror wall, it was nice to be a part of the office.

"You still have your incredible view this way," she turned towards the other line of windows, framing my favorite view of the city. "And now you have the view of the office, too," she reasoned.

It was a big change, but with all the improvements she'd made, I wasn't going to complain about something as little as a privacy wall. When I really needed discretion, I could go into my new bathroom.

"When you do want time to yourself, or have a meeting and don't want everyone to see what's going on, you just hit this button," she tapped on a small keypad on the desk. "And the glass changes to this custom overlay. You can still see out, but they can't see in."

I gasped as the glass transitioned, revealing white cherry blossom flowers with blush buds. From the smile on her face, I could tell this was her grand finale, and it was deserving. I had never imagined something so uniquely perfect.

"Okay, you haven't said a word. Give me something!" She whined as I continued to walk around, stunned that this was my office.

"I'm afraid I'm going to cry if I say anything," I rushed the words, glancing over to see her jumping in circles.

"So, you love it?" She stopped, smiling so big the small dimple appeared on her left cheek.

"I love it so much I want you to redesign the whole floor."

Knowing how excited I was to work in my new office, I wanted to gift the entire staff with an improved workspace.

"Really?" She shrieked.

"Well, first I need to see the final bill," I quickly added. She'd stopped sending the mounting invoices.

"Danny boy paid them," she smirked.

"What? When?" My attitude quickly shifted.

"He couldn't get you on the phone one day, so he called me hoping we were together. When I told him you were giving me shit about the renovation costs, he said to send the bills to his office."

"You didn't think to tell me this?"

"He asked me not to. Plus, I figured you'd have this whole independent look you're giving me now. If I was stuck with your budget, I would've been shopping at Ikea," she waved me off.

Gripping my chest, I bent over as an unexpected roar of laughter fell from my lips. Victoria had always poked fun at my cheap spending habits. It was the reason I hired people to shop for me, certain I could never approve such extravagant purchases.

"Don't be mad. He just wanted to do something nice for you," she whispered, pulling me to her side.

"I still want to know how much it was," I noted with a smile.

"And I still want to know what's going on with you and Daniel. He's worried about you, Em," she turned to face me as her tone shifted from playful to concerned.

"I don't know," I sighed. "So much has changed. I honestly haven't had time to think about it."

After Daniel's silent treatment, my issues with him were no longer the mountain they once appeared to be. When he shut me out, I sought other ways to find answers I thought depended on him.

Strolling into my office after such a long break was less than impressive, borderline offensive. I finally understood why he wasn't thrilled by my impromptu visit.

"Well, you need to make time. That's your husband, Emily," Victoria frowned, confused by my response.

"I'm aware, Victoria. It's just bigger than him, now. I don't feel rushed to fix things on his schedule. It's been over a week since I even spoke to him."

"He said he's been trying to reach you," she argued in his defense.

It was something he'd mentioned in the conference room, but I hadn't ignored any calls or texts from him. "He must have been sending smoke signals," I joked.

"He loves you," Victoria added when I plopped down on the neon sofa.

"And I love him," I answered honestly, leaving out the question of whether love was enough.

After watching me lounge, Victoria thankfully dropped the topic, joining me on the sofa instead.

30

"So, Daniel showed up unannounced, and you learned he secretly paid for the office renovations you love so much. But how does that make you feel?" Dr. Cathway's calm voice was more soothing than the lavender mint tea sitting in front of me.

She had an extensive teacup collection, and I'd spent over ten minutes picking the perfect one. With gold trimming, my mug featured a simple pink design and matching coaster, plucked from a fairy tale.

"I don't know. In a way, I'd forgotten about our problems." I stared at the ceiling, wishing answers were written in the pristine crown molding I presumed to be original.

"Had you forgotten about Daniel?" She asked as she scribbled something onto her notepad, a prop she'd introduced in our second session.

"No."

It was the quickest answer I'd given since we started. I couldn't deny how often and regularly I thought of Daniel, usually dressed in a gray suit or nothing at all. I missed the good parts of our relationship, but had no interest in rehashing all that had gone wrong.

"Maybe you don't want to address the difficult conversations you associate with a reunion."

I'd come to assume either Dr. Cathway was a psychic in a former life, or I was more obvious than I thought. She never failed to call me on my shit, and despite how annoying it was at times, I liked it.

"Let's change course for a second," she continued when I twisted my lips silently. "Why don't you like your husband doing nice things for you? Like secretly paying for your office renovations? That seems to bother you."

"He messed up, and now he's doing these things," I explained.

"So, does he not spoil you with monetary presents when he is in your good graces?"

"Yes, he does. Daniel is always very thoughtful and generous," I assured her, hoping not to misrepresent him.

"Then why do you associate his gift giving in these more difficult times as a consolation of sorts? That *is* how you see it, right? Or am I misunderstanding something?"

"No, you're right. It feels like he's trying to buy my forgiveness." I knew the source of the feeling from the taste of the words.

"Your hesitation; the way you answered, leads me to believe you've just had a revelation of sorts," she correctly read me again.

"It's my dad. He would do that with my mom. It became so obvious, whenever she got a new car, or a vacation home, my sister and I would concoct stories about what he'd done. It was never a gift for good times. There were always strings attached."

Thinking back to Daniel's visit, I tried to remember the way he looked at me, wondering if there was guilt in his eyes. I remembered the sincerity of his apology and dismissed the possibility he wanted to buy my forgiveness. If my sister wasn't such a gossip, I'd probably never know he paid the invoices.

"Understandably, you've placed that assumption on Daniel. Do you think this is also the catalyst for the tit-for-tat nature in your marriage?"

"What 'tit-for-tat' nature?" I could hear the defensiveness in my voice.

"When you discuss your marital issues, it seems you are aiming for fairness. Everything is centered around evening the score. Take today, for example. You describe your husband's vulnerability as vindication. Rather than meeting him with understanding, you chose to escort him out."

"He did the same to me!"

"That's the tit-for-tat nature I'm speaking of. You describe your relationship as though it is a fight. When Daniel says, or does something that hurts you, you in turn look for a way to reciprocate the injury."

"It's not fair for him to expect anything more after the way he treated me," I argued.

"Have you ever considered you might be seeking the wrong outcome? Marriage is more about balance than fairness," Dr. Cathway paused as I took in her powerful statement. "How did you really feel when you saw Daniel? What were your true thoughts?"

The more I thought of him, the more one detail stuck out. It was all I could think of, and so I told Dr. Cathway. "He was so sexy!" I rolled my eyes miserably before taking a sip of tea.

"You often talk about good qualities in your husband as if they're hindrances. Do you not enjoy having an attractive spouse?"

"It makes it hard to think. I can't block out the way my body reacts to him to focus on my mind. In here, I can sift through my thoughts, and find the words to express myself. With him, I feel suffocated by his presence and just want to surrender," I looked up, hoping my words made sense to her.

"Do you think Daniel values your feelings?" She tilted her head as she asked this.

"Yes. I know he does." I answered quickly.

"And do you value his?"

This one stumped me. I'd never thought of Daniel requiring much attention in that capacity. He was a leader, an astute businessman, and very traditional in his ways. When prompted, he never seemed to hide his feelings, but without my pushing it wasn't something he freely discussed.

"He doesn't really talk about his feelings," I finally answered.

"I think you're misunderstanding the question," Dr. Cathway began, her subtle way of addressing my deflection. "I'm not asking about Daniel's actions. I'm asking if you value Daniel's feelings. And before you answer, know that if you tell me you do, I'm going to follow that up with a request for supportive evidence."

"No."

"No, what?"

Now, she was being annoying. "No, I don't value Daniel's feelings," I stubbornly admitted.

"I think that's a big admission. We should stop there for the day," she suggested.

My sessions with Dr. Cathway were indisputably the fastest hours of my life. It seemed her limestone ranch possessed time shifting powers that continuously left my head spinning.

"But what do I do about that?" I begged for answers I knew she would refuse to give.

"It depends what you want," she shocked me, steering away from her usual template answer about not having solutions.

"What do you mean?"

"Well, if you want to continue not valuing your husband's feelings, you don't need to do anything. But if you do want to value his feelings, I'd start by trying to identify how he feels."

Dr. Cathway closed her notebook, heading to the kitchen, as she did after every session. I followed slowly, contemplating her advice. It was a routine we were developing. I washed the teacups, leaving them on the drying rack before she came behind me with a folded towel, carefully drying each dish before placing it in the cabinet.

"You can be very hard on yourself at times, Emily," she spoke in a softer tone than usual.

"You think so?" I challenged. I'd always felt I let myself off the hook at every opportunity.

"You police yourself more than you do those around you. Constantly, you're looking for an angle that makes you a manipulator, or insensitive. When it comes to other people, you assume the best. Why don't you give yourself the benefit of the doubt?"

"That's too dangerous. If I gave myself a way out, I'd take it every time," I laughed softly, knowing myself too well.

"But maybe that's not the case." She squinted, looking to me with concern. "You love your husband. You miss him. Even if that emotion is only manifesting in a physical form, it doesn't mean you won't be able to maintain your other, more introspective emotions, by appeasing your desires."

"You think I can have sex and still seek a resolution on our problems?" I asked for clarity.

"Why don't you?"

"Because I've had sex with my husband."

Dr. Cathway gave me the first unguarded smile since I'd met her, flashing perfectly straight teeth as she rose to close the cabinet.

"Well, to recount your thoughts back to you, because you know that is what I do, right?" She asked the same question she'd ended the prior two sessions with.

"Yes, I get that now."

"You told me you had problems with your husband's lack of planning for your birthday last year, and that it bothers you when he focuses on work as opposed to pouring into your marriage. Is that correct?" While I wasn't sure where she was going, I knew it would leave me exposed.

"That's correct," I answered slowly.

"But you've had sex with Daniel since these events took place, right?"

"Yes," I smiled, realizing her intended point.

"Then it appears you can experience sexual gratification without dissolving your feelings. You are just choosing to focus on said gratification rather than addressing those feelings."

"So, I should do both?"

"I'm not here to tell you what to do. But hear me out – you do have the power and emotional intelligence to experience sexual pleasure while also expressing how you feel. They do not have to happen simultaneously, and one does not cancel out the other. You can have both, if you want."

"Sex has always been the barometer of our relationship," I explained, disbelieving her dangerous proposal. "When things are bad, it's a drought. If I open myself up to him sexually, he will naturally think things are resolved."

"That's why communication is so important. Clarity brings about clear expectations, Emily. When you're open and honest about what you want, there's no place for confusion."

"Dr. Cathway, did you just give me my first answer?" I teased, nudging her with my hip.

"You better get out of here before I charge you for another hour!" We both laughed.

After Daniel's ambush, it was nice to unpack. Although there were still lingering questions floating throughout my mind, I was much lighter when I left Dr. Cathway's office.

With my driver waiting, I headed to lunch with my mother, ready for an unadulterated perspective on my husband's antics.

31

Whispering to the driver as he held the Mercedes car door, I could tell my mother disapproved of my restaurant selection before she crossed the street. Joan's on Third had been one of my favorites since I bought Cherry Blossoms Publishing. Close enough to the office, but far enough to ensure I didn't bump into employees, it was perfect.

"Mom! Over here!" I waved, unwilling to leave my table unattended.

Joan's had indoor and outdoor seating, but I preferred the patio tables. You couldn't secure the seat until you received a numbered place card after ordering, so I waved her over from the round wooden table.

"Darling, I thought I had the wrong place. This is..." My mother's smile turned downwards as she looked around, the distaste obvious.

"Mom, it's delicious. Just sit down," I fought back the urge to laugh.

"Emily, do they even have a decent bottle of wine here?" She frowned, sitting across from me in the wooden chair.

"They don't serve wine, but –" I stopped, holding my hand up as she stood from the table, waving to her driver. "Mom, sit down!" I aggressively whispered, tugging on her wrist.

"Yes, ma'am?" The driver appeared, even stockier than I'd remembered.

"Be a doll and run to the liquor store," she leaned over.

"Mom, that's not necessary," I whispered across the table.

The two exchanged a look, with my mother nodding authoritatively before the brown skin man excused himself. Pleased, she turned back towards me, her smile reappearing.

"So, is this one of the eclectic places you like to go?" She asked with a tight smile.

"This is far from eclectic, mom." I raised my hand, alerting the waitress at the end of the patio dining area.

"Are you ready to order?" She approached us with a wide smile.

"Yes, please. We'll have a bottle of sparkling lemonade, and I want to take my mother inside to order from the buffet line," I smiled.

"Buffet?" My mother's face hid nothing.

"Come on, mom," I pulled her inside while the waitress assigned our numbered place card.

Arm in arm, I walked her around the small deli style display of foods, pointing to my favorites as she pierced her lips, glancing around with suspicion.

"I love the mac and cheese," I pointed to the exposed pan behind the thick glass.

"It's cold, Emily," she sneered.

"They heat it up, mom."

"Do they make anything fresh?"

"Yeah, you can order something from the menu, but this is what I always get." I ordered a small portion of macaroni and cheese and a piece of vegetarian lasagna.

"I'll order from the menu. I didn't plan on eating leftovers," she rubbed her fingers together uncomfortably until I finished.

Back at our patio table, she glanced over the menu as the waitress waited patiently to take her order. "To be clear, this will be made as I order, correct?"

"Yes, ma'am. Everything from the menu is made to order," the waitress cheerfully explained.

"Okay. I'll have the French toast, please," she politely handed the menu to the waitress before turning to me. "So, how is your day going?"

Smiling at the waitress as she gathered my menu, I waited for her absence to answer. "It was a really busy morning," I paused to remove the plastic topper from the glass pitcher of lemonade.

"Yes, I remember you telling me the overzealous New Yorker had finagled a meeting with you," she recalled just as her driver arrived, discreetly handing her a Starbucks paper bag.

"Thank you, darling," she accepted the bag before gently placing it on the chair next to her. Reaching her dainty hand into the bag, she retrieved a plastic Starbucks cup containing a clear liquid and placed it on the table.

"Mom, I know that's not –"

"Tell your story. The obnoxious publisher from New York," she waved her hand in circles, encouraging me to continue before pouring a bit of what I knew to be vodka into each glass of lemonade.

"He's actually not obnoxious. At least not as much as I thought. He explained more of the reason he got into publishing, and it helped me better understand him." I sipped the lemonade, which was even better with my mother's addition.

"Good, right?" She smiled, sipping from her own glass.

"His name is Quentin... Well, he tells me to call him Q. He's completely self-made, one of those 'from the ground up' stories," I smiled, recalling the memories he shared about his grandmother. Maybe it was guilt for the head start my parents' success had afforded me, but I always admired the dedication and faith it took to build something on your own.

"And he's jaw dropping handsome, right?" She interrupted me.

"What?" I feigned shock, hoping the real answer wasn't written on my face.

"I talked to Victoria while you were parading him around the office as Daniel watched. Was that part of your act?" She boldly asked.

"Mom!" I screeched, annoyed by her suggestion.

"You're telling me, you really didn't know the man was there watching you?" She smiled mischievously.

"No! I had no idea. I don't need to make Daniel jealous," I argued.

"But you did," she claimed just as the waitress arrived with my meal.

Gritting my teeth, I bit back my rebuttal, flashing a polite smile as I waited impatiently for the waitress to leave me alone with my mother.

"I absolutely love our mac," the blonde woman excitedly added, placing my plate on the table.

"Yes, it's my favorite." I managed, tapping my fingernails against the table, pushing aside the glass pitcher to make room for my lasagna.

"And your French toast should be out in no time," she turned to my mother, who didn't even acknowledge her.

"I was in a meeting, mom. How was I supposed to know Daniel was going to pop up?" I sliced into my lasagna. "He didn't even call to let me know he was coming."

"Hmm..." She hummed, sipping her lemonade.

"He said he's been reaching out to me, but I haven't gotten any calls," I recalled his claim as I took my first bite of lasagna, inhaling deeply as the explosion of flavors sent me into foodie heaven.

"Because I blocked him."

My eyes shot open with shock, certain I'd misheard her. "You what?"

"Finish your food, dear," she pointed to my plate.

The waitress reappeared. This time, with a tower of French toast and a glass maple syrup dispenser on a brown tray. Again, I tapped the table, anxious to reconvene our conversation as the waitress took her time placing the plates on the table.

"I think you're both all set. Is there anything else –"

"That's it. Thank you," I blurted, unable to wait another second. The blonde smiled, seemingly unbothered by my rudeness, before walking away.

"Don't make a big deal of this," my mother brushed me off before I could begin, carefully slicing into her French toast. "You needed some time to think, and Daniel wasn't going to give it to you."

"When did you even... How did you block him?" I asked, reaching for my cell phone.

"After lunch at The Ivy. You said he was a jerk, he needed to learn a lesson. According to Victoria, he has."

Half listening, I scrolled through my settings, unsure of how to block someone. Finally, I found the correct tab and sure enough, there was his name in red font.

"Mom," I started, shaking my head, but words failed me. It was such an invasion of privacy, yet I was grateful for her overstep. She was right, I did need the week to myself. With all I had going on at the office, I hadn't thought much about his lack of communication.

"Oh, stop. You're not mad." She insisted.

Tapping on the phone, I unblocked his number before returning to my texts, waiting for the missed messages to emerge. He said he had been trying to reach out to me, and while I was glad I wasn't sucked back into his vortex, I did want to know what he'd sent.

"They don't just reappear, Emily. They're gone." She chuckled behind her vodka lemonade.

"You're enjoying this, aren't you?"

She smiled. "You kids think I don't know how to use a phone, and here you are unsure of how to block someone. It is pretty clever, if I do say so myself."

My imagination began to run wild wondering what Daniel had texted. How many times had he called me? There was so much I didn't know, and honestly would never be able to find out. Already looking forward to my next session, I yearned to hear Dr. Cathway's take on my mother's behavior.

It changed everything about Daniel's unannounced visit, filling me with guilt. Not only because I'd been inadvertently ignoring him, but also because now that I knew, I wasn't ready to reopen the line of communication. Quickly tapping on my screen, I searched for his name before blocking his contact again.

"How did he look?" My mother interrupted my actions, a childish grin spreading across her face.

Unable to hide my reaction, I matched her smile until we were both giggling like school girls. "Good as always."

"At least you were cute. I like this color you've added. Is it permanent?" She asked. I knew she hoped it wasn't. My mother never approved of us doing anything drastic with our hair.

"It will fade."

Picking from one pasta dish and then the other, I let my thoughts drift. This wasn't typical behavior for me. I was dying to know what Daniel was thinking. Throughout our entire relationship, I had never been unavailable to him. Remembering the look on his face in the conference room, I began to feel empowered by what he described as desperation.

"I miss him," I finally admitted to my mother.

"Of course, you do. He's your husband. What exactly do you miss about him, though?" She pressed, the pull at the corner of her lip revealing her lustful assumption.

"I do miss that," I smiled, deciding against sharing my recent wet dream, or how acquainted I'd become with the handheld shower head in my suite.

"Just be careful, sweetheart. You're upset with Daniel, but everything up to this point can easily be forgiven. Don't add infidelity to the mix," she warned.

"Mom," I gasped. In all our troubles, I'd never considered cheating on Daniel.

"Emily, you can't see your eyes when you speak about this

Quentin, but I can." She glared into my eyes before finishing her lemonade. Pushing her plate of barely touched French toast to the center of the table, she unceremoniously ended our lunch date.

Her warning stole my appetite. The shame built in my abdomen as I questioned my behavior with Quentin. Sure, he was handsome, and I did enjoy our banter, but was it sexual? I didn't think I was attracted to him, but now that my mother mentioned it, I couldn't release the thought.

32

Of all the new looks Monica had delivered to my hotel suite, my favorite was a black Alice + Olivia dress. Subtle sex appeal was my style, and the fit and flare cut personified just that. Faux pearls connected the mock neck top to the bottom of the dress, leaving one inch of skin exposed at the belly and another just above my knee. Paired with black Gianvito Rossi corset pumps, I felt like a million bucks walking into the office.

Crystal's reaction to my arrival always revealed how well I'd done with my wardrobe selection. The look on her face said I'd hit it out the park.

"Don't start," I failed to hide my bashful grin as I approached her desk.

"I'm going to start an Instagram page for these fashions if you keep it up," she playfully teased, reaching for her clipboard before following me into my new colorful office.

Pushing my hair behind my ears, I exposed the large pearl earrings, a graduation gift from my mother. I settled into the desk chair, waking my computer with a shake of the mouse.

"Seriously. You look so refreshed. Whatever you're doing, keep it up. And if you can, bottle some up so we can make a fortune," Crystal joked as she settled onto the neon sofa.

"You're already working on another raise?" I referenced the well-deserved salary bump she'd recently received.

Crystal covered her mouth to muffle the laughter as I pulled up my schedule, frowning at the many appointments. "Today's jam packed, huh?" I looked over the meetings, tapping my chin with the tip of my manicured fingernail.

"Yes and no," Crystal answered, jumping into professional mode. I'd grown to value our relationship even more. Beyond her assistant duties, Crystal had grown to be one of my closest friends. Spending every day together had created a bond I often took for granted. I was certain I could not be as successful without her.

"Everything in the afternoon is optional. They're mostly brainstorming sessions you'll be sitting in on. You can stay as long as you'd like, or not go altogether. Completely up to you. The most important thing is Christian's proposal. The deadline for your approval is tomorrow morning, so you need to read through everything before the day's over," Crystal explained, sliding a paper copy of the schedule onto my glass desk.

"I see," I noted, logging in to check my emails. Christian's proposal had been sitting on the coffee table of my suite for the past four days, but I hadn't dedicated any time to reading through it.

"Madison is first up," Crystal looked over her shoulder before continuing. "She is dying to tell you something. She's been really secretive about it, waiting for you to get in," she leaned over my desk, speaking lowly.

Raising my eyebrows with disinterest, we shared a look before I rolled my eyes, sending us both into a fit of laughter.

A knock on the door silenced us, as Madison appeared on cue. Crystal diverted her eyes to her clipboard. "You also have two messages. A Matthew called, but he wouldn't leave any info," she read from her notes.

"Matthew?" I racked my brain but came up empty.

"I told him you'd be in soon and he said he'd call back," she said. "Oh, and Mr. Gamble called. He said he'd try your cell."

My stomach fluttered as I nodded, hoping my panic wasn't visible. "I'll call him back. Thanks, Crystal."

Over the course of the night, I'd contemplated unblocking Daniel's number but ultimately decided against it. I wasn't ready to face the music, finally initiating the talk we both knew needed to happen.

"Come on in, Madison," I waved towards the door, causing a bright smile to spread on her blushing face.

"You're not going to believe what happened!" She began, walking quickly towards my desk. "Quentin sent these over!"

Extending her hand across my desk, she flashed two tickets to the Lakers game. "It's one of the last games of the season!"

"Oh? Are you a basketball fan?" I smiled, trying to muster up a little energy to match her excitement.

I'd never been much of a sports fan, so the idea of sitting through a basketball game was anything but appealing. Madison's face dropped as she sucked her teeth with disappointment.

"Oh, come on! It's the Lakers!" She argued. "And he's got one of those VIP suites. You don't even have to watch the game – I've heard the restaurants are top of the line, and everything is on the house!"

I nodded, my mother's warning still ringing loudly in my ears. Quentin had made it clear that he wanted to do business together, and while I thought it could be promising, I didn't want to have any extra time with the man for leisure.

"I've drawn up the analysis you asked for. I knew you would want to discuss the details with Quentin. He thought it would be more fun to meet at the Staples Center. I have to say, I like his thinking," she reasoned, placing a thick folder on my desk.

"This is a lot of analysis," I lifted the folder, already overwhelmed by the report.

"Don't worry. I'm going to walk you through everything. If there's more to discuss after we go over it, we'll go to the *awesome* meeting at the Lakers game. If not, we'll cancel."

I laughed, knowing which way Madison was leaning. Crystal buzzed through my new intercom system just as I opened the packet.

"Mrs. G, Matthew is back on line one. Want to take it?" She asked.

"Uh, yeah. Let me see what this is about."

Lifting the receiver, I pressed the illuminated button. "This is Emily Gamble."

"Emily! Oh, my god! I can't believe this worked," the high-pitched voice chimed through the line, as I frowned trying to place the voice.

"Who is this?"

"I'm sorry. You probably don't remember me. I'm technically not allowed to do this, so please don't be upset," he continued and I instantly recalled the thin blond man from the front desk of the Britton Hotel.

"Oh, Matthew! Yes, I remember," I smiled, returning my attention to the folder Madison had placed on my desk.

"I tried the number associated with your credit card, but I was told I had the wrong number. So, I googled you, and umm... I'm not supposed to do that," he whispered into the phone.

"Don't worry. What's wrong?"

"You've received a few deliveries. Would you like them sent to your office, perhaps?" He asked.

"Deliveries?" I paused reading the analysis.

"Yes, one a day since you checked out."

Hesitating, I wondered what they could be. Monica had only been given my suite at the Four Seasons for deliveries. "Uh, sure. I'll put you back on with my assistant. She'll give you the details."

"Perfect. Thanks so much, Emily." I could hear his smile through the line.

"No problem. Have a great day, Matthew."

After transferring the call back to Crystal, I sent a quick memo from my computer, instructing her to compensate Matthew for his effort. An alert I assumed to be Crystal's response caught my attention, but instead it was an email from Daniel.

33

Is this thing on?

From: Daniel Gamble
Gamble@TowerEnterpriseGroup.com
Date:May 23, 2018
To:Emily Gamble
Emily@CherryBlossomsPublishing.com

I think this might be the first email I've ever written you. It feels too formal.
I guess I should attach a spreadsheet of all the ways I fucked up. Keep it professional.
Emily, I'm sorry.
Please call me.

Daniel
CEO Tower Enterprise Group

"Okay! Shall we begin?" I turned at the sound of Madison's

voice. She was eagerly waiting, her eyes gleaming with excitement as mine pooled with remorse.

"Just give me one second," my voice cracked as I stood from my desk. Using all the control I could muster, I rushed to the bathroom before my emotions poured out of me.

Locking the door behind me, I placed one hand on each cheek, inhaling deeply as I stared at my reflection. There was something about reading his words that cut so deep.

On one hand, it felt like I'd blossomed into a new and improved version of myself, independent of the husband who once defined me. On the other hand, the strings that tethered us together tugged at a gaping emotional wound I'd been denying.

Daniel deserved a response, that much I knew. My last session with Dr. Cathway reminded me to value his feelings. I just wasn't sure how to do that without neglecting my own. It was clear he wanted to talk, but I wasn't sure I was ready.

So much had happened. I didn't want to unwrap everything; not with all I already had going on. He deserved my undivided attention, and I wasn't prepared to give it to him.

The conflicting thoughts left me confused and exhausted. My desire to see him was strong, but maybe it was for the wrong reason. I wanted Daniel to make me forget what had happened between us, even if only for a night. But that wasn't fair to his needs. I wasn't sure how to rectify the two.

Closing my eyes, I forced the thoughts from my mind. "One..." I whispered before inhaling deeply. With an important meeting on the other side of the door, I had to pull it together.

"Two..." I silently promised to find a resolution if I could just make it through the work day.

"Three..." I felt my shoulders drop with the last breath, opening my eyes to see a less frantic reflection.

Madison nervously fidgeted in her seat as I crossed the room. She wasn't her normal confident self, a trait I always valued in her. While she wasn't the most social person, when it came to the numbers, Madison never shied away from the spotlight.

"Alright, let's get to this!" I clapped my hands on my way to my seat. Madison perked up, reaching for the thick packet sitting on the coffee table.

"If you'll turn to page seven, you'll see why I think this is a great idea. Each point is detailed throughout the packet, but this is a general breakdown," she wasted no time getting to business. Her normal vigor returned, so I excused what I thought was apprehension as I listened closely to her findings.

Madison had gone above and beyond with research, so we opted to skip the morning status to focus on her assessment. Using projections and cost-benefit analysis, she explained how merging with Laney Publishing could serve us in more ways than we initially anticipated.

One of my biggest concerns was sharing executive power. The fear of a constant power struggle made merging undesirable. Madison had considered this possibility and arranged a compromise with Quentin.

A board would be established, with equal representation from each side. In short, we would grant voting rights like a corporation, ensuring fair and equitable decisions on both ends. Sparing no detail, Madison worked her way through the in-depth study, answering my questions with the knowledgeable advice I'd come to expect from her.

We'd just completed the final breakdown of projections when Crystal led a line of employees into my office, each carrying a large bouquet of flowers.

"Matthew forwarded the deliveries, Mrs. G," she announced as I watched skeptically before pointing to different areas to place the beautiful arrangements.

As everyone filed out my office, I inched towards the first vase filled with yellow roses, taking the card from the plastic holder.

I'VE BEEN IN THIS FLOWER SHOP,

TRYING TO CRAFT A CLEVER MESSAGE,

FOR 2-HOURS.

BABY, I AM SO SORRY.

My heart dropped. This was how Daniel had been trying to apologize. There were ten bouquets in total, one for every day since I'd left his office.

I HAD NEVER SEEN THIS FLOWER UNTIL YOU CARRIED IT DOWN THE
AISLE.
NOW, EVERY TIME I SEE ONE, MY HEART SKIPS,
THINKING OF THE BEST DAY OF MY LIFE.
THE DAY YOU BECAME MRS. GAMBLE.
I LOVE YOU.

A flutter in my heart caused me to inhale sharply, gripping the edge of the round glass table the bouquet sat on. The sight of peach ranunculus flowers would always take me back to my wedding day. I had no idea Daniel remembered. He was so nonchalant about our wedding details, always the calm and collected partner I needed. Reading his recollection brought a wave of emotions. Moving to the next bouquet, this one filled with sunflowers, I read the card with tears in my eyes.

REMEMBER THAT TIME I SENT YOU SUNFLOWERS
AND FORGOT TO SIGN MY NAME?
YOU CALLED TO TELL ME SOMEONE
SENT YOU SOME UGLY ASS FLOWERS.
I HAVEN'T SIGNED A CARD SINCE.

A smile spread across my face as a tear slid down my cheek, the emotion too rich to contain. Laughing softly, I recalled the day, very early in our courtship. Always a gentleman, Daniel sent a bouquet of flowers following every date, a gesture I later grew accustomed to.

"I know it's not a done deal, but after hearing all that, don't you think it's at least worth another conversation?" Madison asked, jolting me back to the discussion I'd already forgotten about.

"Huh? Oh, right... We can go to the game," I answered absent-mindedly.

My thoughts were consumed by Daniel, and how neglected he must feel. Not only had his calls and texts gone unanswered, he'd been sending personalized floral arrangements daily, and I had no idea.

"Great! Quentin is sending a car for us, so we can leave from the office. I'm so excited!" Madison gathered her things in a rush, leaving my office as instant regret made it difficult to breath.

I knew it was a bad idea to spend an evening with Quentin, but I had to do what was best for my company if I wanted to be taken seriously as a business woman. I'd have to figure out what was best for me and Daniel later.

34

Quentin sent a limousine to chauffeur us to the Staples Center, which I thought was a bit over the top. At some point in the day, Madison had changed from the t-shirt and jeans she'd worn to our morning meeting. Now, she sat beside me in an olive jumpsuit and black block heels. Her brown hair fell past her shoulders in messy waves.

"Regardless of what comes of these negotiations, I'm just grateful for the opportunity to work so closely with you, Emily." Madison announced, struggling to open the bottle of Rosé champagne left for us.

"It has been fun, hasn't it? I always thought you were the best at what you do. This whole process has really affirmed that for me," I smiled, taking the bottle from her before easily opening it.

"There's so much I can learn from you. I've always looked to you as like a mentor in my head, because one day I want to have my own publishing house," Madison shared, taking a large gulp of the champagne.

"The idea of running a company terrifies me. It seems like so many moving pieces, but you make it look easy," she gushed, finishing her drink before refilling the glass.

I sipped slowly as Madison spent the rest of the ride revealing how much she admired me. Never one to discuss more than the business at hand, I was a bit taken aback by her rare candidness and honesty.

She had a point. For everything the Quentin situation lacked, it was undeniably an exciting opportunity. Madison typically handled acquisitions on her own. Being involved in the process made me feel more like a business owner than I ever had.

Making deals and rubbing shoulders with other executives was how I'd envisioned myself since college. So far, I'd done very little of that. Instead, my time was spent learning the ropes. In the last week I felt the training wheels had finally come off. I was officially leading the course.

The champagne was finished by the time we arrived at the arena. Quentin waited at the gate with a bright smile as we approached. The alcohol left me feeling lighter as I greeted him with a handshake, careful not to be too friendly.

"One day we're going to be partners and you won't be so formal," he joked. "You look incredible as always, Emily. And you too, Madison," he complimented us both as my mother's warning danced in my memory.

For an out of towner, Quentin sure seemed familiar with the Staples Center. He led us to a freight elevator, which took us to a top floor bustling with excited fans.

"It's no Madison Square Garden, but I have to admit, I'm pretty impressed," Quentin confessed.

"Are you allowed to say that and go back to New York?" Madison poked. We all shared a playful laugh.

Pausing in the large walkway, Quentin pointed out several restaurants he recommended. Our passes granted us anything we wanted on the floor, in addition to what was already available in the skybox. "I got this suite right over here," Quentin pointed towards a glassed-in room a few feet away.

"Mr. Gamble!" Madison called, prompting a group of men to turn in our direction. Only one set of eyes stopped my heart.

Daniel's eyes lit up when they landed on mine, weakening my knees. He was dressed for me in a light gray tailored suit. As he glanced from Madison, I saw his eyes narrow once he came across Quentin, quickly excusing himself.

Appearing to move in slow motion, Daniel made his way to us, first greeting my colleagues. "Always a pleasure to see you, Madison," he held out his hand to her.

"I'm so sorry if I embarrassed you. Me and your wife have had a bit of champagne," she giggled bashfully as she shook his hand.

"Don't worry about it," he smiled before turning to Quentin, straightening his posture. "Nice to see you again, Quentin."

"Of course! You want to join us?" Quentin accepted Daniel's handshake. "I've got a suite right over there."

"It looks like we'll be neighbors then. You all enjoy. I just need a second with my wife," he turned to me.

Behaving as though we were alone, Daniel stood before me, his hand falling to my hip as his thumb teased the skin exposed by the gap in my dress.

"I'll catch up with you two," I managed through Daniel's touch. Madison nodded, carrying on undeterred, but I could see the disappointment in Quentin's eyes.

"You're still avoiding me?" Daniel's voice commanded my attention.

"I got your flowers today," I deflected.

"Why just today?"

"I'm not staying there anymore. My mom convinced me to get a suite," I smiled softly. "They're beautiful."

Daniel's grip pulled me closer, suddenly under his spell. "How long are we going to play this game, baby?"

"What game?"

Staring into his eyes, I watched his defenses fall as he lost a fight to remain stern. Hundreds of fans rushed to find their seats before tipoff, but it felt as though it was just us. Daniel pulled me even closer, leaning to whisper as his lips grazed my ear.

"This silent treatment is killing me, Em. Can we please talk? We can go anywhere you want."

His hand held onto me as though I was his lifeline. My eyes closed to savor the closeness I'd missed.

"I have them waiting for me," I looked to the suite, watching as Madison spoke to Quentin excitedly.

Daniel straightened, tilting his head while searching my eyes. "What are you doing here with him?"

"It's a business meeting."

"A business meeting?" He repeated, his eyebrows rising incredulously.

"Why are *you* here?" I quipped, watching his lips curl with guilt as his thumb caressed my hip bone.

"A business meeting."

I was frozen, locked in a trance I didn't want to end. My strength was depleted. More than anything, I wanted my husband.

"Can we talk afterwards?" He whispered into my ear.

"I don't think we'll stay for the whole game. We're just discussing a contract," I explained. The idea of sitting through an entire basketball game sounded torturous.

"Emily, I don't care about this meeting. I'll leave whenever you do. I just need to talk to you."

"Let's see after we both handle our meetings." The pitch in my voice rose with each word.

Daniel watched me closely, amusement dancing on his lips before his hand drifted down my body, releasing me from his spell. "I like this dress."

"Thank you. Monica sent me some new pieces for the hair change."

"You're not wearing panties," he whispered, kissing my ear gently. "I'll see you after your meeting."

With that, he left, leaving me out of breath in a sea of fans. I tried my best to pull it together before walking into the suite to join Madison and Quentin, certain it would be a long night.

35

"To fair negotiations and a promising future for the three of us!" Quentin led the toast as Madison and I held our glasses high.

Much less than the 'VIP suite' Madison had sold me on, Quentin had three seats in a skybox. While there was a security guard checking passes to enter the special area, it was not private. Once you cleared security, there was a room with catered food and an open bar, and then a small section of black leather seats overlooking the arena.

I'd never enjoyed attending sporting events, but the times Daniel dragged me to the Staples Center, we sat courtside. Here, you were so far from the game you had to watch it on the Jumbotron, which didn't seem to bother Quentin or Madison.

They'd both been cheering from the start of the game; Madison for the Lakers, and Quentin for the visiting Charlotte Hornets, whose star guard was from New York City. Taking full advantage of the perks included with the tickets, Quentin had already finished a bottle of the complimentary champagne.

"I honestly never thought we'd get to this point," Quentin said after leading another toast. Moving closer to me he continued, "You're a hard sell, Emily. But I think you'll see this is best for both of us."

A loud horn rang and I glanced up to see it was the end of the first quarter. That was about the time I'd hoped to be leaving, but we had yet to discuss anything more than Madison's high school basketball career.

Annoyed, I looked to the surrounding seating areas. I felt proud to be discussing business as the movers and shakers did, in a skybox at a Lakers game.

The rush of accomplishment left me in a daze, imagining how much my brand could grow with an additional publishing house in New York. I'd always wanted to expand, but the idea of moving to New York was never one I truly considered. I loved southern California, and hated snow, too much to ever relocate to the east coast. Taking a sip of champagne, I felt as though my dream was close to becoming a reality, when I felt his eyes on me.

There was only a thin layer of glass separating each skybox. Just to the right, Daniel watched me intently, drinking what I knew was whiskey from a glass tumbler. The intensity in his eyes left me feeling exposed, but I couldn't look away.

A man tapped his shoulder, and he broke our connection. Daniel's jaw tightened as he nodded quickly before extending his hand to an older man in a gray suit.

I'd always loved watching him in his work element. No one was as charismatic or persuasive as Daniel. He had a way of making people relax, which he said was the key to gaining trust. Completely in his zone, he quickly gathered a small audience. Even with a plethora of attention, I caught every glance he made to ensure I was still watching.

"Here, have a seat," Quentin disrupted my show, pointing towards two empty seats. No one appeared to be using their assigned seats, lounging wherever suited them.

Settling into the comfortable leather, I glanced back again. Still entertaining, I doubted anyone would notice the change in Daniel, but I saw it. His eyes narrowed as Quentin settled into the seat beside me.

Quentin wasn't the first handsome man I'd worked with, and he wouldn't be the last. If we were going to merge publishing houses, I would have to move past the tension. I needed him to relax if we were ever going to trust each other. I willed myself to give him my undivided attention as the horn signaled a timeout in the game.

"What's bothering you about the proposal?" He asked, turning in his seat to face me.

"There's nothing particularly bothering me. I just want to make sure things work best for the both of us. I wasn't looking to merge, so in all reality, you're trying to sell me on something I never wanted." I straightened my back with confidence.

Negotiations with Quentin had left me feeling backed into a corner, and at times, rushed. Madison was my go-to on the subject, but for the first time, her extreme confidence wasn't enough to sway me.

Quentin approached me like we were seeking the same outcome, but that wasn't completely true. I hadn't sought him out. I couldn't allow him or Madison to continue to push me towards something I wasn't sure of.

"I've been waiting on this," Quentin's response caught me off guard.

"For what?"

"You don't get to be as successful as you are without a bit of shark in you. In all our dealings, you've been much nicer than I'd expected. I knew at some point you'd show your teeth," he smiled excitedly.

"I assure you, this is far from me showing any teeth. A merger is serious, and I need to know for sure it's in my best interest before I sign anything," I looked straight into his eyes before taking a sip of my champagne.

"Well, I know you've wanted to expand to my coast as much as I've wanted to expand to yours. There's no way you can be serious in this business without having a presence in New York, and we both know that," Quentin argued, pausing for my reaction, but I just watched him.

"And if I want to be serious about the salacious world of celebrity, I need to be in Hollywood."

"Is that what you want? To be a part of the salacious world of celebrity?"

Shocked, Quentin froze for a brief moment. It was so quick, it could have easily been overlooked, but I noticed him pull the mask of persuasion carefully back into place.

"Unfortunately, it's where I'm at now. With your help, I'll be able to move into more serious genres, getting back to the reason I founded this company. For Laney," he mentioned his grandmother's name. I hoped he wasn't sleazy enough to seek sympathy for her loss through a business deal.

In our last meeting, he claimed to want less to do with the gossip tell-all path he was known for. Now, as the champagne flowed, I felt his true desires shining through.

Loud laughter from the seats beside our section caught my attention. It was Daniel's group. They were filing out the skybox, the smiles of success plastered on each of their faces. My heart dropped seeing him leave, as Quentin continued to dig a deeper hole for himself.

"This is all to honor my late grandmother, Emily," he turned to me. "And it has nothing to do with business, really. That's why I'd be willing to adjust the originally agreed upon split. I want you to have the lion's share, because making sure Laney Publishing is taken seriously is my main priority."

Quentin handed me a new proposal, bound like a novel complete with a leather cover. "That's the real reason I requested this meeting. I wanted you to see another side of me, to understand what I'm all about. This," he tapped the cover, "is everything there is to know about my company. More than even Madison would be able to find."

We both looked over his shoulder to Madison, who was in the

common area of the suite, choosing another dessert. She'd been sure to give us enough space to talk business without going too far, in case I needed her expertise.

"I'll need some time to look it over," I turned to slide the new proposal into my work bag.

"Of course," Quentin smiled, the unguarded smile that made me feel he wasn't so bad after all.

"Excuse me for a moment," I announced, taking my bag with me as I maneuvered through the suite, hoping to catch Daniel before he left.

The top floor of the Staples Center was still abuzz with fans racing to get snacks without missing much of the game. There were parents struggling with children, loud announcements about the next raffle drawing, and too much traffic in every direction. No matter how hard I searched, there was no Daniel.

"You want to order something else?" Quentin asked, placing his hand on the small of my back.

Unsure if it was as direct as I perceived it, I stepped away subtly, not wanting to make a scene. "No, I'm fine," I answered instead.

"Looking for your husband?"

Turning to search his eyes for motive, I relaxed when I didn't see malice. "Yeah, I think he just left with his clients."

"He doesn't like me," Quentin said matter-of-factly.

"Daniel doesn't know you," I corrected him, the truth tugging the corner of my lips upwards.

"I get it. You two are a power couple. You don't need mergers. If I was married, I wouldn't like the idea of my wife giving up half of her company either," Quentin turned to me with understanding in his eyes.

He had a knack for connecting with people, that was obvious. From the way he inserted himself in brainstorming sessions at my office, to picking up on the cues from Daniel.

"My husband is a business man. He understands taking risks for great rewards," I explained, turning to Quentin.

"I really believe that this merger could take us both to new heights, Emily. I really do."

A loud commotion from the suite diverted our attention. The star player for the Hornets had tied the game with less than a minute to go. Like everyone else in the building, Quentin and I rushed to our seats.

36

The game was a nail biter to the final second. After going into double overtime, the Lakers pulled out a close win that pulled even the disinterested attendees like myself from their seats. Screaming with clenched fists, I jumped in my stilettos as the final horn sounded.

"I think we might've made a fan out of her," Quentin proudly looked to Madison, who wore the biggest grin, her cheeks flush from alcohol and adrenaline.

"I'm blaming the champagne," I joked as we all began to reach for our bags. Tucking Quentin's new proposal into my Neverfull bag, I felt better about the possibility of working with him after an evening in a less formal setting.

We left the skybox together feeling confident about our future. There was much to gain from a merger between our publishing houses. I intended to read his proposal thoroughly to understand his business more.

"I think we should have a team building night here," Madison mentioned as the noise from the hallway grew deafening.

"I always try to do team building with my staff. It helps build morale," Quentin leaned in to speak over the pandemonium, but his words were lost on me.

Across the thick traffic with voices too loud to decipher words, Daniel leaned against the wall, scrolling through his phone. As though he could feel me watching, he glanced up, a small smile relieving the scowl on his forehead.

"Excuse me," I said too low for either of them to hear before struggling through the maze of people, determined to make my way to Daniel. Two steps forwards, then another back, I slowly crossed the sea of yellow and purple clad fans until I was directly in front of him.

"I thought you left," I heard the remnants of disappointment in my tone.

"I told you I'd wait for you," Daniel's scowl reappeared, confused by my doubt. He'd never been the type to promise something he couldn't deliver.

"I know, I just," I struggled for the words before a bump from the crowd shoved me into his chest.

"You okay?" Daniel lifted my chin with his index finger, his eyes warm with an emotion I'd missed.

"Yes," I breathed the answer, tasting the champagne on my tongue.

"Let's get out of here so we can talk," he stared into my eyes.

My stomach sank with anxiety at the thought of discussing our issues. So much had happened, and so much was still going on. I wasn't ready to work through it. I needed time, but that didn't stop the way my body was calling for my husband, yearning to feel him.

Thinking to my last therapy session, and the conversation with my mother that followed, I took a leap of faith. If communication was key, and clarity brought about clear expectations, I knew I needed to be transparent.

"I don't want to talk."

Daniel's eyes narrowed before his lips curled upwards, reading my intention. He was always good at sensing what I wanted, but this time he was only half right.

"I miss you," I slid my hand inside his suit jacket, feeling the hardness of his abdomen tense with my touch. His lips split, a sharp breath releasing as he silently fought for composure.

"But I'm not ready to talk," I continued, working through my feelings in real time. "I know we need to discuss everything and find some sort of resolution. I'm just not ready for that yet. I just want... I want to feel you," I admitted, dropping my head with a bit of embarrassment.

I could feel him watching as I questioned my decision, unsure of how he would respond. The tension that had brewed between us was now overflowing, surrounded by commotion. A minute felt like a lifetime as I awaited his response with anxiety rushing from my chest to my fingertips.

"Emily, are you asking me to have casual sex?" Daniel again lifted my chin until our eyes met.

Although it was in fact what I desired, I hadn't considered it that way. There would always be strings between us, we were married. But I was in no rush to repair them. I didn't want to fight, or address what I'd done wrong. I wasn't searching for an apology or accountability from Daniel. I just wanted to feel him inside me, owning my body like only he could.

"I guess so," I admitted shyly, trying to turn away, but he gripped my chin, prolonging his glare.

Looking down, Daniel blinked slowly, sighing loudly. I could feel the lecture forming in his mind, explaining to me how immature and unreasonable I was being.

"Come on," Daniel's voice boomed with what sounded like anger. Gripping my wrist, he pulled me through the thinning stream of fans so abruptly I almost tripped. Racing to keep up with him, I practically jogged in my stilettos until we reached an elevator guarded by a large man wearing all black and an earpiece.

After Daniel shook the man's hand, he pushed a button that opened the elevator doors and then stepped aside. Following him into the elevator car, I hoped to search Daniel's face for any indication of his motive, but he refused to look at me. Instead, he faced forward, his jaw tight as he watched the numbers illuminate with each passing floor.

The elevator doors opened into a garage. Daniel again reached for my wrist, leading me to a white Mercedes Maybach. Without a word, he opened the back door, releasing his grasp. I climbed inside, still confused by his silence. The door slammed before I could settle in my seat. To my surprise, Daniel did not join me.

The car was immaculate, tufted brown leather seats accented the black interior. Two small monitors mounted between the front and back seats displayed the sleek Tower Enterprise Group logo. After admiring the décor and over the top luxury, I turned to watch Daniel, confident he couldn't see me through the dark tint. He was speaking to a man in a black suit who appeared to be the driver.

I couldn't hear their conversation from the backseat. Daniel looked upset, and the man in the suit nodded as though he was receiving instructions. When the driver finally did speak, Daniel looked confused. His eyebrows curved before he turned to the car, causing me to inhale sharply. In two swift movements, he opened the car door, leaning down as our eyes locked with an intensity I felt deep in my pelvis.

"Your place, or... ours?" He flashed a quick smile at the absurdity of the question. My stomach relaxed, grateful he'd discovered the humor in the situation.

"Ours."

He nodded, glancing at me longer than necessary before closing the door and continuing his conversation. When Daniel stopped speaking, the driver entered the car, glancing into the rearview mirror.

"Good evening, Mrs. Gamble," he nodded.

"Good evening," I smiled nervously.

Satisfied with his greeting, he returned his attention forward and pressed a button. A black suede partition rose from behind the mounted monitors just as Daniel climbed into the backseat. Glaring across the immovable center console separating us, I could hear my heart beating in my ears. The adrenaline left me breathless.

Unexpectedly, Daniel reached across the console with both hands, his touch aggressive and impatient. Forsaking my inhibitions, I raced across the soft leather until I was in his lap.

Desperate to taste him, I readily pressed my lips to his. Welcoming his warm tongue, a soft moan celebrated the intrusion. My legs spread to straddle him as Daniel's fingertips ran along my scalp before tightly gripping two fists of hair.

Pulling away, I felt the need to explain myself. "I haven't been getting your calls," I rushed the words.

"I don't care," he growled, pulling me closer as he deepened the passionate kiss. Our bodies melted together, restricted by the confines of the seat.

"It's not that I don't want to talk at all. I'm just not ready," I reasoned breathlessly, again pulling away from our embrace.

"So, stop talking," Daniel urged, tightening his grip on my hair as his tongue slid past my lips. I shrieked from the delightful pain, which seemed to turn him on further. Dropping one hand to my hip, he guided me to his bulging erection. My hips instinctually grinded against him, just as Daniel's hand slid beneath my dress.

Tugging at the fabric, he gripped my bare ass with one hand while fighting the dress with the other. He was right, I wasn't wearing any panties. The gap in fabric made it nearly impossible. Daniel's fervor was too strong for the delicate dress.

"You're going to rip it," I warned him, panting from our embrace.

"I'll buy you another one," he pulled me back to him, continuing to ravish the soft fabric. When he finally managed to lift the dress over my hips, two pearls flew against the leather interior.

"This is a six-hundred-dollar dress!" I twisted to search for the pearls, but Daniel's grip was too tight.

"Hey," he demanded my attention. I turned to face him, seeing the gleam in his eyes. "I'm good for it. Come here," he palmed my ass.

My concern evaporated. I didn't care if every pearl fell from the dress. As I settled in his lap, Daniel's eyebrows rose as his tongue slid across his lips seductively. Staring deep into his eyes, I said the only thing swirling in my mind.

"You bought a new car?"

Daniel's soft smile cracked into a hearty laugh, his hands still caressing me beneath my dress. "You sure have a lot of questions for someone not interested in talking."

Blushing, I turned away to hide the smile tugging at the corner of my lips. Again, he was right. Remaining silent was never one of my strong suits.

"No, Emily. I did not buy a new car," he tried for stern, but I could see the playfulness in his eyes. "I had a moving meeting earlier," he added, pulling at my hips, gently bringing me closer to him. "I went to Malibu with a client and needed the privacy."

We watched each other closely in a prolonged silence that felt necessary. Drifting up the crisp white shirt I'd wrinkled with intensity, I traced the outline of his jaw with my fingertip. Slowly, Daniel moved his hands down my thighs before pulling my damaged dress to cover my ass.

"Why'd you stop?" I protested, already missing his touch.

"As bad as I want you," he paused, leaning forward to kiss my neck before moving his mouth to my ear. He whispered, "I'm not going to fuck you in the back of a rented car."

The sound of his teeth gently clashing against my pearl earring, combined with the warmth of his breath, was beyond erotic. Leaning forward, I tilted my head back, yearning for his attentive kisses. Daniel obliged me with tortuously slow wet kisses from my ear to my shoulder. His hands found their way beneath my dress again, this time from the front.

"Aahh," I inhaled sharply as his thumb circled my bud, applying the perfect amount of pressure while continuing along my neck, creating a swirling pattern with his tongue. My body reacted swiftly, pressing into his hand greedily and leaning into his tongue for more.

"Daniel," I moaned his name in a weak plea for him to stop.

"Hmm?" he answered without pausing his intricate tongue work.

"You said..." My words faded as two fingers leisurely slid inside me. Swallowing slowly, I was forced to breathe through my mouth, in urgent need of air. "You said you wouldn't..."

Undeterred by my half sentences, Daniel continued his seduction, swirling his fingers in my wetness, his thumb still pressed against my sweet spot.

"I said I wasn't going to fuck you," he whispered before trailing the tip of his tongue around the base of my ear. His free hand tilted my hips forward as his fingers surged deeper into my warmth.

"Baby, please," I whined, not wanting to climax without him. My body had other plans, grinding against his hand faster as the waves of sensation grew stronger.

He could sense my nearing explosion, I knew it from the heaviness of his breath. His kisses were more aggressive as his teeth grazed against my skin before sinking into my neck.

"Ahh! Baby!" I cried, lifting myself before winding back, wanting more.

"Don't come, yet," he whispered, continuing to push me forward. I was lost to his movements, a slave to his commands as my body fought against me, searching for the release I couldn't reach without his approval.

"Please..." I begged, knowing he could send me over the edge with one word. "Daniel, please..."

"Shhh... We're home. Let's go," Daniel whispered, slipping his fingers from my slit as he gently kissed my ear. Tugging my dress down, he shifted us before opening the car door. I stumbled to my feet, snatched from my ascension.

"I'll be here, Mr. Gamble," the driver announced. Flustered by his presence, I tugged at the hem of my dress feeling naked.

"That's not necessary. I'm in for the night," he spoke to the driver, but his attention was on me as he wrapped his arm around my waist, relaxing me with his eyes. "I'll text you the pick-up time for tomorrow."

"Yes sir. Good night, Mrs. Gamble," the man nodded in my direction before dismissing himself.

"Relax, baby. The car is completely soundproof. He doesn't have a clue," Daniel pulled me to his side.

"Really?" I turned to him, embarrassingly pointing to the gaping hole at the slit in my dress, a consequence of the two missing pearls.

"One, I'm going to replace that," he pointed to the hole in my dress with amusement. "And two, he signed an airtight nondisclosure. Our secrets are safe with him," he reasoned, leading me to the front door with a satisfied grin I couldn't resist.

37

Daniel locked the front door behind us and then followed me through the foyer. I could sense his impatience, so I took my time prancing in my stilettos.

"It smells different in here," I glanced towards the kitchen, turning to see the passion in Daniel's glare. Refusing to comment, he began unscrewing his cuff links, gently setting them beside a bouquet of flowers on a side table.

"Who sent you flowers?"

Daniel smirked, unbuttoning his shirt. "They were for you."

"They better have been," I rolled my eyes, turning towards the kitchen, away from our bedroom. Before I could take one step, Daniel's arm pulled me back towards him.

I yelped as he hoisted me in the air without warning. "A bit eager aren't you, Mr. Gamble?" I teased, biting my bottom lip as I wrapped my legs around his waist.

"I've missed you," he whispered on my lips before kissing me deeply as he walked through our home. My hands gripped his neck, leaning from one side to the other to deepen the kiss.

"Show me how much you've missed me," I challenged as we

reached our bedroom. Uncrossing my ankles, I released his neck and Daniel gently placed me on my feet.

Standing at the foot of our bed, our eyes were locked as I bent over to unbuckle each ankle strap on my pumps. Daniel pulled his shirt off, dropping it to the floor before unbuckling his belt. I watched intensely as he pushed his pants to the ground before stepping out of them.

Reaching over my shoulder, I unzipped the top half of my dress before adjusting my arms, reaching from a different angle to finish the job. The dress fell in a puddle at my feet. Without breaking our gaze, I unlatched the clasp of my black lace bra, letting it too fall to my feet as Daniel pushed his boxer briefs to his ankles.

My tongue felt heavy at the sight of his thick length gripped in his right hand. Daniel's eyes moved down my naked body hungrily as desire pooled between my legs. I turned to crawl on the bed, but he stopped me, gripping my elbow before yanking me towards him.

His left hand lifted the nape of my neck, forcing me onto the balls of my feet. Devouring me, Daniel kissed me so deeply I struggled for air. Lifting my left knee to his side, I lost my footing, surrendering control as he thrust inside me before falling to the bed.

"Ahh!" My back arched with approval, my hips angling to make room for him.

With my left leg slung over his shoulder, I curled my toes as Daniel dug into me viciously, stretching me without regard. A soft groan escaped him as he fell deeper, his pleasure emitting more clearly with every thrust.

Lifting my hips, I matched his rhythm as our bodies collided with an aggressive lust, the sounds of my wetness serving as the soundtrack. Our chemistry was even better than I'd remembered. Our bodies were designed to fit together. Our fingers casually interlocked before moving to grip limbs, hair, anything to deepen the connection.

"Yes! Yes!" Reaching over my head, I pushed against the headboard to propel my body forward. Feeling his back muscles flex beneath my fingertips as he screwed his body in a wave like motion, a satisfying explosion was imminent. My eyes closed awaiting the inevitable ecstasy.

Positioning himself on his knees, Daniel gripped my thighs to pull my body into a ninety-degree angle. My ankles rested on his shoulders, my extended legs flush against his chest. Roughly, he pulled me in rhythm with his body, slamming into me hard and fast. Watching the muscles in his abdomen contract with his accelerated pace, I felt myself losing control.

"Fuck!" Daniel looked to the ceiling, trying to delay his own pleasure. My pelvic muscles tightened with arousal.

He had always been so perfectly put together. Something about making him unravel had always weakened me. Even with him dominating my body, I felt empowered driving him to the edge so easily. Knowing how good I felt to him, evident from the satisfaction on his face, was as pleasurable as the overwhelming physical pulsation.

Spreading my legs in the air, I arched my back as the waves of sensation overflowed, my release pouring out of me as I cried his name. Diving into me, Daniel pounced on my vulnerability, wrapping his arms around me as he plunged deeper, extending my climax.

His indulgent groans grew louder, intensifying my hunger for more. The vibrations built deep in my chest, leaving my legs tingling with satisfaction.

Emboldened by my orgasmic glow, I wrapped my legs around his waist tightly, rolling until I was left straddling him. The shock on his face was quickly replaced by an approving glare when my hips began to rock slowly.

Biting his lip, Daniel reached up, palming my breast as he lifted his hips to guide me. The new angle combined with my sensitive state was more than I could handle, every move threatened to send me into another whirlwind climax.

"Come here," Daniel commanded, pulling at my waist for what I thought would be a kiss. Instead, his mouth found my nipple.

First, gently circling with the tip of his tongue until the delicate skin hardened. Suctioning his mouth, Daniel sucked hard while his hands tightly gripped my hips, lifting my body before plunging into me.

"Ahhh!" I moaned, the waves of pleasure sending me into a prolonged euphoric bliss. Leaning towards him created a friction along my clitoris with every collision.

With my hand pressed against the headboard, I launched my body back to meet his rhythm. When his teeth grazed against my hardened nipple, I yelped with shock. It was all too much – his mouth, hands, and length pushing me over the edge as my body begged for more.

Lifting his hips from the bed, Daniel plunged into me hard and fast, biting down on my nipple until I screamed through a shattering orgasm I couldn't get enough of. My body bucked like an animal, shoving the headboard as I ravenously raced for more. I didn't notice Daniel losing control until his body tensed, his arms holding me tightly as he released inside me.

The rocking gradually slowed as my body relaxed. On shaky legs, I rolled over, sated. My heart raced as I fell to the bed panting, glancing over to see a wide grin on Daniel's face.

"God, I needed that," he said. His chest rose and fell slowly as he stared at the ceiling.

Rolling onto my side, I watched him in awe, as I always did after he took me to undiscovered levels of pleasure. He was breathtaking, his body a bronzed sculpture of perfection, chiseled at every angle. Even lying flat, his abdomen rippled with distinct creases as his breathing finally normalized.

"You alright?" He asked. I hadn't realized he was watching me watch him.

"I wish I had a cigarette."

"What?" Daniel laughed.

"I've never had one, but it just feels like it would top this off perfectly," I bashfully smiled as the silly thought escaped me without permission.

While I'd smoked a bit of weed in college, tobacco had never been my forte. But now, lying naked beside Daniel, my body still feeling his hands all over me, I craved the foreign respire.

"I have a cigar," Daniel's voice rose at the offer, his eyes searching mine.

"But you can't inhale, right? I don't know how to smoke those," I scrunched my nose disapprovingly.

"Come on," he wrapped his hands around my waist as he pulled me to the edge of the bed. "I'll teach you."

38

Naked in our large closet, we flirtatiously passed each other, needy hands lingering at every opportunity. After thumbing through my vast collection of nightgowns, I tip toed back to the bedroom, lifting Daniel's button down shirt from the pile of our discarded clothes.

I was fastening the last button when he emerged from the closet wearing nothing but basketball shorts, the outline of his slightly erect penis drawing my attention as he made his way towards me.

"That looks good on you," Daniel whispered on the nape of my neck, wrapping his arms around my waist.

"It smells like you." Lifting my shoulder to my nose, I inhaled deeply, closing my eyes.

"Let's get you a fix," Daniel began walking, forcing my feet forward as he led from behind.

The house felt unlived in, much like it had during our separation. It was obvious no one had used the kitchen or living room, both perfectly staged from a weekly cleaning. Daniel's man cave, as I liked to call it, was a different story. Two chairs were angled around a table facing the television, with two empty glass tumblers sitting on the table top.

Glancing over my shoulder I asked, "You had company?"

"Jason came over to watch the game last night," he answered after a brief pause, searching my eyes before releasing me.

A pang of guilt swirled in my stomach, wondering if he thought I was accusing him of something more sinister. Pushing away the sudden need to discuss a topic I knew I wasn't ready to unpack, I sat in the leather chair as Daniel gathered the empty tumblers before setting them on the bar countertop.

"You want a drink?" He called from the back of the room.

"If you're drinking with me," I raised an eyebrow, seeing him turn just before his grin revealed itself.

Watching from a distance, I noticed every muscle in his bare back as he moved about the bar. He selected two square glasses from a shelf, and then reached for a bottle of Macallan whiskey. Turning around, he opened the small freezer to retrieve two large ice cubes from a black silicone tray. Each cube measured about two inches tall, barely fitting into the glass.

Satisfied with his concoction, Daniel carried the drinks across the room as my eyes drifted to his abdomen, admiring the increased definition with every step.

"Alright, we're going to start this with the basics," he sat both glasses on the coasters left behind from the previous drinks. Continuing throughout the room, he made his way to a glass humidor case in the furthest corner, pausing as he pored over his collection of cigars.

After a few seconds he opened the case, retrieving a thick brown cigar from a colorful square box and a large glass ash tray. With a smile playing on his full lips, he walked back to the table. After setting the ash tray between our drinks, Daniel wrapped one arm around my back and the other beneath my knees. Lifting me with ease, he settled into the opposite chair as I found comfort in his lap.

"Rule number one: Do not inhale." He glared into my eyes sternly as though breaking this rule would result in serious harm.

Reaching around me to lift the cigar from the ash tray, he pulled a small lever to reveal a thin glass tray he sat on the table. The tray held a gold plated lighter and a matching tool with a hole through the middle. From watching my father and Daniel smoke cigars, I knew it was for cutting the end. My eyes were more focused on the lighter, one I'd never seen. I could tell it was important from the care in which he held it.

"Where'd you get this?" My right hand covered his as I gently took the heavy lighter into my palm, wrapping my fingers around the cool metal. His initials were engraved on one side, with the words 'From Now Til Forever', on the other.

"Jason gave it to me a while back," he answered casually, leaning in to kiss my neck as he reclaimed his lighter.

"As a gift?"

"Yeah, two years ago, I think. It was either my birthday or Christmas," he squeezed my side as he reached for the cutter.

"Rule number two: You always cut the end of the cigar." He announced before sharply snipping the thick cigar in one swift cut.

"Did he give it to you privately? I don't remember Jason ever giving you a gift," I asked, looking over my shoulder. Their relationship was a bit of a cliché; Daniel the over protective older brother who refused any gratitude from the younger brother he treated as a son.

"You know I don't like when he buys me shit. I think he had it engraved so I couldn't give it back," he huffed and then sparked the lighter, ending the conversation as he held the cigar to the flame.

"Rule number three: You don't just light a cigar. You have to take your time. It makes it taste better," he explained as he slowly twirled the cigar above the flame. After a few seconds, he lowered the cigar so the fire barely touched the surface, continuing to twirl.

"I smoked weed in college, you know. I'm not a complete rookie," I watched the side of his lips curl upward, but he refused to look my way, concentrating on his project.

"Unfortunately, your illegal endeavors won't help you much in this venture. Remember rule number one?" He quickly glanced at me.

"Don't inhale," I answered, sarcastically rolling my eyes.

"Exactly," he nodded slowly, biting his lower lip as he finished roasting the tip of the cigar until it glowed with a bright orange color. "Now, watch me," he instructed, bringing the cigar to his lips.

Holding the cigar with his thumb and index finger, Daniel began puffing fast, five or six times before blowing a small amount of smoke out. He repeated that three times, when he finally produced thick white clouds. Watching his jaw tighten with a mouthful of smoke, and the way his bare chest rose and fell as he released it left me squirming in his lap, ready for more of him.

"You ready?" He misread my arousal for anticipation.

"Yeah," I played along, wrapping my fingers around the cigar as I prepared to mimic his actions.

"Don't inhale, Emily," he repeated.

"Okay," I rolled my eyes, bringing the cigar to my lips before doing just as he had, pulling five times quickly, filling my mouth with smoke.

"Not so much," he frowned, pulling the cigar from my hand.

Attempting to hold the smoke as he had, I instinctually swallowed, filling my lungs with smoke. A roar of a cough burned my throat as it made its way across my tongue. Turning me so my legs fell over the side of his, Daniel patted my back as if burping a baby, and the smoke fell from my lips.

"You're so hard headed," he chuckled, continually patting my back.

"I was puffing like you," I explained through the final cough.

"You have to puff quickly in the beginning, but now that it's lit, you can just puff once or twice," he said before demonstrating, this time even sexier than before.

Leaning back in the chair, he curled his index finger around the cigar, puffing twice before tensing his jaw as he held the smoke in his mouth. When he opened his lips to exhale deeply, a thick white cloud floated across the room.

"See?" He asked, just as a ringer sounded. Handing me the

cigar, he lifted me from his lap, setting me back on the leather seat. "Let me grab my phone. You practice, but don't inhale!"

I waited for him to leave, not wanting any more criticism. The second he crossed the threshold of the room, I brought the cigar to my mouth. Cradling it in the curl of my index finger, just as he had, I wrapped my lips around the soft brown leaf. This time copying his shorter version, I puffed the cigar twice, expanding my cheeks as the thick smoke warmed my tongue. Parting my lips, I pushed the white smoke out, smiling at the outcome.

In a strange way, smoking the cigar made me feel closer to Daniel. It was one of his regular past times I'd never taken part in. Glancing at the gold lighter resting on the table, I ran my fingertips across the engraved letters. There seemed to be so many things in his life that were off limits to me.

It was as though I didn't really know him, only the husband he presented himself to be. Puffing the cigar, I let my thoughts fill my mind like the smoke, uncertainties swirling with curiosity. I had so many questions for the man I'd married, but I knew I wasn't ready for answers.

I successfully puffed the cigar three more times before Daniel returned. He found me leaned back in the chair, my legs hanging over the arm rest, proud to showcase how quickly I'd mastered the routine. With his arms folded across his chest, Daniel smiled as I kicked my legs in the air, narrowing my lips to blow a thin stream of smoke.

"You're a natural," his abs tightened as he chuckled, extending his hand with my phone. "It was yours."

My eyes scanned the short list of notifications on the screen. The message from Crystal brought me to attention. Kicking my legs around the arm of the chair, I placed my toes on the cool hard wood as I read her text.

39

Crystal: Sorry to bother you so late, Mrs. G. Just wanted to remind you that Christian will need an answer for his proposal first thing in the morning.

"Shit!" I leaped up.

I'd completely forgotten about Christian's new initiative and our scheduled meeting in the morning. He was so excited to have my ear. As much as I was enjoying down time with Daniel, I didn't want to abandon my new responsibilities.

"What's wrong?" Daniel took the cigar I'd forgotten I was holding, setting it in the ash tray as he looked over me with concern.

"I need to read a proposal before morning," I lifted the chilled glass, downing the whiskey in one gulp. Tapping on my phone, I began making my way to the bedroom as I typed a quick response to Crystal before switching apps to schedule a ride.

Back in our bedroom, I walked into the closet, rising on my toes to reach a large tote bag on a top shelf. My recent shopping spree had replaced much of my wardrobe, but there were a few things I'd missed in my hotel suite. Stuffing the bag with a few nightgowns, I moved to my vanity, picking two bottles of perfume and tossing them onto the silk fabric.

Consumed by my packing, I didn't notice Daniel standing in the door way, his eyes widened with disbelief. My lips twitched with the urge to smile, seeing him want me was more gratifying than it should be. Quickly, I packed away a small toiletry bag before opening one of Daniel's drawers and taking a pair of his sweat pants.

"Can I wear these?" I asked as I stepped into them.

"You can have whatever you want."

"So, I can keep this shirt too?" I asked, looking down at the button up, already excited to sleep with his scent.

"Whatever you want." He repeated flatly.

Tucking the shirt into the oversized sweatpants, I pulled the drawstring tight, securing them around my small waist. Reaching into another of Daniel's drawers, I found a matching black hoody, sliding my arms through the sleeves before zipping the jacket closed.

Glancing at the full-length mirror, a soft laugh shook my shoulders as I caught my reflection swimming in Daniel's clothing. Sliding into one of the few pairs of sneakers I owned, I completed my outfit.

"How do I look?" I turned to him before sliding my phone into the heavy tote, making my way across the closet with the weight straining my shoulder.

He ignored my question until I was in reach, when he lifted my chin so that I was looking directly into his curious eyes. "You're really leaving?"

A silence swirled between us as I searched for the right words to answer him. Heavier than usual, his eyes trained on me with a longing I wasn't used to.

"Honestly, I did plan to stay, but there's this proposal I need to read by morning," I finally answered with a partial truth. The furrow in Daniel's brow sent a surge of anxiety through my chest, as though he could read me like a book, knowing my intentions never included a night together.

"This is more awkward than I'd anticipated," I added, hoping for a laugh that never came.

"What could be awkward about a booty call with your husband?" Daniel's head tilted, feigning curiosity. Thankfully, his lip curls slightly, a flash of amusement reaching his eye. "Are you good to drive?"

"I called a car," I answered, retrieving my phone from the bag before tapping the screen for updates.

Daniel nodded slowly, his bottom lip disappearing behind his teeth. I could tell he was fighting his words. Parts of me wished he wouldn't. "Do you want me to bring a car to you?"

"Are you going to let me push the 'Rari?" I teased, referencing his prized possession.

"You can have whatever you want, Emily." His voice was strong, but I could sense the desperation buried beneath the surface. Trapped in his glare, I found myself speechless and frozen, regretting my decision.

He hadn't said it, but I knew what he was thinking, because I'd thought it too. There was no reason I couldn't bring whatever required my approval to our house. But, he didn't say a word, and so I clenched my teeth, trapping my thoughts.

My phone beeped with an alert, and I glanced down. "My car's here," I answered without looking back to him.

Daniel moved aside, graciously making room for me to exit the closet. Each step felt treacherous, like my feet were anchored to the ground, yet I forced them onward. A large part of me wanted nothing more than to curl into his arms and go back to bed, where everything seemed to make perfect sense.

As I left the bedroom, I noticed Daniel wasn't following me. I continued, determined to stick with my emotional plan. I wasn't ready to discuss what had happened between us, and I was done pretending things were okay when they weren't. The sound of

Daniel's footsteps stopped me in my tracks, turning on my heels in the kitchen.

"I'm going to walk you out," he explained, pulling a shirt over his head.

Nodding quickly, I swallowed the disappointment, silently admitting I wanted him to stop me. Instead, he followed close behind as I made the walk of shame, ending at the gray Nissan waiting at the end of our driveway.

"Emily?" The young white man asked, tapping on his phone to begin the ride.

"Yes," I forced a smile, moving to open the car door before Daniel stopped me. His arm dropped to my waist, his thumb circling my hip bone as it always did when he wanted my submission.

"Do you still love me?"

40

His words hit me like a ton of bricks. The fact that he could ever think otherwise left me winded. Remorse swarmed my abdomen.

"Of course! Daniel, I will always love you," I assured him, gripping his forearm.

He searched my eyes for a long pause before nodding, rushing his words. "I thought so. Okay, let me know you get there safely."

Opening the door, Daniel looked relieved as he ushered me into the backseat. "Maybe next time, you can stay over at my place," I offered while climbing across the upholstered seat.

Daniel's eyebrows rose with shock at my mention there would be another time, but he didn't say a word. Once settled into the seat, he closed the door, moving around to the driver's window. "Drive carefully. That's my life in the backseat," he advised, nodding towards me.

A flirtatious smile spread across my face, one Daniel returned before straightening. Tapping the roof of the car, he sent my driver on his way. Our neighborhood seemed even quieter than normal. Glancing out the rear window, I watched Daniel. Still standing in the street, he brushed his hair forward with both hands. I could see the deep breath he took just before the driver made a turn. My stomach tensed with doubt, questioning my decision.

As our neighborhood passed by, I waited for the tears I was sure would come. They'd accompanied every difficult decision in my life. Leaving Daniel in the middle of the night was up there with my most conflicted times.

The look of defeat in his eyes as he watched me pack my bag from the doorway to our closet. His apprehension to follow me out, undoubtedly a deep battle within him. One he let me win, choosing not to stand in my way despite the hurt in his voice as he asked if I still loved him.

The memory replayed in my mind with hurt. Suddenly, I realized he never returned the words, as he usually did. My hands worked quickly, digging through the tote until the phone was in my grasp. Tapping until his picture illuminated on the screen, I finally unblocked his number. Bringing the phone to my ear, I hoped he wouldn't ignore me as I had him.

"Hey," his voice was tired, deflated.

"You didn't say it back."

"Say what?" A slight rise in his tone excited me.

"You asked if I still loved you, but you didn't say it back," I explained.

"Oh," he breathed into the phone. I could hear the smirk on his handsome face. "How about I show you instead?"

His answer sent chills up my spine as the driver pulled into the circular driveway of the Four Seasons. After parking, he scrambled out of his seat to open my door, completely out of character for an Uber driver.

"Thank you," I whispered to the driver before returning my attention to Daniel. "How do you plan to show me?"

"I guess you'll have to wait and see," he teased.

"I guess so," I paused, digging through my purse for a tip.

"Oh, no," the driver waved me off, returning to his side of the car with a wide grin. "Your man already tipped me handsomely."

"Really? You tipped the driver?" I smiled into the phone, walking through the glass doors of the hotel.

"I had to give him an incentive," he said plainly.

"How much did you give him? He looked too excited," I frowned on my way into the elevator, knowing how generously Daniel was known to tip. The doors closed, ascending the floors quickly. I was grateful for the lonesome ride, allowing me to continue our conversation in private.

"I guess enough," Daniel chuckled into the phone, his tender laugh warming my heart.

The doors to the elevator opened and I made the short walk before unlocking my suite. "Well, you wanted to know I made it safely. I'm home."

"You're at a hotel, Emily. *I'm* home."

It was a punch to the gut as I entered the freshly cleaned room, sparkling with the touch of housekeeping. My dry cleaning hung in plastic from a rolling trolley at the edge of the room, with a bottle of champagne sitting in a chiller atop the bar as I'd requested.

He was right, and the realization released the tears I couldn't find earlier. Sinking to the sofa, the guilt of my selfish decisions began to overwhelm me.

"I'm sorry, babe," Daniel's voice was calm and soothing. "I respect your space. Enjoy your time there. Get your work done. I'll talk to you tomorrow."

Swallowing slowly, I pushed the emotions down just long enough to ask the question. "Do you still love me?"

Another soft laugh from his end. "I'm *in* love with you, Emily. Always will be."

"You promise?"

"I'm going to show you. Just get some rest."

"Goodnight," I whispered meekly.

"Goodnight, baby."

My shoulders slumped the second the call ended, already missing him. Everything felt like a mistake. From leaving my parents' home in the middle of the night, to moving into this hotel, and even going home with him after the game.

I was in over my head with emotions, playing a game I didn't want to win. How had I let things go so far, fighting for a moral victory that could destroy my marriage?

Suddenly Dr. Cathway's words reminded me of the importance of my alone time. "You need time to heal if you're ever going to recover from the hurt you've experienced. You should not turn to a new page without fully understanding the lesson of the previous."

While the memory of our last therapy session brought a gust of relief, it did nothing to stop the tears streaming down my face as I cuddled along the plush pillows of the sofa, imagining they were Daniel's safe embrace.

Determined to not repeat my previous patterns of sweeping things under the rug, I fought the urge to run back to Daniel. I was done returning to good times while denying the problems lurking deep within. Finally, I allowed myself to release the tears, drifting to sleep with both excitement and fear for what the new page of my life could include.

FANTASIES

THE EMILY GAMBLE SERIES

DEDICATION

To the fans who have grown to know and love Emily and Daniel Gamble as much as me. I appreciate you, and your support. This book is for you.

PROLOGUE

The sun shined a bit too bright for my liking. At only seven in the morning, my entire office was illuminated. A dark emptiness brewed within me, annoyed by the sunlight. After another sleepless night, I was stuck in the grey mood I'd grown accustomed to, forcing myself through routines without passion or purpose.

"So, how'd it go?" My brother's voice jolted my thoughts.

Turning from the view of the city, I watched Jason lounging in the leather seat, casual without a care in the world. My younger brother had always been able to relax in a way I never could. His cool demeanor had served as a motivator more than once in my life; affording him serenity had been a constant driving force.

"How'd what go?" I barked much more aggressive than I'd intended. If even my baby brother was subject to my outbursts, I hated to think how awful I must be to employees. "I'm sorry. I haven't been sleeping well."

"Did you send the flowers like I told you?"

Always eager to help, Jason had inserted himself as my relationship advisor, constantly coming up with ways to help me resolve things with my wife. He'd popped up at my house unexpectedly after my big fight with Emily, and for the first time in my life, I confided in the man who'd idolized me since childhood.

"I did," I scratched my forehead, uncomfortable with discussing things any further.

"It's not gossip if you're talking to your brother," Jason argued, a master at getting his way.

He knew how much I hated discussing my personal life with anyone, including him. Although he was my closest friend, I'd never shared the details of my marriage with him, or anyone else.

"I sent the flowers," I conceded, glancing back to the unobstructed view of Los Angeles.

"And?"

"She didn't get them." I watched the excitement drain from his eyes, letting him sit in it for an extra second before continuing. "She moved to a different hotel, no doubt somewhere in Beverly Hills. Her mom picked it out. But I ran into her at the game last night."

Jason scooted to the edge of his seat as though watching a climactic scene in a movie. "Em was at a basketball game?"

I smiled, remembering how shocked I was to see her there, like a mirage in the desert. My wife hated sports, but she always endured them for my benefit, pretending to enjoy herself. Once I'd laid eyes on her, I couldn't focus on business for the rest of the night.

"She was hosting a meeting in a suite," I began, debating whether I wanted to include the detail that had been bothering me. "She's been entertaining this guy from New York. He's interested in her business in some way, but it doesn't sit right with me."

"Emily being involved in her business; or it including a guy?"

My eyes shot up with defiance, hating the guilt that swirled in my abdomen. I'd never questioned Emily's loyalty for a second, but something about Quentin troubled me. Maybe it was the way he made her laugh when all I'd brought her recently were tears, or maybe it was the connection they shared that I wasn't privy to, being on the outs in her life.

"I've always wanted Emily to go after her dreams. The guy just seems sketchy. Emily can be very naïve when it comes to closing deals. I'm usually the one to protect her from the ugly side of business."

Jason nodded slowly as he listened, leaning back to allow my words to sink in. "So, you see her at the game..." he prodded.

"Right," I sighed, growing more uncomfortable. "I asked to talk to her, but she didn't want to blow off her meeting. I waited an hour for her to finish, and then she basically told me she didn't want to talk."

"What?" Jason slid to the front of his seat again. "Women always want to talk!"

"Not mine," I rose my eyebrows. "She said she wasn't ready to talk, but she did want to go home together."

I looked to Jason, watching his eyes bulge as the realization of what Emily wanted sank in. "Really? And you obliged?"

"Of course, I obliged!"

We shared a laugh, my brother's louder than my own since I knew how the story ended. "But then, she left. Said she had to read over some proposal or something."

Shaking my head, I tried to make sense of it all for the hundredth time since she left. Nothing about her behavior was anything reminiscent of the woman I knew. Emily was always in a rush to make-up, a fixer much like her mother.

This time, she seemed to enjoy the broken space we were in, and I wasn't sure how to read her. The last thing I wanted was for things to continue as they had the last time, or the awful outcome that ensued.

"So, my little sister is becoming the mogul she's always wanted to be," Jason finally responded, a smile playing on his lips. "You've got to play her game now."

"Her game?"

"She wants to be courted... again."

"Courted?" The word felt funny rolling off my tongue referencing my wife.

"She wants you to chase her. Fix the shit you broke," Jason boldly declared, turning away as his words began to anger me.

"What exactly did I break, Jason?" I chuckled at the absurdity.

"You may have had good reason, but you did betray her, D." His words infuriated me, unraveling a thread of resentment I'd been bottling up.

"Betray?!" I barked. "If it weren't for me, her father would be going to prison for at least a decade!"

Noticing my temper was getting the best of me, I forced a deep breath before continuing. My father in-law's legal battle had consumed me for longer than I cared to admit. A lot of time and money had gone to maintaining not only his freedom, but his professional reputation, which to him was even more important.

"Jason, if it weren't for me, that family would be destroyed. Now, he'll only have to forfeit a few contracts, and maybe lose a property. And that's all because –"

"Part of the job," Jason interrupted me.

"What?"

"I believe that's the exact phrase you used, when you let the Laker's deal slip through your fingers to take Emily to Thailand, because she had to be there on her actual birthday. It's the same excuse you give me and mom for spending every holiday with the Delley family. Or, when you bought that warehouse downtown, where no one lives," he continued.

"Get to the point, Jason," I urged him, my patience running thin.

"Making Emily's life a fairy tale has been a part of the job since you married her. You've always secretly worked overtime to make things work out for her, and now you've created a –"

"– monster." I finished his sentence.

"I was going to say diva, but you get it. She's used to you fixing her problems, and we both know your ego enjoys the smile she rewards you with. You like being her super hero, so put on your cape."

I hated how true his words rang. I had made a point of keeping the details of how Emily's life worked from her. It was her father's way, letting his wife and daughters live in bliss while he quietly put out the fires threatening to ruin everything. It was something I'd admired about him since the day we met. He never shielded me from the truth, but his family resided in the gray at all times.

"Just be the man you pretended to be when you met her. Hell. You're actually him now," Jason chuckled.

Again, his truth struck me. When I first met Emily, my consulting firm was barely clearing a profit, dependent on a dangerous cocktail of debt and private investments. The way she commanded a room, never intimidated by status or wealth, was contagious. Emily felt she deserved to be wherever she was, a trait afforded by the lifestyle her father worked so hard to provide her.

To gain her respect, I pretended to have the same confidence, exaggerating my success to the visions I had in my mind, more than the results I'd actually produced. Our relationship became the push I needed, because for Emily, I would do anything.

Having my 'why' was enough for me to break through ceilings that had once held me captive, stunting my growth. Nothing was off limits for Emily, and I adopted that same attitude to make her dream life a reality.

By the time we wed, I was who I had presented myself to be, but she never knew it was all because of her. She was the key to my success; both through motivation and inspiration. Never once did she question who I said I was, giving me the permission I was so desperately seeking. My wife convinced me to become who I was destined to be.

"Oh shit," Jason's obnoxious ringer disrupted my thoughts.

"Ring tones went out a long time ago," I reminded him as he smiled, silencing his iPhone.

"You won't be saying that when I bring them back," he grinned, shoving the phone into his pocket as he made his way to my desk. "I got a meeting. I'll come by after."

"You don't have to keep checking in on me like I'm some wounded kitten."

I hated not being the strong and fearless man my brother knew me to be. Now that he had seen me at my weakest, when the fear of Emily leaving me was the strongest, our roles had reversed.

"How else will I know you've eaten? You're disappearing before my eyes," he joked, ignoring my request for independence as he circled my desk. "I'll check with Tracy, see if we can get lunch."

"She's not in yet. Just call me after your meetings," I relented.

"Cool," Jason fought back his smile, enjoying the privileges of his new role. "From now," he began, our hands slapping together before I pulled him into a hug.

"Until forever," I finished, releasing him. His phone vibrated, and he pulled it from his pocket as he walked out my office.

"One more bit of unsolicited advice," he called from the door. "If Emily wants to date, it probably means she wants to start over. You could use a clean slate, bro. It's a time to rewrite the rules. Take advantage."

The gentle look in his eyes stopped me from dismissing him. Instead, I nodded, watching my little brother leave my office as an idea popped into my mind. Reaching for my phone, I started to doubt myself until she picked up.

"Hey, boss! I'm parking now," Tracy's voice was apologetic. I worried it had to do with my recent attitude shift.

"Don't worry. I have an idea I need your help executing. Come and see me after reading through the day's memos."

"Sure thing," she answered before adding, "should I go ahead and confirm the booking details?"

"Not yet," I paused, knowing I needed to get an answer to her soon. "Just come see me when you're caught up with the morning messages."

"Will do."

After ending the call, I went to work on my end, preparing for what I knew would be no easy feat. Emily had grown accustomed to the best, and I was determined to raise the bar once again.

1

"Boss lady!"

Crystal stopped me mid dash as I moved from one meeting to the next. Only an hour into the morning and I was already swamped, running on fumes after waking up early to read through Christian's proposal.

"I know, I've got the status meeting," I nodded, continuing towards Madison's office. She'd emailed me a list of questions about our upcoming merger, which would double our staff and market share in national publishing.

"No, it's this," she extended her hand with a small white envelope. "You got a weird delivery, I pushed it into your office."

Pushed? My nose scrunched with curiosity as I changed course, entering the colorful office my sister had redesigned to fit my personal style. A chrome rack sat beside my desk with ten identical dresses, just like the black Alice + Olivia one I'd worn the night before. I knew the sender before I opened the note, fighting back a bashful smile.

THE PHYSICAL INTERPRETATION OF APOLOGIZING IN ADVANCE.
IN CASE YOU EVER CHOOSE TO WEAR THIS AROUND ME AGAIN,

AS I HAVE NO INTENTION OF BEHAVING BETTER.
I LOVE YOU.

My husband was never one to spare an expense when it came to making me smile. My initial instinct to call him didn't seem sufficient. Still, I reached into my purse for my cell phone, when the key to my hotel suite caught my attention.

"Is there anything you want me to do?" Crystal asked, reminding me of her presence.

"Yes," I nodded, reaching for a sheet of customized stationary at the corner of my desk. Quickly, I wrote a note before folding the paper, pushing it into an envelope with my hotel key. "Have this sent to my husband's office," I instructed, watching the enthusiasm spread in her eyes.

If there was one thing Crystal loved, it was the games Daniel and I had been known to play with each other. Certainly, a rack of dresses might have alarmed her, but now that she knew the identity of the sender, she appeared more comfortable.

"I'll have it done immediately."

Together, we left my office as I continued to Madison's for our meeting. Like before, she was excited to move forward with the deal, asking if there was any way she could assist me with the amended proposal I'd received the previous night.

I assured her I could handle it, although I hadn't so much as glanced at the thick packet. At times, I wondered if I was getting in over my head taking on so much more responsibility at the publishing house I'd founded for purpose and abandoned for pleasure.

Since my marital problems had resurfaced, I threw myself back into the business, more than I had been involved since purchasing Cherry Blossoms Publishing. It was both a distraction and overdue career, one I'd spent most of my inheritance to launch.

After promising Madison I'd read over the details of the contract before morning, I made my way back to my office. Crystal raised her index finger, calling for my attention as I approached her desk.

"Yes sir, she's right here," she smiled, handing me the phone.

"This is Emily," I frowned, curious about my assistant's teenage giggle.

"You're giving me the key to your place? This feels like a big step," his voice boomed through the phone, seductive as ever.

"Don't get too excited, I can have that magnetic strip deactivated at any time," I shot back, piercing my lips to contain the smile.

"Ahh, an incentive to behave. I see," Daniel's voice deepened.

"I've never known you to behave, Mr. Gamble."

"But my apologies are legendary." His tame words brought a tightness to my pelvis, my thoughts as dark as he'd hoped they'd be.

"What time will you be done at the office?"

"Shouldn't be too late. Can I take you to dinner?"

"I was thinking we could have dinner at... my place," I found the words to describe my makeshift home at the Four Seasons.

"Your place, huh? Are you cooking for me?"

"I don't have a kitchen, but I do have room service," I offered.

"Oh, a lazy date," he teased.

Turning so my back was to Crystal, I moved the phone closer to my mouth as I whispered, "I guarantee I won't be lazy on this date."

Hearing Daniel's sharp inhale sent my thighs pressing together as I closed my eyes awaiting his response.

"I'll be over as soon as I finish here," he responded after a loud swallow.

"Please and thank you."

I reached around, hanging the phone up before continuing to the status meeting. Greeting passing employees, I had an extra twitch of confidence in my step, already anticipating my night.

2

After ending my workday early, I was more than prepared for Daniel's arrival at my hotel suite. Looking at the fresh white fingernail polish that matched my lace teddy and thigh highs, I knew he would approve. He'd texted me just minutes ago to let me know he had arrived. Lying on the bed, I tried to slow my heart rate, closing my eyes in an attempt to force relaxation.

Hearing the soft beep when the electronic lock opened, I felt myself grow eager. Although I couldn't see him enter the living room, I could feel Daniel's presence before he appeared in the doorway to the bedroom. His eyes landed on me before a grin spread across his face.

"Hi," I tried for innocent.

"You look amazing." He walked towards me, wrapping his fingers around my ankle, gently pulling until I sat at the edge of the bed.

In one swift motion, Daniel wrapped his arms around me, lifting me into the air. My legs gripped tightly around his waist as he moved towards the living area. I wasted no time, peppering soft kisses along his neck as I loosened his tie. He didn't stop me, but he didn't engage.

Daniel stopped at the bar, releasing me with a soft tap to my bottom. "Make me a drink."

Confused, I obeyed, walking to the other side of the bar with my eyes set on his. The smirk on his face left me with hope. I'd waited all day for this moment. It was obvious he planned to torture me with delays. After pouring us each two fingers of the Macallan whiskey I'd requested from room service, I slid his glass across the quartz countertop.

"How was your day?" Daniel asked, sitting on one of the two bar stools.

"It was long," I started, making my way to the other side of the bar. "And boring," I added just before sitting next to him.

We were so close my knees bumped against his, and that alone was enough to turn me on. As always, Daniel looked calm, but I knew him well enough to know he was affected.

"How was your day?" I asked, softly nudging him with my knee.

"Long."

He swallowed his entire drink in one gulp, and then set the glass on the bar with a thud. I followed suit, drinking the liquor too fast, instantly feeling the burn in my chest.

"Come here," he pulled me into his arms, lifting me yet again.

This time it was him initiating the contact, sliding his tongue past my lips as he kissed me deeply. It was all I'd been waiting for. My meetings throughout the day were agonizing, unable to focus as I repeatedly relived our night together. What I thought would curb my desires had only intensified the hunger. After one night with Daniel, a night without him felt punitive.

"I missed you," I whispered when Daniel ended our embrace. Carefully, he climbed on the bed with me still in his arms. Lying between my legs, I clasped my ankles against the small of his back.

"You have no idea how much I've missed you, Em."

His voice was raspy, which only excited me more. "I hope you plan on making me forget about those boring meetings."

I felt Daniel's laughter as his chest vibrated against my own. He kissed my ear softly before pressing his face into my neck. It was sweet and intimate, feeling his cool breath against my hot skin. Wondering if he was enjoying my scent, I sat still for a few seconds until the low muffle of his breathing revealed he'd fallen fast asleep.

"You have got to be kidding me," I whispered.

Trapped beneath him, I was stuck with my thoughts. Looking left to right, I noticed the proposal I'd planned to read on the night-stand. There was no way I could reach it with Daniel's weight holding me tightly.

I'd never seen him so exhausted, falling asleep with me in lingerie. Without knowing a thing about his work schedule, I was curious what his day had been like. We always kept our businesses separate. Initially, I thought it was a good idea, allowing us both a sense of independence.

Now, with work demanding so much of us, our autonomy left me feeling in the dark about the man I was committed to sharing my life with. Often, I felt like a stranger in my own marriage. Unlike me, Daniel never needed advice on business, or a moment to vent. He was so well put together, requiring so little maintenance or assistance from me.

While dating, I'd enjoyed the mystery surrounding Daniel. Without stating so, I always assumed the elusiveness would evaporate over time. To my surprise, it didn't. Instead, I was left flashing my badge as his wife to feel less of an outlander. I'd never expressed these shortcomings, because, I guess in the back of my mind I wanted my inclusion to materialize organically.

No one wants to beg for access into the life of the person they love. The ideal scenario is to be let in willingly, even if that access follows a long fight or patient wait. I was willing to endure either, but the thought of asking felt... needy.

The weight of Daniel and heaviness of the unacknowledged gaps in our lives grew to be too much. Carefully, I maneuvered myself until only his arm lay heavily across my midsection, his handsome face so close I could still feel his breath.

"What's going on with you?" I whispered. The sound of my voice brought the slightest curve to his lips before his muscles relaxed as he fell back into a deep sleep.

3

I awoke to Daniel sitting beside me, leaning against the headboard in nothing but his boxer briefs. His brows furrowed as he read the leather-bound proposal Quentin had given me at the Laker's game. I'd barely skimmed it myself, after seeing a lot of the information Madison had presented in her initial analysis repeated.

"Really?" I asked groggily, reaching over Daniel's lap for my cell phone on the nightstand. "You're just going to read my stuff? What if that was confidential?"

"It was the only reading material in the room. I didn't want to wake you with the TV," he answered without glancing up.

Noting the few alerts, none of which required a response, I set the phone back on the nightstand and instead took the remote control. With a few buttons, I switched on the television, turning to Bloomberg. Shockingly, Daniel barely looked up, continuing to turn the pages detailing Quentin's proposition to merge our publishing houses.

"Something tells me you just want to know what's going on with my business."

He was engrossed, as he always was with business. I watched

his eyes scan one page after another, squinting at some points and shaking his head at others. I desperately wanted to know what he could possibly disagree with.

Unlike my lack of involvement with his career, Daniel had always played a major role with Cherry Blossoms Publishing. We met when his consultancy firm negotiated my deal to acquire the floundering publishing house. And since then, he had been my in-house counsel, divvying out business advice whenever I needed it.

Entrepreneurship was far from my comfort zone. Although my father had built one of the most successful hospitality empires in the country, his business was never something he discussed with me or my siblings.

In retrospect, I guess it was for my own good, since my father had recently been arrested for fraud and embezzlement in relation to his business practices. An arrogant chuckle from Daniel made me refocus. I snatched the proposal playfully, annoyed by his word-less reactions.

"That's all you get." I teased. "I hope you enjoyed yourself."

"Eh, fiction's not really my thing," he smirked. Daniel had a way of subtly getting under my skin, letting me know his feelings without directly saying how he felt.

"Fiction?" I shot back, setting the leather book on the opposite side of the bed.

Daniel lifted the remote control from a fold in the luxurious white comforter, increasing the volume of the television as though he hadn't just dropped a major insult. I wished I could let it go, refusing to engage in his little game. But he was the business expert. Dangling an accusation like that left me salivating for more understanding. He knew I could never resist his valuable feedback.

When I was looking to buy a business already equipped with a reputation, business model, and proven track record, he had built one from the ground up. His consultancy firm handled everything from contracts, to mergers, and real estate. As he put it during our first conversation, "If you can afford me, I can fix your problems."

"Are you going to make me ask why you're calling Quentin's proposition fiction?" I rolled my eyes.

"That proposal is bullshit."

He answered flatly, without turning his attention away from Bloomberg. A short sigh of relief escaped me, assuming his reaction was personal. I'd had a growing suspicion that Daniel was uncomfortable with me working with Quentin since they first met. Admittedly, it was a bit awkward for my husband to find me giggling away with a handsome man, even if he was a business prospect.

The talking heads on the television were discussing a minor spike in the cost of copper, and what industries would be affected most. Apparently, it was a great time to catch a sale on stocks in telecommunication, as their industry costs would temporarily balloon. Because many shareholders would sell, their stock price would fall, but undoubtedly return to their peak within 18-months.

"I know you've been out the loop, but I've actually been kicking ass at work lately. My team has vetted Q's company thoroughly. He's the real deal," I assured him, questioning if I'd used Quentin's nickname to annoy him as his subtle insult had annoyed me. Even more, I wondered what my psychiatrist would think of me enjoying the possible rivalry between Quentin and my husband.

"Q?" Daniel finally looked away from Bloomberg. Amused by my attempt to invoke jealousy, he smiled so deeply a small dimple showed in his left cheek.

"Quentin," I corrected myself, seductively climbing over him to get off the bed.

Daniel's hands gripped my lace covered hips at the optimal time to leave one leg on either side of his body. With a gently twist of my hips, I was straddling him, his full attention finally granted.

"There's no opposition in the proposal, Em. It's a glorified media kit for his company, not an actual opening of his books." He stared at me as I tried to fight the smile daring to reveal itself. "It's all fluff, babe."

"Are you serious?" I gawked. "Daniel, there's an entire section dedicated to weaknesses."

Leaning across the bed, I reached for the proposal as Daniel's hand tightened on my hip to prevent me from falling. The white teddy dug into my soft flesh as I secured the book, excited to prove Daniel wrong. Flipping through the pages, I silently appreciated the thickness of the paper. When it came to Quentin's attempt to professionally seduce me, he spared no expense.

Everything with him was top of the line, often overboard. Like when he sent a limousine to pick us up from the office, or decided to have a business meeting in a skybox at the Staples Center. I'd seen several proposals as the head of Cherry Blossoms Publishing, few of them were leather bound.

"Who did this research?" Daniel asked, bringing me back to our debate.

"Everything in here has been double checked by Madison," I argued, searching for the section she'd pointed out as crucial. "Here! See," I turned the thick book of a proposal towards Daniel so he could see the heading that read 'Improvement Areas'.

Daniel, fighting back an arrogant grin, took the book reluctantly, quickly scanning the pages before turning to me with disappointment in his hazel eyes. "All this basically says is he doesn't retain his readers. We both know that's a win in disguise, because you can convert them and increase his market share."

I frowned, taking the leather in my hand as I tried to comprehend the two pages of statistics and graphs as quickly as Daniel had. I'd looked it over briefly, noticing that because Quentin's publishing house focused on salacious memoirs and celebrity tell-all books, he didn't have much of a fan base.

Readers want to grow with an author, witnessing their work improve, boasting that they've been supporters since the first release. It's their dedication and word of mouth that makes writers successful. When you enjoy reading a book, you tell everyone, effectively building an author's reputation and audience.

Quentin's Laney Publishing didn't have that reader loyalty. They sold books to fans of television shows, who were only interested in a bit of gossip, with no connection to the writer. He used ghost-writers for most of his releases, which made author recognition all but impossible.

I was certain we could find a way to turn one book into three, changing the way he published to create return customers, a plan Daniel had just pointed out. I didn't see Quentin's lack of retaining customers as a true negative, but more of a challenge I was confident we could overcome.

"He doesn't own his company outright, Em. You do. How could he think you could be partners when you're not even peers?"

I looked up with confidence, because that was a question I'd already asked Madison. "That's why he wants a board," I said, flipping through the pages again for the proof. "We can keep our clients separate and share distribution. It's a nice blend of autonomy and consolidation. We'll vote for decisions, which would make us more equal in the structure of the business. Plus, I'll get half the value of my company in cash."

It was a concession I was willing to make to recoup most of my initial investment. Daniel was right, there was no way we could establish an equitable partnership as things were. At Cherry Blossoms Publishing, I owned everything, which made my voice reign supreme. At Quentin's publishing house, every major decision had to go through a board of investors since he was not the sole owner of the company.

Daniel lifted me from his lap, setting me beside him before standing from the bed, uninterested. "He wants a board so he can vote you out."

A punch to the gut would have hurt less. Of all the things I'd suspected of Quentin, trying to swindle me out of my company wasn't one of them. He'd been sly from our first meeting, a bit too charming for my liking. But nothing about him felt sleazy or conniving.

"Where's his balance sheet?" Daniel asked, standing at the edge of the bed. When I didn't respond, he continued. "He's been in business for 8-years, but there are only six years of income state-ments, no tax returns, only half a page of disclosures."

I couldn't look up at him, my mind was too busy searching for ways to prove him wrong. It was so like him to come into a situation and assume the worst. Daniel argued that he was a realist, but I always saw it as pessimism. He saw the worst in people, business, and life in general. It was a defense mechanism, preparing himself to minimize disappointment. For me, it was nothing more than a buzzkill.

"I'll tell you what," he spoke in a softer tone now. "If Madison vouched for all of this, ask her to create a proposal as if you were looking to merge your company. Don't tell her what it's for, but tell her you have another company in competition with Quentin. See what she creates for the proposal, then compare that to all the fluff in there." He pointed to the proposal that felt like sand on a summer day, burning my hands.

"You think Madison is working against me?" This was one accu-sation that was sure to be false. Madison had been with Cherry Blossoms before I even acquired it. At times, I thought she loved the company even more than I did. There was no way she would ever do anything to jeopardize the publishing house we loved so much.

"Do you remember the time I negotiated the merger between the two spring water companies?" Daniel asked from the foot of the bed.

"No."

"You remember," he coached. "One was from Colorado, and the other was in West Virginia."

"Daniel, you've literally never mentioned anything to me about any merger you've ever worked on." My voice was monot-one, stripped of all the emotion begging to pour out. He was flaunting the secrecy of his business and how little I knew about it.

"Look," he continued with a shrug, seemingly oblivious to my frustration. "All I know is, they're drowning you in digits with that proposal. Someone is hiding something." He ended the conversation, walking towards the second room.

"Want a drink?" He called over his shoulder without breaking stride.

I wanted to reject him, as punishment for the way he paraded his expertise without regard. I'd been working on this deal for weeks, and he wasn't the least bit impressed. Seeing the muscles in his back flex with each step made me reconsider my defiance, as my legs unfolded beneath me.

"Yeah," I answered, inching across the bed until I was perched at the edge, my feet resting on the coolness of the hardwood floors.

Daniel poured two glasses of whiskey, then stopped to retrieve his suit jacket. Lifting the Italian fabric from the arm of the sofa, he took something from the inside pocket before taking one glass in each hand and making his way to me.

Handing me one glass, I noticed the orange and brown pattern of the wrapper he'd gotten from his suit. "You brought chocolate?" I asked excitedly, taking the gourmet candy bar from his hand.

"I figured tonight would involve whiskey," he said, sitting beside me on the edge of the bed.

Staring at the intricate design on the wrapper, I thought back to when Daniel first introduced me to the chocolate he had found for my father. Like Daniel, my father preferred to drink whiskey, a drink they often shared together. For his recent birthday, Daniel had gifted him with different variations of chocolate bars, which they had found to pair perfectly with the richness of the liquor.

I felt frozen in the past, admiring the packaging of the orange and almond dark chocolate. It was a bittersweet memory, like so many involving my father. A sore subject I didn't like reflecting on. He was facing more charges than I could understand, and unwilling to talk to me or my siblings about the future of his life, or businesses.

Without thinking, I rose from the bed with memories and reality weighing me down. Daniel's hand caught my wrist. "Where are you going?"

"To take a bath," I breathed, as though the decision itself was draining.

Daniel swallowed slowly, watching me with intensity. "Can I join you?"

To my surprise, a laugh fell from my lips. "Seriously?" Daniel had never accepted one of my invitations to bathe together.

"Yeah," he answered quickly.

"Okay," I offered, leading the way to the bathroom. He followed me closely, never releasing my wrist as we entered the dark bathroom.

4

U nlike our light-colored master bathroom at home, the hotel suite opted for grays so dark they could be mistaken for black. Every surface shined like a black diamond, with mystique and boldness.

I'd packed my own bath oils, pouring a little lavender into the running water as it quickly filled the deep bathtub. Daniel alternated between watching me in the nude, and the water, a subtle nervousness to him like a kid nearing the edge of a swimming pool, unsure of his swimming abilities.

I'd been craving Daniel, sexually more than anything. From the look on his face, as he waited to bathe with me for the first time, I realized it was intimacy he missed most.

Stopping the water, I pushed the building guilt away. I was the one who had delayed a reunion between us, needing time to myself more than I cared to mend my marriage. Daniel's gaze of intense longing was a direct result of my neglect.

"Ready?" I asked with a small smile.

Daniel answered with action, stripping his boxers to reveal what I'd been missing. I didn't hide my enthusiasm, watching him climb into the bath before offering his hand. I accepted, settling into the steamy water as Daniel's arms draped around me.

Sitting between his legs, my head rested along his collarbone as our breathing synced to one rhythm. So many questions unanswered, yet my words formed not one. Instead, I lay silent, finally relaxing.

Years of marriage, but we'd never spent a moment submerged beneath warm water, our bodies joined together in a simple bliss I couldn't describe. The silence was welcome, as each of us recalled whatever memory came to mind.

For me, it was us sitting in the same formation, years earlier, as we prepared to furnish our first home together. It was a simple gesture to ensure we could fit together in the bathtub before purchasing it, but deep down it was very symbolic.

I was someone else then, with different goals and expectations for my life. I wanted nothing more than to outgrow the shadow of my father, hoping individual success would allow me to define myself. However, with marriage came a curbed appetite for industry, as my professional ambition diminished.

Dismissing my career to focus on being a wife all seemed like a fairy tale until it was meant to be my reality. Then, it was a weight, wrapped around my neck, pulling me towards a life I wasn't fully in love with.

Making the difficult decisions about what I wanted for my life was no fantasy. In fact, when it was time to put all I'd learned from my mother into practice, it felt more like a nightmare. In a strange conundrum I never anticipated, I did not fit the shoes I had daydreamed of wearing for as long as I could remember.

Choosing the details of our life together – kitchen cabinets, hand painted tiles for the back splash, a huge deep soaking bathtub, soundproof insulation – those decisions I enjoyed. And there were so many details; enough to keep me busy for a full year.

Then, it was time to live it. I thought I'd revel in spending my days as I pleased, while Daniel worked at the office, returning home to a meal I'd spent hours preparing. I wanted to enjoy learning new recipes, managing the house staff, organizing social events with fellow wives, and planning for our first child.

It just wasn't enough for me. Watching Daniel pour himself into his passion, it was clear our lives were disjointed. Forcing myself into a career, I tried to mimic his lifestyle in hopes it would bring us closer. In the end, I was void of comfort. Unhappy spending my days in the office, or at home, felt immensely ungrateful. Being unfulfilled in a space of abundance is a lonely existence, which often left me questioning myself.

"What are you thinking about?"

Daniel's words caused my muscles to seize for a split second, feeling caught in a lie I'd never spoken. In an instant, I relaxed, falling into his soft skin as the water passed over my shoulders.

"Do you remember shopping for bathtubs for the house?" I asked, looking over my shoulder just in time to see the smile spread across his face.

"Of course, I do," Daniel's grin was unrushed, a characteristic I'd grown to value in him. "A soaking tub was on your 'must have list'," he raised his brows with sarcasm at the recollection.

"I thought we'd be taking baths together," I admitted, relaxing deeper into his arms.

"I've always enjoyed my seat in the audience."

To my right, a window framed a view of Los Angeles I wasn't used to. It was a tourist view of the city I loved, up close and personal. The view from our home was much different, overlooking the city from the privacy living in the hills provided.

Daniel leaned in close, allowing his soft and warm words to cascade against my neck. "So, you were thinking about why we never bathe together?"

I smiled, happy he could still read me. While the memory of house shopping together was fresh in my mind, it meant more than the literal recollection.

Debating whether I wanted to delve into the deeper questions, I ran my nails over the top of the water, filling my palm with bubbles.

Lowering my hand into the warm water, I moved in a wave like motion, creating designs in the lavender scented suds.

"Talk to me," he whispered, kissing my neck gently.

I inhaled a shaky breath. "Sometimes, I feel like I don't know you." I said it so quickly, I shocked myself.

My instinct was to bury the confession, so I rushed an explanation. "I mean, I think of us in that bathtub and these ideas I had about marriage. I didn't imagine living such separate lives. I feel intensely connected to you but still like an outsider, all at once."

Daniel sat silent for so long I began to doubt my revelation. I was the one who said I wasn't ready to talk, and here I was pushing us into an in-depth discovery. I was moving to turn, and tell him we didn't need to discuss it now, when his arms tightened around my midsection.

Resting his chin on my shoulder, he spoke softly. "What do you want to know?"

"It's not that simple," I reasoned, leaning into him. "I don't have a list of questions you've never answered, but I sometimes wonder what your days are like. And I feel like I should know."

"You know me better than anyone."

"There's just so much I feel in the dark about," my stomach tensed at the admission. I liked to believe Daniel and I were closer than most couples. But whenever a new detail about him emerged, I questioned that.

Daniel kissed my neck softly, pressing his lips gently into my skin before moving slightly and repeating the gesture. He kissed me repeatedly as I sat in silence, unsure how I could better explain myself. The words didn't come until he pushed me. "You have to talk to me, baby. I don't know what you feel left out about, but I know I'd be happy to tell you."

"What does 'From now until forever' mean?" I asked quickly. The mystery had been sitting at the edge of my subconscious, waiting for an opportunity to reveal itself.

Daniel's body tensed briefly and I feared I might have crossed a boundary. His arms gripped me even stronger, so tight I had to lean further into him for relief. I felt his nose softly grazing my damp neck as his body relaxed again.

"You know my dad left us when I was young," he started.

"Yes," I breathed in disbelief. "Of course, I know your dad left when you were twelve." I turned to face him, citing his age to assure him I'd never forget.

"Well, you're the one acting like I'm a stranger." He argued, pulling me back into his grasp before kissing my neck a few more times.

"My mom was overwhelmed, understandably. Her and my dad had been together since they were teenagers. I tried to help her carry the load by accepting responsibility for my little brother. So, I vowed to take care of Jason from now," he began their saying as I joined in with him.

"Until forever."

"Exactly." He kissed me again, this time in front of my ear. "It just stuck."

"I think it's sweet," I smiled, feeling privileged to know the origin of the deep bond between him and his brother.

"What else?" Daniel asked as though it was a trivia session he was determined to ace. "What else do you want to know about me?"

Charmed by his enthusiasm, I pressed on. "What's the Tokyo deal?" I asked, allowing my curiosity to run wild. He'd been working on a project in Japan for months, but I knew little about it.

This time there was no tension or hesitation. "It's a startup. They're actually based out of Fukuoka, which is like Japan's Silicon Valley. I want to guide their US integration. If they can break into the North American market, the sky's the limit."

"Hmm," I nodded along, always entertained by how excited he got about business.

"My work is boring," he said. "I don't talk about it because it's not much to discuss."

"I like when you talk to me about business. I always learn something," I said, feeling his chest react. I turned to see him laughing softly. "I'm serious! You've taught me everything I know about business."

Biting his bottom lip, he nudged me until I fell back into his chest. I felt lighter. It wasn't so much the answers to his questions that relieved me, but his willingness to share. I knew I'd never know everything about him, but I needed reassurance that nothing was off limits between us.

"Can I ask you something?" He asked, as his hands explored beneath the surface of the water.

"Of course," I answered curiously.

"Have you always wanted to be a mogul?" His words were weak, as if he wasn't sure if he should release them.

"What?" I felt my nose scrunch at the absurdity of his question.

Me? A mogul? I still didn't see that in my future. Even as the CEO of Cherry Blossoms Publishing, I looked to myself more as a boss, but never more than that. Being as involved as I currently was with the business was more than I ever imagined. Before, I'd been a silent partner of sorts. Only the funding came from me. Well, my trust fund. But I never involved myself with the day to day activities or business happenings.

"I think I was just looking for a distraction after everything that happened with us." I admitted.

For a split second, I felt his abdomen flex. And then his hand traveled gently up my shoulder, finding the tips of my hair. His fingers twirled my damp strands around his fingertips, silently encouraging me to proceed.

"It was nice to have a purpose every day," I paused, unsure of how Daniel would accept the other half of that thought. "It felt like I didn't have anything else."

"I do that too," he revealed as his fingertips found my scalp, massaging gently. "Whenever things aren't right with us, I work insane hours just to keep my mind busy. Did it help you?"

"Yes!" I divulged without hesitation or shame. Work had been my saving grace. It was the only reason living in a hotel suite wasn't depressing. I was busy from my waking breath until I dozed off, exhausted. With a multi-million-dollar company depending on me, I didn't have time to overthink things between me and Daniel.

"I don't know that I will love it after a while, though. Sitting in an office all day doesn't appeal to me. Sometimes I feel like a suit, telling creatives how to work their magic."

Daniel hugged me, wrapping his ankles over my legs to lock me into his embrace. "You've always been good at the office. In your first year, you broke all the sales records," he reminded me.

It was a fond memory. When I first acquired Cherry Blossoms Publishing, there was plenty of room for improvement. By optimizing the systems in place, and implementing a few changes, I saw instant results. But since my third year in charge, we hadn't seen much growth. Our sales were stagnant at best, with very little change happening.

"We've barely been steady since," I reminded him.

"You didn't purchase it to be a cash cow, remember? You said it was about 'giving artists a place to share their gifts'," he spoke in an annoyingly high pitched voice to imitate my idealistic hopes.

"I don't sound like that!" I splashed a handful of water towards him, feeling his chest rise and fall with laughter. When the water settled, as I did back into our embrace, I thought of his recollection. "We don't do that either. Cherry Blossoms isn't really the company I envisioned it to be."

Daniel's fingertips continued dancing along my scalp, calming me with every movement. "You always have options."

"Like what?"

"You've already proven you can change the structure," he started.

"Yeah," I remembered. "I guess I have to restructure everything if I want it to live up to my dreams."

Suddenly, Daniel turned me around. Unaffected by the splash of water rushing onto the tiled floors, he smirked as he pulled me towards him. "Speaking of restructuring. We've never really set the rules to our marriage," Daniel said as my legs wrapped around his waist.

5

"R ules?" I asked, confused by the notion. Facing him directly, I was more bashful, lacking the confidence I'd embodied with my back to him.

"Yeah," he massaged my knees with his strong hands. "The set-up we have now is obviously not working. Honestly, I think you mirrored what you saw with your parents, and I just went along with that."

I inhaled his last sentence with a wave of tension that traveled down my throat, curving into my stomach with disdain. "I never want to be like my mother."

The words were laced with vile. So distasteful, my face twisted as I spoke the truth. Remembering my mother in the moment only she and I witnessed, as she shook violently in my arms, destroyed by my father's wrongdoing, I felt disgusted.

My entire life, it felt as though my mother moved from one humiliation to another at the hands of her husband. He was more of an enemy than a partner to her, and yet she constantly defended him, despite never being welcomed to the inner circle of his life.

She didn't seem to know much about his business, or business in general. And she was regularly reminded that she was an outsider to his personal life. My mother was more like an employee. Though high ranking, her clearance was limited to the on goings of his family life – raising his children, planning family vacations, and appearing alongside him at public events.

"What *do you* want to be like?" Daniel asked.

"What do you mean?" I stalled, feeling myself blush. While I was certain of the type of woman I didn't want to become, I was less sure of what type of woman I did aspire to be. My eyes drifted to the small gap between us, as the bubbles in the bathtub dissolved by the second.

I'd never felt so naked in my life. Stripped bare, I had no answer for what I felt should be second nature. How could I not know who I wanted to be? Daniel's index finger lifted my chin until our eyes met again. Instinctually pushing my shoulders back, I gazed into his eyes with the confidence I was known for, even if I didn't feel it in my heart.

"We can write the rules to our marriage, babe." He paused, his finger still holding my chin. "Whatever we want," he added with certainty.

"People will think we're crazy," I felt the frown pushing my eyebrows together.

"No, they'll realize they're crazy for not doing the same," he smiled. "Everyone wants to live by their own rules."

"What rules do you want?" I flipped the question on him, unsure of my own desires.

Daniel reached to the edge of the bathtub, taking one of the rolled washcloths and submerging it into the warm water as he took the lavender soap from the dish. With his eyes locked with mine, he rubbed the two together until the white towel bubbled over with suds.

"Em, I don't know what I'm doing," he began after a deep sigh. "You're the only experience I'll ever have with marriage. So, I can't say that making our own rules will work."

Raising the towel to my neck, he began rubbing the warm cloth across my collarbone as he kept on. "But I know two things – I want to spend the rest of my life with you, and I want you to be happy about that."

"You're always worried about my happiness," I reached for his forearm, halting his relaxing bath as I took the washcloth. "What do you want?"

I watched him process my words, allowing them to crease lines in his forehead as I pushed the washcloth over his broad shoulder, lifting his left arm to carry suds to his wrist.

"You want to know my rules?" He finally asked.

"I do," I said, bringing the washcloth to his chest before moving to his right arm.

"I need to live together." Daniel's words were definite, as though he'd given the idea much thought.

I nodded, but still found the need to debate. "I can see that, but living so close to work has been really convenient."

Before I could finish my argument, he interjected. "Then, we'll move. I want to be with you every night. I don't even like sleeping in different beds, but being in separate houses is unbearable."

"Okay. Living separate is unbearable for you. So, I'll come home," I answered quickly.

"Same bed," he added.

"Same bed," I acknowledged his amendment with a smile. Sharing a bed with Daniel was no concession. Sleeping alone was one of the worst parts of our separation. "What else?"

"If you want to use your maiden name, I'd prefer you change it legally," he searched my eyes as he spoke.

"Are you asking if I want to use my maiden name?" I wondered aloud.

"Well, that's the name you're using. I don't want to force you to change it."

"What do you want?"

"Don't play games, Em. You know I want you to use my name," he recalled.

"Then why would you not state that as a rule?"

"Fine. You're Emily Gamble." He said boldly before cracking a smile.

"Fine." I felt my lips curve upwards. I'd never had a problem taking Daniel's name. In fact, I loved the allegiance it gave, a clear indication we were on the same team. It was when we were at odds that I felt awkward about sharing a name while lacking devotion.

"Anything else?" I chimed, reaching behind Daniel to wash his back.

"I want to alternate holidays."

This rule was the most difficult to accept. I'd never spent a holiday away from my family. Daniel never seemed to care much, but I guess I hadn't given much thought to his preferences. After a moment of reflection, I nodded in agreement as he took the washcloth from me.

Setting the cloth on the edge of the bathtub, he retrieved another from the pile of washcloths rolled and stacked to perfection. His light eyes watched me closely as he dunked the cloth into the water before bringing it to suds with the lavender soap.

"To keep things fair, you get three rules," he said, causing ripples in the water as he pulled me close with a firm hand on my hip.

"Easy," I boasted with confidence, holding my index finger up to signify my first rule. "I want to be let into your life. I don't like feeling like an outsider all the time."

"I'm fine with that. That doesn't even count as a rule," he said, lifting my arm to cover me in suds.

"Fine," I continued to hold my index finger as I watched him carefully. "I want my name added to the house deed."

Daniel huffed. "Really?" He looked to me for a second before shrugging. "Done."

Adding another finger to my count, I continued. "I want you to help me understand business, for real. I don't want to be dependent on you."

This time Daniel hesitated as his head bopped imperceptibly. "Okay," he paused. "I like that one. You got one more."

I took a deep breath, knowing my third and final rule would be the most drastic change for either of us. Looking to Daniel, I locked our gaze before speaking. "I want to go to therapy together."

His hands massaged the suds on my breasts. "Is that a deal?" I asked, unsure if he was distracted.

"Therapy," he spoke the syllables slowly, as though trying to pronounce a foreign word. "Yeah, okay."

"Yeah?" I asked.

"Yeah." He agreed more confidently.

Satisfied with our newly set rules, Daniel reached for the extendable handheld shower head, rinsing first my body and then his. Standing from the water, he lifted me from the tub before heading to the bedroom.

Glancing at the illuminated red digital numbers, I couldn't believe the time. Only four hours before the blaring alarm would sound, signaling the start of my work day.

"What time do you need to be at the office?" Daniel asked, standing at the edge of the bed. I knew what he was asking from the dark lust in his eyes.

"I need to leave by seven," I said through a smile.

"You're going to be late."

6

————

It had been weeks since my older sister Victoria redesigned my office, and I was still finding hidden details. Like, the small secret door hidden in what looked to be a wall panel. By pressing the discrete door, you opened what was a fully stocked bar, equipped with refrigeration.

As I had with every other new discovery, I picked up my office phone to dial my closest sister. As always, she answered quickly.

"What's up, baby girl?" She answered excitedly.

"I found the bar," I rushed my discovery.

"Did you?" I could hear her smile through the phone. "I thought that one would take you longer. How'd you find it?"

"Being lazy and bumping into the wall," I giggled.

It had been a rough morning after my long night with Daniel. I was exhausted, but refused to take a day off. Instead, I came into the office a little late, as Daniel had predicted. Crystal cleared my schedule at my request. Basically, I was at work, but completely unavailable. My assistant was so great at her job, she probably had the entire office under the guise that I was closing some major deal rather than struggling to stay awake.

"You over there sleeping in the office after Mommy bullied you into booking that expensive ass suite? I will happily find use for that hotel room," she teased.

"No. I was at the hotel," I said slowly, pausing before finishing the sentence. "Daniel stayed the night."

"Shut up!" She was gushing now. If I didn't have her full attention before, I definitely had it now.

Just then, my cell phone vibrated loudly on the glass desk suspended from the ceiling. Rather than the photo from our Thailand vacation I was used to accompanying his call, this time a new picture of me lying on Daniel's chest appeared on the screen, one he must have taken the night before. The white bold letters above the photo read, 'My Husband'.

"This is him calling now," I teased. "I'll call you back later."

"Promise me we'll go to lunch this week!" She rushed, desperate for details.

"I promise," I smirked as I ended the call before answering my cell phone.

"Hey," I answered casually, leaning back in my desk chair.

"Damn, I expected you to sound as tired as I feel." Daniel's voice sent seductive chills up my spine.

"Regretting your mistakes so soon?" I shot back.

"I never said I regretted anything." His tone was intimate and yet authoritative.

"I see you updated your contact info in my phone," I changed the subject, twisting in my chair to focus on the city view.

"I was overdue for an upgrade," he challenged.

"I guess you're right. It's been a while since we were in Thailand," I remarked, noticing a message pop up on my computer screen from Crystal. She was asking if she could come in for a quick chat.

"I think I'm overdue for a vacation," I distractedly added as I typed quickly, inviting Crystal into my office.

"Let's go to Thailand," Daniel's quick response garnered my full attention.

"You don't have time for a vacation," I pressed the phone closer to my cheek as my office door opened.

"That must be your way of telling me *you* don't have time for a vacation. Welcome to my world, Mrs. Gamble," Daniel chuckled.

He was right. There was no way I could get away for long enough to fly halfway around the world. The flights alone were more time than I could spare in the midst of a merger.

"I have to go, Crystal needs to tell me something. And from the look on her face, it's important," I watched my assistant look away bashfully.

"I want you to come over to the office." He said, catching me off guard. "To sit in on a meeting."

Holding one finger up to Crystal, I turned in my chair, creating a small envelope of privacy. "A meeting? Why do you want me there?"

"It's a mock merger meeting. I think you'll see what I mean about your proposal," he explained.

Instant excitement made it difficult to remain calm. I loved sitting in on Daniel's work, whether necessary or not. But never in our years of marriage had he ever so obviously attempted to teach me about business.

"What time?" I finally responded.

"Can you be here in an hour?"

"Yes." I answered without hearing what news Crystal had to share.

"I love you." His words were so genuine I felt butterflies.

"I love you too, Daniel." I didn't bother to hide my smile as I turned back to Crystal. "I'll see you soon."

I ended the call, setting the phone down to signal to Crystal she had the floor. Noting the silent memo, she stepped forward, glancing at her checklist.

"Your schedule has been cleared as you requested. The team thinks you'll be monitoring progress and eyeing competition," she read from her clipboard, oblivious to my smile. I knew her so well. "There's only a problem with Madison."

My eyes rolled before I could imagine what the head of my acquisitions team could want to discuss. She had been overly excited about merging with Quentin's company, Laney Publishing, since the idea was introduced.

"I know," Crystal smiled, sharing my amusement. "I told her she could have fifteen minutes whenever I could find it," she said.

"Well, send her in now. I need to be at Daniel's in an hour to sit in on a meeting." I turned to stuff the leather proposal from Quentin into my work bag.

It had been a few days since I received the proposal, but I'd yet to read it. The last thing I needed was for my colleague to see how behind I was on urgent work.

"Okay, I'll get her now. Let me know if there's anything I can prepare for Mr. Gamble's meeting," Crystal announced on the balls of her feet as she turned to leave the room.

"No, it's just a mock meeting," I started before an idea popped in my mind. "You know what?" I caught her attention as she spun back on her 4-inch heels.

"What is it, boss lady?"

"You have a copy of the latest proposal from Quentin, right?" I asked.

"Yeah, I got it this morning," she said.

"Read over it. I want your honest feedback tomorrow morning with notes," I decided as the words fell from my lips.

"Consider it done," Crystal beamed. She'd always wanted more responsibility. This was her opportunity and I didn't expect her to fail.

"Perfect."

I looked to Crystal like the little sister I always wanted. She was one of the few employees I hired myself after purchasing the publishing company. I was fine with Human Resources filling every other role, as Daniel had suggested. But when it came to the person assigned to follow me around, organize my calendar, and be my eyes when I wasn't around, I needed to play a role in their hiring process.

Crystal was the one component of my company I was undoubt-edly confident about. She was with me, and her opinion was as good as my own. "Don't hold back," I warned her.

"I never do." She assured me.

"Don't hold back on what?" Madison's call from the door jolted us.

7

Without missing a beat, Crystal answered Madison on her way out. "Trying to find a new manicurist for the office. You know, to boost morale."

Madison watched my assistant exit before turning to me. "I'm so glad I could catch you. There's so much we need to discuss," she rushed toward the sitting area as I made my way around the desk, joining her across from the coffee table.

Madison sat on the neon yellow tufted sofa, while I relaxed in a red womb chair, kicking my feet up on the matching ottoman. The rug that sat beneath us was like a painting on the floor, filled with vibrant colors that somehow refused to distract. Instead, it tied the inspiring design my sister had created together.

"Oh yeah?" I asked, accepting a piece of paper she extended in what appeared to be panic.

"It looks like Quentin is meeting with other publishing houses. He's serious about the merger, but it doesn't seem to be exclusive to us. We need to move quickly."

"Do you need some water?" I asked, reaching for my phone to message Crystal.

"No, I'm fine," she shook her head. "I just don't want us to lose this opportunity, you know."

I looked over the page, which was a print out of an email correspondence between Madison and someone I wasn't familiar with. "Who is Martell Engram?"

"He's in PR," Madison said before I cut her off by raising my index finger as I continued reading.

The email was written in a friendly yet messy tone, as a tidbit of gossip. Apparently, Martell had heard about the merger we were discussing with Quentin and wanted to give Madison a heads up that he was also shopping the opportunity around to other publishing houses in the city.

"How do you know him?" I asked, glancing back at the printout to remember his name. "This Martell. Are you friends?"

"No, not really," she denied quickly. "We've met once or twice at events throughout the years. I can't vouch for him personally, but I know he's in the know. If a deal is happening, he knows about it. I wouldn't call his bluff."

"I see," I nodded, catching the sensitive skin of my lip between my front teeth as I considered the best possible response.

"Should I call Quentin? Maybe set up a meeting?" Madison asked, her pale cheeks reddening by the second. Her hair was pulled into a ponytail with a pen tucked through her long sandy brown hair.

"No." I answered quickly. While I wasn't sure what I should do, I knew that rushing without a plan was a bad course of action. "Let me think on it. I'll get back to you."

I rose from my seat, signaling the end of the meeting. The forgiving linen rayon fabric of my dress impressed, without one wrinkle displaying the hours I'd been sitting at my desk answering emails. It was another look my college friend Monica had picked for me, one I might have shied away from in the past.

The cognac colored maxi shirt dress was both business and casual, with brass buttons leading from my breasts to just below my knee. Leaving a few buttons unfastened in each direction created a hint of cleavage and a daring split in the otherwise modest look. A fabric belt wrapped twice around my waist defined my shape favorably, while the rolled-up sleeves added dimension.

"I can take that," Madison offered, reaching for the print out in my hand.

"I think I'll hang onto it," I said, as she paused. An emotion I couldn't decipher flashed across her blushed face before she could plaster on a smile.

Crystal reappeared as quickly as Madison exited, closing the door behind her. This time, my assistant was carrying my schedule. Joining me in the seating area, we watched as Madison stood just outside my office, frantically typing away on her phone.

"Do you think she forgot you can see through the glass?" Crystal teased.

It was one of my favorite features in my redesigned office. Victoria had decided a two-way mirror as an office wall was anything but stylish. Thankfully, she understood the utility my old mirror had presented. I liked to be able to watch the comings and goings of the office without being seen.

In a compromise that exceeded all my expectations Victoria had created a wall of windows that transitioned, to a design of white cherry blossom flowers with blush buds, at the push of a button. From inside my office, I could see through the flowers, but on the opposite side of the glass, the design was opaque. To conceal my exhaustion and constant nods, I'd had the feature activated all morning to provide an extra layer of privacy. Now, Madison stood on the other side of my wall of windows, oblivious to the fact that I could see her every move.

"There's something up with her," I said, more to myself than to Crystal.

"Do you think she's pressing too hard for the deal?"

I turned to my assistant, a bit shocked that she too had picked up on Madison's overzealous behavior. After a brief hesitation, questioning if discussing my suspicions were appropriate, I decided to continue. If there was one person I could trust in the office, it was

Crystal. She had been my assistant for years, and not once had I ever questioned her loyalty or commitment to me or Cherry Blossoms.

"She's really pressed, isn't she?" I asked, again more to myself.

"I thought it was because of a crush she had on Quentin, but now I think it's beyond that," Crystal looked to me as though I had an answer. When I remained silent in contemplation, she continued. "Did you promise her some type of promotion in the merger?"

"No." I answered, looking into her eyes. I didn't want her to think I would promote anyone without offering her the same opportunity. She was my right hand in the business, more valuable than any executive.

"Do you think Quentin could have made her any promises?" She asked meekly, understanding the unethical nature of the accusation.

"He couldn't," I reasoned, thinking about it for a second. In the new merger Quentin and I had discussed, we would have equal authority, meaning any promotions would have to be agreed upon by both parties. Then, Daniel's insinuation came to mind. He thought Quentin was attempting to buy my company under false pretenses.

"What's my schedule look like this week? Are there any meetings with Quentin?" I asked.

Crystal opened the leather-bound planner. As she flipped through the pages of daily breakdowns, I noticed an abnormal amount of blank space towards the end of the month.

"What's going on there?" I leaned across the table, pointing to the month view, which highlighted two blank weeks.

"Oh, it's just," she shook her head without looking up to me. "I have to know the outcome of the merger to know how to arrange your future schedule. So, I've been writing everything in pencil until the deal is set, then I can ink it in the calendar."

"That makes sense," I relaxed. Feeling on edge in the office for the first time, I walked towards my desk needing a moment of clarity.

In less than two minutes, I'd gone from reminding myself that Crystal was the most trustworthy employee, to wondering if she was plotting to oust me from my company because of a break in my schedule. I needed to calm down.

"There is only one meeting with Quentin, and it's not today. But, you know Madison is usually the one he coordinates with. She only reaches out to me for your openings." She looked up to me for direction.

"Well, the next time she does that, let her know you'll have to check with me first. Don't just put her on the schedule."

With my hands on the back of my desk chair, I began to put in play a strategy that would reveal any nefarious doings on Madison or Quentin's part. While I didn't want to rush to judgement, it was clear there was something pushing Madison to close the deal. And Quentin had been overzealous from our first meeting. I'd have to do some digging, but I was going to get to the bottom of this one way or another.

8

Tower Enterprise Group was nothing like Cherry Blossoms Publishing. Whenever I stopped by, I felt underdressed in anything other than a suit. Daniel's consulting firm was always busy, with people walking with purpose, heading from one meeting to the next. There was never any laughter, just firm handshakes and informal plans for follow up.

"Mrs. Gamble," Tracy greeted me as I neared her desk.

"Hey," I smiled, looking towards Daniel's office. "Is he in?"

"I am," his voice boomed from behind me. Just as I turned to see him, Daniel's hands were on my waist. "You don't look tired."

Blushing, I looked over his suit selection. A dark navy three-piece suit that framed his broad shoulders, curving along his sides and back. How he could be so sexy fully clothed was beyond me.

"I don't know how you're operating on all cylinders," I said, straightening the Pratt knot of his tie as I leaned in, lowering my tone. "Did you even sleep last night?"

I was shocked when I woke to find the bed empty. Always the early riser, Daniel usually beat me to the office. But, after the night we'd had, I thought even he would need a late start.

"I had to go home to change," he whispered with a slight raise of his eyebrows that said more than his words.

It reminded me of our agreement. One I hadn't given much thought. I'd been so wrapped up in work, I hadn't considered the logistics of getting my things from the suite back to our shared home. But seeing Daniel in all his corporate glory made the task feel more like a reward. I was looking forward to waking up to him.

"I'm going to send Crystal to move my things," I pressed my lips together to hide my smile as I reached for my phone. Daniel didn't hide his appreciation, letting his grin spread until a dimple creased his cheek.

"First, we need to handle something," he said, leading me into his office. "You all set, George?"

A balding white man stood at Daniel's desk, holding a pen. "I'll just need your ID, Mrs. Gamble," he said.

I looked to Daniel for an explanation and he smiled. "The deed to the house," he explained.

I'd forgotten all about the request, but he hadn't. Reaching into my purse, I took my driver's license from my wallet and handed it to George. After a quick inspection, he instructed me where to sign and verified my signature with the one on my license. When I wasn't following his instructions, I was staring at Daniel, silently relaying my appreciation. He wore a proud expression, always a man of his word. In that moment, I didn't think I could love him more.

George notarized the document before placing it in an envelope and assuring Daniel he would file it immediately. The two discussed another matter briefly before George left us alone.

"Thank you," I whispered, wrapping my hands around Daniel's neck. I wished we were in the privacy of our home so I could thank him how I wanted, but this would have to suffice for now.

"Of course," was all he said before a knock on his office door interrupted us.

"Mr. Gamble, are you ready to begin?" A young Latina woman

asked. She was dressed in a navy skirt suit with an iPad in her hand. "I'm sorry. I thought you were alone."

"It's fine. Go ahead and set up in the conference room. I'll be in in a minute." Daniel instructed as I released my grasp.

"Michelle, this is my wife Emily. Em, this is Michelle. She'll be leading the meeting today."

"It's nice to meet you," I smiled as she did the same.

"Same here. I'll see you both soon." She left as abruptly as she'd arrived.

"It's almost time to get started," Daniel said, glancing at his watch.

"Okay, let me call Crystal before I forget." Quickly, I reached for my cell, selecting her office number from my favorites.

"I was just about to call you," Crystal answered, speaking in a low tone.

"Why? What's wrong?" I stiffened.

"Let me go in your office," she said. "Okay, Quentin just showed up at the office." Her breathing was labored.

"What? But I thought we didn't have a meeting," I said, confused.

"You don't. Madison came back to your office right after you left and I told her you'd stepped out. I could tell she was disappointed, but didn't know why. Then, not even fifteen minutes later, Quentin strolls in."

"Did he come by my office?"

"Yeah, that's where he came first, which is strange. He usually meets up with Madison first. I asked if you were expecting him and he said he'd talked to you about stopping by. I told him you weren't in, but that Madison was, and he went down to her office." Crystal reported.

"Oh shit," she said, with the ruffling sound of movement. "I locked the door. They're at my desk looking for me." I could hear the amusement in her voice, imagining her watching the scene unfold from the privacy of my office.

"How do they look?" I asked, needing her to be my eyes and ears.

"Stressed."

"Hmm," I bit my lip, noticing Daniel watching me closely. "Give me a minute to think and I'll call you back with a plan."

"No problem. They're heading back towards creative now. Is it okay if I stay in your office to avoid them?"

"Of course. I'll call you in a few minutes."

I ended the call conflicted. It was the first day after my new agreement with Daniel and I already felt pulled in two directions. Daniel would never take off midday to come to a meeting at Cherry Blossoms. Yet, here I was, clearing my schedule without thinking of the repercussions.

I still hadn't read over the proposal. Despite my building nerves, I thought the merger had great potential. My dad always said that in negotiations, the first contract was a rough draft. Details in the initial proposal didn't at all make me want to reject the opportunity.

This was the first major deal I'd ever had, and from Quentin's perspective I could see myself looking like amateur hour. He'd shown up at my office and I wasn't there. Even worse, I hadn't read the proposal. At this point, I wouldn't be shocked if he did move on with another publishing company.

"What's going on?" Daniel's calm voice soothed me in a way I didn't know I needed.

"Quentin is at Cherry Blossoms," I said, hearing the shame in my voice. I should be there, to greet him, and discuss the merger.

Daniel's jaw flexed as he looked towards his office door. "Did you two have a scheduled meeting?"

"No. I checked my calendar before I came over, and there's nothing scheduled."

"So, he just popped up?" His brows let me know of his disapproval.

"Madison got intel that he's shopping the deal with other houses. She thinks that if we don't move quickly, he'll move on without us. I don't want to rush anything, but I can't let this deal fall through."

Daniel paused. I could see the restrain on his face. "What do you want to do?" He asked, rather than dishing out the advice I was so used to.

I took a deep breath, thinking of my options. "I want to look like I know what I'm doing."

It was honest and vulnerable. I'd never felt confident in business, even my own. At every meeting, there was an underlying layer of self-doubt, wondering why I deserved to be sitting at the head of the table. Now, in the biggest deal of my career, I felt ill equipped and in over my head.

"You do know what you're doing." Daniel's response was swift. His eyes pierced mine with sincerity, putting me at ease.

"I haven't even read the proposal," I admitted, fully expecting him to scold me. Daniel would have stayed up late, and came in early to make sure he got his work done. I lacked his work ethic, and it appeared to be my downfall.

"So." He shrugged instead. "He needs you. Not the other way around. There's no other publishing house he could merge with to give him the same metrics as Cherry Blossoms. It's a bluff."

"No," I shook my head, reaching into my bag for the printout I took from Madison. "She got this email from some guy in PR."

Daniel's eyes narrowed as he read the email. "Mr. Gamble, they're ready for you." Tracy said from the doorway. Daniel raised a finger to signal we needed a minute and Tracy nodded.

"Can I keep this?" He asked, looking from the letter to me.

"Why?" I asked sarcastically.

"You know why," was all he said as he refolded the paper and placed it into his suit pocket. "Look," he glanced at his watch again. "Tell them you're here for a meeting. Invite them to meet you here in an hour."

"Here?" I heard the rise in my voice. "You're going to be in the meeting?"

"Not if you don't want me to."

The idea made me nervous. I'd never conducted business in front of Daniel. If I felt out of place with my employees, I assumed the feeling would amplify in front of my husband.

"What's holding you back?" He wondered aloud.

"Can you let me do things my way?"

His jaw line softened as he looked to me with kind eyes. "I promise."

I quickly texted Crystal the plan as Daniel and I walked to the conference room. His team was gathered around a long mahogany table facing a projection screen that displayed a line graph. Nervous energy circulated the room at Daniel's presence.

"This is Emily Gamble. She will be sitting in on this meeting without bias or influence."

"Understood," the woman from earlier responded as we took our seats at the head of the table. "There are iPads for each of you. We've created a simple app for you to follow along with the intel as we go through the data. Feel free to type any questions or feedback directly into the note tab on the right side of the screen."

I picked up the iPad, impressed with Michelle, but even more with the presentation. The app was sleek and professional. I easily navigated to the proposal, opening to the line graph displayed on the screen above.

"You can begin," Daniel announced with an authority that made everyone stand taller.

9
_____

Watching Daniel in action was a master class in business. He was extremely observant, taking notes throughout the presentation and asking limited questions. During the meeting, he would scribble short notes for me about what statistics indicated and how you could leverage them.

As the team emptied out the conference room, each stopped to thank him for his time, or brag about a new contract they were working on. The Latina woman I now knew as Michelle asked for a bit of feedback on her leadership.

"You created the app?" He asked. Her smile answered positively. "It's a really nice touch. No one likes staring up at a huge screen. You've given clients an easy way to dissect the data at their own pace. I left some notes there for you." Daniel told her before instructing her to take a step back.

"You led well, but don't be afraid of delegation. If you can't trust the people you put in place to execute, they shouldn't be in those positions," he said. Michelle nodded as though decoding the message before thanking him and leaving us alone in the conference room.

Daniel turned to me with what appeared to be nervousness. "Not too boring, right?"

"I loved it," I beamed. He was so fitting as a boss. I bet no one ever questioned his expertise. From the way he handled himself, it was clear he was in charge. "I took so many notes," I smiled, tapping my notebook.

"Good," Daniel relaxed. "I saw it on the schedule and thought it could be a good thing for you. If you've never seen a merger, you don't know what to look for."

Holding the door to the conference room, Daniel continued. "Do you see how we compared the two businesses against each other, like they were competitors, even though they're looking to join forces? You can't only think about what you'll gain. There's a con to every pro."

"That's what you do before mergers?" I asked as we walked down the long hall back to his office.

"That's what we do for clients looking to merge. We show them what's in their blind spot before it's too late."

"That's what your day's like, huh? Sitting in on those?" I wondered, more curious about his work than ever.

"No, I never go to those," he chuckled. "I just went because I wanted you to sit in."

"That's why they were all so nervous and excited," I smiled.

"Yeah, they're not ready to present to actual clients. For now, they only do research. Michelle just got promoted so she's building her own team."

"She built that app? That's amazing," I remarked, still impressed by Michelle.

"She's a wiz with IT. That's where she started, but I think she wants more than sitting around a bunch of nerds developing software," he said, smiling when I giggled.

"She seems like she could do more. She's impressive."

Daniel nodded to a passing man vying for his attention. "Tracy gave me the file. I'll look it over tonight."

The man looked pleased as he thanked him before turning

down another hallway. I admired the way Daniel moved in his office. It was apparent that he was in the know with everything, or at least it looked that way. He had been running his own business much longer than me, but sometimes I feared I would never be as skilled as he was.

"Mr. and Mrs. Gamble," Tracy greeted us as we arrived at Daniel's office. "Mr. Q and Madison have arrived. I've already served them drinks. They're waiting on you."

I could feel the nerves building in my chest. It was nothing like the cool and confident demeanor Daniel embodied walking into a meeting.

"If you believe it, they will." Daniel's words caught me off guard.

"What?"

"You're in your head about how you look to them. But if you believe you're the leader of Cherry Blossoms Publishing, then they will too."

Taking a deep breath, I nodded, trying to steel my nerves. "I know you've been holding back all day. But, can you please just give me some advice?"

"You sure?" Daniel asked.

"I'm positive."

"Don't feel pressured to speak. Silence backs more people into corners than words ever could. And don't ever feel rushed into anything. You're in control, and things move at your place. You don't have to explain that."

"Right," I nodded, though still a bit unsure.

"Do you want me to come in with you?" He asked.

"Yes." I answered quickly.

"Okay, let's go. Remember, *he needs you*," Daniel extended his hand, forcing me to lead the way into his office.

"Sorry to keep you waiting. We just wrapped our meeting. How are you?" I announced us as we entered Daniel's pristine office.

Madison and Quentin, who looked to be in the middle of a conversation, abruptly turned and stood to greet me. Having Daniel beside me, I suddenly felt taller, more confident than ever.

Quentin was dressed in a black suit, with his curly hair looking a bit unruly. Madison had removed the ponytail and pencil from her hair, letting her sandy brown hair flow down her back.

"Hello, Quentin," Daniel said, extending his hand.

Quentin accepted with a smile that didn't quite reach his eyes. I could sense he was less than happy about Daniel's presence.

"Always a pleasure to see you, Madison." Daniel then shook Madison's hand as her cheeks reddened.

"Hey, how you doing?" Quentin asked Daniel. "Are you joining this deal now?"

"No, you're just using my office," Daniel shot back. To my surprise, he then walked to his desk rather than joining us at the sitting area. He was pushing me to hold my own, and in that moment, I felt sure of myself. Daniel would never send me into something he didn't think I could handle.

I sat opposite Quentin and Madison, facing Daniel, who was sitting behind his desk, slightly turned to face his computer.

"Mr. Gamble will be sitting in on this meeting without influence or bias," I announced, drawing Quentin's attention back to me and Madison. I glanced up just in time to see Daniel's smirk of recognition as I repeated the phrase he'd used earlier.

"Well, it's good to see you. I didn't mean to bombard you," Quentin began after we shook hands. We were seated in the soft leather chairs Daniel reserved for special clients too exclusive for conference room meetings.

"Well, I'm eager to hear why you popped up. We didn't have a meeting on the schedule," I explained, watching him look to Madison before responding.

"You're right. It wasn't supposed to be formal. I figure we're about to be family, we should be able to drop by," he reasoned, flashing that flawless smile of his.

"It's no problem," I assured him. "So, why'd you want to drop by?"

It was clear he was thrown off by the shift in dynamics, and I liked it. Quentin had caught me on my heels more than once, at times making me feel a bit cornered. Now, I felt the playing field was even, and it left him wavering. He looked from me to Madison and then she spoke up.

"Well, Quentin just wanted –," she started before I interjected.

"Please, Madison," I started without taking my eyes off Quentin. "We don't want to speak on Mr. Bolden's behalf."

He grinned, aware I was calling him out. "Mr. Bolden? Come on, Emily. Call me Q." When I only offered a polite smile, Quentin began explaining. "I wanted to see if there were any questions I could answer about the proposal."

"I'm taking my time reading through it. There's a lot of important information there. I don't want to rush anything. But if any questions arise, I know where to find you."

Now that I suspected Quentin was working with ulterior motives, the last thing I wanted was to make him defensive. I needed him to be his normal arrogant self. If I was going to successfully combat him, my strategy would have to be subtle and calculated.

"Of course. I'm happy to help." He paused, looking to Madison briefly before returning his attention to me. "I just really want to close this deal. I don't want to worry you, but there are more offers on the table."

"*More*?" I questioned. "There was already an offer on the table?"

"Well, uh," he stuttered a bit. "The current deal between us."

"I didn't offer you anything," I said with a soft giggle.

"There's interest," he clarified with a smile. He was comfortable again. Just like I needed him.

"From who?"

"I thought by now, you'd trust that I don't kiss and tell," he teased, leaning forward as he rubbed his hands together.

Sitting back, I nodded slowly, forcing myself not to respond. This was a tactic of his I'd fallen for several times. He could be so provocative it was borderline inappropriate. Mentioning how I should trust his discretion within earshot of my husband was worthy of an emotional objection. Yet, I gave him nothing, choosing silence over wit. I could sense my indifference forcing him to reveal his hand. Daniel was right about words never having the effect of silence.

"I just don't understand what's happened since the last time we talked," he said, scooting to the edge of his seat.

"You didn't strike me as the insecure type, Quentin," I responded with concern, sitting up and crossing my legs. "It's only been a few days, and you're already worried?"

"Not worried, just eager." His green eyes brightened as he licked his lips. I was grateful Daniel couldn't see him as all his bravado returned.

Quentin again looked to Madison, who looked down at her fingers. Next, he turned around to see Daniel, who was typing away at his desk. I knew my husband well enough to know he was paying close attention to our conversation. When Quentin turned back to me, Daniel glanced up and winked.

"Maybe we should go to lunch," Quentin suggested.

"That would be nice," Madison chimed in.

"I actually have some business to go over with Madison this afternoon. Let's put something on the schedule after I've finished combing through everything."

Seemingly defeated, Quentin rose to his feet, ending the meeting. I followed suit, extending my hand. "I'm having a party soon. You should come through," he suggested as we shook hands.

"Oh yeah? What's the celebration?" I asked as we turned to leave.

"I was hoping it would be our merger," he rose a sarcastic eyebrow. "You should come too," he said towards Daniel's desk.

"What's that?" Daniel looked up, although I was sure he'd heard every word.

"I'm hosting a party. You two should come," Quentin repeated.

"I just go where the wife says," Daniel said coolly.

"I bet you do," Quentin smirked. "Anyway, it was nice to see you, Emily. We'll talk soon."

He turned to leave and I watched him go before shifting my

attention to Madison. "I want to see a breakdown of our business. In great detail, as if we were proposing a merger."

"For Quentin?" She asked. "He's already well versed in our business. I don't think he needs any further convincing." She giggled, but quickly stopped when I didn't join her.

"You keep a breakdown of us on file, right?" I asked although I knew the answer. As the head executive of acquisitions, Madison always had a current breakdown of our business.

"Of, of course," she stuttered.

"Perfect. Email me an up to date version by end of business."

"Will do," she said on her way out the office. I watched her leave, closing Daniel's office door before exhaling deeply. I was proud of how I'd conducted myself, but also glad it was over.

"What?" I asked when I noticed Daniel watching me with a wide grin. He was leaning against the glass top of his desk with his arms crossed, having taken his suit jacket off.

"You killed it!" He began clapping as I made my way to him.

"Stop it," I rolled my eyes, feeling my cheeks warm with embarrassment.

As soon as the meeting began, the nerves eased away. I was in my element conversing with Quentin in what was always a battle of wit. Madison had been less of a teammate, but she had shown to be enamored by Quentin from our first meeting.

"Did you notice how he kept stumbling over his words when you held your ground?" He asked, a flash of his professional leadership shining through.

"Yes! He didn't know what to do when I sat silent." I remembered, feeling excited. "And did you see Madison? She was no help at all."

"She even sat on his side of the table," he added.

I hadn't realized that. I thought through the meeting with skepticism. "He kept looking to her like she was his partner. Do you think they're working together?"

"I think you should watch her closely," Daniel warned me.

I nodded, soaking it all in. I needed to cross reference our company breakdown with the proposal to see what was missing in Quentin's paperwork. That would help me strategize and make sure I didn't get the short end of the deal.

My mind was racing with ideas when I again noticed Daniel watching me with a grin painted on his face. "What is so funny?" I wondered.

"You," he said, reaching for me. I was in his grasp before I could respond. "When I thought of us having a clean slate, I envisioned showering you with gifts, not business advice."

"Well, you know, I like gifts too." I said innocently, as his arms engulfed me.

"I should've known not to listen to Jason," he said so softly I wasn't sure if I was meant to hear it.

"Jason?" I asked, wondering what his little brother had to do with anything.

"Yeah," he sighed. "Jason was determined to get us back together."

"Really?" I twisted to free myself from his grip, needing to face him. I never knew Daniel to share details about our personal life with his brother. In a way, I was relieved to learn he wasn't going through everything alone.

"Yeah, you know he loves you."

"Vic is the same way," I smiled, thinking of my sister's excitement when I mentioned I'd spent the night with Daniel.

"I can't be mad, though. It was Jason's advice to rewrite the rules," he admitted, looking to me with lust in his eyes. I knew he was thinking of the fact that we would be going home together tonight.

My pocket vibrated and I checked my phone to see a new message from Crystal. "Speaking of the new rules," I looked up to Daniel, who was watching me closely. "We have our first therapy session."

"When?" His eyebrows shot up.

"Now."

"Now? Babe, I have," he started.

"Crystal already checked with Tracy. You're free for the next two hours and I only need you for one." I explained, watching the emotions slide over his face.

Daniel inhaled deeply before moving around his desk. "I have ideas for the other hour," he announced, lifting his suit jacket from the chair back before methodically sliding his arms into each sleeve.

10

Sitting beside Daniel as he drove to Dr. Lorraine Cathway's office, I could sense the tension as he navigated throughout west Los Angeles in silence. In true Daniel fashion, he didn't put up any fight about the impromptu session. Besides, he wanted to write our own rules, how could he be the one to break them?

"Are you nervous?" I wondered as we neared the small office that looked and felt more like a private home.

"Should I be?" Daniel asked while making a right turn.

"No," I answered quickly. "I mean, I've only had a few sessions myself, but I think they're more beneficial than anything."

"Good," was all he said before returning to the silence.

Unlike his normal routine, there was no music playing in the car, leaving me with my thoughts. I wasn't sure how a therapy session with Daniel would go. Dr. Cathway had been great at helping me talk through some of my problems, but it was because I *wanted* to work through them. I needed Daniel to be on board with this fully, not just going along to please me.

We arrived, and Daniel began looking around doubtfully. "This is it. I was confused the first time I came, too."

Daniel nodded, turning the car off, before taking a deep breath as he turned to open the door. I did the same as I made the short walk to the red front door. Although we were early, the receptionist let us right in.

"Come on in," Dr. Cathway called above the slow whistle of a teapot. "I've just made some lavender tea for us."

Daniel was looking around the unorthodox office that could easily be mistaken for a small apartment. I wouldn't be shocked if there was a bedroom in the back of the place. It was the only thing missing.

"Dr. Cathway, this is my husband Daniel," I introduced the two as we neared the small kitchen.

"Hello, Mr. Gamble," she smiled, stretching her flawless chestnut complexion. Carefully, she poured into three delicate tea cups sitting on matching saucers. It was a white China set with gold trim. A simple yet elegant design.

"The pleasure is mine," Daniel offered as we settled into the bar stools at the counter.

"I hope you like lavender tea as much as your wife. I've found it to be a relaxing start to the first session."

Dr. Cathway handed a cup to Daniel and myself and kept the last for herself. Together we all moved to the seating area. Daniel and I shared the black velvet Victorian sofa, placing our steaming tea on the coffee table separating us from the doctor, who sat in an upholstered chair.

I'd always admired her long silver hair, which she had pulled into a chignon at the nape of her neck. Dressed in a cream-colored blouse with pearl buttons, she was as poised as ever observing the two of us. I wasn't sure if Daniel picked up on it, but I knew the process well enough to know she was already making mental notes about us. Her patience and attention to detail was unmatched. Nothing got past her. That was the reason I wanted Daniel to go to therapy. We needed a mirror to better see ourselves.

We had decided to work on our marriage, writing our own

rules, but we needed a referee to alert us when we were out of bounds.

"So, where should we begin?" She asked with a warm smile.

I looked to Daniel, who was slightly turned towards me. His hand rested on my thigh, gripping firmly despite his laid back demeanor. I could sense his discomfort and wanted him to relax.

"I think it might be better if I started," I spoke first. "Daniel is a bit of a pessimist, so I think he'll need time to warm up."

"Oh, am I?" He asked as his fingers massaged my thigh.

"Well, you know, you expect the worst in people and situations, and then they have to prove you wrong," I tried to explain. Daniel's eyebrows rose as though this was news. I felt myself sinking.

"As a rule of thumb, I think we should only focus on expressing our own feelings. Speak for yourself, Emily. I don't know Daniel well, but he strikes me as a man that can speak for himself," Dr. Cathway said.

"I am," Daniel assured her. "And I'm not pessimistic," he squeezed my thigh, making me squeal with laughter.

It was the release we both needed, removing the tension from the room. More relaxed, I leaned into his side, ready to update Dr. Cathway on life since my last session.

"I've been working a lot more these past couple of weeks. And I really feel like I'm coming into my own in the office. I've got projects I'm excited about and new ventures on the horizon."

For the next thirty minutes, I detailed the trials I'd been facing at the office, and Dr. Cathway advised me on ways to find balance. We discussed journaling in the morning to help guide me through the day, and again at night to quiet racing thoughts. She noted how far I'd come and encouraged me to continue before changing pace.

"Daniel, you've been quiet the entire session. I'd like to hear from you. How do you see me helping you two?" Dr. Cathway asked, shifting her posture to face Daniel.

He perked up, leaning forward as he spoke. Each of his words seemed purposefully selected as he crossed his fingers in his lap.

"Emily seems to find great value in her meetings with you," he turned to me as he said my name and I offered an encouraging smile. Like Dr. Cathway, I too had noticed his silence, but wasn't going to push him to participate in the first session.

Daniel returned his attention to the doctor as he resumed. "I want us to define our marriage for ourselves. It's something we didn't do from the start, but I'd rather begin later than never at all. Emily wanted us to go to therapy together," he said, returning his attention to me as he finished. "And I'm willing to do whatever it takes to reconstruct our marriage."

"I see," Dr. Cathway said. Though her face revealed nothing, I could hear the smirk in her tone. "And what issues do you think the two of you need to uncover and resolve for this reconstruction to take place?"

Daniel's face softened as he looked to me. "Honestly, I'm just trying to navigate this fresh territory we're in."

He was answering her, but speaking to me. I heard him clearly. He wanted to tread lightly, and I completely understood that. I too was actively trying not to disrupt the calmness between us. It had been a tumultuous year, to say the least. And there was still so much uncertainty – with my family and my business – I needed us on good terms.

Unimpressed, Dr. Cathway didn't respond. Her lack of a reaction prompted Daniel to add, still looking to me, "We've just gotten back to..." his words trailed off as our eyes connected deeply, not needing the ending of the sentence.

"Having sex?" Her words jolted Daniel. He sat up, looking to the doctor and then me.

"Ya'll talk about *that*?"

I looked away to contain my laughter. The shock on his face was so genuine, as though I'd betrayed him in some way.

"We talk about whatever Emily wants to discuss. After all, that is the only way I can help. Daniel, if you're serious about restructuring your marriage, you should take these sessions seriously."

She commanded his attention. I watched silently as the two of them finally interacted. "What can I do to show you I'm serious?" He asked, always searching for solutions.

"Well, I understand you want to start again. What action are you looking for from Emily to show she's truly committed to the new direction?"

I swallowed slowly, unprepared for her to give him such leverage. I'd brought him into this relationship, but Dr. Cathway appeared to have no loyalty to me. I waited impatiently for Daniel's response as my hands tensed in my lap. What would he ask of me to prove I was committed? Would I be willing to give in to his demands? Why didn't I get any demands?

"I'm not sure," Daniel answered after a long pause.

"I think that's something you should think about. There is an action you're expecting or looking forward to. You should put that on the table."

I could see his mind turning over the advice as he nodded imperceptibly. Dr. Cathway lifted her tea cup, sipping casually, satisfied with herself.

"What about me? I haven't set forth any expectation. I don't have an action," I said, feeling cheated.

"I thought this was an expectation on your part. Daniel is here, right? Ready to restructure. What have you done? Where is your action, Emily?"

I looked to Daniel, who was still staring straight ahead. He felt my stare, but didn't turn. Watching his chest rise and fall I began to doubt my decision to come to therapy together. It was more than I'd bargained for, and nothing like I'd expected.

"It looks like you both have some homework for next week." She said before sipping her tea again. This time, her smirk was visible behind the dainty tea cup.

11

———

Alexandria's was a familiar chain restaurant, but completely out of character for my sister. When Victoria invited me to dinner, I assumed it would be low-key, but this was anything but.

"You came!" Victoria shouted as I whispered my reservation name to the hostess. "She's with me," my sister explained to the relieved employee as she waved her off, leading me towards the back of the restaurant.

"Why are you so excited?" I asked her, looking to her tight grip on my wrist.

Struggling to keep up with her feverish pace, I moved on the tips of my toes to stop my heels from loudly announcing each step. The restaurant floor shined like mirrors, evidence of regular polishes on the large white square tiles. Glancing around at the patrons, all dressed as though denim were a requirement, I tried to make sense of her restaurant selection.

It wasn't the type of place my sister usually wanted to dine. Barely my senior, Victoria was all about the reputation of the places we frequented. She was known to research a chef before going to dinner, after which she would request their presence to shout their praises and show how informed she was.

This place needed no research. I doubted there was even a chef to speak of. A group of line cooks, each well versed in the art of reheating frozen cuisine, felt more fitting. Before I could force my sister to explain her random yet urgent dinner request, she stopped on a dime at the final table in the restaurant.

It was positioned in a way that would make a customer feel left out, totally removed from the rest of the dining area. The lone table was separated by a wide walking path, used by waiters transporting dishes and drinks from the kitchen to awaiting diners.

Less of an explanation than a shock, I stood staring at the rest of my family members, with the one I thought closest still clenching my wrist. It was as if she could read my mind, physically stopping me from following the instinct to bolt. It had been an incredibly long and draining day. The last thing I needed was whatever they had in mind.

"Vic, I do not have the energy for this," I whispered.

"I know, but I knew you wouldn't come if I told you about it," she reasoned, taking one step towards the table.

"What is this? An intervention?" I snapped, tugging my hand from her grip.

"Of course, she thinks it's about her," my older sister Denise huffed. "Hi, Emily. We've been waiting thirty minutes for you to arrive."

"Hi, Denise," I said as sarcastically as she'd spoken my name. Things were always so weird between me and Denise. Sometimes, I paused trying to remember why we were so short with each other. I'd never been able to develop an answer, but that didn't stop us from giving each other a hard time. "I didn't know you were waiting, because I didn't know you would be here."

Moving around the large table, I settled into an empty seat beside my mother while Victoria excused my tardiness, although no one seemed interested. "I told Emily dinner was a half hour later. I thought one of you would be late."

My father sat at the other head of the table, appearing much more confident than he had the last time I'd seen him. It was all too much that day, seeing the agents move throughout the house taking what they wanted with so little regard. To us, it was a family home, but they treated it as nothing more than a crime scene.

The cries from my mother still rang loudly in my memories. It was the weakest I'd ever seen her – broken by my father's deepest betrayal. I'd avoided him since that day, despite my mother and even Daniel's wishes that I at least hear him out. I'd argued there was nothing he could say to change the way I felt. Now, I would finally learn if that was true.

"I guess you're all wondering why I called you here." My father's voice bellowed, fighting over the seemingly endless traffic of waiters entering and exiting the kitchen only a few feet away. "And here of all places," he looked around with a chuckle that felt more like an act than true amusement.

"No, I used to love this place, Daddy," Olivia chimed excitedly.

As the oldest daughter, only my brother Elliot was older than Olivia. She'd always taken the role as a second mother, and this instant was no different. Much like our mom, she found it neces-sary to support my father, and make him feel comfortable despite the discomfort his actions had caused all of us.

"Well, it was one of your favorite restaurants when you all were younger. Me and your mother always loved bringing you here, seeing your little eyes light up," he looked to the other end of the table. Following his eyes, I saw the tight smile on my mother's face as she recalled the memory.

Even for me, upset and ambushed, I could remember how much we loved the chain restaurant as children. What now felt gaudy was fancy to us then – the white shiny floors matching the pressed collared shirts of the waiters, who always remembered how much we loved Shirley temple drinks with extra cherries. It was an ode to our mother, who always requested her martinis 'extra dirty', which I found to be a wildly inappropriate way of requesting more olives.

"Of course, as our empire grew, we introduced you to better restaurants, but we never forgot about this place," my father continued.

It was his use of 'our' that struck me as strange. Up until his arrest, facing federal charges of fraud and embezzlement, everything he had built was solely his. Never once did he credit my mother for any of his success, although she raised us and gave him the idea to create experiences rather than typical hotel rooms. On the brink of bankruptcy, she'd helped him change his entire approach to hospitality. But we only heard that story in her bitter tone, when my mother griped about my father's transgressions, and his audacity to ever betray her.

"To forget where you've come from is to forget the people you came with," my mother added.

It was clear they were going with the united front theme. From the way they looked across the length of the table, maintaining eye contact, I almost believed them. But the memory of my mother, alone and broken by the news of my father's fraudulent business practices, made it impossible for me to view them as a team.

They were nothing like me and Daniel, open and involved with each other. Watching my parents continue their act made me even prouder of my husband and the way he had brought me into Tower Enterprise Group, helping me improve my own business. He didn't want me dependent on him, forced to survive off whatever he was inclined to throw my way. Daniel empowered me to build my own empire, so I would never be grateful for inclusion in something he'd consistently denied me access to.

"And that's why we've always been intentional about our diversification," I heard my father say, quieting my thoughts.

"Your father's lawyers have warned him that something like this would happen for years. He's been prepared," my mother said, in what felt like a rehearsed speech.

"Hell, we've been waiting!" My dad chuckled again. Only Elliot, who sat to the right of him, and Olivia at his left, laughed along. I silently wondered if they truly believed him or just felt obligated to laugh because they were sitting so close.

No one operating a business legally prepares for fraud indictments. That was bullshit, and you didn't need a business to know it. Turning, I looked to my mother, watching her chest rise and fall. She was still focused on my father, refusing to face me.

"I certainly was not prepared," my mother said as she turned to me with sad eyes. My stomach tightened with guilt. I'd been weaponizing her vulnerability against her, silently chastising her for being so broken.

Now, it was my turn to avoid eye contact as I shifted in my seat to look towards my siblings. None of them had been there to witness her breakdown, or the way she talked about my father as though he was the enemy. I was alone with her, and she'd trusted me with her grief in a way she couldn't with her other children. I only hoped she knew I had not, and would never, tell any of them about that day.

"But we've managed to work our way through," my mother's voice was strong now, nothing like that day.

"Life has been great for you all," my dad took the attention again, forcing us to look from one end of the table to the other, keeping up with this tandem speech. "But, believe it or not, me and your mother have had plenty of battles before this."

This time, my sisters' all turned to each other as we shared a look of confusion. While money wasn't an issue for us growing up, we weren't under the impression that our family was without problems. My father's infidelities were well documented in our house, and vehemently included in the lessons of men and marriage shared by my mother.

With no interruption from my mother, my father finished. "Along with the hospitality division, we have other businesses to get us through trying times like the one we're in. In addition to our real estate and investment portfolio, we own fourteen of these franchises," he lifted his hands as though the cheesy restaurant was a grand reveal.

I didn't know they owned it, or any for that matter. But I was so upset with my father, everything he did seemed to disgust me. He could have very easily told us he wasn't broke without the song and dance.

"You don't need to worry yourselves," my mother finally addressed the reason for the meeting. "We want you to know that we're fine, financially at least." She smirked, and as the only person sitting next to her, I nodded while plastering a smile on my face, suddenly understanding the courtesy laughter Olivia and Elliot had awarded my father.

It was like seeing her for the first time. Not as my mother, but Christine, the wife of Malcolm Delley. She had her own story, and my father was her partner. Regardless of how little I agreed with their tactics, it was clear that they were a team, and I was merely in the audience.

I'd spent so much of my life worried about my parents and siblings' reactions and opinions, I could barely make a decision on my own. There, at that table with all of them, I realized we were all on our own, living individual lives. Mom and dad had their own issues to deal with. The best thing I could do was focus on me, and my marriage. It didn't matter who disagreed, no one sitting there was my teammate, only spectators.

"We're going to get through this," my father proclaimed with excitement.

"And we'll get through it as a family," my mother smiled, satisfied with their performance.

Just then, my father alerted the wait staff who hurried to the table with bottles of wine in hand. "I had this brought in, Emily. It's your favorite Chianti," he looked down the table at me.

In that moment, I wanted to be angry and defensive. It was so easy to feel that way when my father wasn't staring into my eyes with the desperation that now tugged at my heart strings. He was hurting, much like my mother, looking to us for comfort and support.

"Thanks, Daddy," I heard myself say. I could see the deep

exhale from across the table. His broad shoulders relaxed for the first time all night.

"You can get the pimp Alfredo!" He added for good measure, recalling how I mispronounced my favorite meal the first time I ordered for myself. Anyone raised in a large family knows that living down a moment of humiliation is more than difficult. The best you can do is embrace it, which was what I did, creating an inside joke that even decades later left all seven us laughing uncontrollably.

12

"This is the new talent you were excited about?" I asked Christian as I looked over the roster he'd handed me, not bothering to hide the disappointment in my tone.

After weeks of preparation for his new venture, to promote undiscovered talent in the lower publishing seasons, he was finally ready to present. It was my third meeting of the day, and I was already feeling mentally exhausted.

My days were beginning to run together, with so much happening at the office and then even more at home. Daniel and I were still on shaky legs after our first therapy session three days ago. We'd barely discussed the dinner with my family, because his work schedule was even more chaotic than mine.

He'd been going into the office early, and hosting video calls from home, working to close the deal with the Japanese startup. I tried to give him space professionally, making key decisions on my own when it came to my business.

After finally working through the proposal from Quentin, and comparing the data to the breakdown of my own business provided by Madison, I could see what concerned Daniel. Much like a first date, Quentin was doing all he could to present the best version of himself. Unlike Daniel, I wasn't so offended by it. He'd be a fool to expose everything without a little prodding. Just as I would be a fool to take him at face value.

Still, I was excited about the prospect of merging our businesses to increase the cash flow from Cherry Blossoms Publishing. Currently, my investment in the company was far from liquid. Any major changes, including the interior design revamping my sister was scheduled to begin, required another investment into the business. More money that I didn't have.

While my bank account was flush, it was not from my earnings. Daniel was financing my lifestyle, a dependency I did not wish to become permanent. Cherry Blossoms Publishing was my sole income stream, and it was only rich in valuation. On paper, I was successful, but it wasn't the type of capital you could spend in stores. Merging with Quentin would cash out half of my portfolio, empowering me to invest in new ventures.

My father and Daniel both made sure to keep several streams of income pouring into their accounts. I wanted the same. But until I could withdraw some of my investment, I was locked into Cherry Blossoms, and so was my cash.

"You don't seem impressed," Christian winced.

I exhaled deeply as Crystal appeared in the door way to my office. Holding one finger up, I held her off for a minute. "Each of these writers has already been published, Christian. They all have agents. How can they be new talent?"

He'd spent more time formatting their stats than searching for undiscovered writers we could develop. Beneath their emboldened names were short lists of professional highlights, including previous releases and associated book sales. Under that, he'd listed all their accolades and even a few honorary degrees.

"Well, we've always tried to steer clear of completely breaking a career. We need to see some level of success before we can get behind them, right?" He asked with confusion.

Another sigh. "I guess you're right." I conceded.

It wasn't Christian's fault that the culture he had been hired into was not in line with what I wanted at Cherry Blossoms. Why were we always so focused on sales and not talent? Not once had we published anyone's breakout hit. Instead, my team wanted to find the most popular writers and get behind their follow up. It was cowardice. Nothing forward thinking about it.

"Let me look it over and read some of their work. I like the direction," I said with a tight smile. Christian could tell I wasn't pleased, and he gathered his things quickly to rush from my office.

Crystal held the door for him as she peaked her head in. "Mr. Gamble's on the phone."

Nodding, I hurried to pick up the line, knowing he'd been on hold for a while. "Sorry, baby. I didn't know you were–," I started.

"We're too busy." Daniel interjected, the frustration in his voice apparent.

"I would have taken the call if I knew it was you," I explained. Daniel had a standing rule that if ever I called, I got through. It was the reason I usually called his cell, hoping to avoid his assistant interrupting an important meeting for an unnecessary call from me.

"I told Crystal not to interrupt you. So, don't get mad at her," he breathed heavily into the phone.

"Is it a bit overwhelming not being the only mogul in the family?" I teased, hoping to lighten the mood.

He paused, and I could feel him relax, even if just a little. "We're going away."

"Oh, are we?"

"Yeah," he answered quickly, convincing himself. "There are too many distractions in the city. I need you to myself."

"And do I get you to myself?"

"I'll tell Tracy I'm unavailable," he assured me.

"Okay," I breathed into the phone, suddenly excited to go away with him. "When?"

"I'm picking you up from the office at five."

"Today?" I screeched, feeling unprepared. "Where are we going?"

"Not far," he said, a soft laugh letting me know he'd completely relaxed. "Just be ready at five."

"Whatever you say," I bit my lip, seduced by his spontaneity.

"Stop flirting," he ordered before kissing his teeth. I laughed, realizing I needed a reason to relax as well. Leaning back in my chair, I felt the stress fall from my shoulders. "What else do you have for the day?"

"Victoria is about to come by," I groaned, rolling my eyes as I remembered the appointment.

"Relax," Daniel urged. "You always have a good time with your sister."

"Yeah, but usually it's not after she ambushed me into a family meeting I wanted no parts of," I reminded him, feeling myself grow frustrated again. "If they really wanted to have a family meeting, why wouldn't they have you there?"

"I told your dad it would be better with just the seven of you," he said casually. I sat up in shock.

"Wait," I paused as my office door swung open. "You knew about the dinner?"

"Baby sis!" Victoria's voice chimed as she strutted towards my desk in five inch heels.

"Sounds like your sister's there. I'll see you at five. Love you!" Daniel rushed off the phone, amused with himself.

I shook my head, placing the receiver down in disbelief. I couldn't contain my laughter, recalling how Daniel brushed off my frustration after the family dinner. He'd reasoned that we needed to be on the same page, arguing my father was only trying to keep everyone in the loop.

"Of course, he knew," I said to myself.

"What are you smiling about?" Victoria asked as she settled into the chair opposite my desk.

"Your brother-in-law," I admitted.

"You've been pretty tight lipped about you two," she said with disapproval.

"And you've been pretty tight lipped about family ambushes," I shot back.

"Oh gosh!" She groaned, throwing her head back dramatically. "I knew you were going to make this a thing."

"Come on," I stood from behind my desk. "We can catch each other up on our secrets while I show you the office."

For the next hour we walked through every square foot of the eighteenth floor, better known as Cherry Blossoms Publishing. Victoria wanted to see every office, conference room, and even the bathrooms. By the time we finished the tour, she had more ideas than I could visualize to transform the space.

She'd updated me on how worried my family was about my silent treatment towards our father, even though I didn't think it was that big of a deal. I was the smallest and youngest of the bunch, yet everyone behaved like they feared me when it came to confrontation.

She was happy to hear me and Daniel were working things out, but I decided not to tell her about our decision to begin couples therapy. The last thing I needed was her asking what we discussed with Dr. Cathway. I did tell her about Daniel's impromptu idea to get away. Naturally, she thought it was romantic, wishing her husband Mike would do the same.

"The entrance is just not right for the vibe you want," she announced as we arrived back to the front of the office.

"You do realize you said that about every space I showed you, right? My conference room is depressing, the hallways are too dull, the communal areas lack character, and the lighting throughout is uninspiring," I reminded her of the critiques she'd rattled off throughout the tour.

"You told me you want a revamp, and the only way I know how to do things is all out. If you want this place to really be your own, we're going to have to change everything," she explained.

"That's the problem," I sighed, leading her back to my office. "Is this really my place?"

"What does that even mean? Of course, it is. You just need to design it in a way that reflects your energy. Just like your office. Remember how stiff it was before I redesigned it?"

"Of course, I do," I said. Victoria's design in my office had helped me fall back in love with Cherry Blossoms. It was the first injection of my personality into the company that often felt like a stepchild. "But if I have to change something for it to fit me, was it ever truly mine?"

"Excuse me," Crystal interrupted us before we entered my office. "Mr. Gamble scheduled a delivery from Monica for your getaway, it should be here by three. And he asked me to remind you how much you love him."

"Thanks, Crys," I laughed, continuing into the office.

"Daniel needs to write a fucking book on marriage. I'm surprised there aren't flowers in here waiting for you," Victoria joked as my office door closed behind her.

"He knew about the meeting and didn't tell me," I raised an eyebrow as I led us to the sitting area in my office. With the press of a button, the windows clouded, revealing the cherry blossoms design. Cloaked in a bit of privacy with my big sister, I poured us each a midday drink.

"That makes sense," she said, accepting her glass. "I was worried you might want to bring him, but daddy said all I needed to do was get you there and Daniel would stay out the way. You know those two are thick as thieves," she said.

"That might not be the best choice of words." I could barely get the joke out before we both fell into laughter. As we settled down, each taking a sip of the dark Brandy, I returned to her previous comment.

"If there's any book Daniel needs to write, it's how to make up without ever discussing what caused the break up."

Victoria pursed her lips and I knew she could read between the lines. "You two still haven't discussed Lana?"

At least her name didn't have the same sting as it once did, when I thought she was having an affair with Daniel, extorting him for six figures. When I learned the truth, that it was my father she threatened to expose, I was both relieved and devastated. Not only did my father have a secret, but my husband had worked behind my back to assist him with containing his fraud.

The way I reacted was wrong, but my instincts were right. Daniel had chosen to work with my father rather than being completely honest with me. Although I no longer harbored resentment for his actions, I still wanted to know why he didn't include me in his decision making.

"Not a word," I answered my sister, finishing my drink.

13

"**W**hat's wrong?" Daniel asked, glancing away from the winding road to watch me dig through my Never-full bag, searching for my favorite moisturizer. A rush of relief fell over me when my hand grasped the small glass bottle.

"I thought I forgot this," I held it up, watching the smirk indent his cheek. He gripped the steering wheel tightly with his left hand, while his right rested on the center console. Leaning back into the seat, I placed my hand in his, interlocking our fingers. "I don't think I have enough stuff."

It had been my concern since Daniel insisted I only pack toiletries for the trip. Sticking to his spontaneous plan to get away for the weekend, he'd picked me up from the office, along with the package sent over by my best friend Monica. As a stylist at Neiman Marcus, she did most of my personal shopping. But to my surprise, her picks arrived in a locked suitcase, with instructions from Daniel that I could only open it upon arrival at our destination.

"I'm trying to tell you," he peeked at me quickly before returning his attention to the road. "You have everything you need."

"How can I be sure without knowing what's packed?" I countered, mentally wondering what could be in the suitcase.

"Do you trust me?" He asked without looking away from the road.

"Yes," I answered quickly.

"Then, don't worry," he grinned, continuing his stoic stance.

He was adamant about keeping me in the dark, refusing to even share our destination. I'd been confused since he merged onto 101-North, rather than 101-South, which led to Malibu, my predicted weekend escape. That was close to an hour ago, as we sat in stand still traffic, lined with other cars destined for the same short term escape from the city of angels.

Accepting my fate of surprise, I melted into the Italian leather seats of Daniel's Ferrari, watching the beautiful scenery pass us by. It had been an eventful week, filled with twists and turns – the biggest of course, was our decision to start over.

Daniel called it writing our own rules, a concept that seemed foreign to me. How could we write the rules to an institution that had begun long before we ever existed? Marriage needed no explanation. The rules were written in ink. Or, so I thought.

Looking over to my husband, I twisted for a more comfortable position, content with watching him drive. The way he navigated the car was so sexy, switching lanes with a tense jaw, flexing his biceps as he rounded the curvy path. My thighs pressed together at the sight of him.

Daniel was dismissive of his looks, never buying into the hype surrounding him. He didn't react to the women who fawned over him, as many men would. Instead, he flashed a courteous smile, committed to his busy demeanor that only made him more attractive.

It was what caught my eye the first time I saw him – his lack of attention towards me. I was with Monica, my college roommate, at a mansion in the Hollywood Hills. We were searching for the perfect venue for my 25th birthday party. The space had everything I wanted, including an infinity pool overlooking the city. Daniel sat with the owner of the property at the bar, wearing a black suit that proclaimed his importance.

I thought he was older than me by the way he dressed. I knew he was older than me from the way he dismissed me. Barely balancing on five-inch heels, I pranced towards the bar to approach the mysterious man refusing to look my way.

"You need something?" He asked, glancing up from whatever he was writing. He saw through me. I could feel it from the way his eyes took me in with an inhale and looked away before the breath reached his lips. "I'll get Reggie."

That fast, he was gone. Undeterred, I made a deal with Reggie, the owner of the property. I wanted Daniel to attend my party. And for that guarantee, I booked his property to host my twenty-fifth birthday.

Daniel arrived like it was a favor to a friend, again paying me no attention until I approached him directly.

"You came," I walked towards him with the confidence only success could bring.

"Of course," he flashed the first smile. "Happy birthday."

"Thank you," I felt my cheeks expand further than normal. "So, your friend told you about my proposition?"

"Reggie isn't my friend. He's my client," Daniel corrected me without pause.

"Oh?" I wondered, sipping my kamikaze drink. "What do you do?"

"Are you falling asleep on me?" Daniel asked, lifting my hand to his lips before kissing the back of my hand softly.

"No," I assured him, a bit flustered from the memory of our first conversation. "But I'm about to be. Are you driving to San Francisco?" I wondered, the disapproval clear in my voice. I was never one for a road trip, always opting for short flights over scenic routes.

"Relax," he goaded. "We're almost there," he bit his bottom lip while pulling at the steering wheel to take the Garden Street exit.

My eyes lit up, finally realizing where we were headed. "Santa Barbara?" I asked in shock.

"Now, that you know, I need to turn on the GPS," he said, tapping on the screen to direct us towards a saved address. "Have you been? You never mentioned it."

"No," I announced excitedly. "My parents used to go all the time, but they never took us. I always thought of it as a grown-up place," I laughed at the admission.

"This weekend," he started, glancing over to me as he followed the directions to take a right turn. "Is for grown-ups," he finally finished as we entered a quiet neighborhood filled with breathtakingly beautiful homes.

When we arrived, I had my doubts, suspiciously eyeing the residential street dotted with Toyota Priuses. The house was too large for a party of two. My reservations faded when Daniel opened the front door to reveal a minimally decorated home, open in every sense of the word.

From the moment you stepped into the home, your eyes were drawn to the backyard, which looked ripped from a postcard. While Daniel tried to show me around, I found myself following the view.

"This is beautiful," I whispered without permission as we finally stepped out the sliding glass doors that led to the massive backyard. The entire living room moved outdoors with a push of collapsible doors. It was the first time I noticed the 12-meter-long pool overlooking the vast forest.

"Where are the neighbors?" I asked, turning to Daniel.

"According to the owner, the stay is free if we ever see them," he said, fighting to hide his grin.

I would never take that bet. Glancing around, there was no way to convince me I'd encounter anyone from the hillside view. It felt like a private slice of paradise.

"Let's see the place," Daniel draped his arms over my shoulders as he stood behind me. Leaning into his hard chest, I urged myself upright, suddenly feeling exhausted from the sheer beauty.

Together, we walked through the property, finally seeing the master bedroom, which like all the other rooms centered around the view. There was a large king-sized bed, with white sheer drapes hanging from the poster frame. A standalone bathtub was in front of the bed, where a television should sit. A massive bouquet of white roses in a red stained glass vase sat on a small table near the entry. My eyes glazed over as I made my way to the beautiful display, taking the card with trembling fingers.

To My Mogul Wife:
Nothing works for me without you.
You're the inspiration and motivation for everything.
I'll spend my whole life thanking you,
And it still won't be enough.

I turned to Daniel with blurry vision, feeling overcome by emotion. He'd gone above and beyond to surprise me with an incredible and much needed break. Satisfied with my reaction, he cradled the nape of my neck while wiping a loose tear with the pad of his thumb.

"Let's have a good weekend together," he leaned to kiss me softly. "We've earned it."

I nodded in agreement, not trusting myself to speak without releasing the waterworks. Daniel took my hand, and we explored the beautiful property together. In total, there were four bedrooms and six bathrooms, plus a living room, a den, and a dining room. On the furthest end of the property there was an outdoor theatre with a gigantic projection screen accompanied by two beach loungers.

The kitchen was a bit small for the house, an all-white galley style aimed towards the backyard. Daniel assured me it was large enough for the chef and staff he'd hired for the weekend. His assistant had been given strict instructions to hold his calls, and I told Crystal to do the same. It was a weekend for the two of us. One well deserved and overdue.

Finally, able to open the suitcase Daniel had arranged for me, my hands were met with the softest fabrics. Silk and lace covered the top of the suitcase. Lifting each colorful piece, I marveled at the expensive robes and lingerie. Beneath that was a layer of swimsuits and cover-ups. Ruffling through the light clothing, I turned towards the doorway.

Following Daniel's voice to the kitchen, I saw him speaking with a man in a chef jacket and two women that appeared to be his assistants. "Hi," I forced a smile.

"Hello, Mrs. Gamble," they all spoke out of order as I tugged at Daniel's arm.

"There are no clothes in the suitcase," I whispered too loudly to contain the conversation.

Daniel laughed, all but confirming the selections were no accident. "What do you mean there are no clothes?" He asked as he led me to the master bedroom before calling over his shoulder. "Dinner in two hours, chef?"

"Yes sir," the man called back to him.

"I mean there are no clothes!" This time amusement swirled around each word, rising on my toes to face him.

He smiled with genuine joy in his eyes before lifting me from my feet. My legs wrapped around him as his lips sought my neck, attacking the soft skin with aggressive kisses.

"I told you, you have everything you need." He whispered as we entered the bedroom.

Locking the door behind him, Daniel undressed quickly, leading me to the bed as I remained fully clothed. "You're mine for the weekend. We're not going anywhere, so you don't need any clothes," he explained before silencing me with all-encompassing kisses.

14

"How were your pancakes?" Chef Derek asked. He was tall and bald, with a tawny golden complexion. His broad shoulders served as evidence of the football career Daniel had told me about. The two met as collegiate athletes at Stanford.

"They were delicious," I rolled my eyes with approval, struggling to think clearly with Daniel's hand gripping my thigh beneath the table.

My wardrobe selection had proven to be more than adequate, since we spent the bulk of our time in the master bedroom. We had yet to leave the property, with all meals brought in, and any requests delivered within an hour.

A white chiffon cover-up fell over my matching bikini as I eyed the pool. We'd spent countless hours jumping into the deep end, where I learned of Daniel's summers as a lifeguard growing up in his hometown of Chicago.

It was strange to learn so much about the man I'd loved for years. Then again, I hadn't realized he didn't know about my years playing tennis, spending every summer weekend traveling throughout California for a different match. Small details woven together created a fabric of trust. The things you forgot about were necessary components of intimacy.

"You ready to get in?" Daniel asked with a squeeze of my thigh. I was slightly sore from the night's adventures in the bedroom, but didn't mention it for fear of him holding back the next time we were alone.

"You want to race again?" I asked with the excitement of a child.

"Baby, you can't beat me," he smiled, relaxed and sated.

"I can!" I argued, determined to beat him at least once before we left. "I just needed to warm up."

"Come on," he released my thigh, and my entire body felt cheated. "Derek, thank you! And you too, Kim and Anita," Daniel called to the chef and his staff as he pulled me towards the backyard.

The cleaning staff had placed pool towels on the loungers at the edge of the pool. Before I could undress, Kim met us with a bucket of ice housing a gold bottle of Ace of Spades. In her other hand, were two champagne flutes. I looked to Daniel before thanking her, constantly impressed with his little touches.

"What?" he asked as he pulled his t-shirt over his head.

"Did you plan all this? Or should I be thanking Tracy?" I teased, knowing how much of his life was supplemented by the help of his assistant.

"I haven't talked to Tracy once since I left the office," he said proudly. Daniel never had a problem unplugging from work. It was a characteristic I often overlooked. Unlike most workaholics, he valued his off time. I was never in competition with his career.

"You haven't checked your email once?" I pushed, watching his cheeks expand with a guilty grin.

"Just once, after you fell asleep last night," he admitted.

"Did you have anything?" I wondered.

"Nah," he scrunched his nose. "A contract approved, but nothing that needed my attention."

Looking out to the forest, which appeared to be endless, I felt immense gratitude to have a successful husband who was still captivated by me. From my mother's lessons of marriage and men, I would have thought the combination impossible. The way she put it, powerful men were entitled by design.

My mother would describe a lifestyle where people jumped to provide every need before you could ask as though it was a hindrance. She excused my father's infidelities, claiming the convenience and endless temptation was too much for a man to constantly reject. He was too busy to concern himself with her needs, or at least that was how she saw it.

Whether he knew it or not, this short trip together had proven to me that Daniel was not that way. He still cared about impressing me. Every small gesture he'd made felt monumental in our plight to rebuild our union.

"Have you checked with Crystal?" He asked, squinting as he looked up to me from the lounge chair. After a late start to the morning, the sun was already shining brightly.

"More than once," I bit my bottom lip, releasing the guilt I'd been holding onto. Every time I was alone, whether on the toilet or watching him swim, I peeked into my email account hoping for nonexistent updates.

"Any news?" He asked, standing in nothing but his trunks.

"There's never any news," I said with disappointment. "When I'm there, I'm welcomed in every room. But when I'm not, I'm not. The entire business moves on without me."

Daniel stepped forward, wrapping his arm around me so his hand rested on the small of my back, lending his strength to my insecurity.

"What about Crystal? She's there to be your eyes and ears," he offered advice, pressing into me.

"She can only watch what she's invited to. None of the executives include her on memos," I revealed.

"You just need to adjust the culture. Make it function the same when you're away as it does when you're there," he assured me.

The idea would be a monumental feat, transforming a company that barely felt like my own. It had been more than half a decade since I acquired the company, and I still felt out of my league. I was the representative of a company that didn't represent my views or desires.

I kissed Daniel on the cheek, recognizing his need to protect and defend me. He'd always wished to provide a safe passage to success.

"I don't know what I need," I said before quickly maneuvered from his grip, diving into the pool before he could stop me. Feeling overwhelmed with an unachievable task, I sought refuge.

When I was younger, swimming was playful and carefree. The older I got, the more I realized how seamlessly it could clear my mind. My arms moved in large circles, propelling me forward with the calming soundtrack of rushing water brushing against me from all angles. In twelve meters, I released all the tension that had built, feeling relieved and optimistic.

Daniel met me at the other end of the pool, much more relaxed than I. My heart was pumping through my chest, out of breath from the exertion. He wrapped his arms around me, relieving me of the duty of treading water.

"Tell me what you want," Daniel's voice was warming as the sun beamed down on the pool.

"What do you mean?" I asked, wrapping my arms and legs around him in what felt like the standard formation for our weekend together.

"Tell me what you want, so I can go get it," he reiterated, breathing deeply to calm his heart rate.

I stared at him with an understanding I wasn't sure he would appreciate. Daniel had always done as my father, seeking to solve my problems without ever empowering me to solve them on my own. That wasn't the life I wanted for myself, but I wasn't sure how he would react to what I did want.

Releasing my grip on him, I treaded water for myself. Unable to reach the floor of the pool, my arms and legs worked overtime to remain at eye level with my husband. He watched, amused by my added effort as he accomplished the same feat with ease.

"That's the thing," I started, moving to the edge when I found treading water too intensive.

Daniel followed me to the edge of the pool, remaining in the depth, as his arms moved so minimally he failed to disrupt the stillness of the water. He was his usual calm self, watching me flail from a safe distance, ready to swoop in and save me at a moment's notice.

"Come here," he reached for me before I could continue. Unable to resist him, I latched back onto his body, allowing him to lead me into waters too deep for my comfort.

"Talk to me," he coached, his hands gripping me in all the right places.

"I don't want you to get it for me," I gushed.

His eyebrows bunched with confusion, unable to comprehend my request. My head fell back with amusement. It was everything I expected. Daniel had no issues with taking on my dreams and desires, but allowing me to flourish on my own was foreign.

Again, I pushed away from his body. This time, I forced my legs and arms to work more efficiently so that treading water didn't exhaust me. "You asked me what I wanted," I reminded him, waiting for the recollection in his eyes before I continued. "What I want is to get something on my own."

His eyes squinted before his hands reached for me. Relaxing into his grasp, I held him closer, kissing his neck to assure him that my dream of independence had nothing to do with my love for him.

"You really do want to be a mogul, huh?" He whispered in my ear.

The smile that spread on my face was happiness, but also understanding. It wasn't completely about what I could achieve, but how I achieved it. I wanted what Daniel had, a company built from the ground up. Win or lose, I wanted to take my destiny in my own hands.

Leaning back, I gazed into his eyes. Treading water, I felt more grounded and connected than I had in years. Daniel's jaw relaxed as he caught his bottom lip in his teeth.

"I can be too much, huh?" I wondered. "I know I'm constantly changing my mind and making impulsive decisions," I reasoned.

He cut me off with a deep kiss, taking my breath away. "You are exactly who I fell in love with."

With that, he swam to the edge of the pool, supporting me with the expertise of a lifeguard. Dripping water throughout the living area, he carried me to the bedroom, repeating the pattern of our holiday that led us on a loop from the bedroom to the dining room, and then the pool, before repeating it all again.

15

The start of a new week always provided a boost of optimism. It was a fresh start, filled with promise and a comfortable distance from the exhausted version of myself that ended the previous week. But this Monday was different. More than rejuvenated, I felt reborn after a weekend in Santa Barbara with Daniel.

I returned to the office to see Crystal's feedback to the potential merger with Quentin's publishing house. She validated my suspicions about the proposal, but like me, she still saw opportunity. Together, we had begun making alterations to give Cherry Blossoms the upper hand in negotiations.

It had been a while since I'd heard from Quentin, which was rare for him. There was a little anxiety brewing, wondering if I'd overplayed my hand by making him wait in silence. When Madison told me about him courting other publishing houses with the plans for a merger, I felt the deal might get away from me.

While the proposal he sent wasn't going to provide all I wanted for Cherry Blossoms' future, I believed we could find a way to build the company I had always envisioned. I needed Quentin to make it a reality.

After sending the revised proposal over to my godmother, who also served as my legal counsel, I moved on to the stack of books we'd be publishing in the next quarter. Not one struck my interest in the first thirty pages, which was always my barometer for finding a good book.

If the reader wasn't drawn in within the first chapter, they'd move on. But my team didn't seem to understand that, based on the writing they'd approved. Now, already through production, there was nothing I could do to change what they'd put in motion. Still, I wanted to make sure future quarters were different.

"You wanted to see me?" Crystal asked after knocking softly on my office door.

"Yes," I waved, motioning for her to join me. As always, she had her clipboard, which flipped open to reveal two folders she stuffed with information about my schedule and upcoming commitments.

"Do you still read Unsigned Writes?" I asked, referring to a popular writer's forum.

Dedicated to showcasing up and coming writers committed to maintaining the integrity of their work, as well as their rights and royalties, it was a haven for undiscovered talent. In the years between my college graduation and the acquisition of Cherry Blossoms Publishing, I spent countless hours reading and reviewing the work of writers I'd never met.

Crystal was recommended by a friend when I was interviewing assistant candidates. Once I discovered she too was an enthusiast and respected reviewer on Unsigned Writes, I hired her on the spot. She would listen to me for hours, as I brainstormed what I desired for the publishing house.

Discovering new talent and launching their careers, without demanding too much of their intellectual property, was all I wanted. Six years into running Cherry Blossoms, and it still wasn't quite what I had imagined.

I'd always understood that change would take time, so I didn't expect things to turn around overnight. My team was comprised of the best literary scouts, marketers, and editors in the publishing industry. Sometimes, I just wished they would go against the norms of the industry they were so versed in to try a different approach. If teaching an old dog new tricks was challenging, teaching an old executive new strategy was damn near impossible.

They cared too much about sales and proven track records, and too little about talent or passion. Of course, Cherry Blossoms was a business, and their careers depended on profitability, but for me it was about more than that.

It made me think of Daniel, and how he saw me as an entitled brat who never cared about money. In a way, it was embarrassing, but it was also an advantage. My privileged upbringing allowed me to view opportunities without limitations. I could think outside the box, with a brazen courage to try things differently, knowing I was far from one mistake away from financial doom.

"I do," Crystal answered with a cautious smile. She quickly added, "But not at work," as though she might be in trouble.

"Well, I need that to change," I said, picking up a pen and pulling my custom stationery pad from the edge of my desk. "I need you on there all the time. And I need to know whose work you look forward to reading."

She looked at me quizzically for a second and then leaned forward. "Are you serious?"

"I'm dead serious." I looked up, locking eyes to let her know how sincere I was. "When I brought you on, it was never to answer phones or maintain my schedule. We both know you can do more than that. I guess, I thought Cherry Blossoms would organically become more like the company we used to talk about in those coffee shops," I wondered aloud.

"I never considered what it would take to fully transform this place into my vision. I can admit it's not there. Have you seen the books we're releasing next quarter? None of them pulled me in like the work we used to love on Unsigned. They all lack..." I wiggled my fingers hoping the word would drop into my hands.

"Hunger," Crystal answered for me.

"Exactly! They're the words of accomplished writers. There's an arrogance that comes with success, and the pages just reek of it. Actually, everything we're putting out reeks of it."

"Well, in your defense, it takes a while to change a culture," Crystal said, always on my side. Then, she leaned in and lowered her voice as though someone may hear us through the soundproof glass surrounding my office. "And you've had a lot going on in your personal life."

We'd never discussed what she could surmise about my troubles with Daniel, but I suspected she knew something was awry. As my personal assistant, Crystal served as my eyes and ears, privy to my personal and professional schedule, arranging every aspect of my life. There was no way she didn't know about the challenges in my marriage, even if the details were murky.

"I think I've finally sorted the personal bit out," I offered a small smile, silent appreciation for her continued discretion and unwavering loyalty. "Now, I want to make the waves we imagined when you agreed to do this with me."

Crystal had been with me since I acquired Cherry Blossoms. No one ever knew her as more than an assistant, but we had a clear understanding that she was my right hand in the business. She knew what I wanted the publishing house to become, and her salary and bonuses reflected how much I valued her. However, that still didn't feel adequate. I needed to make her position official.

"Don't worry, boss lady. I've always been in this for the long haul," she smiled as she opened her clipboard to reveal folders. Quickly, she flipped through papers before landing on whatever she was searching for.

"Next quarter's work is already in production. If we can vet, sign, and approve a new writer within the next month, you may be able to add a new project this winter."

I jotted down my thoughts while listening to her speak confidently, like she'd been waiting on this moment for a while. "I want to hear all about that, but first I need to make sure you get this contract drawn up," I handed her the stationery.

Her perfectly arched eyebrows curved as she read my notes. "Is this for real?" She asked, glancing up in disbelief.

"Crystal, we both know you are more than an assistant. I want you to continue to manage my life, because you're the best at it, but you do so much more. You need a title that reflects that."

"I agree," she started, her voice weak with emotion. "But, director of talent relations?"

"I want you to take on more responsibility. Scouting talent, onboarding them, and making sure they feel appreciated. You know what I'm looking for," I explained, feeling more confident about the impulsive decision.

"But," she shook her head slowly. "I don't need a raise. You just gave me a bonus," she reasoned.

"If you're taking on more, you need to be taking home more." I said flatly, a lesson Daniel had taught me in my first year of business. "Going forward, I want you copied on any email sent to me, and formally invited to every meeting."

Crystal nodded, finally accepting I was not backing down. Placing the sheet back into the folder, she closed the clipboard and placed it gently on her lap. "There are a few new writers I think you'd like, but one I'm sure you'll love."

I perked up with excitement, ready to get to business, but a knock at the door drew both of our attention. We turned to see my mother, who had never visited my office before.

"Hello, Mrs. Delley, what a pleasure to see you," Crystal jumped back into her assistant role with ease.

"Hey, Mom," I said with concern. "Is everything alright?"

"Yes, I just wanted to see my baby girl. Is that alright?" She walked into the office, wearing a white and black vintage Chanel tweed suit.

"Crystal, I'm going to take my mother out to lunch, but I want to read this writer's work you mentioned. And I'd like that contract drawn up by the end of the day." Crystal and I both stood, abruptly ending our meeting, thanks to my mother.

"I'll have her writing printed out and ready for you to take home tonight," she smiled. I could see she too felt the excitement I had coursing through my veins. "But, Emily, you didn't write anything next to the salary."

"I trust you to value yourself appropriately," I grinned, watching her turn on the balls of her feet with enthusiasm.

Crystal knew the business better than anyone. But more importantly, she knew me. I trusted her to handpick talent I would believe in. She understood my grand vision for Cherry Blossoms Publishing, placing less emphasis on maximizing profits and expanding market share.

Heading to lunch with my mother, my mind was still back at the office, an avidness I'd never felt for business. I was eager to read what Crystal claimed I would love, especially after a day of finding it difficult to like anything my team had selected.

16

S on of a Gun was a perfect representation of everything Los Angeles. The restaurant served fine dining, with a laid-back design aesthetic, forcing patrons to sit with strangers at long communal wooden tables. The buzz surrounding the restaurant led to a reputation that drew people from as far as the valley. Of course, there was never enough room for everyone wishing to try the elevated casual dining. At the end of the day, if anyone could get in, no one in LA wanted to go.

"This is," my mother glanced around as we stepped through the door. With a nod to the bartender behind the high counter, I secured two coveted seats at the bar in the back of the thriving restaurant. "Nice," she finally finished her sentence. Underwhelmed as always with my restaurant selections.

Unlike most cities, restaurants in LA didn't have a lunch wave that died down as everyone returned to business in their offices. Here, the meetings happened in restaurants, bars, and concert halls. And business, like everything else in the city, happened 24-7.

Sitting next to my mother, I glanced around at the patrons. There was a couple in the corner, leaning so close together, I initially thought they were kissing. I couldn't help but wonder what they did for a living to both be free midday on a Monday.

At the main picnic style table in the middle of the small restaurant, there were three sets of diners. The first, two men deep in discussion. I'd know they were talking business, even if I hadn't heard one of them mention how his accountant 'was part magician the way he found loopholes,' on our way to our seats. It was the way they spoke with their hands, leaning in to every word.

Two women sat with drinks a seat apart from the male diners, providing a buffer of privacy in the shared seating. If I had to guess, they worked in fashion, probably celebrity stylists. Each was dressed impeccably, in the way that feels intentional and careless at the same time. They were effortlessly stylish, laughing every few sentences, existing in their own bubble.

The last set of diners were closest to us, which meant we were privy to their conversation. A young man with a smooth complexion, the color of milk tea, was pitching a television show. The older woman, closer to my copper complexion, with box braids pulled into a bun, seemed intrigued. He had a notepad with a few visuals he'd drawn up, sliding it across the table to help her see his vision. I could almost feel his nerves as he awaited her feedback.

That was the thing about LA, everyone was excited about something. And no one wanted to do anything ordinary. The worst thing you could be here was 'normal'. Custom was the only way, whether you were talking cars, clothes, or careers.

"We'll have two martinis." My mother ordered when the bartender approached. "And make them extra dirty." She winked with her second request, as she always did.

"So," she finally turned to me. "You're avoiding me."

She wasn't asking or accusing; merely giving me an opportunity to excuse my bad behavior. She'd been doing it since I was little.

"I've been busy with work," I explained.

"Yes, your sister tells me you're going to redesign the entire office. That sounds pricey. What's the point of it?" She scoffed while accepting a menu from the wait staff without thanking them.

"I'm debating it now, but I wanted to change the feel of the company. It's a bit stuffy still. I know you've never seen the place," I tried not to sound offended.

"Nonsense," she brushed me off. "Do you think your father and I would allow you to purchase a company without first seeing what all it entailed?"

I sat dumbfounded. It always bothered me that she never visited my office. To hear she saw it before I even purchased it made no sense. "You did? Why didn't you say anything?"

"I don't know if you remember yourself then, Emily, but you were a rebel without a cause. Anything I liked, you hated. Anything I despised, you avoided. But something I was unaware of? That was your sweet spot. You went to Howard because it was the furthest you could get away from me," she smirked as the bartender delivered our extra dirty martinis.

"That's not true," I lied. There were plenty of reasons I wanted to attend Howard University, but putting a minimum of four hours between me and my mother was pretty high on the list.

"Oh, don't worry. It never bothered me. You see, I too get sick of you," she laughed with her shoulders before taking a sip of her drink.

"I don't think you're supposed to say that to your children," I said, a bit annoyed.

She looked at me over the sharp edge of the round glass. "I don't think you're a child, sweetheart."

I had to laugh at that one, finally taking a sip of my drink. Something about my mother's wit was comfort to me. How strange that what you were used to could become your security, despite how dangerous it may seem to others.

"It was a time in your life when you needed to feel independent. You needed to believe that it was solely your choice – a sink or swim decision that you were willing to handle on your own."

"And you let me?" I asked dumbfounded. My parents had never been good at allowing their children to make bad decisions. So, I wondered if this was her subtle way of admitting that buying a publishing company with my inheritance was a good idea.

"Emily," she placed her hand over mine, looking through me. "Your father and I will never let you fail. Even when you feel you're free falling, trust that we've done everything to provide a safety net for you."

My breath was slow, labored with curiosity. She was speaking in codes I couldn't quickly decipher. What safety net could she possibly have in place for my company? And after my father's issues, were they still safe?

"Two more, honey," my mother said with a raise of her index finger when the bartender turned towards us.

"Mom!" I huffed. "I haven't even finished this one."

"Then, you should hurry. You don't want to look like a lush with two drinks." She took the olive lined pick from her now empty glass. "Update me! What's going on with you? What must we discuss to get our weekly lunches back on track? And what are you doing with these brows, dear?" She roughly rubbed the pad of her thumb over my eyebrow.

I was overdue for an appointment. In fact, I was overdue for all my appointments. "I've been busy, mom," I griped like a teenager. "I don't know if you've heard, but my family is going through some things," I whispered like I was sharing a rumor.

"Emily, name one way your life is affected by your father's situation."

She turned to me with the challenging gaze she'd mastered in my upbringing. It was all knowing and defiant. I looked back to her with confusion.

"You can't be serious," I said with disbelief before finishing my drink.

"Oh, but I am," she smiled with her eyes. "So, tell me. How has your life been altered? Just one way will do."

She paused, her stare growing more confident by the second. "Did anyone take anything from you? Were your accounts frozen? Have you so much as spoken with a lawyer?"

"You may remember the woman extorting my husband," I bit an olive too hard at the recollection.

"One day, you're going to realize that your overreactions do not amplify a problem. Your husband received and responded to an email, Emily. It did not have to affect you. You just let it." She smiled at the bartender as he delivered our next round and continued without hesitation. "Besides, you're back home now. Daniel has proven to be trustworthy, and all is right in your world."

I clenched my teeth with frustration as the waiter approached. "Can I get you two anything?" The blonde woman asked.

"Sweetheart, order for us. I don't feel like bothering with another of these eclectic restaurants you're so keen on choosing." My mom slid the menu to me as she added, "They do make a good martini, though."

Taking a deep breath, I tried to relax, despite my mother pressing my buttons intentionally. "We'll have the oysters, two lobster rolls, and the Parmesan fries. Thank you."

The waitress accepted the menu and left quickly, leaving me with my mother, who was halfway done with her second martini.

"Emily, this isn't a battle you want to take on," she looked to me with what felt like pity. "Your father is working to resolve his issues, but none of them affect you. Besides, I was only reminding you to keep yourself up. He may let you give him hell, but your husband is a handsome and successful man. Get your eyebrows done."

It was a reminder for brow maintenance, but a warning of much more. She was reiterating one of her oldest lessons to me and my sisters. As a teenager, I filed this one in the 'Tribulations of Dating a Rich Man' folder. According to my mother, marrying a man of privilege meant you had to be on top of your game at all times. She believed you had to consider yourself forever dating, competing against every woman dying to take your spot.

"I don't give Daniel hell," I shot back.

"Oh, yes you do. Sometimes I think he enjoys it." She smiled, amused with herself. "But, honestly, I think he just loves you. I'm glad to hear you two are back on good terms. What's the status with this handsome guy from New York?"

"Please don't mention Quentin and Daniel in the same breath, like they're in the same category. Quentin," I over pronounced his name since she refused to use it, "is a business associate."

"And what business are the two of you looking to go into?" She asked with peaked interest.

Part of me wanted to conceal my new endeavor, but the other part, always seeking her approval was a bit too proud to hide it. I wanted her to know how involved I was with my business, acknowledging the major strides I'd made.

"We're in talks of a merger," I tried to sound as casual as possible, reaching for the pick with olives as I watched her from the corner of my eye.

She may not have said it, but I could see she was impressed. "Really?" she pressed her lips tightly together. "I didn't take you as the marrying type when Daniel came around, but to do it twice just feels excessive."

"What are you talking about? A merger is nothing like a marriage," I argued.

"You're right," she said in a tone that let me know she was not at all conceding. "A divorce is much cleaner than a dissolution."

She bit an olive from the pick, shaking her head slightly. I watched her closely, now hanging on to her every word, despite how incurious I wanted to be. "Think of it like that and you'll be smarter this time around."

"Is that so?" I turned to her. It never ceased to amaze me how impressed I was by my mother. She had the power to take me through all emotions – joy to frustration, followed by annoyance to admiration. "And how could I be smarter, mom?"

"If I could do it again," she paused for effect. "I would only marry if I could guarantee my own independence."

I nodded, but she wasn't done yet. "And I'd make sure I owned him."

"Owned him? Mom, that sounds a bit abusive, even for you." I huffed, finishing the last of my olives.

"A fair split is very rare, Emily. Almost impossible in any type of relationship. But if I'm in charge, I at least have the option of being fair. If the shoe is on the other foot, I'm at the mercy of someone else. And that's a position I never want to be in."

I was replaying her words in my mind when the server arrived with a large silver platter of oysters on ice. Regardless of how much she drove me crazy, my mother's value and wisdom was undeniable.

17

After a day at the office, and lunch with my mother, I was exhausted by the time I got home. Dropping my keys on the table in the foyer, I kicked off my heels with a deep sigh of relief. It was the start of the week, but I was already looking forward to the weekend.

When I entered the kitchen, Daniel was watching me, holding his cell to his ear. "Yeah, I know," he said into the receiver. "Look, Em just got home. And she's already got her shoes off, so I know she's tired."

I smiled, dropping my work bag onto the kitchen island with a heavy thud before making my way to him.

"Yeah, let's do that," he said, opening his arms to welcome me. He'd showered already, wearing a thin white t-shirt and black joggers, rather than the suit he'd left the house in. "'Til forever."

He ended the call with who I now knew was his little brother, wrapping his arms around me as he kissed the top of my head. "Jason says 'hi'."

"Why didn't you say that when he was on the phone, so I could've said 'hi'?" It was always funny looking up to him. Without heels, Daniel was a full foot taller than me, towering over my petite frame.

"Then, he would've wanted to say something back, you would've snatched the phone, and I still wouldn't have you to myself," he leaned down to kiss my lips.

I inhaled his scent, feeling myself relax in his arms. It was all I needed after a day like the one I'd had. As much as I loved lunches with my mother, having them in my new role felt like a burden. Typically, I'd end the day after two martinis with her. But now, I had meetings I couldn't cancel, which meant returning to the office for another few hours of work. I was wiped.

"Do you want to go out to dinner?" Daniel asked.

"No!" I answered quickly. "I don't want to go anywhere. I wish it was the weekend," I groaned, which seemed funny to Daniel.

"Was it that bad?" He asked, kissing me softly again.

"I don't know how you do it." Inhaling deeply, I rose onto the balls of my feet to wrap my arms around his neck. "Long hours, endless meetings, constant emails, useless small talk. I'm drained," I closed my eyes, leaning into his chest.

Daniel held me close before moving forward. My feet followed his as he led to the back of the house. "Where are we going?"

"You need a drink, Mrs. Gamble," he said, placing his hands under my arms. The tips of my toes grazed the wooden floors as he carried me to his man cave. Resting my head against his chest, I was too comfortable to argue.

Walking slowly through the house, into his den decorated with sports paraphernalia, Daniel navigated in the darkness. Once we arrived behind the bar in the corner of the room, he activated dim lights using a remote control.

"What would you like to drink, wife?" He asked as my arms lowered to hug his abdomen tightly.

"Pinot." I answered in a pouty tone.

"Ah," Daniel turned, draping his arm over my back to move me along as he leaned for the wine fridge. "So, a classy bad day, huh?"

After retrieving a bottle of Domaine Faiveley 2015 Pinot Noir, he returned to the counter. "How did you beat me home?" I asked, looking up to him as he worked to uncork the bottle, pouring a small portion into a glass before offering it to me to test.

"I missed my Friday session with Nick," he explained, referencing his personal trainer. "I had to make it up with a 2-hour session today."

Approving the wine with a hum of satisfaction, I turned to set the glass on the counter, feeling the hardness of his torso. Daniel never let his appearance slip, once telling me his physique was a business investment. As he put it, 'How am I supposed to convince someone I can take care of their business if I can't even take care of myself?'

"My mom scolded me for not having my eyebrows done. She thinks you deserve better than that," I looked up to his handsome face, watching his lips contort with amusement.

Glancing down, his forehead creased as he ran his fingertip over my eyebrow. "I thought you were going for a new bushy look," he teased.

"Daniel!" I playfully hit his side, laughing as he positioned his arm to block my harmless jab.

"What else did your mother have to say?" He asked while pouring the dry wine into a decanter to breathe.

"She thinks I drive you crazy," I revealed, watching even closer for this reaction. Vibrations from his abdomen matched the smile on his face. Unable to contain the laughter, he tried to bury his face in my hair.

"That's funny to you?" I asked, straining to see him as he turned my body until my back leaned against his chest. Holding the decanter in one hand, and two wine glasses in the other, he guided me to the seating area with soft nudges against my backside.

"Your mom is hilarious," he finally said as we settled onto the sofa that could only be described as manly. The thick, butterscotch colored leather was shiny and a bit stiff when he'd purchased the furniture. But as he'd anticipated, time and use had softened it into a smoothness that felt more like cashmere.

"So, you're not going to deny that I drive you crazy?" I pushed, crowding him despite having ample space to spread out.

"I wouldn't describe it like that, but I could imagine someone on the outside not understanding us." Now, he was watching me, tugging my legs until they rested across his lap.

"What's not to understand?" I felt myself growing defensive.

"Relax," he fought the smile pulling the corners of his lips. "Your mom just likes to give you a hard time because she's the reason you're so dramatic."

"I am not dramatic!" I yelped, watching his head fall back with laughter. Even I had to recognize the irony.

Daniel leaned forward, filling both glasses much higher than they would in a restaurant, before handing one to me. "To my mogul wife, working long hours in dramatic fashion!"

I raised my glass to meet his, smiling as they collided before forcing myself to sip slowly. As mentally drained as I was, gulping the expensive wine felt more appropriate. Trying not to think of my schedule for the following day, I stared into the glass of wine, admiring the moody color as it moved around the glass slowly.

"I don't know that I want to be a mogul," I blurted out.

To my surprise, Daniel didn't laugh. Surely, this was as dramatic as you could get. Two weeks hadn't passed since my declaration that this was what I wanted to do, and yet I was already unsure of myself.

"And that's okay," he said instead. I turned to see him watching me with an unconcerned yet caring look in his eyes. "It's okay to change your mind. But you don't have to make a decision immediately."

I nodded, enjoying another sip of the Earthy wine. "I do want to be a mogul, but Cherry Blossoms just isn't mine. The more time I spend there, the more I want to change. Now, it feels like I want to change everything." It almost felt like news to me.

"What's wrong with changing everything?" Daniel asked, taking my foot into his free hand, gently massaging the ball of my foot.

"Well, nothing I guess," I admitted with a small shrug. "It's just, would I rather buy a house and completely gut it, or just build the house I want from the ground up?"

Daniel's brows rose as though he understood me. I watched him sip the wine, waiting for his response. "They say change is harder than creation."

"That's what I'm feeling. It doesn't seem smart to uproot everything. It's an uphill battle."

"What would you change?" He asked, setting his wine glass down. "You know, idealistically, if there were no issues."

"Oh gosh," I groaned imagining how differently I could run my company if there were no impediments. "There's little things, like the interior design, that I would love to change. But more than anything, it's the culture, and structure of the business that don't fit my vision."

Always attentive, Daniel listened silently before pulling at my ankle to bring me closer. "You can change everything, baby. It's yours."

"I know," I rushed. But the truth was, I didn't know that I could. Many of the employees were set in their ways. The culture was in accordance with industry norms. What I wanted to do wasn't what any other publishing house was doing.

"How about this," Daniel started, this time reaching for my hip as he manipulated my body until I was straddling him. "You think of how you want to change things, and I'll help you make it happen. You know, without intruding on your independence."

That was the man I married. Always eager to fix everything. Daniel was solution based, ready to brainstorm ways to win in everything he attempted. Lowering myself, I fell into him, the hardness and warmth of his body welcoming me.

"Can I ask you something?" He asked, distracting my darker thoughts. His eyes were inquisitive and yet unsure.

"Yeah," I answered without neglecting my desires. Leaning down, I kissed his lips softly, watching his face soften as he kissed me back.

"Would you want to build a house?" He asked with his lips still pressed against mine.

"Are we still talking about Cherry Blossoms?"

"No, we'll talk about that when you're ready," he leaned up to kiss along my jaw line. "I think we should move."

"But you love this house," I reasoned, glancing around at the room he'd so painstakingly decorated. My eyes caught on a framed autographed poster of Muhammad Ali, a gift I'd moved mountains to purchase for his birthday a few years back.

"It's been good to us," he admitted as his hands found their way into my hair, massaging my scalp while pulling me closer to him. "But I like the idea of a fresh start. New scenery did us well," he rose his hips so I could feel him. I knew he was referencing our weekend away, and how electric things were between us.

"There's no denying that," I smiled bashfully. "But, you can't build in LA," I argued. The city was at capacity. It wasn't Arizona, where new neighborhoods would pop up on undeveloped land.

"Let me rephrase," he grinned, never deterred by my semantic arguments. "Would you want to move?"

"I'm not against the idea," I said after brief consideration. My short stay in hotels had taught me the convenience of living closer to the office. When we purchased our home, I thought our life would be more in line with the cliché plan – kids, career, and bi-annual vacations. Now, with Daniel convincing me we could potentially create the life we wanted, I could see moving into a place more custom fit to our lifestyle.

"That's good enough." Daniel flashed a small smile, but I could tell he was more excited than he let on. My curiosity wondered how long he'd been considering the question, but my body was more focused on other things.

"Now, can I ask you something?" Pressing my body into his, my heart rate increased, feeling him harden between my legs.

"Of course," he smiled.

"Just how tired are you?" I strained to fight back my smile, watching the lust swirl in his eyes.

"I'm never *that* tired," he grinned, pulling my face down to kiss me deeply. Lifting me from the sofa, we deserted the wine, leaving the den in such a rush we didn't turn off the lights.

Daniel moved faster than the leisurely pace he'd carried me into the den with. Just as we reached the kitchen, he slowed. "I almost forgot," he said softly.

Unwilling to release him, my ankles remained clasped behind his back as I turned to see what he was reaching for. He lifted a white envelope and handed it to me.

"What's this?"

"Open it," he smiled, setting me onto the kitchen island. Following his instructions, I unfolded the flap, pulling the single sheet from the envelope as I read what looked to be a contract.

Hovering over me, Daniel pointed to a line at the bottom of the sheet. "You're on the house deed."

"You did it?" I asked, suddenly feeling emotional.

"Of course, I did it. I would've always had it that way. I didn't know you cared," he explained.

"I didn't. My mom did." I admitted, feeling a bit silly for forcing him to go through the trouble.

"Well, it's done. And it makes sense for you to be on it."

"It doesn't matter much now, though. We're moving, right?" I smiled.

"You'll be on that deed, too."

I looked to him with an appreciation blooming in my chest. There were so many moving pieces in my life, so much suspicion. But one thing I was certain of was that Daniel was for me. He had never given me any reason to question that. I was desperate to feel him, needing to express the love I felt so deeply.

"Let's take a shower," I suggested, biting my bottom lip with intentions I knew he could see. Without a word, Daniel lifted me from the counter, carrying me to our bedroom with an urgency I appreciated.

Daniel undressed quickly as I fought my burgundy shift dress before joining him under the waterfall shower head. He turned to me with a salacious grin, his body glimmering as water cascaded down his defined torso.

Always in control, he gripped the nape of my neck, taking my mouth with long strokes of his tongue. I moaned lazily, leaning forward with my hips to feel his growing erection. The glass wall of the shower quickly fogged from the steam of the water that couldn't compare to the heat burning within.

I dropped to my knees in the center of the shower, too far from the wall for Daniel to reach support. Wrapping my lips around his manhood, I took his length to the back of my throat, twisting my head to swirl my tongue around him. Widening his stance, Daniel gripped a handful of my hair for leverage, barely rocking his hips forward.

"Mmm," he hummed when I suctioned my jaw, feeling him harden against my tongue.

The warmth fell over us like a tropical waterfall, an erotic soundtrack to my dominance. It was the only time I felt completely in control of him, owning his pleasure. Looking up as he strained to contain himself, I watched his abdomen tense and relax in rhythm with my movements. His hips began to rock faster as my hands wrapped tightly around his thickness.

I stroked him gently at his base, focusing my tongue on his most sensitive region. Slowing his hips, he gripped my hair tightly, pulling me away. "You're gonna make me cum," he warned.

"I know," I said, out of breath, but silently begging for more. My hands continued pumping him, moving in opposite directions as his hips restarted. His grip on my hair loosened slightly, as a pearl of salty sweetness emerged.

It was all the encouragement I needed, leaning in quickly to taste the tease of his release. Emboldened by the soft sounds of his pleasure, barely audible above the water crashing around me, I worked him.

"Damn, baby," he grunted. My hands were moving rapidly, my head swirling from side to side. Opening my mouth, I felt him throbbing against my tongue, excited by the tension. Releasing my grip, I cupped his balls in one hand and sucked long and fast, letting my mouth do all the work.

"Fuck!"

I could hear the submission, as he gave me what I wanted, coming long and hard while growling my name. My sex clenched with desire, so turned on from bringing him to climax. Still aroused to a full erection, Daniel was far from done.

"Come here!" He pulled me to my feet before lifting me in the air.

The coolness of the glass wall against my back was a shock, but it was the way he spread my body, demanding room, that made me shriek with delight.

"Ahh!" My legs and arms wrapped around him as his forearms reached behind me. His hands gripped my shoulders, pulling me into each of his pumps as he slammed into me relentlessly.

"Daniel! Baby! Yes!" I cried, already to the point of climax within seconds.

Long, deep strokes carried me to the point of no return as he reclaimed dominance, sending me into a fury of cries begging for more. I could never get enough of him, never tire of his expertise with my body. He had the power to change the course of a day with ease, turning stress to vapor like the steam of a shower.

18

"**W**hat are you doing up?" Daniel's groggy voice jolted me.

"Go back to sleep, baby," I urged him, holding the book flat against my chest.

"You're still reading? What time is it?" He reached for me, wrapping his arm around my waist.

Glancing at the nightstand, I answered him in disbelief. "Just after five."

I'd stayed up all night, reading like a teenager, completely losing track of time. Crystal had prepared a collection from her favorite unsigned writer. Taking the time to bind her work like a book, I'd gotten lost in one short story after another before diving into the first eight chapters of what the writer described as her debut novella.

As Daniel drifted back to sleep, I sat up, fully awake. Deciding to get the day started, I quietly maneuvered from under the blankets. Glancing over my shoulder, Daniel was fast asleep as I crept into the bathroom.

Standing under the waterfall shower head, I felt energized despite the sleepless night. My thoughts kept drifting back to the fictitious characters I'd read about, wondering how they were handling the issues they'd faced throughout the story.

By the time I stepped out the shower, I knew I had to learn more about this writer. All Crystal had included was her name, Ivy. She clearly had experience developing both characters and intricate plots. I was drawn in from the first line of the story, promising myself I would only read one more chapter before calling it a night.

That started just after eleven, when Daniel had fallen asleep. Thinking I'd get a head start on tomorrow's schedule, I reached into my work bag, surprised to see the book. I'd completely forgotten about my request for Crystal to compile the writer's highlights. Now, I was eager to read more.

Daniel was just waking up as I entered the bedroom, already scrolling his phone for news. "You know, they say you shouldn't check your messages when you first wake up," I warned him.

"Oh yeah?" He answered without glancing up. His voice was raspy, deepened. "And what do they say about staying up all night reading?"

"It makes you smarter," I joked, climbing on top of him. He grinned, tossing his phone on the bed, finding my hips with his strong hands.

"I don't think you've ever gone into the office earlier than me," he said with his hand tracing up my body. "I'm proud of you."

"Crystal found this new writer," I smiled at just the thought of Ivy. "I read everything she sent me in a night."

Daniel's brows rose as his lips curled in a soft smile. "That's good. Maybe she's the inspiration to help you define the next chapter of Cherry Blossoms."

Pressing my lips together, I fought the giddy joy I felt bubbling at his suggestion. Ivy was just what I wanted for the company. She was who I had in mind when I decided to purchase a publishing house. Even without meeting her, I knew our paths were aligned.

"I think you're right." I finally agreed. "I know what direction I want to go in."

"Let's talk about it over dinner after therapy tomorrow," he suggested.

"Tomorrow?" I was already excited to discuss everything, unsure I would need another day.

"I have to work late tonight. But I know I'll need some alone time with you after one of those sessions," he said before inhaling deeply.

"We never talked about the first session. Was it rough for you?"

"It's uncomfortable," he admitted. "I wanted to go to dinner last week, but you had the family dinner."

"Oh yeah," I smirked. "Your betrayal."

"Stop," he pulled me towards him, burying his grin in my hair. Rolling me onto my back, Daniel's lustful gaze let me know he had no plans of letting me get to the office early.

Two hours later, I was walking into the office with a pep in my step despite the lack of sleep. Feeling energized and excited for the day, I'd chosen a fire red tuxedo dress with black lapels and buttons. Black sky high pumps completed the look, as my hair sat in a curly bun atop my head. I was ready to tackle what I expected to be a packed day.

"You just got a delivery, Boss Lady!" Crystal squealed. Peeking behind her into my office, I noticed the large bouquet of roses on my desk, taming my smile as I asked about the day's plan.

"So, we're meeting with Quentin and Madison today, right?" I asked, already dreading another interaction. I wasn't prepared, but knew it was time to continue the negotiations I'd been putting off.

"No," she frowned, looking on her desk until she located her clipboard. Reading from the top sheet she explained, "Quentin said he wanted to follow your lead and take things slower. He asked if you would be able to attend his party this Friday," she looked up to see my reaction. And then added, "I told him I'd let him know by the end of the day."

"Let me think about it," I said, biting my bottom lip. He wanted to take my lead? I replayed the words in my mind, searching for the double entendre I'd come to expect from Quentin.

"Okay, perfect," Crystal jotted something down. "And you're still on for your meeting with Victoria soon."

I glanced at my watch, having forgotten about my sister's appointment. She was scheduled to show me the ideas she'd come up with for redesigning the office, something I'd failed to give any further thought since our last meeting.

"I think I'm going to take her out of the office," I thought aloud.

"No problem. I can arrange a restaurant if you'd like," Crystal offered, correctly reading my mind.

"Somewhere with French toast," I requested with a grumbling stomach. "Anything else?" I said with one foot towards my office.

"Yeah," Crystal started, suddenly a bit nervous. "Did you have a chance to read anything from that writer I suggested? I know I sent a lot," she shook her head dismissively.

My smile grew instantly. "Crystal, she's brilliant!"

Watching her shoulders drop as she exhaled loudly, I realized she'd been concerned about it. It was the first project in her new position, and I was blown away.

"I want to sign her," I said with certainty. "Like, as soon as possible."

"Well, I thought you might feel that way," she started. "And since Quentin cancelled, you're free this afternoon."

I nodded, wondering where she was going. Crystal was always confident and comfortable in her position and associated tasks. Now, I could sense she was challenging herself, venturing into foreign territory.

"I contacted her, and she agreed to meet later today," she finally revealed with an excited grin.

"Are you serious?"

"Yeah," she beamed. "I told her I'd check with you and get back to her."

"Oh, I'm all in!" The excitement between us was electric. "Set it up for three. Let her pick the place and we can head out together at two."

"*Together*?" Crystal's thin eyebrows rose as she tried to make sense of my plan.

"You found her, you're going with me to sign her." I answered matter-of-factly before heading into my office. Without turning to see her reaction, I knew she was ecstatic. Crystal had always wanted to be more involved with the business.

By finding Ivy, she'd proven to be as valuable as I'd always known. Now, we just needed to build our own roster of writers we believed in, because of the way their writing made us feel, rather than how many books they'd sold. It was going to be nothing like what Cherry Blossoms had been in the past, but everything I wanted our future to entail.

With a pink rose petal between my fingertips, I called Daniel. He answered on the second ring.

"Hey, Gorgeous."

"Thank you for the roses," I smiled into the receiver.

"Thank you for a perfect start to the day."

I paused before asking, "Do you want to go to Quentin's party this weekend?"

"Do I want to go or will I go?" He countered without hesitation.

"He cancelled our meeting today," I explained. "Said, he wants to take things slower and invited me to this party."

"So, is it business or pleasure?"

"I think it's supposed to be a friendly business gesture," I offered, though I wasn't exactly sure of Quentin's intentions.

"You sound like you're on the fence," Daniel said before changing to a more authoritative tone. "Legal approved this?" After a pause, he added, "I'll look it over and get it back within the hour."

"This is silly," I laughed to myself, realizing I was intruding on his work day. "You can handle that. I'll talk to you about it at home."

"I always have time for you." He answered so quickly I wasn't sure he was speaking to me until I recognized the tenderness of his tone.

"I just know you're busy," I reasoned.

"I'm never too busy. I needed to talk to you anyway," he paused and then I heard a door close. "I looked into that email you gave me."

"What email?" I asked, searching my memory.

"A guy named Martell Engram emailed Madison about your deal."

"Oh yeah!" I recalled, eager to know what he'd learned. "Is it true? Is Quentin shopping the deal to other publishing houses?"

"It's true that's he's shopping his company," Daniel confirmed. "But it's not for mergers, he's looking for investors."

"Investors? His financials are good." It was one of the reasons I wanted to merge with Quentin's Laney Publishing. He had the cash to buy out half of my ownership, liquidating a significant portion of my assets.

"They are," Daniel confirmed again. "I researched that too, and his financials all check out."

"Then, why would he want investors?" I wondered.

"That's what's not making sense," he said, in a disapproving tone. It was no secret that Daniel was not a fan of Quentin's. "Maybe you can ask him at his party."

My stomach tensed as the softness of a rose petal teased my fingertip. "I'll just give it some thought. I'm not sure if I want to go yet."

"Well, you decide. If you choose to go, I'll be there."

"I love you."

His deep inhale let me know he understood how much our newly rekindled communication meant to me. Being able to call Daniel, even for the smallest things, was my safety blanket. I loved the reassurance and confidence he gave me. Just knowing he was there was enough to set me at ease.

"I will love you forever, Emily."

"I'm going to smell my roses for a bit. I'll call you later," I smiled.

"I'm going to replay this morning in my mind."

"You're a mess! Bye!" I giggled as I sat the receiver down.

19

"I'll be right back with your orders," the waitress smiled, taking my menu and then Victoria's before leaving us.

"So, why are we so incognito?" She whispered once we were alone. "Do you not want everyone to know about the design?"

Biting back a laugh, I sipped from my cappuccino, tasting the bitterness of the extra shot of espresso. "Honestly, I was just hungry. Show me what you got," I nodded towards the large bag she'd brought with her.

Following Crystal's recommendation, we were on Melrose at Blu Jam Café to try what she promised was the best French toast in the city. Per usual, I chose to sit outside, enjoying the soft breeze of an LA morning. I never understood escaping one office for another. I liked watching the city, wondering where everyone was going in less of a rush than the typical major city.

A young dark skin girl was across the street, struggling but managing to control the leashes of what looked to be a dozen dogs. She was thin, with full hips and a plump bottom that made me envision she was a transplant from the south. Quickly, I developed a story of her dreaming to be an actress from grade school.

Like so many others, she'd packed up everything and drove

across the country to chase her dreams. Sure, she walked dogs down Melrose for money, but that wasn't her destiny. She was a star, just undiscovered.

That was the story for so many in Los Angeles. The possibility was what kept the energy pumping throughout the city. You never knew who would become the next big actress, or singer, producer, or writer, but you always felt the proximity to talent. It was everywhere you turned, impossible to ignore.

A guy who looked fresh out of high school approached from behind Victoria. He was tall and lean, with blond hair like Zack from *Saved by the Bell*. I imagined he was popular in high school, maybe the captain of the football team. Now, he probably surfed at Venice during the day and played guitar at night. Before my imagination could continue, he stopped at a storefront a few meters away, unlocking the door to let himself in.

Entrepreneur? I wondered silently. I hadn't pegged him to be in business. Maybe he was just a store manager working to save up until his band hit it big. I smiled to myself, randomly motivated by complete strangers. God, I loved my city.

"Now, don't get freaked out by all the color. It'll still be professional," Victoria reclaimed my attention. While I'd been people watching, she had unfolded her sketchbook, revealing a detailed drawing that looked nothing like the current décor in Cherry Blossoms, but everything like the vision in my mind.

"You made this?" I asked, pulling the page closer.

It was perfect. A bright green courtyard served as the center of the office, with a mural welcoming visitors into the office. Running my fingertip over the artistic mural she'd sketched – a vibrant graphic novel style image of a man and woman kissing. Their eyes were closed, but you could see the passion on their faces regardless. The woman's hand rested on the nape of the man's neck, luring him closer, a longing clear but calm.

"It doesn't have to be this exact image. I just think a colorful mural would be a great way to set the tone," she offered with a self-conscious delay.

"I love it." Seeing my sister's design was the validation I needed to believe I could change everything. Angling the page, I noticed the different colors of each room, defining the spaces in a way that felt both separate and inclusive.

One office had what a small label described as turf flooring, but from the image, it looked like grass. Four swings hung from the ceiling, with a large white board and bean bags at the edge of the room.

Currently, there was a mural of a playground in the creative segment of the office, but this was three dimensional. It was the perfect setting for creative brainstorming. I could essentially transport my team back to childhood, when their imaginations were a superpower. That's what we'd need to build what I wanted. We would have to dream everything, because it had never been done before.

"I know the courtyard looks crazy, but I've been researching ways we can set up a realistic looking garden indoors. Maybe losing a little office space, but completely transforming the feel." Victoria explained, turning the sketchbook to point and explain her design.

She'd just finished describing the break room that looked more like a small convenient store when the waitress appeared holding two large plates. Closing the sketchbook, Victoria carefully tucked it away in her bag.

"Here's your breakfast quesadilla," the waitress announced, placing Victoria's dish in front of her. "And your French toast."

"That's not French toast," Victoria scrunched her nose as she looked across the table at my plate.

"This is our signature dish – the crunchy French toast." The waitress perked up. From her excitement, I imagined this was a common response. It didn't resemble any French toast I'd ever seen, that was for sure.

"It's made with a French brioche, soaked in our secret batter and covered in crunchy corn flakes," she explained with precision that assured she'd spent all morning reciting the recipe.

"Well, it smells delicious. Thank you," I leaned in to read her name tag, "Lizzie."

"You're very welcome. If you need anything else, just give me a wave. I'm kind of swamped inside, but I'll keep an eye on you two out here," she smiled before leaving us alone.

"You know I have to taste that, right?" Victoria reached with her fork before I could answer. She moved an entire slice of French toast onto her plate, which was welcomed given the generous portions.

"And I'm going to need some of these," I leaned over, feeling the unforgiving fabric beneath my arm strain as I reached for a spoonful of grilled potatoes.

From the silence, only interrupted by approving moans, I had to assume my sister was as hungry as me. We finally slowed when our bellies were too full to continue, occasionally picking at a lone square of potato until the waitress reappeared.

"Please, take this food before I eat another bite," I held my hands up like the final bell of a cooking competition had sounded. The amused waitress took both plates, nodding as I asked for two green teas to go.

"How did you find this place?" Victoria asked, holding her phone carefully over the name embossed on the black dining table, snapping a photo for later reference. "This is a hidden gem."

"Crystal recommended it. I just told her I wanted French toast," I explained while wiping what I hoped were the last remnants of maple syrup from my lips.

"Speaking of gems," Victoria huffed. "Crystal is a lifeline. I don't think there's anything that girl doesn't do."

"Tell me about it," I agreed, remembering my night spent reading the amazing work from the writer she'd introduced. "She's my partner in the office. I just promoted her to a more fitting title, because she's always been more than my assistant."

"She earned that," Victoria smiled. "Whenever I need anything, she tries her best not to involve you unless it's completely necessary. You need people who don't constantly need direction."

"You're right," I agreed as the waitress appeared with our teas and the bill.

After paying, I walked with my sister down Melrose, choosing to extend our meeting a little longer back at the office. Her design had sparked something, and I wanted to continue the conversation.

We were only a few paces from my white G-Wagon when I spotted the 'for sale' sign in the passing window. Noticing my interest, Victoria tried to read my mind. "Please don't tell me you have more ideas for developing real estate."

I laughed, noting how a few weeks ago that reminder might have hurt. When things between Daniel and I were less secure, and memories of the warehouse we'd developed left a sour taste in my mouth.

"No," I answered, pushing softly on the door that swung open with little effort. "I just want to see what's out there."

"This is nice," Victoria whispered, looking up to the high ceilings as we entered the storefront. The place looked halfway through a renovation. It was much smaller than the current Cherry Blossoms office, but it sat alone rather than a floor within a high rise.

"It is," I too whispered, a rush of adrenaline reminding me we were trespassing. "This is the type of space I need for Cherry Blossoms – something in the city, amongst the dreamers and doers."

"What?" Victoria shrieked. "You couldn't fit half your employees in here," she argued.

"Maybe I don't need half of them," I shrugged, watching the shock shift to curiosity on her face.

"Can I help you?" A loud voice boomed from the back of the building, sending us both into a panic. We ran in our high heels, behaving like unruly teenagers as we rushed to the street. We were at my truck, laughing too hard while climbing onto the leather seats, before the face of the voice revealed itself.

"Oh, my gosh!" She patted her chest dramatically. "I just had flashbacks of getting caught with boys in the basement."

"Mom used to flip out!" I cried, hitting the steering wheel hard at the recollection.

When we were younger, the rarely used back door to the basement might as well have been a secret tunnel as far as we were concerned. Victoria and I would regularly sneak friends in, often allowing them to stay the night. Our mother was never a strict disciplinarian, but when our father was out of town, she really checked out. More focused on tracking his whereabouts, she didn't particularly care what we were doing as long as we were home. That is, until she discovered our secret tunnel, sending half a dozen kids into a frenzy whenever she chose to supervise.

"I swear she knew," Victoria shook her head as I started the engine before pulling into the slow but steady traffic. "There's no way she couldn't have heard us down there."

"I'm convinced mom was aware of everything. She just knew what we could handle, and let us learn our lessons on our own."

Victoria's laugh paused, and we sat with my heavy presumption for a few breaths. We'd always considered my mother to be the soft one, assuming we were getting over on her with secrets she could see through. From everything that had happened with her marriage, and the truths of our personal relationships, my mom had proven to be well within the know.

After a short ride to the office, I was pulling into the garage. Parking in my regular spot beside the elevator, I reached for my purse as Victoria maneuvered her large portfolio bag from the backseat. Together we walked across the concrete lot, our stilettos broadcasting our presence.

"She knew about Lana," I finally added, looking over to Victoria as we stepped into the empty elevator.

"I know." She looked to me with sad eyes. "She was really worried it could come between you and Daniel. I mean, at the end of the day, it didn't really have anything to do with either of you."

"Lana didn't have anything to do with either of us," I agreed as the elevator doors closed. "But the way we handled it said everything about us."

20

"This is where she wanted to meet?" I asked, feeling over dressed and out of place. Although Crystal said it was a café, the sneakers hanging on the wall made it feel more like a shoe store.

"Yeah, she said it's her favorite place to write." Crystal smiled as she looked around, leaning to whisper to me without taking her eyes off a group sitting across from us. "It's like a secret society of artists. I'm not sure how true it is, but I heard there's an indoor skate park at the back. You need a passcode to enter."

I followed her eyes to a group huddled around a circular booth table. An overweight Asian man, who appeared to be in his mid-twenties, was leading the discussion, pounding his fist onto the table. It was clear he was yelling, but I couldn't make out the words over the booming bass blaring through the speakers. Despite his visible passion, not a strand of hair in his immaculately styled topknot moved.

"This music isn't very relaxing," I leaned in to tell Crystal.

Taking a deep breath, I forced myself to relax. The last thing I wanted was to scare Ivy off by appearing to be out of my element in an environment she clearly enjoyed.

"I know," Crystal said as she turned to me, concern on her face. "We need to get you a drink. You've got to calm down. You look disapproving as hell," she laughed, raising her hand to call a waitress over.

I was shocked they even had a wait staff, but didn't mention it to Crystal. She ordered three espresso martinis before running through her plan for the meeting once more. We'd decided it was necessary that I do most of the talking. Crystal had already developed a rapport with Ivy online. I was the one she would be wary about.

"Oh shit," Crystal stopped mid-sentence, glancing at the door. "That's her."

Looking towards the entrance, I found myself both shocked and unruffled. I hadn't spent too much time considering what Ivy looked like, but sitting in the bar like café, I realized I always expected her to be stunning. Slim like a model, she wore a white linen dress I imagined revealed a bit more in better lighting. The darkness of the café did little to hide her aura. Heads turned as she walked towards us, her long locs dyed bright pink at the tips. Half fell down her back, and the rest sat atop her head in a stylish bun. As she approached, I was taken by her flawless skin, bright like she'd spent the previous week soaking up rays on a beach in the Caribbean.

"You must be Emily," she looked me up and down and I instantly regretted wearing the bright red tuxedo dress. I was quite literally a 'suit' in a room full of artists.

"I am," I smiled, seeing the humor in my outfit for the first time. "It's a pleasure to meet you, Ivy."

Even with the music two decibels above appropriate, I could hear the sharp inhale from Crystal at my right. I'd made a mistake, but I wasn't sure what. "No," she whispered, cringing from embarrassment.

I turned to see the beauty in white extending her arms towards me, each hand balled tightly into a fist. On the skin between her knuckles, old English font spelled out my mistake. 'JUST FOUR', the tattoo read.

"My name is Four," she explained with a smile that revealed a gold outline on her bottom row of teeth. When my face revealed my confusion, she added, "It's roman numerals."

"I'm an idiot," I laughed. I'd been calling her Ivy since reading her work, which she only signed with a lowercase letter 'I' and V". "Of course, Four," I closed my eyes, mentally updating my memory so I would never repeat the mistake.

"No sweat," she turned her attention beside me. "Hey, Crystal."

"Thanks for coming," Crystal grinned as we all picked seats.

The woman who's looks matched the effortless beauty of her words sat across from us. She smiled at the waitress when she arrived with our drinks, a familiarity between them let me know they weren't strangers.

"Oh, my kind of ladies," she sipped from her martini as soon as it was in front of her. "I don't even like coffee, but it's the only alcohol they serve."

"I know," Crystal huffed, taking a sip. "They're determined to caffeinate you."

We all laughed together, eyeing each other over the glasses of our drinks. "Crystal, I already know a little about you," the woman I now knew to be named Four turned her attention to me. "So, tell me about you."

Taking another sip to buy myself a little time, I quickly considered the best way to describe myself. A few months ago, I might have started off by telling her about Daniel, and being his wife. Years before that, I would have started with the success of my father, introducing myself as his daughter. After spending the last few months working hard at Cherry Blossoms, I felt my title there most fitting. Yet, that wasn't what came from my shockingly confident voice.

"I think the term 'fan' is demeaning. It creates this distance and inequitable relationship between writer and reader. I like 'supporter' better, because it's more indicative of how I felt when I read your work last night." Turning to Crystal, I saw the smile tugging at the corners of her lips and knew she was proud of me. "Crystal is the director of talent relations. She gave me your latest novella and I read it in one sitting."

Four blushed, taking a sip of her drink before finally saying, "I appreciate it."

"When I finished, I wanted everyone to know about it. I told my husband, who hasn't seen me so excited about a writer since we married. And at the office, I told Crystal, hoping she could connect us, because I want to support your work, and tell as many people as possible about how great you are."

I hadn't planned it, but it was a pitch. Without mentioning what I wanted, it was clear I was selling myself. Maybe I was trying to buy Four, or at least her talent. From her lack of excitement, I doubted my approach was worthy of the accomplishment I felt for making it through the speech without clamoring over my words.

"When you say 'office', you're referring to Cherry Blossoms Publishing, right?" She asked without so much as a smirk.

"I am," I answered, unsure of her intention.

"You own it, right?"

"I do."

Four finished her drink, and so I did the same. As I set my empty glass on the table, she looked at Crystal and then to me. "I sent that novella to Cherry Blossoms Publishing. Got some generic message saying they only accept work from agents."

I nodded, knowing exactly what she was insinuating. I was a part of the problem for artists – making it damn near impossible for their work to make it to the masses without prior success. Agents only worked with writers with a track record. And you could only build a track record by having your work published. And you could only get your work read by a publishing house if it was hand delivered by an agent.

The loop had frustrated me since I purchased Cherry Blossoms. It was the reason finding new talent was so challenging, but the standard for the industry.

"That's why Crystal's role is so important," I reasoned. "She's more in line with my vision – to cut out the middle men and work directly with writers."

"So, you're saying my work is finally good enough to no longer need an agent to vouch for me?" She shot back with sarcastic excitement. It was clear the espresso in the martini wasn't the only bitter taste in her mouth. "You know, your staff won't even look at a writer's work if they're not signed to an agent, who of course takes a cut of any deal they broker."

"Yes, I know." And I knew where she was going.

"It's not to save time or cut back on bad submissions," she kept on. "The two of you are in cahoots with each other to split the profits of the people who actually do the work. Publishing houses don't tell stories. Agents couldn't string two interesting sentences together. But as a team, the two take upwards of half a writer's revenue."

"The suits." I said flatly. It was a term artists used to describe the machine that had become a necessary evil for their work to see the light of day.

"So, your outfit is intentionally ironic then?"

"Actually, no." I signaled to the waitress, drawing her attention to the table. "I stayed up all night reading a novella written by a woman I thought was named Ivy, and then me and my husband had some amazing sex, so I felt pretty invincible when I was getting ready for work."

Four stared at me for an intense moment before breaking into a loud laughter. I smiled, grateful to finally see her lower her guard. "I wasn't sure if I liked you," she said. "But bomb morning sex making you wear a bright ass tuxedo dress to work is fucking boss."

"I want you to come on board," I cut to the chase. "We have to publish your work, but I need you as more than a writer. You'll work directly with Crystal. We're going to build something. I'm not sure what yet, but I want you to sign on anyways. We'll figure out the details later."

"What can I get you?" The waitress asked.

"Are you paying?" Four asked me.

"Are you in?" I countered.

"If you're paying," she reiterated without pause.

"Of course."

"I'll have two more, and so will they." She said flatly.

"So, six more espresso martinis?" The waitress repeated.

"Yes, ma'am," Four flashed her golden smile. The waitress left with our order and Four turned to Crystal.

"I told you, you'd like her," Crystal grinned.

"She's alright," Four teased.

"Hello! I'm right here!" I leaned towards them, and we all fell into another round of laughter awaiting our martinis.

21

Only two sessions into therapy, and I was already regretting beginning the process. After another full day at Cherry Blossoms, filled with meetings and updates, the last thing I wanted was to discuss my marriage with Dr. Cathway over hot tea.

And yet, that's exactly where I was. Beside Daniel, who again sat with tension in his shoulders, his eyes more on me than the doctor.

"How has this week been?" Dr. Cathway asked after neither Daniel nor I volunteered a starting point for the day's session.

"It was fine," I answered in a high pitch, unsure if this was a loaded question bound to go in a direction I wasn't prepared for.

"It's been a pretty good week," Daniel said firmly.

"I'm happy to hear that. Did you have the opportunity to further dissect anything we discussed in our first session?"

I looked to Daniel, and then back to the doctor without speaking a word. In truth, we hadn't mentioned much about therapy. Besides Daniel insisting we follow every session with dinner together, I couldn't remember discussing the conversation Dr. Cathway started the previous week.

"What I don't want," Dr. Cathway began, setting her iPad on the small table beside her. "Is to create a space for you to begin conversations you fail to finish."

My eyes were trained on her, but I could sense Daniel's gaze. As much as I knew she was right, I could feel the irritability rising in my throat. While it had nothing to do with Dr. Cathway, I wasn't in the mood to be scolded.

Unbothered by my glare, she continued. "Even more, I don't want to spend an hour on surface level conversation. We all know there are issues between you two that you're avoiding."

Daniel shifted in his seat, his discomfort palpable. My stomach tensed with anxiety. Dr. Cathway was a trusted safe space, but I could sense she was seconds from exposing information I'd confided in her.

"I'm not completely against enjoying an hour of small talk with you two," she offered a small smile before sipping from an elegant tea cup. This week she'd chosen a teal colored set. Watching her closely, I wondered just how many tea sets she owned. Each one proved to be more beautiful than the last.

"But you're both busy, so if we're going to do this, shouldn't we do it right?" She looked from me to Daniel for an answer.

"I agree." Daniel shocked me with his response.

"And what about you, Emily?" She focused on me.

"Yes, I want to do this right," I answered as my throat tightened.

"So, you're comfortable with me bringing forth topics we've discussed in your individual sessions?" She asked the question she'd warned would precede any divulgence of information we'd previously discussed.

When I first requested couples therapy, Dr. Cathway asked whether I wanted her to broach topics discussed in our private sessions with Daniel. I decided I did, knowing these were the issues we really needed help with. Still, she insisted on asking before each occurrence, providing an opportunity to back out.

Swallowing slowly, I nodded. Reaching for my tea cup, I gulped the liquid, now barely warm after sitting for a quarter of the session.

"Alright, then," Dr. Cathway lifted her iPad and stylus. "Lana Boyden."

She dropped the name like a bomb, waiting to see the destruction as Daniel's body shifted towards me. I turned to face him, looking into hazel eyes that squinted with questions he wasn't prepared to ask with an audience.

"Daniel, I'm sensing a feeling from you."

He turned to her after a long gaze in my direction. "I feel I'm walking into a room, where a conversation has been had about me. Now, I'm just trying to figure out how much of my life has been discussed between the two of you."

I could hear the battle in his voice, fighting for control. He was being ambushed, but I felt the same way. I didn't walk into the session prepared to discuss the woman who's name still led my teeth to clench with fury. On the other hand, I knew Dr. Cathway was right to force us forward in our discussion.

Daniel and I had experienced the honeymoon bliss that followed our battles. Bliss fueled by avoidance as we actively skirted around the difficult conversations that were so necessary.

"Emily, would you like to answer your husband?"

"Well," I looked into the empty teacup, wishing there was another sip to delay my response. "I started coming to Dr. Cathway after the last meltdown between us, but I told her about me filing, and all of that."

I couldn't face him. Instead, I spoke to Dr. Cathway, my eyes pleading with her as though she could save me. No one liked uncomfortable conversations, but for me they were especially intolerable. My hands held the fading warmth of the teacup tightly, searching for soothing. My breathing was labored, and my voice weak. The urge to cry was unbearable, leaving me embarrassed and defensive.

"Meltdowns between *us*?" Daniel asked, emphasizing my decision to place the blame on both of us.

As though he needed to set the record straight, he turned from me, facing the doctor as he continued. "Emily has meltdowns. She doesn't like having difficult conversations. So, she runs. Abandons everything she's built, just to escape confrontation. I am left with the job of chasing after her, trying to convince her to explain why she's being so erratic."

The word erratic cut like a knife. In my mind, erratic was one step from the looney bin. Is that what he thought of me?

"Erratic?" I heard myself interrupt him.

Now, Daniel faced me. "What would you call leaving your mother's house in the middle of the night without telling anyone?"

"Because I saw the emails from Lana," I shot back. I hated addressing her on a first name basis, as though we were familiar.

"Yes, let's talk about that," Dr. Cathway interjected, commanding our attention. We both faced her, eager for her take. I for sure was happy she decided to call him out about the emails, which were in fact the root of the problem.

"This woman attempted to extort you. And while I have my ideas, I would like to know why you chose to keep this from your wife," she prodded.

I turned to Daniel, seeing his jaw tighten before his Adam's apple rose and fell slowly. "I wanted to protect her." The words barely escaped.

"And why do you think Emily needed protection?" Dr. Cathway asked what I had been trying to figure out for weeks.

"Look at her!" Daniel's voice boomed as he pointed his hand in my direction before refocusing on Dr. Cathway. "She's over-whelmed by an uncomfortable conversation!"

"That's not fair! Why are you yelling at me?" My voice cracked, looking to Daniel as a tear rolled down my cheek.

"Em, I'm sorry," he closed his eyes, pressing his fingertips to his temples.

"This isn't acceptable." Dr. Cathway's face was stern, more than I'd ever seen. Leaning across the coffee table, she offered me a tissue.

"That's what I tell him. Whenever I ask him about this, he gets so upset. It's impossible to even have a conversation. Why is he so angry?" Wiping another tear, I could hear the tattle tell nature in my tone.

"No, Emily," she looked directly into my eyes as she spoke. "You don't get to shift the conversation based on the way Daniel expresses his feelings. What you're doing is emotional manipulation."

My heart sank. From the corner of my blurred vision, I could see the shock on Daniel's face. I sat stunned, feeling a pinch of betrayal that Dr. Cathway would be so hard on me.

"We're working backwards," she continued. "Trying to understand why Daniel hid information from you, but that doesn't absolve you of the unreasonable behavior you exhibited. Raising his voice doesn't diminish what he's saying. It's no more distracting than your tears. This is uncomfortable. Embrace that. He is working through his emotions as well. If you want to understand where he is coming from, don't police how he shares."

"Wow," Daniel slouched into the sofa before turning to me. "I think this therapy thing is backfiring on you."

"This is not a competition." Dr. Cathway spoke before I could respond. "Neither of you will be crowned the winner. You're on the same team. Don't you understand that?"

I nodded, feeling like an adolescent. A silence of understanding fell over the room, which I imagine Dr. Cathway purposely allowed to linger. When we were at odds, it did feel like a battle, one I wanted to win. I did everything to prove I was the most damaged party, requiring both remedy and retribution.

"When we're at odds," Daniel finally broke the silence, his voice calm and deliberate as he spoke to Dr. Cathway. "It feels like a slow death. A vital organ is deteriorating, and I feel myself sinking. Emily knows this. She knows I cannot function properly when there's discourse between us. She is not a part of my world, she's it. And she," he continued.

"Let's not speak for Emily," Dr. Cathway gently interrupted him. "Try to speak from your perspective – how you feel, what you know."

Daniel agreed. "I feel like my access to her is snatched away. It's dangled as though she knows I don't want to survive without it. And even when she does re-emerge, it's incremental. I have to earn back her love."

Dr. Cathway listened, squinting her eyes as though every word Daniel spoke was of monumental importance. Her body shifted to me, but the words fell from my lips before she could prompt me to answer.

"I'm not withholding anything," I said to Daniel. He remained facing forward, so I too turned to face the doctor. "Daniel says I shut down, but I don't think he really gets what I'm doing."

"Let's not insinuate what Daniel does or does not know," she stopped me.

I paused, looking for another way to express myself. "When I feel hurt, I shut down all emotions. It's a defense mechanism. But it's not as easy to turn back on. When we come back to each other, it takes a while for me to warm up. I can be open, and my love never falters, but it's hard for me to be..." I faded as I struggled to give the illusive feeling a name.

"Intimate?" Dr. Cathway answered with the most caring expression I'd ever received. I felt so seen and understood I wanted to cry.

"Yes," I swallowed after hearing my voice crack again. "It takes a while for that to return." I whispered the realization, afraid the words would release more tears.

"But we've been intimate every day," Daniel held his palms up in confusion.

"We've had sex." I corrected him. I'd always been able to share my body with Daniel following a fight, but that didn't mean I was ready to share my soul again.

"Mmm," Dr. Cathway acknowledged, as though we'd hit a breakthrough. "And those are different."

"Very different," I agreed, focusing on her rather than looking to Daniel.

"The way he spoke to me," I closed my eyes, trying to shake the memory from my mind. "The vile language. He was beyond angry. I just can't understand how he could ignore me at one of the lowest points in my life. That hurts."

"Still?" Daniel asked softly. "You're still hurting, babe?"

I couldn't trust myself to look at him without crying, so I answered facing Dr. Cathway. "Yes."

Another silence fell over the room. Slowly, I inhaled, holding the breath for a few seconds as I had learned in previous sessions with the doctor. With each exhale, I felt myself relaxing.

"Is that a shock to you, Daniel?" Dr. Cathway asked.

He paused, looking to the ground as he brushed his hair with his palms. "I guess so," he finally answered. Looking up, he continued. "Emily is strong. She's so... defiant. Rebellious even. I never imagined she could feel a way and not voice it."

"Are you doubting her feelings?" The doctor asked.

"No." Daniel answered without hesitation before turning to face me. "No, baby, I'm not."

He reached for my hand, and I accepted, needing his touch. I hated being so vulnerable, admitting things I wanted to remain concealed.

Daniel returned his attention to Dr. Cathway. "It's just embarrassing to know how badly I hurt her," he softly shook his head as though he too was recalling our break down.

"I've been thinking everything is okay between us, and she's still hurting," he spoke more to himself. His words were fluid, like he was letting us in on his thought process. "She puts on a strong front, but I can't battle with her. I just can't," his words faded as he leaned back in his chair, still gripping my hand tightly.

"I had too much to handle. And she picked a fight and ran," he said. "She left me in the middle of the night. At her parents' house, I should add. Looking like a fool!"

He released my hand, and I realized I wasn't the only one still hurting. "Worse than a fool, she made me look like a victim. Her family was actually sympathetic," he chuckled, but there was no humor in the recollection.

"Did that upset you more?" Dr. Cathway finally interjected. "Being a victim?"

"I'm not a victim." Daniel winced at the accusation.

"I agree," she nodded, closing her eyes. "I misspoke. I meant, did being perceived as a victim upset you more than Emily leaving?"

I watched Daniel as he looked down at his hands resting in his lap. His fingers were interlocked as his thumbs circled each other. When he looked up to Dr. Cathway, his voice was a mix of confusion and desperation.

"I do everything for her."

Finally, he turned to me. "Emily, I do everything for you. There's nothing you've ever asked of me that I didn't make happen. Being with someone else, or leaving you, has never even crossed my mind. I can't think of anything I've done to make you doubt me," he spoke with a sincerity that tugged at every one of my heart strings.

"You haven't done anything," I assured him.

"Then why don't I get the benefit of the doubt?" He asked.

Stumped, I looked down to my fingers. "It seemed so clear when I read the emails."

"Do you realize you were wrong now?" He asked.

"Yes," I admitted. "Of course, but you were hiding something from me." I looked into his eyes. "Do you realize that was wrong?"

"I do." He blinked slowly with the admission.

"I think this is a great place to stop for the week." Dr. Cathway broke the silence.

"What?" Daniel asked too loudly. "We're just getting somewhere!"

Spontaneous laughter belted from the depths of my belly. His reaction mirrored my feelings so accurately I was taken aback. In all my sessions, I'd never experienced what we had in an hour. It was actual progress, more than Daniel and I could have achieved alone. Dr. Cathway smirked as she sat her iPad down.

"In here, we identify wounds, pick at scabs, and learn techniques to care for them. But the real healing will happen at home, when no one's watching. Just today, we've addressed emotional manipulation, and how that is unbeneficial to this wound." She looked at me as she said this, and then shifted to Daniel. "And although you want to keep Emily comfortable, it's important that you express yourself and trust her to be able to handle herself. As much as you may want to, you cannot protect Emily from herself."

Dr. Cathway stood, leading us back through the apartment styled office. We needed the push to rise from the Victorian sofa. Daniel and I walked in silence after thanking her and making pleasantries about seeing her the following week.

It was his idea that we ride to the session together, and as we reached his Audi, I was grateful for his foresight. I felt exposed and vulnerable. The last thing I wanted was to be alone.

"Now, do you see why I want dinner to follow these sessions?" He asked as he opened the passenger door.

"Yes," I breathed as I plopped into the seat.

"I felt this way last week, too." He said quietly before closing the car door.

22

D aniel settled beside me at the restaurant, resting his head on mine, and I didn't object. We were both drained. When the waiter arrived, I ordered wine for the both of us, desperate to unwind.

"That was intense," Daniel finally said.

"It was," I agreed, enjoying the weight of him. "She took the training wheels off today."

"How did you find her?" He asked, straightening as the waiter approached with two glasses of Chianti wine.

"Crystal found her for me."

"Will you be ordering a meal as well, or just cocktails?" The older white man asked politely.

"We're eating," I forced a smile, weakly reaching for the menu. I felt zapped, though most of my exertion had been emotional labor.

"Our meal of the day is lobster bisque risotto, a specialty from the chef."

"I'll have that," Daniel handed his menu to the waiter with a relieved smile.

Glancing at the cover of the menu, I knew I didn't want the task of picking a dish either. "Make that two," I handed my menu over. "And a Caesar salad."

"Sure thing," he said before dismissing himself.

After a gulp of wine, I felt myself relaxing. My stomach had been bound up with tension since we left Dr. Cathway's office. Leaning into Daniel, I felt his arm drape over me, his hand falling to my hip.

"Crystal did a good job finding Dr. Cathway," he said. "I like her."

Sitting up, I smiled, feeling proud of myself and Crystal. She'd proven to be invaluable in both my personal and professional life. "She's the best. I just promoted her so she can have a more fitting title. I don't think I ever intended her to just be an assistant."

Daniel's brows furrowed for a few seconds and then he nodded as though he'd caught up. "You're talking about Crystal."

"Yeah," I reached for my wine. "Who'd you think I was talking about?"

"Well, I was talking about Dr. Cathway. I like her," he explained.

"Oh, yeah, she's good too," I chuckled, feeling the tart cherry flavor of the wine hit the back of my throat.

"So, what does Crystal's new role entail?" He turned to face me and I felt slightly nervous. Daniel was so experienced with business, discussing my ideas sometimes felt elementary.

"I'm not sure about any of this," I warned him.

He bit his lip to stop the smile that creased his cheek, revealing his dimple. "I'm not going to pick apart your ideas, Em."

"I don't think you will," I shook my head. "It's the opposite, really. You're an executor by nature. Whenever I have an idea, you go about making it happen. I'm not sure I want any of this to come to fruition immediately."

"Okay," he said sternly. "I'll just listen. And when you're ready for me to move, I'll move. But not before you give the order."

I finished my wine before turning to him, lifting one knee onto the leather seat. "Well, let me ask you this," I decided to change course before revealing my idea. "What do you ultimately want for Tower Enterprise Group?"

"To sell it." He answered flatly.

"What? But that's your company!" I argued, not expecting that response. "You love what you do."

"Baby, I'm a capitalist. Tower Enterprises is just a business, it's not me. I like building things up, and when the stars align and I can make a good profit, I sell."

"But what would you do if you sold it?"

"Build something else."

The stories I'd heard from him and his brother always painted Daniel as entrepreneurial. Tower Enterprise Group was his latest venture, one he'd built on his own. Yet, he spoke about it without sentiment, as though it held no space in his heart, only his checkbook.

Recently, I'd felt drained because Cherry Blossoms Publishing had begun to sit the same way with me. Gone were the days when I had this immense passion to transform it into what I wanted it to be. Instead, I was beginning to envision an entirely new company, something I could build from the ground up like Daniel had.

"I think I know what I want to do with Cherry Blossoms," I started, swallowing slowly as I prepared my thoughts.

"I'm all ears," he leaned in, crossing his arms with an intense glare that let me know I had his undivided attention.

Sitting with it, I thought of what I didn't like about Cherry Blossoms. There was so much I loved about my company, but the structure and culture didn't fit with my vision at all.

"Cherry Blossoms is outdated. I don't want it to run like a traditional publishing house. Everything is so professional, but it should be creative." I paused, wondering if it sounded too idealistic. Daniel was listening closely, so I continued. "I wanted a publishing house that was more about the writers than the bottom line. My whole team, all they care about is sales. No one is searching for new talent or trying to develop writers. They want to sign popular writers and make them more famous. It's not the same."

"So, you want a cooperative, where you work with the writers rather than maximizing profits?" He asked, leaning forward to retrieve his glass of wine.

"Like, Tower Enterprises. You don't focus solely on making the most money from your clients," I argued.

"Right, but I have incentives, babe." He sipped the wine before explaining himself. "I'm working with my clients on a common goal. And my contracts are written to reward my team for the best results. My success is directly tied to the success of my clients."

His business wasn't comparable to mine. As a consultant, Daniel worked with his clients to anticipate and solve their problems, in either individual or recurring agreements. We developed artists, partnering for the long haul of their careers. At least, that was what I envisioned.

"I used to think I could transform Cherry Blossoms into the company I wanted. I thought I could redesign the office and change the culture. I figured if I changed the way we operated, the business would follow," I explained.

"Makes sense," he said, raising a finger to alert the waiter before lifting my empty glass, silently requesting another.

"I don't think that will work, though," I admitted, watching his reaction closely. Daniel would always find a way to make my plans work, regardless of the cost or collateral damage. But what good would it be if the new company I wanted cost me the thriving company I already had?

"Why not?" His face gave nothing away, although his gaze narrowed just slightly as I continued.

"To create the company I want, I'd have to self-destruct Cherry Blossoms. It's not just a principle or two I want to change, it's everything. It kind of feels pointless to spend the time and money getting rid of everything I have just to build it all over again. Wouldn't it be better to just start from scratch?"

"It depends," Daniel started, pausing as the waiter delivered another glass of wine. He picked up the conversation once we were again alone. "What exactly do you want to change?"

"Right now, we're so archaic." I began, rattling off issues until I ran out of breath. "We have little online presence, depending almost solely on agency partnerships. Writers are getting a small portion of royalties, when I would rather be their partners. We treat them like employees, setting deadlines and minimum submissions. I want to let the artists lead the process. There's no way anyone sitting in an office can tell them how to create."

"So, you want a co-op?" He asked again, searching my face when I didn't respond. "A member owned business between you and the writers."

It was the first time I'd considered it, but it felt right. "We claim to have that type of relationship with writers now, like we're all a family. Every publishing house does. But we don't. The way we talk about writers, as commodities, it really irks me."

"So, you'd want to split profits evenly?"

I hadn't thought that far. "I don't know about that part. I don't want to cheat them, but I don't even know that I deserve the Lion's share."

Daniel's brows rose as he unfolded his arms, reaching for his glass of wine before taking a sip.

"Is this so radical, that you need a drink?" I giggled, reaching for my own glass.

"It's just not what I was expecting," he reasoned. "How do you see this happening? When?"

"I'm not sure, but I don't want to keep putting it off," I said more to myself than him.

"Can I give you some advice?" He asked cautiously.

'Yes, please."

"You need a team – handpicked by you. A change like that is going to take a lot of moving pieces, and you have to accept what you don't know. You want artist partnership, so you need an artist to represent that perspective. You want to go digital, you need someone to lead that. And you need a bridge, between the old and the new, someone who understands where Cherry Blossoms is and where you want it to go."

I smiled, thinking of Crystal and Four, and how perfectly they fit two of the descriptions he mentioned. Even before hearing his advice, I was already moving in the right direction. It gave me more confidence in the decisions I was making.

"I think I'm onto something," I said, watching pride swirl in his eyes. "I'm going to need you, but I'm not sure how yet."

"Whatever you need, I got you."

I quickly began working through a plan that had been formulating in my mind. "I kind of have an idea, but I'm not ready to share it yet."

"That's okay," Daniel said quickly, leaving me assured.

"I know I need a new company, but I don't want it to have anything to do with me. My name shouldn't be on the paperwork anywhere. Can you do that?"

"Of course. When do you want it?"

"As soon as possible," I decided on the spot.

"Consider it done. Just remember, you can structure the business however you want. Your team can get in line, or you can find a new team." He offered. "Whatever you choose, you know I'm here. You can't fail."

"My mom recently said something like that," I smiled, recalling the conversation. "I didn't know she'd seen my office before, but she said her and my dad always make sure to have a safety net for us."

"Right," Daniel agreed. "And since you moved into the eighteenth floor, the property value has skyrocketed. There's no way you could ever lose."

I sipped the wine, processing his words with confusion. "The property value?"

"Oh, I thought the safety net was your parents owning the building," he returned my confused stare.

I carefully placed my wine glass on the table. "My parents own what building?" I asked, swallowing slowly.

"Wait," Daniel placed his glass beside mine. "You didn't know your parents own the entire building you work in?"

"You did?"

494

Daniel smiled, despite the shock and mild animosity I began to feel. I loved the idea that my parents wanted to provide security for me, but the secrecy of it all was uncomfortable.

"When we were setting up your deal, your dad demanded all these unusual requests in the agreement." Daniel squinted, remembering details from so long ago when his consultancy firm negotiated my agreement to purchase what is now Cherry Blossoms Publishing.

"He wanted the lease in your name personally, which I argued was irresponsible. Of course, I didn't want you to fail, but if the business did go under and the lease was in your name, you would be responsible for the financial obligation personally. Whereas, if you leased through your business, bankruptcy would minimize your personal exposure. Then, he wanted your lease to allow for subletting, which I knew was out of the question."

"Why? What's wrong with subletting?"

"Think about it," he leaned closer to me. "If I own a property, I want the right to say what businesses can operate in my building. Otherwise, there could be conflicting tenants, or even a lessee whose views conflict with my own. By allowing subletting, as the owner, you're giving up too much control."

"But I have the option of subletting in my lease," I said, even more confused.

"Exactly. When the request was approved, I researched who owned the building. The concessions they were making just didn't make sense."

"And you found out it was my parents?"

"Yeah." His Adam's apple rose and fell slowly as he watched my reaction.

"Why didn't you tell me?"

"Baby, we weren't even dating then. I was only working with you. I considered that to be personal, not professional. Besides, it only made the deal better for you."

I sat in silence, trying to make sense of my parents' decision.

Not only to purchase the building I worked in, but to refrain from telling me.

"And, honestly, I assumed you knew." Daniel added.

"No, I didn't." I sighed, unsure of how that would change my desires for my business. In a way, I was my own landlord. There had to be a way to make that work for me. My mind began working overtime as the waiter arrived carrying two oversized pasta bowls.

23

"I'm really excited that you're ready to move forward!" Madison could barely contain herself as she flipped through my edited proposal.

After speaking with Daniel and Crystal about what I wanted the future of my business to look like, I was looking forward to merging with Laney Publishing. Quentin had a lot of experience working directly with writers, something I hadn't considered when we first began discussions. Of course, his forte was more salacious, reality TV star tell-alls and exposes. But he knew about taking an undiscovered talent and selling books. I wanted to focus on that more than we currently were.

"I wanted to be thorough working through everything." I reasoned.

Madison smiled, but I could tell from the look of concentration on her face, she was barely listening to me. She was too focused on reading the changes I'd made to Quentin's merger proposition, each of which had been marked in red font along with a sticker for indication.

In Quentin's initial proposal, he'd listed the valuation of my company based on the previous year's sales. However, Cherry Blossoms was currently on track to see a seven percent increase in earnings. I wanted the valuation to reflect our anticipated growth, increasing my asking price.

Other changes were more superficial, like the cost of the design renovation, as quoted by my sister. I'd requested it to be approved in advance, rather than requiring approval from the board we'd agreed to set up for decision making.

My recommendations about the board were the most drastic adjustment I'd made to the proposal. Quentin wanted executives from each publishing house to automatically receive seats on the board, and voting privileges. I proposed they have access to meetings without the ability to vote on decisions for the first twelve months following the merger.

"How about you look over the changes. We can meet before I present it to Quentin on Friday," I decided.

"You're going to the party?" She asked with a mixture of excitement and shock.

"Yeah, I think it will be a great place to finally give him my updated proposal."

Madison agreed, still struggling to grant me her undivided attention. I had to lead her out the office, she was too intrigued to stop reading. Before she left, I made one final request. "Don't mention anything about the revisions to Quentin before I deliver it to him on Friday."

She paused for a moment. "Of course," she answered before leaving.

With one part of the puzzle in play, I called Daniel to make sure he was ready to move forward with the rest of my strategy.

"Hey, baby," he answered quickly.

"Hey, you busy?"

"Not too much. Is everything okay?" I heard the concern in his tone, which somehow set me at ease. I could always relax knowing Daniel was making sure things were okay.

"Yeah," I paused, suddenly wishing I'd planned for the meeting to take place at his office. At least I'd be able to see him in his element, even if only for a few minutes. Nothing was more thrilling than watching Daniel boss people around in a three-piece suit. "I just wanted to make sure I was still on to meet with Michelle."

"You are," he answered slowly.

"And you're sure you're okay with this?" I wondered, remembering how highly he'd spoken of the IT specialist.

"I've told you a hundred times – if there's anything I can do to help you, I'm in."

"Okay," I said, as I had all the other times I asked. "But if you change your mind, you can let me know."

"Don't forget," he paused and then added, "you're the one who has to lure her away."

"Hey, Emily!" Crystal called from the open doorway. "Michelle is here."

"My meeting is here," I said to Daniel. "I'll call you later."

"You got this," he spoke confidence into me as I waved Michelle into my office, placing my phone in the top drawer of my desk.

"Can I get you something to drink?" Crystal asked as I welcomed Michelle to the sitting area. I motioned toward a red womb chair for her to join me, as I sat across from her on the neon yellow tufted sofa.

It was the first test of my new plan. To achieve the nearly impossible task I'd assigned myself, I needed to secure my team.

"No, I'm fine," Michelle said as she sat down. "It's great to see you again, Mrs. Gamble."

"Please, call me Emily," I smiled, feeling the nerves dissolve. "And this is Crystal. She'll be joining us in the meeting. She's my right hand in the business, and I trust her to keep this confidential."

"Confidential?" Michelle asked.

"Yes. What I'd like to propose to you isn't something many know about. I'm going to fully transform my position in the publishing industry. As far as I can see, everyone is stuck in the past, which makes the future wide open for the taking.

"I want to create a space for writers to flourish, without focusing so much energy on metrics. They'll have the opportunity to connect directly with their readers, building a strong network with less distractions. Of course, we'll still have the best team supporting their vision, but we won't get in the way of their art. And that's where you come in." I motioned my hands toward Michelle. She was nodding along to my speech, but now she looked a bit nervous.

"I want you to come on board and be a part of my personal team. We need everything to go digital, and I was extremely impressed with your app development at Tower Enterprise Group. Daniel tells me you're brilliant, and I think you'd be the perfect addition to this new direction.

"Now, before you answer, I want you to know what we're offering. I'm willing to double your current salary and offer you a stake in the company. It will be a meeting of minds with you as the lead tech. Crystal," I motioned to my right, "will serve as the director of talent relations, handling all things administrative and marketing. We have a brilliant writer named Four who will represent the creative aspect, and I will serve as the financial and managerial backing."

Michelle's eyes widened. "I'm sorry, is that drink still available?" She asked Crystal.

We both laughed softly. Crystal rose from beside me, "Coke or something stronger?"

"Will it look unprofessional to request a real drink at," she glanced at her watch, "two in the afternoon?"

"Do you drink Brandy?" Crystal asked.

"I will today," Michelle smiled, exhaling deeply. "Wow, this is not at all what I was expecting."

Crystal poured three glasses of Brandy, distributing them to each of us before adding her piece. "Before you decide anything, it's important that you understand that Emily is the leader. We're going to support and execute her vision as a collective, but this is Emily's company."

"I get that," Michelle said. "But it would be something we build together?"

"Yes." I answered quickly. "I want this to be something we are all committed to, which is why I would ask you to sign on for a minimum 5-year contract. It won't happen overnight, but if we do this right, it will be worth all the hard work we put in."

"I have always wanted to build something," Michelle said, shaking her head slowly as though she was in disbelief. "This is like a dream come true. Just the opportunity to work with someone as established as you is…" she again exhaled loudly, shaking her head.

"You can take some time to think about it," I offered, assuming it would take a bit more convincing.

"I don't need any time. Where do I sign?" She frowned as she looked from me to Crystal.

We turned to each other in shock. "Are you sure?" Crystal asked. "We haven't even gone through the contract particulars."

"I'm positive," she said definitively before downing the Brandy in one gulp.

"Well, alright!" Crystal praised, lifting her glass. I did the same, throwing back the Brandy with relief.

"But, I have to know," I started as I set my empty glass on the table. "What did you think I wanted to meet with you for? You seemed nervous."

Michelle's light skin blushed as her lips tightened. "I thought maybe I was looking at your husband too closely or something. I was fully prepared to tell you, he is fine, but I don't play for that team." She admitted through a playful giggle, and me and Crystal exchanged a look before laughing loudly.

24

"I'm still not sure if you really wanted me to make this, or if you're silently making fun of me," I said nervously as I triple checked my ingredients.

"Why would I make fun of you silently?" My mother paused to position herself better before groaning, "That takes the fun out of it." She stretched her tiny frame to reach the liquor on the top shelf. After flicking the bottle of Ciroc vodka with the tip of her fingernail, she grasped the glass cylinder tightly.

"There's a full bar in the back," I mentioned as she reached for a glass. Too busy stirring my blend of browning ingredients, I hadn't offered to help when I noticed her searching through the cabinets. After insisting on having dinner with me and Daniel, rather than our weekly lunch date, I was shocked when she asked me to cook spaghetti. I'd learned the recipe for my sauce in a cooking class I'd taken with Daniel while vacationing in Rome.

Always unimpressed, my mother barely batted an eye when I made it for her our first week back. It was all I could talk about, boasting how nothing was from a jar. Back then, I even made the pasta from scratch. Now I'd adjusted the recipe to prevent spending an entire day in the kitchen.

I still started the sauce with freshly diced onions, garlic, and overly expensive extra virgin olive oil, before adding a cup of red wine. And I chopped my eggplant, zucchini, and mushrooms fresh as well, just as I'd learned in the class. But now, years after our 2-week trip that started in Milan, I'd made a few adjustments to save time.

In Italy, it seemed nothing was rushed, especially when it came to fashion. I was blown away by the quality of fabrics and design when we first arrived in Milan, where Daniel insisted I only window shop. He said it would be pointless to add to our luggage at the beginning of the trip. Too concerned that my favorite boutiques would sell the one of one creations that left me drooling, we compromised by having each store hold my purchased items until we returned to Milan for our departing flight.

After spending a tipsy weekend in Tuscany learning about wine and cured meats, we ventured to Florence by train. It was a crash course in art, filled with museum tours and my favorite – the art of gelato.

Afterwards, we ventured to Rome, where we visited all the clichéd tourist sites. Daniel led us through the eternal city with a physical map for 4-days. We learned to cook my now signature dish on our final evening. The following afternoon we took a bullet train to Naples, just to taste pizza in its birthplace, before returning to Milan to collect our purchases and fly home.

"What childless family needs to store liquor out of reach? Who are you hiding it from?" My mother quizzed while unscrewing the top.

"Can you even be a family without children?" I wondered aloud. I'd never truly considered Daniel and myself a family, but instead a couple. Children were what solidified a family.

"Of course," my mother answered like my question lacked merit. After downing her pour, she refilled her glass and another, offering it to me. "You know how you love and protect Elliot?"

Unwilling to remind her of my distaste for vodka, I accepted what I could tell was too much without an argument. "Yes, but me and Elliot are not a family, mom. He's my brother. We are a part of a family."

The sizzling sound of my browning vegetables alerted me to add the diced tomatoes before covering the pot. My mother was looking toward the vases that lined the top of the cabinets, but it was clear she was viewing a memory in her mind rather than the souvenirs from my travels.

"When me and Malcolm first got married," she smiled. Whenever she spoke about my father affectionately, she called him by his first name rather than title. "We did everything together."

She sipped the vodka, inhaling and exhaling so deeply that her small frame seemed to rise and sink with the breath. "He didn't even have a passport when I met him," she smiled at this recollection. A laugh shook her shoulders, but never fell from her lips. "I'd traveled extensively, you know."

She turned to me for validation, and I quickly nodded. It was common knowledge in our family that my mother had studied abroad, majoring in French. During her semester there, she'd visited a handful of countries, all of which she would later revisit with my father in tow.

"Your dad was like a sponge," she continued. "The more he saw, the more he wanted to see. He picked up languages fast. Much faster than me." She sipped the vodka. "He knew a bit of Spanish, and that somehow made Italian come naturally for him. He was always adaptable like that. And we would go everywhere. But that was only in the beginning." Her tone shifted from upbeat to what sounded like sadness.

"We always traveled as a family," I argued, walking to the refrigerator.

Glancing at the shelves, I noted how poorly I'd been managing groceries. More time at the office meant more takeout, and dinner meetings, and vegetables spoiled before I could cook them. I took the bottle of Lemonade from the door shelf, pouring a little into my mother's glass before adding to my own.

"No, we vacationed," she corrected me. "We stayed in resorts, and always in major cities. When it was just Elliot, we could still move around a bit. But by the time you were born," she huffed at the memory. "We would have so much luggage, sometimes we'd need a shuttle van just to get to the hotel."

I couldn't help but laugh, easily recalling the chaos of family vacations growing up. In my mind, everything was ideal, but my mother clearly had sacrificed for us.

"Me and Malcolm were a family before you all came along," she insisted, as though she now believed it herself. "If I could do it again, I think I would've kept it that way."

"Geez, mom!" I shrieked, only partly serious. I sipped my drink, squinting when the bitter lemon flavor hit the back of my tongue.

"I'm serious," she laughed. "Being a mom has been the high-light of my life, but it also marks the end of a life I really enjoyed."

"Did dad want kids?" I wondered.

"We both did," she said with assurance. "But we didn't imagine raising kids the same way. Your father saw kids as an addition. I saw you as adjustments. I couldn't carry on my life as it was," she explained.

"And you think dad could?" I asked, lifting the pot lid to stir the sauce. It was beginning to bubble, so I lowered the heat slightly, allowing the ingredients to merge.

"Oh, men are selfish." She scoffed, taking another sip of her mixed drink. "Your father was always going to do what he wanted. Everyone else had to fit within his plan. He was considerately uncompromising."

"That sounds like an oxymoron," I noted, finishing my first drink.

"Not really," she extended her hand, holding her glass for a refill. "He was kind and generous, but unwavering in his life path. I admired it." She paused and then added, "Still do."

"What about you?"

"Oh, I was a sacrificial lamb," she could barely get the words out before laughter rattled her thin frame. "I gave everything to my children, happily. I dedicated my life to raising you all and making your dreams possible."

"Do you regret it?" I tried to hide the fear in my voice. As much as I enjoyed honest and mature conversations with my mother, a part of me doubted I could handle knowing that she regretted having children.

"Not at all," she interrupted the silent questions swirling in my mind. "But it's not that simple. It's like going to London, and having a wonderful time, then asking if you regret not going to Paris instead. How could I say if I've never been? And I loved my vacation, nonetheless. But, of course I do sometimes wonder what Paris would have been like. Would I have liked it? Would I have wondered about London while I was there? Could my life remain the same had I not experienced London at that exact moment?"

She looked up to me, her eyes searching mine for understanding. "I get you," I smiled softly.

"You know, sweetheart," she started, placing her glass on the counter. "You can have it all, just not at the same time. There will always be a bit of mystery to life, and I like to think of that with awe. It's exciting to imagine how my life could have been different if I'd put myself first. There's no sadness to it."

I listened silently, realizing she did not want pity from me. In a way, I guess I'd been questioning my own life decisions in the same way. Was buying a publishing house the best decision at such a young age? Was it worth it to transform a business when it was already financially successful? I couldn't know unless I tried.

"And the future is the most exciting mystery," she added in a hushed tone. "Nothing is ever off the table, you know."

"So, if you could write the future however you wanted, what would it look like?" I asked, expecting her to take a few moments to consider the question. Instead, she answered without hesitation, as though the words were already simmering on her tongue.

"Move to France," she stopped to clarify. "The south of France, deep in the countryside."

"Really?" I smiled at the thought of her, back in her element like the twenty-something version of herself who studied abroad there.

"I'd teach English to young children, maybe kindergarten," she added although I hadn't asked. "And I'd learn new recipes, from scratch, the way they cook over there. Those markets with all the different cheeses and olives used to be my favorite. I think I'd move to Avignon, and torture your father with short trips around Europe."

"Well, you just said nothing is ever off the table," I reminded her. "You could start living for you now," I suggested just as the front door opened and closed loudly.

Daniel entered with a bouquet of white roses in one hand, and a bottle of red wine in the other. "What'd I miss?" He asked with a smile.

My mother lit up as she always did when she saw Daniel. Whether she admitted it or not, he was her favorite child. I wondered if it was because she never had to sacrifice for his love or happiness.

"You know, just a little girl talk," my mom smiled as she walked around the kitchen island to greet him.

"And vodka," I added, lifting my glass as I checked on my sauce.

"Deal me in," Daniel playfully requested, engulfing my mother in a bear hug.

25

———

"This is dangerous," Daniel ran his hand up my thigh. The slit in my skirt was so high, his fingertips grazed the matching forest green panties when he traced the laser cut fabric. Geometric cut out shapes revealed my copper skin tone beneath the Aliette blazer and matching skirt. It felt like armor, which was exactly what I needed for the charge I was leading.

"I thought you liked it," I reminded him of his earlier compliment as the driver arrived at the destination.

"I do like it, but I'm really going to like taking it off," Daniel leaned in, his whisper melting the anxiety that had built during the short car ride.

"Here you are," the driver announced.

"I'll text you, Cliff," Daniel spoke in a much more aggressive tone, earning a head nod from his trusted driver as the back door opened.

"Welcome," a man overdressed in a black tuxedo and white cloth gloves opened the door. Daniel climbed out before offering his hand, which was necessary to maneuver in the constricting and revealing suit.

My patent leather black heels matched the oversized bag I'd

chosen to carry the revised proposal I was hand delivering to Quentin. Glancing around, I noted the line at the end of the building, assuming it was for everyone not on the list the thin blonde was hassling Daniel about.

"Gamble?" She reiterated, her loud tone an obvious side effect of the booming music. The bass was intense even from outside the theatre that had been transformed into a nightclub, for what I still wasn't sure Quentin was celebrating. The woman scrolled her manicured nail on an iPad before glancing up at Daniel and then to me. "You're Emily Gamble?"

"Yes," I answered, looking to Daniel.

For a moment, I paused, taking in just how handsome he was. Dressed in all black, his suit curved along his back, too perfectly tailored to ever fit another body. As always, his hair was cut to perfection, along with his mustache and small patch of hair on his chin. I'd suggested matching the black button down shirt and tie, wanting us to coordinate. Now, standing beside him, confidence oozed through my pores.

"I'm so sorry. I should have been looking out for your car. My name is Heather," she apologized with sincerity before personally escorting us inside. "Quentin wanted to make sure you have the best time tonight."

The room felt large and intimate at once. From the entrance, I could see a bar so long it lined the entire back wall of the party. On one end was a dance floor, where couples moved gracefully together, as though it were a black-tie gala. The rest of the room was filled with small circular high tables, where groups gathered around, looking important.

Waiters moved efficiently between tables, carrying trays of champagne flutes, while others held an array of drinks I imagined to be custom orders. It was very Hollywood, the type of event Daniel frequented more than me. As he would explain, this is where business was done in LA, in dimly lit rooms with alcohol flowing freely. I was unimpressed.

Heather handed me a fob, much like the key to my G-Wagon.

Only, this one had just one button, which she explained was to call for service. GPS tracking would allow our dedicated server to find our location. To demonstrate the abilities, she pressed the button, making small talk with compliments about my outfit. Before I could thank her, a young man wearing a white collared shirt with a black tie arrived.

"Hello, I'll be helping you for the night. Can I get you a drink?" He asked, flashing a practiced smile towards me and Daniel. His dark brown skin glowed in the low light, with long locs pulled into an intricate pattern before falling down his back.

He reminded me of Four, and her beautiful locs. I wondered if he was also an artist, as the hairstyle seemed to be a statement itself. Then, I wondered what Four would think of a party like this. If I was unimpressed, she would probably be disgusted. To think I could potentially be discussing her career in an atmosphere like this left me feeling uneasy.

"I'll have Macallan," Daniel announced over the loud music.

"Eighteen-year or Twenty-one?" The young man asked, referring to the age of the whiskey.

"Is that really a question?" Daniel shot back with a smirk.

The young man returned a bashful grin. "I have to ask," he reasoned with a shrug.

"I'm Daniel Gamble," he extended his hand, turning to me, "This is my wife, Emily."

"It's nice to meet you," the young man said to me after shaking Daniel's hand. "My name's Dean."

"Dean?" Daniel repeated the name with skepticism.

"Deonte," he admitted. "They told me to use Dean when I'm serving, or I'd be repeating myself all night."

Daniel nodded, offering a smile I knew wasn't genuine. "Well, Deonte, I'll take the twenty-one. My wife will have Ace of Spades."

"Sure thing," Deonte smiled before excusing himself just after Heather did the same, confident we were in good hands.

As soon as we were alone, Daniel leaned down, speaking

discretely into my ear. "Who the fuck would tell a server to use a fake name?"

"He's probably from a hired catering company," I offered, certain he was blaming Quentin for the tasteless advice.

"Here comes the man of the hour," Daniel added before straightening.

Following his eyes, I saw Quentin approaching. The polar opposite of Daniel, he wore a white suit with black lapels and a matching black tie. His hair was a bit longer than the last time I'd seen him, with soft curls lined to perfection.

"I can't believe you made it," Quentin said when he reached us.

"Of course," I shook his extended hand. "I just hope you won't be partying too hard to handle sensitive documents." Reaching into my bag, I retrieved the leather-bound proposal I'd had drawn up while he greeted my husband.

"How are you, Daniel?"

"Good to see you, Quentin," Daniel's tone was icy as the two shook hands. "So, what are you celebrating?"

"Hopefully, getting in bed with your wife," Quentin's jovial tone did little to help the delivery of his joke. With the proposal in my grasp, I looked to Daniel with caution, hoping he didn't allow Quentin to get under his skin.

Daniel's glare was fierce. "Is that what you consider this? I look at it more as begging for a seat at her table."

Quentin smiled, pausing for a moment. "I wouldn't call it begging. I'm willing to pay for it."

"I heard you're begging for help in that department, too." Daniel smirked now. "I spoke with Martell Engram recently," Daniel dropped the name of the man working with Quentin to find investors.

"Mrs. Gamble," Heather called my attention just as the conversation was heating up. I turned, walking two steps from the men so she didn't hear their conversation. Quickly peeking over my shoulder, I watched as they continued, desperate to know what they were saying.

"Yes?" I asked, hoping to get rid of her quickly.

"We have a table ready for you in the VIP section," she gestured towards the back of the room.

"No, we won't be here that long," I assured her.

"Well, I can still hold it for you. If you change your mind, you can always use it. You're in the first private room." She smiled brightly, pushing her blonde hair behind her ears. "And your car is on standby right out the door you entered. You have priority parking for your convenience."

"Sounds great, Heather. Thanks," I rushed the words before turning to Quentin and Daniel.

Deonte was arriving with our drinks, effectively ending the conversation. I kicked myself as I returned, accepting my glass of champagne.

"I'm glad to see Dean is taking good care of you two," Quentin smiled.

I knew Daniel wouldn't let it slide before he began. "Oh, this is Deonte," he corrected him. From the look exchanged between Quentin and the waiter, it was obvious this was not the first time he'd learned the young man's name.

"Oh," Quentin slowly looked away from the waiter, "I must have been mistaken."

"Yeah, Deonte's worked some of my events before," Daniel looked to Deonte and then Quentin.

"Is that right?" Quentin directed his attention to Deonte.

"There isn't a venue in LA I haven't worked," Deonte offered, exchanging a look with Daniel before tucking his tray beneath his arm and leaving. I felt for him, thrown between a war of egos that had nothing to do with him.

"If you two are done," I interjected, extending the proposal to Quentin. "Here's my revised proposal. Hopefully, we can meet to discuss the details next week."

"I hope so," Quentin accepted the heavy leather bound file. "Daniel, will you be joining us for that too?"

"Someone has to pay the bill," Daniel responded without hesitation. I had to look away to curb my laughter.

"That's a low blow," Quentin teased.

"I'm only joking," Daniel smiled coyly. "My wife will cover your lunch."

"You have to read over it first. I made sure all the adjustments are clearly marked so you can spot the amendments, but there's no rush." I found myself playing referee as the men glared at one another with building animosity.

"I appreciate that," he said, tucking the book beneath his arm. "As I was telling your husband, I'm in the midst of closing a big deal. So, I'm happy to value Cherry Blossoms favorably. I see the promise, and know you're worth every penny. You'll find I'm flexible on most things, but I really think we should keep the board as we initially planned. Giving executives power will strengthen morale."

I nodded, forcing myself to remain expressionless. There was no way he should already know of any suggested changes in the proposal, like the details he'd just alluded to. I'd made sure to keep everything under wraps, but like always, Quentin's arrogance revealed too much.

"Just give it a look. We can discuss everything when you're ready," I said, extending my hand.

"We're done talking business?" He smiled.

"I just wanted to hand deliver the proposal. Have fun with your party," I slid next to Daniel, allowing my hand to fall into his.

Quentin's smile faded instantly. "You're leaving? You just got here." He looked around nervously. "I have a table set aside for you and everything."

"We have another event to get to," I lied. He was on his heels again, and I liked it.

"I should have known you were too well dressed for my little party," he joked, trying to loosen up.

"Welcome to LA," I winked, squeezing Daniel's hand slightly before turning towards the door. We walked hand in hand through the hall, placing our untouched drinks on the tray of a passing waiter before exiting the loud party and returning to our waiting car.

26

Daniel handed me his suit jacket before climbing into the backseat and settling beside me. "I do not fuck with him! Back to the house, Cliff!"

The driver signaled, quickly maneuvering through the parking lot before turning into light traffic. That was the thing about LA, no matter what time of day or night, there was always a possibility you'd wind up in traffic.

"I know, baby," I whispered to Daniel, curling beside him as his arm fell over my body, his hand resting on my ass. "Just trust me. He's only part of my plan."

"I have never come so close to losing my cool," he inhaled slowly with a tense jaw.

"That comment about getting in bed with me?"

"Who the fuck says that?" He barked, his hand tightening on the softness of my body.

I'd never tell him, but I liked seeing him this way, territorial and enraged. It was so unlike him to lose his cool, but Quentin had pushed him to his limit. My hand slid up his thigh as his chest rose and fell. The tension was leaving his body beneath my touch.

"You know I don't trust him," he added, his tone already less aggressive. "And you don't need the merger."

"He'll buy out half of my company," I reminded him. "I need the cash flow."

"For what?" His grasp tightened with each word.

"I have other things I want to invest in," I explained. "I can't do any of that without liquidating some of Cherry Blossoms."

"You can't be serious," his hand relaxed. Instantly, I missed his commanding touch. Turning, Daniel glared at me with furrowed brows. "You're telling me you're hurting for money?"

"I didn't say that," I assured him. "I know we're comfortable, but I want to contribute. Everything we have is yours."

"Everything I have is ours."

I exhaled slowly, hoping to back things up. This wasn't a discussion I wanted to have. I couldn't make Daniel see things from my perspective. He didn't want me taking unnecessary risks, but from my position, every risk was unnecessary.

"I'm not concerned about Quentin," I assured him, allowing my nails to run along the smooth silk of his Tom Ford suit until I reached the growing hardness between his legs. "And you shouldn't be either."

"Don't start, Em," he warned.

"What?" I played innocent.

"There's not even a partition," he growled with annoyance. Daniel didn't negotiate when it came to discretion. If he couldn't guarantee our privacy, there was no way he would consider anything risqué.

Throwing his suit jacket over his lap, I added a barrier before my hands continued exploring. "Is that better?" I whispered.

He didn't answer, but he didn't stop me, which was all the approval I needed. We were only a few miles from the house, but I wanted to kick things off before we arrived.

"What were you two talking about? I heard you mention Martell –," I tried to pry for information before Daniel's hand fell heavily over mine, stopping both my words and movements.

"If you want to talk business, we can," he looked to me with an ultimatum in his eyes. There was no way he was going to entertain a conversation about Quentin while I teased him.

"Okay," I agreed softly, leaning to kiss along his jaw. Shockingly, he didn't stop me. Instead, his hand released mine, while the other grabbed a handful of my ass. My tongue traced a line from his neck to his ear as the driver turned into our neighborhood. Daniel let me continue my flirtatious game until we arrived in the driveway.

"Have a good night, Cliff." He said to the driver before rushing out of the car, leading me to the front door aggressively.

We'd barely cleared the foyer, when his hands found their way to my hair, pulling me close as his mouth conquered mine. It was the culmination of a tension brewing all night.

"Take this off," I pleaded as his hands explored my body.

Daniel paid me no attention, gripping my long hair in a fist as he jerked my head back to kiss my neck. A loud moan escaped me when his teeth sank into my skin with a hunger I craved to fulfill. He was leading us to the bedroom, pressing his body against mine as he forced me forward.

My fingers worked quickly to undo his cuff links before tossing them aside. By the time we neared the foot of the bed, I'd unfastened every button on his shirt to reveal his sculpted chest. It amazed me how attracted I was, like the first time I'd ever seen his perfect build.

Turning, I lifted the back of my blazer to reveal the zipper on my skirt. "Unzip me, please."

"You're keeping that on," he said, turning me around to face him. I watched closely as he tugged at the belt keeping the blazer closed. Instead of loosening the fabric, he tightened it, leaving me even more confined.

I watched him undress in confusion, but from the look in his eyes I was certain he knew what he was doing. Stripping down, he glared at me as he removed every piece of clothing. My thighs pressed together, struggling to soothe my growing arousal.

"Baby, I can't move in this," I whined when he finished undressing.

"I know," was all he said before taking my mouth, kissing me passionately. Kneeling, he gently removed the stiletto from my right foot. I gripped his shoulder for balance, enjoying the soothing massage after a night in 5-inch heels. After releasing my foot, he kissed my calf and then my thigh before removing the other stiletto.

It was sweet and intimate, but extremely seductive. Forcing me to wait, he teased me with labored affection when my desire was urgent. As he rose, he kissed the back of my thighs through the cut outs in the skirt, biting gently on my ass. My teeth clashed with my bottom lip, yearning for him.

"Please, take this off," I pleaded, desperate to spread myself for him.

Turning me around, he stared at me for what felt like eternity. He pored over my body with lust, started at my cleavage and then drifting down to my panties. His gaze traveled back up my body, and I felt the slickness between my legs as my sex clenched, eager to feel him.

He eyed me like a puzzle, silently. And then he tugged at the skirt, careful but demanding. Wiggling my hips, I helped him move the fabric until it was just high enough to expose my panties. Satisfied, Daniel lifted me onto the edge of the bed, and I fell to all fours, the only position I could manage. The skirt was a restrictive net around my legs, pressing my knees together.

Glancing over my shoulder, I saw him admiring me and my confidence grew. Extending my arms forward, I arched my back, poking my ass out.

"Just like that," he growled as he climbed onto the bed, positioning himself behind me.

I'd never been so excited to hear lace destroyed when his hands reached between my legs. There was no warning or smoothness to the way he slammed into my body. I almost climaxed from the extremeness of the intrusion.

"Ahhh!" I cried loudly, pushing back to him for more. He didn't hesitate, sliding out of my wetness before thrusted deep into my warmth again.

With his hands on my hips, he positioned me perfectly to hit my g-spot with every stroke. The restraints on my legs somehow intensified the pressure, rushing me towards an explosion.

"Daniel! Yes!" I cried as my body raced towards a cliff of ecstasy.

His rhythm was panicked, unchoreographed lust. Our bodies collided with chaotic precision, each of us moaning with every surge. It was perfection. Needy and sloppy. I leaned into him, calling his name for more until I was overwhelmed. With fists of sheets, I felt myself losing control as I reached my peak.

Unable to spread my legs to lessen the explosion, it was centralized and extreme. I came violently, biting the sheets as my legs fought the tight fabric of my skirt.

"Another one," Daniel called, slapping my ass as he pumped me hard and fast.

Tears stung my eyes, mixing with mascara as I pressed into his body for more. Greedily, I clenched around his thickness, pulsing with the aftershocks of an explosion. He was relentless, gripping my waist to keep me in place for his onslaught.

"Come on, baby," Daniel's voice was weaker. I could hear the groans of his own pleasure, which always turned me on even more.

I loved to know I could please him, take him to levels that stripped him of bravado, leaving him with nothing but my name. We raced to climax together, with his hands gripping my body so tightly I could feel the imprints of his fingers.

"Now, baby! Now!" He growled. I came instantly, crying as he stiffened inside me, jerking with his release.

Folding over my body, he gently kissed my ear before sliding out of me. Finally, he unzipped my skirt, freeing me from the restraints, and I collapsed onto the bed. Daniel watched me with a satisfied grin. His naked body glistened with a coat of sweat.

"You love me?" He asked with confidence.

"Too much," I answered, feeling my eyelids grow heavy.

27

It had been two years since I first laid eyes on the beauty. Although so much had changed, my heart still swelled at the sight of the property that had caused so much turmoil in my marriage. From the street, it looked like a warehouse, but the inside was another story.

Each of the four floors housed a loft condominium. I'd designed them to stand apart, respecting no budget Daniel set with profits in mind. Instead, I created the most beautiful spaces I could imagine, treating the property like my own private dollhouse.

That was until everything came to a head when our finances began to crumble, partly due to my impulsive purchase of a property that quickly transformed into an endless expense. Determined not to allow it to destroy all he'd built, Daniel worked overtime to fix my mistakes before firing me from the project altogether.

During an uncertain time in our marriage, I conceded complete autonomy to Daniel. In our new agreement, he had sole authority to design and sell the condos as he saw fit. It was a desperate act on my part, hoping to persuade him towards reconciliation. However, almost immediately, I began to question my decision, and Daniel's motives, wondering if he planned to swindle me out of my fair share.

The memory made me cringe. How I could ever doubt Daniel's integrity was beyond me. In all the years we'd been together, he'd never given me a reason to question his honor, and yet I had, without regard.

Walking into the small nook Daniel had added since he took control of the construction, I realized how many small details I hadn't considered. Such as mailboxes for each unit, and a place to leave packages. Daniel thought of everything, creating a separate entrance area.

"Baby?" His voice boomed as I opened the door to the first-floor apartment I'd named Margaret, or Maggie for short.

"This looks amazing," I gasped, my eyes wide to take in all that he had added. It was humbling to see how well Daniel had done without my input.

The grin on his face as he walked towards me was contagious. I found myself smiling as he lifted me in the air. Without knowing the cause of his excitement, my lips clashed with his, quickly intensifying the kiss as my legs wrapped around his waist.

Daniel kissed me deeply while walking across the loft, careful to avoid hitting the glass top to the dining table as he made his way to the kitchen. I was undoing the top buttons of his shirt when he suddenly pulled away.

"Are we christening Maggie?" I asked. My hunger for him was so easily awakened. The way he wrapped my hair around his fingers, tugging gently as he tilted my head to his liking weakened me.

"She's not ours anymore," he grinned, gripping my hips tightly, a cue to unravel my legs.

He set me on the ground and the disappointment of releasing him left me with a sigh. "What do you mean she's not ours?" I asked, pushing my hair behind my ears, certain his rough hands had left me disheveled.

"I mean, she's not ours," he reiterated, handing me a small white envelope while holding on to a larger manila folder.

I opened it with cautious curiosity, looking to him with suspicion. It had been so long since I saw Daniel so giddy. His hazel eyes lit up as he watched me, biting his bottom lip in a struggle to contain his growing smile.

When I finally opened the envelope, the breath left my body. Inside was the receipt of a wire transfer, almost as much as my entire inheritance, thrice the investment we'd spent on the property.

"You sold them all? We made this much?" I asked in shock, looking back to the receipt, and then again to Daniel. I didn't expect to sell the condos for nearly as much, although the potential profit was never my reason for purchasing them.

"We made double that," he said, finally allowing the smile to spread across his handsome face. The dimple in his cheek deepened. This was the news he had really been waiting to share.

"Double?" I wondered, now more curious about the folder in his hand.

"Yep," he tapped the folder against his free hand, teasing me for the second time. "I figured we should invest half. And I think you'll need a little capital for your new venture."

Finally, he handed me the folder. Inside were the documents incorporating GIA Inc. I flipped through, not understanding most of the legal jargon, but clear about the premise.

"Just like you asked, your name is nowhere on the paperwork, but you legally own it outright." Daniel answered the question I was too stunned to ask. It was one of the final pieces I needed to set my plan in play.

"Gia?" I wondered about the name he chose for my new business.

"I was trying to find an acronym for your new move, seeking more independence. 'Get It Alone' popped in my head. When I realized the initials spelled Gia, I went with it. That condo changed everything between us."

The memory freed butterflies within my stomach. It was such a tumultuous time, when our marriage was in danger of collapsing. I took a leap that day, offering myself to him, in what I could now see was the spark our relationship so desperately needed. That day, in the third floor loft I named Gia, set us in motion for the beautiful recovery we were now experiencing.

Unable to express how much it meant to me, I threw my arms around Daniel's neck. Not only had he done what I'd asked, but he did so without knowing exactly what I wanted to do with it or why I even needed a new corporation.

"Thank you," I whispered as a tear slid down my cheek. I was terrified to start something new, but excited to move forward with a plan that set my heart on fire.

"Congratulations," Daniel said softly, wrapping his arms tightly around my waist.

"We did it," I leaned onto my toes to kiss his neck as another tear passed my lips.

We stayed like that, embracing tightly, silently celebrating what neither of us needed to say. This property had nearly shattered our marriage, but we didn't quit, even when I wanted to. Together, we had decided to fight and that moment felt like victory, after two years at war.

28

———

With the windows to my office tinted with the white cherry blossom design, I felt secure discussing confidential details with Four, Crystal, and Michelle. Huddled around the neon table in the corner of my office, we began to draft the details for a vision that had quickly evolved from mine to ours.

That was my dream. I never cared to be the head of a company, but instead a part of a movement. I was more interested in collaboration than a title of superiority. I wanted to build something with people who had a similar vision. People who wanted to make a change.

"I get what you want logistically here," Michelle pointed to a graphic. "But that will change the interface of the app. Are you good with that?"

These were the types of questions we were spending day after day answering. As the three of them continued with discussions, I watched employees passing my office. Traveling between meetings, oblivious to what we were working on behind this clouded glass, or how it would affect them.

At times, it felt neglectful to withdraw from the current state of

Cherry Blossoms, focusing more on the future. As far as I could see, things would shake up enough once Quentin came on board, so there was no reason to wait until we closed on the deal to begin adjusting.

"There are some weak links that need to be weeded out," Four announced as she struggled to get out the white hammock. "I've been sitting in on the meetings, brainstorming sessions, everything. People can sense change is coming, but not everyone is going to adjust."

"Who knows how they'll feel once they see the full picture, though," Michelle said. It was my hope, however unlikely, that everyone would happily follow my new direction.

"I have to agree with Four. There are some people I just can't see accepting more change. It's unreasonable to think we can have the same staff take us in a different direction," Crystal looked to me with concern.

Every step forward seemed to reveal a new obstacle. Time wasn't on our side, which made everything urgent.

"Crystal, what time does Quentin want to finalize things?" I asked, drawing her away from the group.

Reaching for the leather planner she used as my calendar, she placed it beside me. "He called to set it up the same night you delivered the proposal," she remembered as she flipped through the pages.

If I hadn't known any better, I'd assume he'd spent hours reading through the changes, too excited to delay discussion. But he'd let on about a detail he shouldn't have known, which all but confirmed my suspicions about Madison. She'd already shared my plans with him, so there were no surprises. He was just antsy to move forward.

He had already sent over his amended conditions, most of which we were expecting. The board was the major area of contention, which we'd found common ground on. We would both have an equal representation, as he had initially requested, with our current executive staffs each automatically earning a seat.

I'd agreed to his request for executives to immediately gain voting power, in exchange for a 2% premium in addition to my asking price to acquire half of Cherry Blossoms. It was a win/win. He got the board, and I got more cash without sacrificing any further ownership.

"Here it is," Crystal pointed at the calendar. It was for the end of the week. "Do you think we can be ready by then?" She asked.

"We'll have to be." I tried to sound confident, but there was still so much to be finalized. I had to make a few changes to the agreement, have it looked over by legal, and back to Quentin within days.

A knock at the door caught all our attention. Turning to see Daniel in the doorway was a welcomed surprise. "Did I walk into a covert mission?" He smiled, making his way across the office.

He was so handsome I found pride in his appearance. As though it was some reflection of me, I beamed as he neared me, leaning to kiss me softly. "Hi, gorgeous."

"Hi, baby." I smiled at him for a few seconds before remembering the other women in the room. "Of course, you know Crystal and Michelle," I said, watching his eyes turn to each of the women with a familiar smile and nod. "And, this is the writer I've been telling you about. Four, this is my husband Daniel."

"The infamous Four," he extended his hand across the table. "Not to be mistaken with 'Ivy'," he turned to me with a grin. The women erupted in an undeserved roar of laughter as he looked to Crystal.

"I'm just wrapping up," I glanced at my watch, shocked to see how far we'd run over the schedule. We were supposed to finish half an hour before Daniel picked me up for our therapy session.

"No worries. I'll let you finish," he casually ran his fingers through my hair as he passed me. "Crystal, can I talk to you for a minute?"

Crystal and Daniel left the office as I watched after them curiously. With our anniversary just weeks away, I wondered if he was working on a surprise. Before I could get too lost in my imagination, Four disrupted my wishful thinking.

"Emily, your husband is fine!" She gushed.

"I told you," Michelle said in a melodic whisper as she packed away her notebooks and laptop.

"So, my husband has been a topic of conversation?" I playfully asked, gathering my things from the table.

"I hate to break it to you, E," Four began, using a nickname she'd picked for me. "But a man like that is always the topic somewhere."

We giggled as my pride somehow transformed to slight embarrassment. Of course, I knew women fawned over Daniel, but it was different hearing it from women I counted as friends. Then, I realized how quickly Michelle and Four had grown from colleagues to friends, and how rare it was to get to work with people you actually liked.

Outside of Crystal, coming into the office had always been a drag. I constantly worked against the misconceptions associated with being a young, black, powerful woman. It was refreshing to feel relaxed in my office, still working, but without the stress. Whenever I was with Michelle, Four, and Crystal, I felt validated. They provided security in my position, a new comfort I valued.

"Are we still on for a late meeting this week?" Four asked with her knapsack slung over one shoulder. Wearing her traditional loungewear, she looked plucked from a Caribbean island in her colorful nylon dress.

"If you two can keep your giggles to a minimum," I teased, knowing we would be meeting at my house.

"I'll agree to anything for another peek at that fine specimen of a man," Four batted her eyes as I playfully shoved her shoulder when she passed me.

"I'll email the changes to you, Emily," Michelle noted, always the most professional of the two.

"Perfect. I'll be looking out for them," I responded, collecting Crystal's things. I stacked her notebooks together, placing her notorious clipboard on top. Then, I reached for her planner, noticing the two-week block in my schedule. She'd previously mentioned she was waiting to see how the merger would affect my schedule, but I wanted her to change that.

"Hey," I said, approaching her desk. Daniel was standing at the edge as she typed away on her laptop. They both looked to me with welcomed caution, as though they were expecting me but had no plans to continue whatever they were working on. I set her things on her desk in a neat stack. "I know we talked about this two week gap after the merger is finalized, but I think it's best to be available. You can schedule meetings and statuses for that time."

Crystal nodded, quickly looking to Daniel, and then back to me. "You got it." She finally answered, but I could feel there was something left unsaid.

"Ready?" Daniel asked, flashing the smile that always put me at ease.

29

I selected a chamomile tea for the day's session as a celebration to calmer times. Daniel and I had reached a deserved moment of triumph, void of any drama or tension. We were finding our groove, settling into the next chapter of our life together.

After months of uncertainty, I was grateful to reach serenity. Without new disagreements, we could unpack old issues. The tea represented our growth, and the relaxing nature we had developed. As we sat across from Dr. Cathway, I was optimistically excited about where the day's session would go.

"Is there anything from the previous week either of you wish to discuss?" She asked, tapping on her iPad with a stylus.

I inhaled deeply, feeling relieved. For the first time, there was nothing bothering me. Every other session had been a release of animosity and discourse. Finally, we were at ease and stress-free.

"Emily is determined to go into business with someone I cannot trust. And my lack of approval is having no impact on her decision making."

Daniel's claim was a dramatic and immediate end to my peace. The entire ride over from the office had been quiet and uneventful, only for him to reveal such a heavy revelation before the tea could cool.

"That's worthy of a discussion," Dr. Cathway said, looking away from her screen to give Daniel her undivided attention.

"I've done everything to let her know how I feel about the deal she's negotiating. I've given her the proof that this guy can't be trusted. She's witnessed the tension between us. And yet, she is determined to move forward with the merger," he listed his grievances.

Admittedly, none of it was news to me. I knew how Daniel felt about my business with Quentin. Saying I didn't care wasn't accurate, but I certainly didn't care enough to change course. There was a lot to be gained from merging with Quentin's publishing house, including market share and most importantly, capital. I could grow my company significantly by joining forces with him, even if he was a bit shady.

"How does all this make you feel, Daniel?" Dr. Cathway's nurturing tone, the one that had set me at ease many times before, annoyed me. She was coddling him about something that had nothing to do with him.

Part of me wanted to argue how little I knew about Daniel's business, and who he partnered with. He didn't involve me in anything unless it added value to him, and I never questioned who he worked with or why he accepted clients. His business was his business, and I deserved the same autonomy.

On the other hand, I had involved Daniel, whether selfishly or not. He was an asset for me in this deal, but not a partner. His feedback was appreciated. However, it didn't afford him the power to veto my decisions.

"I would never make a business deal that would make Emily uncomfortable," he argued.

Unable to silence my opinion, I huffed with disbelief. Daniel turned to me with shock in his eyes. "You think I would?" He challenged.

"I don't think you would ever find yourself in that position. You don't involve me in your business," I explained, as if it wasn't obvious. He knew I had no say in what happened at Tower Enterprise Group.

"Does that make you feel left out, Emily?" Dr. Cathway jumped in.

"No," I turned to face her. "I don't need to be involved in Daniel's business to believe in him or his vision. I trust him blindly. But when it comes to me, Daniel needs to know every aspect of the plan to judge if it's the right move. And only then will he support me."

"That's not true," he interjected.

"Daniel, you're literally arguing that I don't know what I'm doing, when you in fact don't know what I'm doing. You have no idea what I'm working on, but I've told you I have a plan."

His jaw tensed as he fought to contain whatever argument was rolling on his tongue. I watched impatiently, daring a dispute. He knew I was right. So used to leading, it was unbearable for him to watch me make decisions without constantly seeking his guidance.

Taking a deep breath, I remembered Dr. Cathway's words. We were on the same team, and the point was to succeed together, not a competition between us. "Look," I started in the calmest tone I could manage. "You told me you wanted to support me in being a mogul myself. You told me you supported this."

"I do."

"Well, what I need from you is the blind trust I give you. I trust you to run your business independently. I'm not involved in every move, but I still believe in you. Just believe in me. I'm learning how to create something on my own, and I can't do that if you're telling me what moves to make," I reasoned.

"But what point does it make for you to struggle through obstacles I've already mastered?" He asked, perched at the edge of the sofa. I could see the agitation in the tightness of his shoulders.

"You can't teach me everything, Daniel. Some things I need to learn on my own."

This was too much for him to accept. He leaned back into the black velvet, shaking his head. "Does this make sense to you, Dr. Cathway?" He brushed his hair with his palm awaiting her answer.

"Let's start with what doesn't make sense to you," she flipped the question back to him, one of her favorite techniques to force reevaluation.

Daniel sat up, tense with frustration. "Emily is new to business. I have helped her along every step of the journey, in every way I can. Now, she's cutting me out, and I'm supposed to be okay with that?"

"I'm not cutting you out," I said, thrusting myself into what felt like a conversation about me, as though I wasn't sitting beside him.

"You are." He answered without facing me.

"I'm trying to do something on my own," I clarified, feeling my stomach tense with discomfort.

"Why?!" Daniel's voice boomed through the room.

"Let's analyze that, Daniel," Dr. Cathway cut in as the tears began to sting the corners of my eyes. "Why is Emily trying something on her own so uncomfortable for you?"

"Because I'm here," he argued with his hands held high. "And I'm supposed to," he barked the words before abruptly stopping, clenching his jaw tightly.

The curl in Dr. Cathway's lips let me know she was pleased, but I had no idea why. "Keep going, Daniel. Finish your thought."

He turned away, looking to the left side of the room. There was a window showcasing the slow traffic of the residential street. Daniel chose to watch it rather than look at either of us.

"You know what I was going to say," his voice was deep now, solemn with what I sensed to be defeat.

"So, you realize we've visited this previously?" She asked softly.

"Can someone clue me in?" I was annoyed, again left out the conversation.

"Daniel," Dr. Cathway urged him.

He turned to me begrudgingly, taking a deep breath before he spoke. "I feel responsible for protecting you, Emily. I don't want you to make a mistake if I can avoid it. Quentin is bad news. I've seen people like him take advantage of situations, and I know that's what he's trying to do."

"Do you think Quentin is smarter than me?" I asked, braving myself for his answer.

"Hell no!" He responded quickly. "That's what makes all this so frustrating. I know you have to see through this."

"I do." I told him confidently. "And I'm using that to my advantage. I just need you to trust me on this. I trust you on everything."

His eyebrows shot up in disbelief. The memory of Lana Boyden and the way I reacted to reading her emails hit me like a ton of bricks. Before I could explain, he reminded me.

"Emily, you make a judgment and react before I even know what's bothering you.

"I just meant in business," I added quietly. "I need you to trust me in my professional life."

"And I need you to trust me in our personal."

We sat silent for a moment, and I reached for my tea wishing it was spiked. Every session had a way of leaving me exhausted. My heart was pumping incredibly fast. The emotional rush left my head spinning. The tea was the perfect temperature, cool enough to gulp, but warm enough to relax my body.

"Emily, it seems you have your ask. You want Daniel to trust you blindly in this current business deal," she looked to me for approval.

"Yes," I said quietly.

"And Daniel, we've previously discussed your need for an ask as far as trust in your personal relationship goes. Have you decided what that ask will be?"

"Not yet," he sighed, leaning forward for his tea. The teacup was minuscule in his large hand. Tilting the fine china, he finished it in one swallow.

"I'd like you to seriously consider it this week. Emily needs a way to prove her commitment to you in your personal life. And you now know how to prove your trust to her in her professional venture."

"This shit sucks!" Daniel groaned, padding his hair again.

It was the perfect blend of innocence and honesty that left me amused. A soft laughter started with a trembling of my shoulders, and finished with my head falling back with yet another release of emotion.

Daniel was always so well put together. To watch a master of words find himself ill equipped, unable to adequately express himself, was rich. The most mature person I'd ever known had been brought to childlike complaints. The hilarity of the situation was not lost on me, seeing my logical husband corrupted by emotion.

"Well, Mr. Gamble, you surely know how to make your wife laugh. I think you've mastered ending our sessions on a good note.

"It doesn't feel that way," he stood, exhaling loudly before lifting both of our teacups and heading towards the kitchen.

"I think this was another great session," Dr. Cathway said to me as we followed behind Daniel.

"They get harder," I said.

"They're supposed to," she smiled softly before we said our goodbyes.

Leaving the office with Daniel, I waited until we were alone on the short walk to the car to reveal what had shocked me. "I didn't know you were so upset about the deal with Quentin."

"Now you know," he answered without looking to me, continuing to walk at a brisk pace that took effort on my part to keep up with.

"Are you mad at me?" I asked nervously.

Daniel chuckled in a humorless way. Slowing his pace, he reached for me, keeping in step. Wrapping his arms tightly around my frame, he enveloped me in a firm hug. I could feel his emotion in physical form.

"I'm enraged." He whispered in my ear as he continued walking. I followed him blindly, backpedaling quickly, unable to see where we were going.

"And you're still going to let me do things my way?" I asked in a tone of innocence.

Another deep breath. "I am."

"And you'll still love me?"

"Of course," he assured me before kissing the soft skin just below my ear.

"Even if I fail?" I wondered.

"I'll never let you fail." He said before releasing me and opening the passenger door to his beloved Ferrari. I hadn't even realized we'd completed the walk. When I stood staring at him, refusing to get into the car, he finally smiled. "But, yes, if by some miracle you do fail, I will still love you. Now, let's go eat."

Satisfied, I leaned up, kissing his cheek softly before settling into the car. Daniel closed the door, shaking his head as he walked to the driver's side. I smiled remembering my mother's claim that I give him hell, hoping he liked it, as she had suspected.

30

"What the hell are you going to do with this?" Victoria asked.

My sister was at least two meters away from me, but the emptiness of the room coupled with the twenty foot vaulted ceilings, allowed her voice to travel with clarity. I'd found the property after leaving a meeting with Crystal and Four.

North Fairfax Avenue mostly offered street parking, so walking a few minutes to your car was standard. One day, my walk led me to an amazing space available for sale, just off the avenue. The neighborhood was filled with hipster clothing stores, small galleries, and cafes like the one I'd met Four in.

Much like the property I'd purchased with Daniel, this space looked like a warehouse from the street. However, this time looks were less deceiving. Inside, it appeared to be a deserted factory, ripped of everything from the flooring to the machinery it once housed.

"It'll be great," I smiled, happy to see her disapproval.

If she thought it was perfect at first glance, I knew it wasn't what I wanted. The vision for my future only existed in my mind. It took likeminded people like Crystal, Michelle, and Four to understand.

Victoria was nothing like my partners. She was a capitalist at heart, much like my husband. That was the reason I had to shield them from the full extent of my master plan. They would never approve of all I had in store, but their input was necessary. Sharing pertinent details was the happy medium. I needed this building, and my sister's interior design skills to transform it into a place that harnessed dreams.

"Emily, what do you even see happening here?" She asked while opening the dirty glass door that led to the back patio. I watched, waiting for the familiarity that never came.

"Remember you talked about having an outdoor space in the middle of the office?" I reminded her, leading to the glass door on the other side of the overgrown garden. Victoria followed with caution, stepping quickly as though a snake, or even a lion, could reveal itself at any moment. "You said it would be great for creativity."

"That was for Cherry Blossoms," she rolled her eyes, out of breath from her exertion. Now, examining the second half of the building, she seemed to catch on. "Wait. You want to move here?"

She turned to me and I could see the creative wheels begin to turn in her mind. She looked to the high ceilings, and lack of walls, cultivating an inclusive environment perfect for creating. It was bare, giving her a blank canvas to design her full vision.

"Something like that," I whispered, hoping not to distract her with details of my business. I just needed her to sign on to the project. As we walked the rest of the building, I knew she would.

Towards the back of the expansive property, there were three small rooms perfect for offices. At the end of the hallway, a heavy door led to a stairway that felt abandoned. As I had the only other time I visited the vacant property, I propped the door to the stairway open before quickly climbing to reach the second floor.

The view was different than what I was used to. I found myself watching the hipster crowd below transit on bikes, skateboards, and foot. It wasn't an office view that left you feeling accomplished, but one of ambition, en route to success.

"This could be your office." I turned to see my sister wandering around the back end of the room. It was larger than my current digs, providing more than enough room for the colorful design she had already created. Only this time, my personal office would not exist in a setting that felt separate. Victoria had shown she could design the Cherry Blossoms office from top to bottom. This was her opportunity to make it happen.

"Now you're coming on board," I smiled, walking towards her. "I've been talking to Daniel about building the company I want to exist." I shared, unsure if she was listening. Victoria continued to eye the details of the building without reacting to me.

"I'm glad to hear you two are working on things," she turned to me with caring eyes. "Sometimes you get all worked up and you react without thinking of the consequences."

"There's a lot we've had to discuss." I tried brushing past her attempt to blame me for everything.

"Daniel is a good man, Emily. I think you need to trust him more."

"I'm a good woman," I countered, feeling myself grow irritated. "I'm the prize, Victoria. Not Daniel."

Unable to keep a straight face, she shook her head as her flawless skin stretched into a grin. "Modesty has never been your strong suit," she giggled.

"Seriously," I continued after lightening the mood. "I know Daniel is a good man, but I'm not going to live my life afraid to lose him. I need to communicate better, but so does he."

"And you're working on that?" She asked with a hand on her hip.

"We are," I held my chin up, leading us to the back of the room. "Do you think this is enough space for a bathroom?"

Looking around, she eyed the ceiling and then the floor before making her assessment. "We'd have to check the plumbing, but anything is possible. The only question is cost."

"Don't worry about that. I'm negotiating something," I started, before deciding to keep the particulars to myself. "I just got a big check from the condos, so I'm overdue for a splurge." I watched her eyes grow.

"You sold them?" She shrieked.

"I did," I paused and then corrected myself. "Well, Daniel did. He handled everything."

"That's what marriage is about. Sometimes Daniel is better equipped to deal with a problem," she spoke in the tone that reminded me she was the big sister.

"Well, this," I motioned around the room. "This is mine. From start to finish I want to be hands on with this project."

Even with the building stripped, I could see the vision for my new company. It would be inspiring and bold, nothing like a traditional office.

"When would you want me to start with the design?" Victoria asked.

"My plan is to put in an offer this week. As soon as we close, I want to get started."

She looked to me with a question in her eyes, but before she could speak my phone sounded loudly. My ringer only alerted unrecognized callers, so I pulled it from my pocket with suspicion as the number flashed across the screen.

"Hello?" I answered, scrolling my mind for any calls Crystal had scheduled that may have slipped my mind. Since I had begun spending more time out of the office, she had taken to forwarding my calls to help me connect with new partners and potential hires. It was in this haze of overworked exhaustion that I heard the words that drew me back to reality. A bold introduction that paused my breath in a place that had felt so comforting only seconds prior.

"It's Lana," a female voice said with authority, pausing for effect before adding her last name. "Lana Boyden. I think you're familiar with me."

31

"Lana Boyden?" I asked in disbelief.

Victoria's eyes let me know that she too could never forget the woman's name. The one who had attempted to extort my husband after learning of our father's misdoings within his hospitality empire. My sister rushed towards me, moving her mouth silently, but my mind couldn't compute what she was trying to convey.

"Let's not play, Emily. You know who I am, and I know you well."

"Is that right?" I countered, holding up my index finger in a feeble attempt to calm my sister.

Unwilling to be pushed aside, Victoria pulled my wrist until the phone was away from my ear. She tapped on the screen and then Lana's voice carried throughout the empty office.

With the speakerphone amplifying her condescending tone, Lana continued. "I should have come to you first. Women need to connect more, especially in the enterprising fashion we both exist in," she said. My eyebrows shot up at the idea that she would liken the two of us.

Learning from Daniel, I sat silent, forcing her to continue. "I imagine you have ideas about me, but I would bet they're not all true. You see, I grew up in a successful family, too. My father is in finance, and I followed his footsteps. I reached out to your," she paused, and then readjusted. "I've always wanted to get in touch with your side of this puzzle."

I realized in her misstep that she had no idea how much I knew about her involvement. What she had exposed about my father was on the news, but no one ever reported on her attempted extortion.

Victoria, hearing Lana begin to set her plan in motion, began moving her hand across her neck, the Universal signal to cut communication. It was the advice I knew everyone in my family, especially Daniel, would lend. Lana had proven herself to be an adversary, and any communication with her could potentially complicate my father's legal troubles.

Still, I found myself curious, engaging in the conversation Daniel never cared to hear. "What pieces could you possibly have to offer?" I finally asked, purposely adding a sense of doubt.

"I think this type of information is best divulged in person," she said coolly.

"Yeah, that's fine. Send it to design!" I yelled to no one, watching the confusion spread across my sister's face. I paused before returning to the call with Lana.

"I'm sorry. My assistant came in. What was that?" I asked, hearing her shuffle on the other end of the call. I wanted her to think I was busy even if I wasn't. I knew women like Lana. They flustered easily, and I needed her to feel like the one in need.

"Can you find a time to meet? I'm free today if you can," she started.

"I have an hour in my schedule today and it starts in fifteen minutes. Can you meet me at–," I stretched the word, trying to think of a good location. "There's a restaurant called the Sea Club on Melrose. Do you know it?"

Lana's soft laugh came through on my end, although I couldn't be sure if she saw the irony. The Sea Club was where I imagined she'd met Daniel months before, to share what I assumed would be the same information. Only, this time I was going to let her divulge whatever Daniel stopped her from sharing.

"Yes, I'm familiar," she finally answered, her demeanor much subdued.

"Meet me there at twelve," I ordered, ending the call before Lana could respond.

"Emily, what are you doing?" I heard Victoria behind me as I stormed towards the exit, already dialing Crystal.

"Hey, I was just about to call you," she answered with an excitement I couldn't entertain.

"Before we get there," I started, waving my sister to follow me down the steps. "I need you to call the Sea Club and get me a private room. I'll be there in about fifteen minutes and I have a very important meeting. Tell them to treat me like I own the place."

Without any further explanation, Crystal obliged. "Got it. Meeting for two or more?"

She jumped right into assistant mode and I loved her for it. With me and Crystal, there was never ego, only trust. "Just two."

"It's done. Call if you need anything. I don't want to miss a text."

"I think that's it. I'll call you when the meeting is over."

I ended the call to face my sister, who was blocking the front door. "What are you doing? Emily, this woman tried to tear our family apart!"

"Vic, I have to get to this meeting," I tried to brush past her, but she shoved me to hold her stance.

"Don't you remember what this did to you and Daniel? Lana has made her position clear. She is against our family. Anything you do with her is a threat to everything you care about," she argued words I knew were true.

A few weeks ago, 'Lana' would have been the one word answer to explain the dissolution of my marriage, if I'd gone through with my impulsive reaction. She was the root of deceit between myself and my husband, a secret we still struggled to discuss.

"Victoria, this is not the time," I argued, looking towards the door, but deciding against charging her again. Victoria had always been slightly bigger than me, standing two inches taller, with hips that left me envying her curves.

"Daniel has done everything to show you he's committed to your marriage, and you keep pushing him away!" She yelled with what sounded like anger. "When are you going to show him the respect that he deserves?"

I stood in silence, shocked that this was how she felt about my marriage. In all the disagreements we'd had, I never felt that respect was one of our shortcomings. It was a younger version of my mother screaming at me in the abandoned warehouse, not my sister.

The meeting with Lana forced me to ignore my sister's allegations. Turning towards the back of the building, I jogged to the exit.

Knowing where I'd be going, I dressed accordingly. Wearing black Chanel ballet flats, I nearly sprinted towards the back door. Unable to keep pace in her stilettos, Victoria called after me.

"At least call him, Emily! Don't leave him in the dark again!" She yelled just before the door closed behind me.

Ignoring her warning, I rushed to my car, pulling out of the alley just as she exited the building. In a second, our eyes caught, the glare so impactful words didn't need to be exchanged. I saw my sister's exhale of exhaustion as I sped past her, racing towards Melrose to meet Lana.

32

Waiting for Lana to arrive was the longest ten minutes of my life. She strolled into the Sea Club with five minutes to spare, pausing at the hostess stand before being led to the back. I'd purposely positioned myself in the private dining room facing the entrance of the restaurant.

Reaching for my glass, I took a sip of water as she neared me with an air of confidence that made me nervous. I was beginning to doubt myself, wondering why I decided to meet her, when she entered the glassed-in dining room.

"Emily," she flashed a perfect smile as I stood to greet her. We shook hands professionally before she sat across from me, ordering two glasses of wine.

When I first learned of Lana through the emails in Daniel's phone, I researched her online. Disappointingly, I only found a few photos on the website for her family's business. I could tell then that she was pretty, which only made it more difficult to dismiss the possibility of Daniel's infidelity.

Sitting across from her, it was clear the photos did her no justice. Lana's golden complexion shimmered as she flipped her long wavy hair over her shoulder. She was taller than me, and thin.

It wouldn't shock me to learn she'd tried her hand at modeling. She had the body and face for it.

"I'll just have water," I insisted, rejecting her offer of wine. The waiter nodded before leaving us alone.

"Oh, come on," she urged. "We'll need a little drink for what we have to discuss. Don't worry," she leaned in close. "I know your accounts are probably frozen, so this is on me."

Genuine laughter fell from my lips at her insinuation. Some of my father's portfolio was placed on severe restrictions due to his legal troubles, but my finances weren't affected.

"Lana, I don't know if you came hoping for a battle of insults, but you're not going to get it." I spoke as calmly as I could manage. "I don't know anything about you. I didn't dig for dirt on you. And quite frankly, I don't know why you called me. If you want a drink, help yourself. It's on the house."

I glanced at the clock hanging to the right of our table, pointing my manicured nail. "What I do know, is I have a meeting in an hour, and it'll take me thirty minutes to get there. So, once that big hand lands on the six, your time is up."

She stared at me for what felt like a full minute. Inside, I was panicking, wondering if she could see how insecure I felt. I knew nothing about finance, or even the charges my father faced. Everyone kept me in the dark about everything, but she didn't know that.

As far as Lana knew, I was who I appeared to be on paper – an entrepreneur with a packed schedule. The waiter returned with her glass of red wine, and she didn't bother to thank him.

"Since she's paying," she turned to the waiter. "Bring your best bottle of Cabernet."

"Sure thing," the young man said as he excused himself.

"You know, I may have exaggerated a bit on the phone," she began, struggling to cross her legs beneath the dining table. Nervously straightening the silverware, she launched into her prepared spiel.

"You and I aren't much alike. You see, my father didn't give me anything. I went to a state school, and then started working at his firm. Everything I have, I've earned." She said boldly.

"Well, maybe your father didn't have as much to give," I reasoned. It was an argument I'd heard a million times before. At every stage of my life people tried to shame me for my family's success.

"You know, I used to think that, too." Lana spoke slowly, deliberately. "That maybe my dad just wasn't as wealthy as some of my friends' parents who gave them everything."

She glared at me in a way I knew made people uncomfortable. My gut reaction was to rush to counter her statement, but there was no need. Silently, I repeated Daniel's advice from my meeting with Quentin, *she needs you*. After a pregnant pause, Lana kept on.

"Now, I realize he knew exactly what he was doing. My father wanted me to know the value of things. That's nearly impossible when you have everything handed to you."

The waiter returned with her bottle of wine and one glass. With a glance at my watch, I sighed, feigning boredom. Truthfully, I was anxious to know what Lana had to share. She was better informed about my father's case than I, whether she knew it or not. I couldn't let on how clueless I was.

"Lana, I can't stress how little I know about you. There's no issue between us. I saw you on the news, and you seem to know what you're talking about. When you called me today, I was in the middle of something very important. This," I motioned between us, "is not important to me. You probably planned this speech, and I bet it's good. But I don't have time to hear it. I don't care what your dad taught you about valuing a dollar. I don't care where you went to school. Frankly, I don't care about *you*. You've undoubtedly stalked my life, so you know I run a multi-million-dollar company, which will not be affected by my father's legal troubles. You have nothing to hold over my head. So, get to the point."

I watched her façade of confidence slip and felt my own boost. She wasn't more equipped than me, she was just convinced she had the upper hand. After proving I wasn't afraid of her, her whole demeanor shifted.

"You're right. I did research everything about your life when I found a discrepancy in your father's accounting. Something didn't add up with his resort chain, and I knew it had to be going somewhere. Large sums of money don't just disappear.

"What I found was less exciting than I'd hoped for. There were no mistresses or secret children. I would have loved to shatter your little fairy tale life. No, turns out your father is just a run of the mill crook, taking a little money from one account to balance another. Small potatoes, but still illegal.

"Honestly, I didn't think much of it. But after researching so much about you and your husband, I decided my silence was worth something. Between the two of you, I thought asking for a million would have been reasonable, but your husband wasn't even willing to hear me out."

"Is that what pissed you off? Did my husband's dismissal rub you the wrong way?" I wondered, curious where her animosity stemmed from.

"Your family flaunts wealth like you're untouchable. Your dad treats employees like servants, never bothering to get to know the people responsible for his success. Your husband treated me the same way." She spat the words with fury.

"You should have come to me first, Lana. But you got in your feelings and threw away your opportunity." I reached for my glass of water.

"The offer is still on the table, Emily," she announced proudly, reaching for her wine. I nearly choked, unsure of how to continue. I wanted nothing more than to clear my father's name, but trusting Lana was a fool's errand.

33

———————

"It's too late, Lana. You're working with the authorities. What good could you do for me?" I asked, struggling to keep my cool.

"I would hope by now you can see how calculated and strategic I am. I've become very close with the agent in charge of your father's case, and I'm sure with a little urging on my part, he would be willing to drop the charges. That is, of course, if you're willing to make it worth my wild."

I smiled. "Please don't sit here pretending you have pull with a federal agent. I'm familiar with the case. You're nothing more than a witness. How do you expect to influence anything?"

This seemed to amuse her. Pulling her phone from her pocket, she tapped on the screen before enabling the speakerphone. It rang loudly as she looked across the table with an arrogant smirk.

"Agent Cutler," a deep voice on the other end announced with the strictness of a military sergeant.

"Hey, baby," she spoke softly.

"Lana?" The voice asked.

"Oh, now you don't know my voice?" She spoke in a subtly seductive tone.

"Of course, baby." He paused. "Your number didn't show up."

"I've got it blocked," she explained.

"That's smart."

"I've been thinking," she started, pouting her lips as though he could see her. "I don't know about this case with the Delley guy. I think it might be better to make it go away."

The man sighed into the phone. "Lana, we've already tried this. The son-in-law wouldn't bite."

"I'm thinking there could be another way." She stared at me fiercely. "And I think it may be enough to make that house in Cabo happen."

The man was silent for a moment. "What do you need me to do?" He finally asked.

"Before I put anything in play, you can still make all this disappear, right?" She asked.

"Hell yeah. No one was even looking at this guy. Bosses don't care about charges like this," he huffed.

Each breath felt like an accomplishment as the conversation went on. How they could speak about my father like a pawn on a chessboard, casually discussing his future, was infuriating. Swallowing slowly, I forced a deep inhale, careful not to let on how uncomfortable I was.

"That's what I thought, baby." She commanded my attention, pressing her lips into a straight line before raising an index finger. "But, if this doesn't go right, I'm going to want a little revenge." Her eyes narrowed.

"Like what?" He asked.

"If you can take charges away, you can add some, right?"

"That's even easier. Just go at them hard. And let them know, this is the final chance. If they turn down this offer, we'll throw the book at that old man."

"Don't worry," she said softly. "I've got my prey within sight, and I doubt they'll be hard to kill."

"Let them know you have them. You hacked into their database. Every key stroke is ours." He boasted before she hurriedly ended the call. I could feel the sweat dripping down my back, my heart racing a mile a minute.

"What do you want?" I tried for confident despite how small I felt.

"Well, the initial offer was one hundred thousand." She said, lifting her phone from the table before carefully placing it back into her pocket. "Can you believe your husband passed on a deal like that?"

She reached for her wine, taking a sip as she looked up in disbelief. "I mean, this entire thing could have been erased for what he spends on suits in a year."

"How much do I have to pay?" I reiterated, growing tired of her gloating.

"A quarter mill, Emily. Two hundred and fifty thousand dollars." She demanded, taking another sip of wine.

"And if I give you this, what can I expect?"

"Have it to me within twenty-four hours, and all charges will be dropped."

"How can I guarantee you'll follow through?" I pressed her.

"Emily, you heard James. He has your father's life in his hands." She was taunting me now.

She knew I would pay. How could I not? My parents' lives were upended because of her, and now I had the opportunity to fix things. "How do I get the money to you?"

Lana smiled as she reached into her purse, revealing what looked to be a business card. She handed it to me carefully. "Use these."

I read the card vigilantly, noting the instructions that included wiring the money to a bank account and texting a telephone number upon completion. It was clear she had thought of every-thing, confident in her extortion plot. I flipped the card over to see the phone number that I instantly recognized as the one Lana had dialed. I turned to put the card in my purse when the glass door swung open so abruptly, I thought it might shatter.

"Emily, let's go!" Daniel's voice was violent as he stood beside me.

"Daniel," I breathed his name, trembling from his dramatic entrance.

Too impatient for my pace, he began lifting me with a tight grip on my bicep. Quickly, I gathered my things, throwing everything in my purse as I made sure not to leave anything on the table.

"Nice to see you again, Daniel." Lana said in a condescending tone.

He turned to her with venom in his eyes. "Lana, I've told you before. Leave my fucking family alone."

"Talk to you soon, Emily. Don't worry about the wine. I'm sure you'll pay me back," was all Lana said before Daniel rushed me from the room.

With his hand wrapped tightly around my arm, he steered me through the dining area. I could feel the anger in his touch. The moment we were outside, he released me.

"Emily, what are you doing? That woman cannot be trusted!" He barked.

"I know," I breathed, feeling as though I might pass out. "I was getting her to tell me," I faded, my heart pumping too fast to speak.

"I can't believe this," he shook his head. "I wouldn't even know you were here if it wasn't for your sister. Don't you realize she's working with the government? Anything you tell her can be used against your father."

"Do you know James Cutler?" I asked quickly, seeing the recognition on Daniel's face. "Is he involved with my dad's case?"

"Yeah," he said slowly. "He's the lead agent."

"She's working with him," I tried to explain, looking through the glass door of the restaurant, worried she might hear me.

"Em, baby," Daniel exhaled loudly, exasperated. "It doesn't matter what she said to you. None of that will matter. It's only what you can prove."

"I can!" I shrieked, reaching into my purse. "She called him, this is his number!" I shoved the business card to Daniel. He accepted it, scrunching his eyebrows as he looked it over. "I recorded everything!"

Reaching for my phone, I quickly emailed him, myself, and my father the voice note, afraid it could possibly be destroyed. "He said he can make all the charges go away, or add more. She asked for two hundred and fifty thousand."

Daniel's eyes widened as he stared at me. His phone vibrated with an alert and he took it from his pocket. "She says that? On here?"

"It's all on there! She calls the agent, they even mentioned trying to extort you. It's all there!" I was out of breath and weak. Never had I been so scared in my life.

"Come here," Daniel led me towards the parking lot. His grip was kinder, but still aggressive. "Cliff, take her to the house." He ordered his driver.

"Where are you going?" I asked.

"I need to see your dad," he explained. "Give me your keys."

I scrambled, digging into my purse before handing him the key fob. "Is this going to be enough?" I asked, feeling my emotions build.

"I don't know," he admitted, shoving me into the car. "I'll be home when I finish."

"Be safe," I yelled to his back. He was already gone, racing towards my G-wagon.

34

My home office had long been neglected. It looked like a design home, perfectly decorated with nothing out of place.

I'd begun to add a few things to make it my own since I was now finding reasons to sit at the glass top desk. After responding to a few important emails I was looking over an outline Crystal had sent, trying to keep myself busy.

It had been four hours since I left Daniel at the Sea Club. Three hours since I called to check on him, only to reach his voicemail. Two hours since I soaked in the bathtub with Jhene Aiko blasting through the speakers, desperately trying to relax. And an hour since I texted Daniel for the third time, begging for an update.

There was nothing more I could do. Waiting was the only option, but that didn't make it easy. My mind kept creating scenarios, fearful that I had made things worse for my father. Lana was too confident to go down without a fight.

From the time I set my phone on the table, hidden in the leather-bound proposal, I feared she was on to me. I just wanted to get her on the hook for extortion. I never expected her to call the agent, proving she was even more deceitful than I expected. If she was the star witness against my father, I couldn't understand how they could possibly move forward after hearing the recording.

My phone rang loudly. I'd adjusted the silent setting to make sure I didn't miss an alert from Daniel, but instead it was Crystal.

"Hey," I answered, hoping she didn't detect the disappointment.

"Good news!" She said excitedly, oblivious to the stresses of my day.

"What?"

"The adjustments went through!" She shrieked. "We're all set for the meeting on Friday!"

"Are you serious?" I asked, grateful for the distraction.

"I can't believe it either," she said, breathing heavily into the phone.

"Did you call Michelle and Four?" I asked.

"They're here at the office," she added before their voices chimed in.

"We did it!" They yelled.

"We did it!" I yelled back, proud of myself for moving forward with a plan that at times felt impossible.

"Okay, we'll let you go. I just had to update you. See you tomorrow!" She said excitedly before ending the call.

"What did you do?" Daniel's deep voice sent chills down my spine as he leaned against the door frame.

"Baby!" I leaped from my desk, rushing towards him. "What happened? Are you okay? Did you get my calls? I texted you." The questions poured out of me in rapid succession.

His soft smile gave me hope as he wrapped his arms around me. "I had to give them my phone."

"Them? The police? The lawyers? My dad?" My questions were endless.

"Calm down," he chuckled, leading me through the house.

"Calm down? How?" I shrieked. "It's been hours since you left."

"Well, I can only answer one question at a time, baby," he said softly, hugging me closer as he kissed my neck.

In the kitchen, he lifted me onto the island, turning towards the tall cabinet where we stored liquor. He returned with two glasses, pouring light brown whiskey into each one.

"You did a good thing," he finally said.

"Are you serious?" I moved to get down, but Daniel's hand on my hip kept me in place. I could barely contain myself after four tortuous hours of concern, worried I'd created more problems for my dad. Calm as ever, Daniel handed me the glass of whiskey.

"Nothing is confirmed yet," he started. I knew it was to prevent me from getting too optimistic. "But, it looks like that recording will get the charges against your dad dropped."

"What? Like, completely?" I could hardly believe my ears.

"I'm not sure," he urged me to manage my expectations, but it was useless. The thought of my mother getting out from under the mess my father had created was all I could focus on. "We had the extortion angle, from the emails you read, but that wasn't enough."

"Then what did it?" I wondered. I figured Lana's blatant request for money would exonerate my father. She was the star witness of the investigation. Discrediting her seemed like the best strategy to dismantle the case.

"After Lana asks the agent about trumping up the charges, he mentions something about hacking." Daniel said before gulping the Whiskey. "We'd never been able to determine where the government was getting their evidence. Lana was their only listed source."

"They got it illegally?" I asked, beginning to understand why Lana rushed off the phone so fast.

"They'll never say that," he said, pouring another drink. "But they've started negotiations, something they weren't willing to do before. I think your dad will have to pay a fine, but that's it."

I leaned back, feeling the stress I'd been carrying fall from my shoulders. Inhaling felt like my first taste of oxygen in weeks. Reaching for my glass, I ignored the rich flavors of the whiskey, welcoming the burn as the liquid traveled through my chest.

The relief was intoxicating, especially knowing I had helped make it happen. Confronting the woman threatening to bring down my family was terrifying. But I didn't let that fear stop me. Seeing it all pay off was the validation I needed. Following my instinct was not only acceptable, it was necessary.

"You okay?" Daniel's voice brought me back to reality. I opened my eyes to see him staring at me with a mix of concern and caution.

An innocent laugh escaped me as I straightened, wrapping my ankles around the back of his legs to pull him closer. "I'm great," I finally said. "I can't wait for all this to be over."

Daniel continued watching me, his forehead creasing as his hands trailed up my arms until he was cradling my neck with both hands. "You're not mad at me?" He asked, standing between my legs as they swayed back and forth.

"No." I searched his hazel eyes for understanding. "Why would I be mad at you?"

"I didn't trust you," he said with a tinge of shame.

Exhausted from the rush of adrenaline following the meeting with Lana, I hadn't even considered Daniel's actions. I knew the moment I left for the meeting my sister was going to alert him. And there was no doubt in my mind that he would not approve of my decision.

It was no coincidence that I didn't consult him, or my father, before meeting with Lana. Neither of them would have deemed it a good idea.

"Daniel, you couldn't have known she would be so brazen. I still can't believe she called a damn Federal agent in front of me." I rubbed his arm, hoping to comfort him.

"Emily, this is literally what we've been discussing in therapy." He paused, watching me try to make sense of it. "You had a plan, and I didn't trust you. I could've ruined everything the way I barged in the meeting. You would never do that to me."

Realizing his point, I rolled my eyes. "Daniel," I sighed, exhausted from the day. "We have enough going on with us. I don't want to make an issue when there isn't one. You're safe. My dad might be able to benefit. And Lana Boyden can kiss my ass."

There was no relief in his half smile. After pouring two more drinks, he handed one to me. "Drink this," he said. We raised our glasses together, and I finished the drink without reluctance.

"Where are we going?" I asked when he lifted me from the counter.

"I need to apologize properly." He carried me to the room at a leisurely pace before lying me onto our bed.

Daniel was never in a rush when it came to pleasure, but now he notably took his time. Moving painfully slow, he kissed every inch of my body, starting from my ankles. His touch was both familiar and electric. The feel of his soft lips against my skin sent shock waves throughout my body.

By the time his tongue reached my thigh, I was tired of waiting, ready to feel him. "Please," I whispered.

What started as a request quickly grew to begging when he removed my lace panties. Wasting no time, he massaged my bud with the pad of his thumb, using his tongue to explore my slit. Pressing my toes into the soft linen, I greedily pushed my sweetness into his mouth, closing my eyes as he indulged without reprieve.

My moans grew louder as I neared my climax, rolling my body to grind against his tongue at all the right places. Unable to contain myself, I released the need to fight, fully surrendering to his pleasure. Daniel didn't race towards my explosion. Instead, he continuously worked me into a frenzy, lazily releasing me before I reached my orgasm.

Each breath was heavier than the last, a fight to climb a mountain of satisfaction repeatedly. My body enjoyed every second of the pleasurable torment.

"Yes," I moaned loudly when he pushed me to the brink for the fourth time. I could feel myself falling over the edge, too far gone to turn back, when he stopped abruptly.

Climbing on top of me, he sank into my warmth. So aroused and hungry for him, I climaxed instantly, clenching tightly as he stretched me.

"Fuck!" I heard him bite out, his face buried beneath my hair.

Hearing his labored breathing as he pumped into me, chasing

his own climax, I wrapped my arms around his neck. Daniel's fore-arms moved beneath my thighs, spreading my legs to explore me freely.

Gone was the finesse and stalling. Now, he ravished me, caring nothing about how dangerously close I was to another eruption. My heart raced, my body tense, as I cried out in ecstasy.

"Take me, baby," I begged. Wanting him to have all of me, I held on tightly, thrusting my body to collide in sync with his rhythm. We moved mechanically, in opposite motion, creating a friction with euphoric passion.

"This is forever," he growled as his hips began to buck with an animalistic need I recognized.

"Yes! Yes!" I screamed. "Forever!"

Feeling him lose control inside of me sent me into another orgasmic wave of delirium. We rocked continuously, milking every drop until his weight collapsed. I held him, kissing his neck, feeling the subtle endless thrusts as he searched for more, taking all of me.

35

"When was the last time we've been on a date?" I asked, swinging Daniel's hand dramatically as we walked through the Farmer's Market at The Grove.

"You're making me feel guilty," he raised an eyebrow as he looked over to me.

"Should I be less happy?"

"That would make me feel like a better husband," he nodded quickly, sending me into a fit of giggles. I'd felt like a teenager since he woke me up that morning, asking if we could spend the day together.

When we first started dating, I accepted Daniel's hectic schedule. He was always busy, and in a way, I admired that. My father was the same way, so I associated a packed schedule with success.

With his arms now wrapped around me, he whispered in my ear. "I think they have your peach ice cream."

My chest puffed with excitement as I looked to the old-fashioned ice cream parlor. With white and red vertical stripes and matching awnings, Bennett's Ice Cream had been my favorite stall in the farmer's market for as long as I could remember. While Los

Angeles didn't experience drastic changes in weather, we were subject to food seasons.

Every summer I looked forward to Bennett's peach ice cream. They made everything from scratch, including the waffle cones that were sometimes still warm to the touch. Standing in line, I looked up at the menu, although I already knew my order.

"Can I help you?" The young girl at the cash register asked when it was our turn.

"I'll have a single scoop of peach ice cream, on a cone, with a little caramel at the bottom, please."

"And how about you?" She looked up to Daniel. He pressed his lips together, declining with a shake of his head as he reached into his back pocket, retrieving his wallet.

The Grove was an LA staple, located in one of the most popular neighborhoods. Paparazzi was known to stakeout, praying for a glimpse of celebrities. Television shows regularly filmed there, using the outdoor shopping center as a backdrop of the city. On this weekday afternoon, it was rather quiet.

"This has been the best day ever," I smiled as we continued leisurely to the park with my ice cream in tow.

Daniel grinned looking over to me, "You're easy to please."

"You must be kidding," I laughed, licking the creamy ice cream filled with real chunks of peaches. There were plenty of ways I'd heard myself described. 'Easy to please' was never one of them.

"No," he said seriously. "Once you get on your bad side, there's hell to pay. But when things are good, the smallest things make you smile."

"Like peach ice cream?" I asked, feeling a slight soreness in my cheeks from a day of smiling.

"You just want me," he said, looking to me with sincere eyes. "Time together has always been most important to you. And time apart has always been our downfall."

"That makes me sound needy," I argued, flattening the mound of ice cream with my tongue.

"We're all needy," he shrugged, continuing down the wide path leading toward the empty dog park. "Of all the things you could need, I'll take quality time."

"But you don't have much time," I reminded him.

"I'm learning I have to make time."

Tossing the remnants of my ice cream into a passing trash can, I reached into my purse, using hand sanitizer to cleanse my hands. "If you need to make time for me, what do I need to do?"

"You want me to do my homework and yours?" He teased.

Playfully shoving him, he caught my hand, pulling me into his arms. Daniel was my home. The most comfortable place in the world.

"I love you," his words felt like silk against my ear.

"I love you, too." I turned to kiss him.

"You don't need to change anything. You're a good wife," he finally answered.

"You're a good husband," I assured him.

My phone vibrated, disrupting the moment. Unable to resist Daniel's request to spend a day together, I'd cancelled everything. Crystal was handling all my meetings, texting and emailing updates when necessary. My eyebrows rose at the sight of her text.

"Is everything okay?" Daniel asked.

"Quentin got back to me about the adjustments in my proposal. He approved everything," I said with disbelief. I thought there would be more pushback about a few details I'd changed in the latest version.

His jaw tensed, as he turned to look away. What was just a sweet moment now felt bitter. Running my hand up his chest, I tried to bring him back. "Talk to me," I begged with a whisper.

"You know." He said flatly, still turned.

"Do you want to look over everything? Will that make you more comfortable?" I asked.

"No."

"Why not?"

"Because you don't want me looking over everything. I'm not

going to overstep your boundary and make you uncomfortable to appease me. I can't win like that."

"Win?" I questioned. "We're on the same team, Daniel."

He paused for a moment before finally looking to me. He was fighting something, trying to hold back. He closed his eyes, and I knew he had lost the battle.

"This is what I don't understand," he started, holding his hands out in confusion. "You said it was about cash flow. You wanted the buyout. Then we sold the condos. So, that problem is solved. What does he bring to the table now?"

"Is that why you gave me the investment? You wanted me to cancel the deal with Quentin?"

"I gave you the money because it's yours. And I wanted you to invest in whatever it is you're building." He paused, watching me closely before he finished. "But, yes. I did hope it would eliminate your need to work with this clown."

I turned to walk away, feeling betrayed again. After one step, I stopped myself, realizing the pattern I was following. I didn't want to run every time I felt uncomfortable, especially after learning how badly it hurt Daniel.

Turning to face him, I took a deep breath. He was tense, defensive even. "You told me you'd trust me blindly."

"I am trusting you. I have to smile while I do it, too?" His words were harsh, but I knew he wasn't upset with me. It was the situation and the helpless position he was in. My instinct was to punish him with distance for not tailoring his delivery. Now that I could read him clearly, I felt more empathetic than offended.

"Husband," I began, noticing his jaw relax. It was the most common way we addressed each other during our first year of marriage. In that newness, still in disbelief we'd acted on our passion, our titles served as a reminder that we were connected.

"Wife," he reached for me. Back in his arms, I was so grateful I didn't throw gasoline on the fire by ignoring his concerns. "This is harder than I thought it would be."

"Does it help knowing I appreciate you giving me this space?"

Burying his head beneath my hair, he pressed his lips to my neck. "No."

Laughter rattled my body, amused by his honesty. It felt good to allow him an emotional moment without penalizing him for how it made me feel. I was already looking forward to telling Dr. Cathway how well I'd handled my emotions.

"So, when are you closing the deal?" Daniel asked, releasing me after a long pause.

"At the end of the week," I said, feeling nervous and excited.

"Can I take you?"

"Of course," I smiled, happy to know he would be there.

His hand dropped to mine, our fingers interlocking as we continued down the path. "I didn't think the money would make you cancel the merger. I just didn't like the idea of you closing a deal for money. That's never been your approach to business."

Swinging our arms, I looked up at him. "And you didn't want me going to another man to solve a need."

"I will never be okay with that." He said sternly. "If you want to explore business options, or grow your reach, I understand. But you needing anything drives me crazy."

"I think my mom was right," I smiled. "I do drive you crazy, and I do think you're starting to like it."

He smirked, glancing down as he pulled me towards him. "I just like *you*, and you're crazy."

36

Arriving at my parents' house felt surreal. I hadn't been back since the news of my father's legal troubles came knocking on the front door, literally. This time things were different. My parents had summoned everyone to a family meeting and no one was sure what it was about.

"Again, with the valet?" I groaned as we pulled into the driveway.

"That probably means it's good news," Daniel offered, slowing to a stop.

"You seriously don't know what this is about?" I begged.

My mother announced a family dinner three days prior, and since then me and my siblings had been speculating possible reasons for the meeting. Of course, my father's legal troubles were at the top of our list. We'd all been waiting on an update, but neither of my parents offered anything.

In times like this, Daniel was usually my secret weapon. My father might not share details of his business dealings with his children, but he often confided in Daniel.

"I promise," Daniel assured me again.

"I'll take it from here, sir." A young man said through the window.

"What's your name?" Daniel asked as he stepped from the Ferrari 458 Italia Convertible, his pride and joy.

"Ian." The young man smiled at Daniel, accepting his extended hand.

"I'm Daniel. It's nice to meet you," he said.

"Same here," Ian smiled before climbing into the car.

"You introduce yourself to everyone," I giggled as we walked towards the front door.

Daniel shrugged as we ascended the few steps. "You never know when you'll need people. It's better to be on their good side."

We walked into a minimal set up, nothing like I'd expected. There were no decorations or staff rushing around. Instead, the house looked sparse. As we passed the den at the front of the house, I peeked in, noticing the empty bookshelf. It still didn't make sense why the agents needed to take so much from my parents, claiming it was potential evidence.

"You're here!" Olivia called excitedly from the front room.

My oldest sister had always looked like a mother. Taking the reigns as a teenager when our parents went away on business trips had prepared her for motherhood. With my niece Ava cradled in her arms, she came to greet us in a black and white checkered dress that stopped at her knees.

"Oh, my gosh," I gushed, reaching for Ava, who wore a tiny replication of my sister's dress. "Look at her!"

"Wash your hands before you touch my baby!" She snapped, leading us to the kitchen. "Mom's been waiting for you to get here. She's worrying me."

"Can you tell if it's good or bad news?" I asked while washing my hands before leaving the sink to Daniel.

"She's determined to tell us all at once," Olivia explained.

"Now can I hold my baby?" I asked, already pulling Ava from her arms.

"She's not a baby anymore," she whined while hugging Daniel.

"Yesterday, I caught her trying to stand up. She's trying to walk, and then she'll be leaving me for college!"

We laughed walking into the living area where the rest of my family was already gathered around the large dining room table. To my surprise, there were pizza boxes stacked in the center. I expected caterers and buffet trays with more food than we could manage.

Trying to hide my disappointment, I looked around the room in confusion. There were no floral arrangements, no ice sculptures, or any other extravagant party favors my mother was known for.

"A little surprised?" My mom asked from the head of the table.

"Kinda," I admitted as Olivia took Ava from me. "I was expecting more of a show. I can't remember the last time you ordered pizza."

"Come on and sit down." She waved us over. "We've got a lot to talk about."

Although we were five minutes earlier than my mom requested, Daniel and I were the last to arrive. After hugging my mother we moved around the table greeting each of my siblings.

When I hugged Victoria, who sat beside my mom, there was an awkwardness I wasn't used to. She was my closest friend, but she'd sided with Daniel when I met with Lana. Even more, she'd ridiculed the way I treat him, claiming I was disrespectful. Our spat was a hurtful memory I'd kept to myself. We hadn't spoken since that day and now the tension between us was unmistakable.

"You look nice," she said, tugging at the navy oversized silk dress that fell from my shoulder.

"You too," I smiled tightly, kissing her cheek, biting back what I really wanted to say.

Her husband Mike stood and hugged me before offering his seat. "Here, babe. Go ahead and switch me seats. I know you want to sit next to Emily."

I looked to my sister with an understanding that neither of our husbands knew about our growing rift. She switched places with

Mike, and I sat my purse in the empty seat beside her to continue greeting everyone.

My sister Denise, dressed in a bright red maxi dress, sat beside Olivia's husband Andrew. I leaned to kiss her cheek and she wrapped her arm around me. "I have some big news!" She said loud enough for everyone to hear.

My big brother Elliot was beside the head of the table designated for our father. He stood, hugging me tightly before hugging Daniel. I wanted to ask about his girlfriend he'd introduced at the last family function, but figured it better to keep to myself.

"My baby girl!" My dad announced, opening his arms to welcome me as he walked from the staircase that led to the wine cellar. He usually reserved this type of greeting for Daniel. I couldn't refuse the excitement bubbling in my chest. He too hugged me tightly, whispering in my ear, "Thank you."

While he hugged Daniel, I moved around the table to my seat as my sister Denise began to share her good news. She was rambling on about a rap album she had been credited as an executive producer on. Apparently, a song from the album had gone viral, and she was expecting a hefty payout.

My mind couldn't focus on her story, too busy replaying my father's words. He'd thanked me. And the only thing I had done to deserve that was meeting with Lana, discovering she was working with the agent investigating him.

"Now that all my children are here," my mom began as soon as Daniel sat beside my father. "We've got a lot to discuss as a family."

The room fell silent as we listened with bated breath. Building the suspense, my parents shared a smile before my father stood.

"I'll start with my announcement." He said. All of us turned to him, eager for an explanation. Appearing more like himself than he had in a while, he was dressed in a casual jogging suit, relaxed and comfortable.

"I know you've all been worried about the legal troubles I faced with Delley Resorts, but the truth will always prevail. We knew it was only a matter of time before our lawyers could explain any accusations. I'm happy to let you know that all charges against us have been dropped!"

The room erupted in a symphony of exasperated sighs, cries of disbelief, and a slow clap of applause from my mother. She too stood as Elliot leaned towards my father.

"Everything is dropped, dad? You're scot free?" I heard him ask.

"Just a little fine, son. But no charges, no forfeitures, or anything of the like. They just needed to see we have nothing to hide." He explained before turning to me and Daniel with a glare that let me know we now held a secret between us.

The alarming sound of silver on glass turned my attention to the other end of the table. My mother stood with a champagne flute in one hand, and a fork in the other. "And I too have some news."

The entire table shifted, facing my mom who beamed with excitement. She was dressed in a leopard print caftan over a black silk dress. It was as homey as her fashion sense allowed. She'd stopped dying her hair, allowing the gray strands to highlight her dark tresses.

She glanced at me with a small smile before turning her attention to the rest of my family, ready to reveal the reason she'd called the family meeting.

37

"You've probably noticed a lot of the furniture in the house is missing," my mother turned, raising her hand around the room. Most of the décor was absent. Hanging artwork had been taken down along with vases and photo frames.

"I thought the Feds took it," Victoria whispered to me.

I smirked, unable to fall back into our playful nature I was used to. Noticing my apprehension, she pressed her lips together in acknowledgement. She knew I was upset with her, turning away from my glare to refocus on our mother.

"Well, your father and I have decided to leave for an extended vacation," she grinned, looking down the table at my dad. "We're going to spend the next year living in France!"

A harmonized gasp swept over me and my siblings. While I knew most of them were mixed with disapproval, I was ecstatic. When she shared her desire to live in France, I thought it would always remain a dream. To hear she was going to live out a chapter she fantasized about was heartwarming.

"I'm so happy for you, mommy!" I called, raising my glass.

"I'm happy too, but where? When? This is all so sudden," Olivia said.

"I just need to know if we're allowed to visit," Victoria joyfully asked, raising her glass.

"I will always have space for my children," my mom announced proudly. "We've found a beautiful chateau in the countryside, with four bedrooms and a guesthouse. So, you're all welcome."

"Yeah, but me and your mom need some privacy, too," my dad joked, sending us into a roar of laughter. I noticed him lean towards Daniel while we were all distracted, asking my mom questions about their prospective move. "I'm thinking of subletting the house while we're away. Not sure if I should do long term or short vacation rentals."

"I'll run the numbers for you. See what the options look like," Daniel quietly assured him.

We were all excited with the news, making plans to visit them soon. You could see how happy my mother was, finally able to go after a dream she'd tucked away.

"Can we talk?" Victoria turned to me.

"Yeah," I said, turning to Daniel. "I'll be right back."

"You okay?" He asked with concern wrinkling his forehead.

"Yes," I leaned to kiss his cheek. "Just going to talk to Vic."

The kitchen was the only room that didn't feel empty. With a glass of wine in hand, we both lifted ourselves to sit on the counter.

"I know you're mad at me." My big sister was never one to mince words.

"I'm not mad at you, but I think we need to discuss how you feel about me." I chose my words carefully, trying not to get emotional.

"It's not how I feel about you, Emily. It's just how you act," she started.

"That's me!" I shouted louder than intended.

"No." She turned to me with love in her eyes. "Your behavior does not have to define you. That's something you can always change. I just want you to think before you act. I was there, remember? I saw how quickly you leaped into action. If you took a minute to think of the consequences, you might've made the same decision, but it would've been based on reason not impulse."

"And you think I don't respect Daniel?" I asked flatly, remembering her harsh words in the abandoned warehouse.

She lowered her head, taking a deep breath. "I wish I felt different." She glanced up at me with what felt like remorse.

My stomach turned at her response. I'd expected her to walk back her words and apologize. "I don't even want to hear this," I moved to lower myself from the countertop, but she stopped me by placing her hand over mine.

"Emily, he is always there for you. Daniel does everything to make sure you're happy. Why don't you appreciate that?"

"I do!" I snapped. "Why are you praising him for caring about my happiness, anyway? That's like the bare minimum, Vic. He's my husband. Of course, he should try to add to my happiness."

"All I'm saying is that sometimes it seems like you take that for granted," she spoke softly, trying to combat my growing temper. "Men are egotistical, Em. When you act without checking with him first, it comes across like he's not in control."

"Of me?" I huffed as I pushed myself from the counter, turning to face my sister. "He's not! If I need to pretend to be someone I'm not in order to make a man comfortable, that's not the man for me. What me and Daniel have isn't a façade. You don't have to worry about me losing him for being your wild baby sister. He's seen all the sides of me, even some you haven't. And he still loves me."

Victoria didn't answer quickly. She stared at me until the confidence I felt diminished beneath her frown. "Go ahead and just say it," I urged her. "This silence is making me anxious."

My sister only smiled, staring at me for a few extra seconds before jumping from the counter, draping her arm over my shoulder. "You always were the big little sister," she said softly. "I don't know why anyone ever thought you needed protecting."

"Is that your way of apologizing?" I looked up to her, feeling myself settle.

"Oh, I'm not apologizing!" She snapped. "I may have been

wrong, but I'm not sorry I advised you to keep your husband in the loop. And I'm damn sure not sorry I called him when you wanted to go play Sherlock Holmes."

I giggled, bumping her with my hip as we walked to rejoin our family. "I do respect him, Vic."

"I know you do," she said. "But sometimes you forget how much you love him. I was there in that hotel room, Em. The thought of losing him devastated you. I can't ever let you do something to jeopardize breaking your heart."

I nodded, understanding her point of view. If I'd learned anything in my trials with Daniel, it was that I valued our partnership. Losing him felt like losing myself, a pain I never wanted to taste again.

"Family photo!" My mother called. "I want to remember this moment and have it framed in France!"

We all gathered around as she arranged a camera with a self-timer, sprinting to join us before a snapshot of our lives was captured forever. The day my father's nightmare ended, and my mother's fantasy became more than a daydream.

38

"Hey," I started, waiting until Daniel turned away from Bloomberg.

"What's up, babe?" He glanced up quickly.

"Regardless of a change in leadership, a company will still be bound to contracts they signed before the change, right?" I wondered aloud.

Daniel squinted, completely turning away from the television. "Are we speaking hypothetically or specifically?"

"I just want to know hypothetically," I said. "To apply it to a specific situation."

The left side of his lips curved upwards. "Typically, yes. A company will be bound to whatever agreements they enter regardless of ownership. Like, when you purchased Cherry Blossoms. Everything that had already been agreed to, you had to fulfill. But once the timelines of those agreements expired, you weren't obligated to renew them."

"Timelines," I whispered to myself, turning on the balls of my feet with an idea.

"You're welcome!" I heard from the living room.

"Thanks, babe!" I called over my shoulder, certain he wasn't truly upset.

It was the third time this evening I'd come to him with a vague question. In a roundabout way, we'd developed our own set of boundaries. I knew Daniel was happy to advise and assist when-ever necessary, and he knew I didn't want him serving as training wheels.

"What'd he say?" Crystal asked when I entered the formal dining room. Michelle and Four both looked up interested.

With the French doors closed, the room had become our unoffi-cial headquarters. The papers spread across the table made it look more like a war room. When designing the house, Daniel and I had decorated based on theory, imagining what we would need. In practice, a formal dining room had proven to be unnecessary. We almost always ate at the breakfast nook in the corner of the kitchen, or in the living room, in front of the television.

Now, however, the dining room was vital. It had become our private meeting space – away from Cherry Blossoms, where we could talk freely.

"It'll work!" I announced excitedly.

Loud sighs of relief fell over the room, as Michelle clapped her hands enthusiastically. We'd created what we believed was a perfect plan to build the business we knew was necessary. Writers deserved to reap the rewards of their success. In the current model, publishing houses and agents were taking a large slice of the pie. We wanted that to change, and with the plan we had, it would.

Each of us had our different roles to manage. Crystal oversaw everything administrative and branding. She focused on defining our vision. Michelle, of course, handled everything tech. Daniel did not exaggerate when he said she was a wiz. There wasn't anything digital she couldn't build. Four was the rolodex. Born and raised in the city like me, she knew everyone. Discovering new talent was her forte, and she had already presented a dozen new writers for us to work with.

I brought us together, founding and funding our brainchild. No one expected me to know everything. We were all figuring things out in real time, allowing each other space to grow and learn. Nothing about it felt like work. That was how hours could pass with us, huddled around laptops, building what we wanted to exist.

"Your food's here," Daniel announced, knocking on the door to the dining room.

"Thank you," Crystal jumped into work mode. As she took the large bags from Daniel, we reorganized the cluttered table to make room for our dinner.

"Did you order one of everything on the menu?" Daniel jokingly asked as he stepped into the room we rarely used.

"I told her this was too much," Four said, rummaging through one of the four bags of takeout.

"It's fine," I waved her off. "Just set them out. Did they give us plates?"

"Yeah, here they are," Michelle lifted a bag with plates and cutlery.

"Come on, babe." I motioned towards Daniel, pulling a chair for him. "I got shrimp lo Mein just for you."

"I'm allowed in here? I thought this was top secret," he teased, accepting a plate from Michelle.

"It is top secret," Michelle insisted. "But we trust you."

"I don't know," Four chimed in. "Do we need him to sign an NDA?"

We all laughed, working together to open the white carry-out cubes filled with Chinese dishes.

"Seriously, this would all be simple for you. I've seen some of the projects you work on," Michelle finally said to Daniel.

"You don't need me," he quickly countered. "Ya'll are going to kill whatever it is you're working on."

"Yeah, but you know more about this than any of us," Crystal chimed in, passing a box of orange chicken to Four.

"You run a consultancy firm, right?" Four asked.

"I do," Daniel answered. "Thank you," he accepted a dish from Michelle.

"So, this type of stuff is what you do all day, right?" She asked.

"What type of stuff?" He raised his eyebrows, glancing up as he moved a portion of Lo Mein onto his plate with chopsticks.

"Wait." Four turned to me. "You have a whole genius over here and you're making us learn everything on our own?"

"It's going to mean more if we do it ourselves." Crystal jumped in to defend me.

"With all due respect," Michelle lifted a chopstick, demanding the floor. "He has been helping. Just tonight, he's solved like five problems for us."

Daniel turned from each of us as we rattled off our arguments. "Yeah, but only hypothetically," he noted the distinction he'd forced me to make every time I asked a question.

"So, you really don't know what we're working on?" Four asked with one loc falling over her face. The pink ends had faded to a dark fuchsia since our first meeting.

"Not a clue," Daniel smirked.

"Generally, I'm against the construct of marriage," Four began as she cracked open a fortune cookie. "But I like what you two have going on. You have your shit, and Emily supports that. And she has her shit, and you support that. But she doesn't need your approval to do her own shit. Does that make sense?" She looked around the table to see nodding heads from all the women.

"How's Jamal handling this? Is he in the know?" Daniel asked. It never failed to amaze me how he could remember the name of every person he met. He'd only been introduced to Crystal's fiancé once, but he regularly asked about him in small talk with her.

"We're all sworn to secrecy," Crystal answered proudly.

It was our rule – until everything was finalized, we would only discuss the details amongst ourselves. Daniel seemed pleased, though I imagined it must be difficult to bite his tongue and stay in the dark about something happening right before his eyes.

With his hand resting on my thigh beneath the table, I felt his support, whether he said it or not. I was going out on my own, trying something new. It was scary and unbelievably rewarding all at once. For the first time in my adult life, I was proud of myself professionally. I only hoped I didn't gamble away my future betting more than I could afford to lose.

39

The ride to the office was silent, but the tension was loud. I'd agreed to let Daniel drive me to the meeting with Quentin, but now I wasn't sure it was a good idea. Although he had committed to trusting me blindly, the tightness in his jaw assured me he was not happy about me merging businesses with Quentin.

Pulling into my parking spot, he sat with the engine running for a long moment. "Wait," he said, grasping my wrist when I moved to open the door. I sat frozen, preparing for a lecture.

"Emily," he breathed my name. I knew Daniel was serious or upset when he used my first name, rather than nicknames or terms of endearment. "This is not a good idea."

I paused, waiting for more, but it never came. "Okay, baby. I know where you stand. Now, can we go upstairs so I can do this?"

Daniel leaned against the headrest, looking to the roof of the car for what felt like a full minute. Then, he took a deep breath and abruptly turned to open his door. I followed suit, rushing to his side as I slid my hand into his on the way to the elevator.

We were alone in the elevator car, our fingers interlocked, when he looked over at me. "This is not going to go how you think it is, Em. I'm trying to tell you, but you're blocking me out."

"I'm not blocking you out, babe. I promise. I hear everything you're saying. I've been preparing for this. Trust me, I know what I'm doing."

The elevator doors opened to Madison and Quentin waiting. "Today's the big day!" Madison clapped her hands excitedly.

"It is," I smiled, eager to finally close the deal.

We were finalizing the merger of our publishing houses after weeks of contract negotiations. Quentin wore a tan suit that accentuated his green eyes. His hair was cut low, making him appear slightly more mature.

"Are you here to walk her down the aisle?" Quentin asked Daniel with a big grin.

"I need a moment with my wife," Daniel said instead, nodding towards my office.

"Okay, but we're all set up in the conference room," Madison explained impatiently.

"It'll only be a minute," I assured them as I hurried to keep up with Daniel.

"Is everything okay?" Crystal asked as we neared her desk, a rush of concern in her eyes.

"It's fine," I forced a smile.

Once we were in the office, he locked the door, pacing as he brushed his hair with his palms. Setting my purse on the glass desktop, I pushed the button to activate the cherry blossoms design on the windows. Madison and Quentin were speaking closely just outside my office. I studied them, trying to read their body language, until Daniel commanded my attention.

"Baby, please listen to me on this," he urged. The emotion in his voice was evident. "I know you're learning on your own and want to make this decision by yourself. I've seen you working long hours and I respect your independence. I really do," he continued.

"But?" I smiled, placing my hands on my hips. "Go ahead, baby. Just tell me so you can clear your conscience."

Nothing about Daniel's apprehensions upset me. I knew he was fighting his natural inclination to protect me. He was my partner, and I expected him to insert himself whenever it could reward an advantage.

"He's not who you think he is, Em," he said. "He says he started a publishing company to honor his grandma, but that's bullshit. Laney is the name of his ex-wife, who invested her life savings to start his company. He cut her out the business the second he didn't need her."

He paused, waiting to see if that information would sway me. When it didn't, he piled on. "He tried this exact play in New York, but it fell through when they caught on to his antics. He's not a good guy, Emily. You do not want to go into business with him."

Slowly, I crossed the office until I could feel the fury permeating his body. Daniel was livid, which turned me on. Maybe it was knowing how passionately he cared about defending me. With my hands on his forearms, I looked deeply into his eyes.

"I know you have my back, Daniel. I love you for that," I said.

"Then why won't you listen?"

"I am listening. Trust me," I rose to kiss him softly. He barely reciprocated the gesture, his jaw too tight with rage. "Remember, you're supposed to trust me blindly."

"I am."

"A smile would be nice," I giggled, leaning up to kiss him again. This time he leaned into me, kissing like he planned to convince me through seduction.

"Just give it a little thought. You don't have to do this right now," he suggested after leaving me breathless.

"Just trust me. This shouldn't take long," I kissed him once more before going to my desk. With my purse in hand, I took a deep breath. "We're only going to sign the contracts and then we can leave. I have something I want to show you."

Daniel didn't respond, but I could feel him watching as I made my exit.

"You don't mind if Crystal joins, right?" I asked while standing at her desk. "She's been sitting in on all my meetings."

"The more the merrier," Quentin grinned.

Together, the four of us walked to the conference room. Madison and Quentin had already assembled the entire board, complete with Quentin's executive staff and my own.

"Nice to see all of you. Thanks for coming," I announced before taking my seat at the conference table. I was stationed in the center, with my half of the board lining one side of the table. Madison sat beside me, nervously pushing her hair behind her ears. Crystal sat on my other side, placing her clipboard on the long chrome table.

"This is the start of something big for all of us. I just want you to know this is only the beginning. In time, we'll learn names, but for now please know how passionate I am about getting to know every single one of you." Quentin nodded and smiled, satisfied with his speech.

Then, came the boring part. Lawyers placed one contract after the other in front of us, requesting our signatures. Bright yellow stickers with an arrow marked where my signature was needed. Occasionally, I would look up, as Quentin sat across from me signing the same documents. Each contract was notarized on the spot. There was no turning back.

By the time we finished, my hand was fatigued, but not too much to accept the receipt of the bank transfer worth half my ownership in Cherry Blossoms Publishing. "If that's it," I said with a smile, standing to leave. "I guess we can adjourn."

"I'd actually like to go ahead and have the first board meeting," Quentin announced instead.

"Really?" I huffed, but he didn't smile.

"Really." He said flatly.

I sat reluctantly, looking down my side of the table for any sign of recognition, but everyone appeared as confused as me. We'd all planned for a short meeting to finalize the merger, but Quentin had other ideas.

"As the first order of business, I'd like to propose removing

Emily Gamble from the company." He looked directly into my eyes as he said it.

My heart fluttered with shock. I could hear the gasps from my side of the table. Everything moved in slow motion. Daniel's advice replayed in my ear, realizing what he suspected about Quentin was true.

"I move to buy Emily Gamble out of her fifty percent stake, at current value. She will immediately be removed from all things related to what will now be known as Laney Publishing House." Quentin said.

"You can't do this." I heard myself say, my voice deep with concern.

"You're right," Quentin said smugly. "I can't do it alone. We'll take a vote. All in favor of the proposition to buy out Emily Gamble and remove her from Cherry Blossoms Publishing, effective immediately, please raise your hand."

As expected, his entire side of the table raised their hands. I looked to my left, feeling a sigh of relief when no hands were raised. Turning in the other direction, there still were no visible hands, and I began to feel the tight grip around my heart loosen. He needed someone from my side to vote in his favor, and my team was proving to be loyal.

"I agree," Madison's voice caught my breath as she raised her hand with a smirk. "Business is business," she shrugged as I searched her eyes for an explanation.

"Well, there it is." Quentin announced gleefully. "Can we get those amendments?" He asked his lawyer.

"I built this company into the business it is," I argued. "You only want to steal it because of the hard work I've put in!"

"That's true." Quentin acknowledged. "You've done a good job. I'll take it from here."

"But you don't even care. Cherry Blossoms means nothing to you!" My voice cracked with emotion.

"You're right again," he chuckled. "That's why I'm giving you the name. If you think of it, I'm actually being rather generous with you."

"Generous?" I shrieked. "How can you do this? I welcomed you into my world and treated you with nothing but respect!"

"Respect?" He huffed. "Maybe you should talk to your husband about respect. I was actually going to walk away from this deal, especially when you raised the price. But I've never wanted to beat someone as much as I want to beat him. I'm really looking forward to the look on his face when he hears about this. As a matter of fact, bring him in," Quentin ordered as he pointed towards the door. A man I didn't recognize opened the door and a few seconds later Daniel emerged.

"Daniel! My man!" Quentin called with a devious smile. "I didn't want you to miss this."

Daniel's scowl narrowed, searching the room until our eyes met. With the slightest tilt of my head, I begged him not to react. The last thing I wanted was to give Quentin the satisfaction of seeing us defeated.

Daniel's chest rose slowly before he exhaled, moving to stand behind me without speaking a word. His presence was all the comfort I needed, knowing that regardless of what Quentin did, I would be okay.

"You're stealing my company because of some stupid pissing contest with my husband!?" I yelled, unable to contain my indignation.

"I'm not stealing," he said, signing the last document. "I've paid for half of your business. Now, I'm paying you market value for the other fifty percent stake in the company."

"Mrs. Gamble," my in-house counsel leaned in to whisper in my ear. "You do not have to sign these now. We can fight the legality of the vote. But if you sign now, you're conceding."

I nodded, thinking for a moment as Quentin slid the documents across the table. I accepted them, feeling the coolness of the chrome beneath my fingertips.

"The legality of the vote?" I repeated, looking over to my lawyer. "All he needs is someone on my board to vote with him, right?"

"That's right," Quentin answered.

"Well, we have some contracts, too," Crystal added, opening her clipboard to reveal two folders. I slid one across the table to Quentin, and sat the other in front of Madison, clenching my teeth tightly at the sight of her.

Still high on arrogance, Quentin opened the folder wearing a smug smile. I watched closely as it faded. "What the fuck is this? A severance?"

"It is," I paused, waiting for his eyes to reach mine. "If you think of it, I'm actually being rather generous with you." I smiled repeating his words.

"I own you, Quentin." I proclaimed boldly.

"Emily, that's harsh," Crystal piped up with her palm pressed to her chest, feigning outrage.

"You're right, Crystal." I held my hands up in concession. "I own your company, Quentin."

It was amusing watching him grow more uncomfortable in his seat, turning to look to his lawyer, who shared an equally confused glare.

"I didn't trust you from the moment I met you," I said calmly, crossing my legs beneath the table. "But, business is business, right Madison?"

Her cheeks were beet red, always revealing more than she wanted. I'd discovered her deceit early on, although I never did uncover why she had chosen to side with Quentin.

"Your company has good metrics, Q," I paused. "Can I still call you Q? Is that alright?" I asked, continuing before he answered.

"I truly wanted us to be partners. Share in distribution, and expand our market share. If everything went fine today, we would have done just that. I never planned to reveal I owned your company, or use that against you. I just didn't trust you to be fair, so I had to protect myself."

"You don't own my company," Quentin shot back, looking at his lawyer again.

"Your financials were stellar. I couldn't understand why you would be looking for investors," I continued.

"But it's a good company," Crystal reasoned.

"Exactly," I looked to her. "And we're always in the market for a good deal. So, I invested."

"You invested?" Quentin asked.

"Sure did," I smiled. "How much did we buy up, Crystal?"

She flipped open her clipboard, running her fingernail down a printout. "Fifty-four percent."

"Is this making sense, yet?" I asked Quentin.

"G-I-A," he whispered. I smiled watching him put the pieces of my puzzle together.

"You forgot about the board," Crystal whispered loud enough for the entire room to hear.

"Oh, right," I nodded dramatically. "You got so caught up trying to compete with my husband, you got sloppy."

Quentin looked on the verge of passing out. It took every ounce of self-control to contain my laughter. "You were so eager to steal my company, you approved every alteration we proposed. But the last one was where you really messed up. You see, in the latest version, it states that the board will consist of the executive staff of each business as of 11:59 PM the day before the contracts are signed."

"That's on page seventy-six," Crystal added.

"In the middle of the night, I had a strange feeling in my gut. Something about the way you and Madison have been meeting privately and discussing details about my business just didn't feel right. So, I removed Madison Fuller from my executive staff, replacing her with Crystal Richardson."

My lawyer demanded the floor. "That's correct. I have the memo here."

"You had the memo, too." I spoke directly to Quentin. "You just thought you were so clever. Like, I couldn't see through your bullshit."

We sat in a stare off as fate sunk in. "That said, I have still chosen to be fair. Each of your severance packages are beyond what you deserve."

"We need to cast another vote reflecting the actual board, as of 12:00 AM today," my lawyer announced. "Everyone in favor of voting Emily Gamble out of Cherry Blossoms Publishing, please raise your hand."

No one on my side voted against me. And this time, only a few hands rose on Quentin's side of the table. I stood, finally satisfied. "As for the Laney Publishing board, we can discuss why you wanted to oust me from my company at a later date. For now, this meeting is adjourned."

The room was stunned as I turned, falling in stride with Daniel without bothering to respond to Quentin's pleas. Now that my husband knew the truth about the merger, it was time to share the rest of my plan.

40

"**R**ight here," I pointed to the abandoned building.

"Are we seriously not going to talk about what just happened?" Daniel asked after another silent ride.

"I want you to see this first," I leaned over to kiss his cheek. "Just come in. It'll all make sense."

Leaving Four with the task of furnishing the new building had proven to be comical. Knowing my sister would soon redesign the space, I'd asked her not to spend much. Apparently, she took that extremely literal.

Daniel and I walked into the large room at the entrance to find a fold out table and plastic milk crates scattered around. A large sheet of white paper hung on the back wall, with handwritten sections designating a vision statement, possible logo designs, and random lists. The only thing Four seemed to spend money on was a high-end sound system that blasted Sza's *Ctrl* album at nightclub volumes.

I could feel Daniel's glare at my side, his patience running thin. Refusing to tell him about the new building, I wanted to show Daniel what I had been working on. Just then, Michelle descended from the stairs.

"You're here!" She raised her hands before yelling at Four to turn the music down.

"How long have you been standing there?" Four asked after cutting the sound system off. "I was in the zone!"

"I was just taking it all in," I said, trying to fight the urge to laugh at her design choices.

"Crystal already ordered some things from Ikea. They'll be here by the end of the week," Michelle said with a look of embarrassment.

"Do you know how many people just throw out furniture in LA? We can furnish this entire place without spending a dime. All we need is a truck and a little time. Plus, the annual garage sale in Inglewood is coming up, and I always find good stuff there." Four reasoned with sincerity.

The front door opened behind us and Crystal ran in. "That was amazing!" She rushed to hug me. After remaining professional in front of the audience, it felt great to hug my friend, who had believed in me every step of the way. Crystal had worked endless hours to research and execute the biggest gamble of my life.

"Are you okay, Mr. Gamble?" Michelle asked, still refusing to call him Daniel. After working at Tower Enterprise Group for years, she could only see him as her boss.

"I'm just trying to make sense of this," he said, his eyes wide with shock.

"E, you still haven't told him?" Four asked in disbelief.

"She didn't have to. Quentin wanted him there to witness everything," Crystal revealed as she pulled a milk crate and sat down.

"He did not!" Four exclaimed.

"Oh, I recorded the whole thing, we're watching it tonight!" Crystal smiled, reaching for her phone.

"Pull up a chair, Mr. G," Four motioned to one of the milk crates.

Daniel followed her gaze, then crossed his arms defiantly. "I think I'll stand."

"Suit yourself," she shrugged.

"Mr. Gamble, you know we've been working on something really big, right?" Crystal started.

"I know you've been working," he admitted. "And now I know Emily never planned to merge with Quentin, and that's a relief."

"Everything you told me about Quentin today, I already knew," I explained. "We've been doing our own recon, just like you taught me."

"I tore his company apart finding the best ways to expose him," Michelle added. "And to be honest, he does have a pretty solid business. He's been dishonest mostly about his earnings, but not in the way you'd expect. He actually attempted to make himself seem less successful."

"I know." Daniel said flatly. "If he was honest about his business, investors wouldn't support him merging with Cherry Blossoms."

"Well, we were struggling to find out how we could use that to our advantage," I cut in. "And nothing was making sense, until I thought of what you'd told me about Martell Engram. If Quentin was looking for investors, we could buy a portion of his company. And he was locked into the valuation he was shopping with me," I continued.

"So, you could get it for a discount," he said, following along.

"We love discounts over here, Mr. G," Four piped up.

"Call me Daniel," he said, warming up.

"To be honest, Quentin has a more thriving business. He has the digital market share and online currency Cherry Blossoms lacks. So, we had to make it about more than numbers on a balance sheet," Crystal said nervously.

"You were kind of our bait," I smiled. "Quentin got so wrapped up in this competition he'd concocted with you. He started making stupid concessions just to close the deal."

"And that's when he lost." Michelle added.

"I got all that from the most entertaining board meeting I've ever attended," Daniel said, looking up at the vaulted ceilings. "But, what's this?"

"Oh, right," I giggled, forgetting the second half of the plan. "We talked about me changing the culture at Cherry Blossoms, and how it could be more difficult than building something new. This is the new."

I held my hands up, realizing it didn't yet look as inviting as it would in due time. "We're going to build a writer's incubator."

"You know how Silicon Valley has all those events for creatives to come and hone their skills, find investors, and launch with funding? We're doing that for writers," Michelle explained.

"It'll be like an artist haven, and if they decide to go the corporate publishing route," I began.

"You'll funnel them to Cherry Blossoms." He finished.

"Exactly. But if they don't, we support that, too."

Daniel nodded slowly, computing all the information he'd just received. It was difficult keeping everything from him, but the pride I felt was totally worth it. I'd realized I wasn't locked into making something work for me when it was clear it couldn't.

Cherry Blossoms Publishing, as it was, would never be the business I envisioned. And that was okay. I didn't have to sell what was working to create something new. Even more, I was launching a business I was passionate about, from the ground up.

Satisfied with our explanation and grand reveal, Michelle, Crystal, and Four left me alone with my husband. There was still a nervous tension between us, as I tried to read his reaction.

"Anything else?" He asked.

"You didn't see that coming, did you?" I had to know.

"I thought you were going to leverage your parents owning the building to raise the asking price." Daniel said.

"I thought of that, but I didn't want to lean on them."

"You really wanted to 'Get It Alone', huh?"

I thought for a second then nodded, unable to tame the proud grin that spread across my face. "You're not mad, right?"

"No, I'm not mad." He said, leaning down to kiss me. "I'm proud of you."

"Thank you," I kissed him again.

"But I know my ask," he whispered on my lips.

"Your ask?"

"Yeah," he kissed me once more. "Remember Dr. Cathway said I needed to give you an opportunity to prove your commitment?"

"Oh," I giggled. "What is it?"

"Japan."

"Japan?" I leaned back in his arms.

"Yeah," he paused. "I have to go close the deal and I want you to come."

"When?" I asked, shocked that he too had been holding onto secrets.

"Now."

"Now?" I shrieked. "Daniel, we're just getting started. I can't take a long break like that," I reasoned, thinking of all the things I needed to get done.

"Crystal!" Daniel called across the room. The ladies had already returned to work, but she quickly joined us. "How does my wife's schedule look?"

"Completely empty for the rest of the month," she announced proudly.

"The two weeks," I said to myself, remembering the black out in my schedule. "You two have been planning this for a while, huh?"

"Just a few months," Crystal admitted with a bashful smile. "You deserve a vacation, boss lady!"

"So, then it's settled?" Daniel asked.

I looked to him, the man of my dreams. Daniel had shared his business and expertise to teach me how to build my own empire. It was everything I wanted, to learn and grow together, in love. He'd proven his commitment to support me in whatever I chose to accomplish. Now was my chance to return the favor.

"I guess we're going to Japan!" I finally said, rising on my toes to kiss him with all the passion I could manage. We were doing it. Creating the lifestyle we wanted, writing our own rules.

And it was sweeter than I ever imagined.

Read the epilogue and take a deeper look into Emily Gamble's life by reading intimate journals written throughout the book. This behind the scenes glimpse into her life will encourage you to answer a few questions about your own.

The bonus download also features visual looks from the fashion worn in the series.

Read it here:
www.CherryBlossomsPublishing.com/diary

ACKNOWLEDGMENTS

A difficult time in my life served as the catalyst to write the first scene of this book, which catapulted me into the world of writing. I am extremely proud of myself for this series. Naturally, Jarrell is next in line of acknowledgements. He is the first one to read my words, encourage me to continue, and build me up in times of despair. "I bet you think this song is about you!" You're not Daniel! Get over yourself. (Smile)

To my best friend Attilah, who has been the twin sister I've always needed. You hold every secret with grace. Thank you for buying every book after getting a free copy beforehand. I don't know about anyone else, but... You know the rest.

My siblings are my life partners. Thank you Nadir, Khalilah, and Aaliyah. I love you beyond words. My first bio was being your baby sister. Ya'll made me cool. Nothing could ever top that.

My parents are my original love story. Tim and Nadine inspired me to travel around the world at the start of my marriage. I always wanted an adventure like you two. Thank you for loving each other. It was always palpable. Your decisions and commitment had an incredible impact.

My mother-in-law Janice used her rare and valuable book club selection to pick this book. A first. She had all her friends buy my book, which at the time was a lifeline. Thank you for supporting me, our marketing director from day one.

My social media family has held me up in ways that I cannot put into words. You've supported me before I knew this would be a book, let alone a trilogy. You read the books, shared them, and made the trilogy what it is. We did it! I appreciate you so much! Drinks on me, wherever we link up!

ABOUT THE WRITER

Amirah J. Cook is a hopeful romantic with a passion for sharing Black love stories that resonate across cultures. A true global citizen, she's written from places as inspiring as Bangkok, Thailand, and Florence, Italy. The first book of her trilogy debuted while she was exploring the shores of Split, Croatia, and the following two were crafted and polished in the lush beauty of Bali, Indonesia. She currently resides there with her husband, the talented artist and entrepreneur Jarrell E. Cook.